# WITH DREAMS
## OF PAYNE

With Dreams of Payne

Copyright © 2022 Gemma James

Cover design by Gemma James

Previously titled *Epiphany*

ISBN: 9798410057493

This book is a work of fiction. Names, characters, and incidents are either products of the author's imagination or are used fictitiously. Any resemblance to actual events or persons, living or dead, is entirely coincidental.

# WITH
# DREAMS
# OF
# PAYNE

## GEMMA JAMES

*To my mom. Thanks for always being there.*

# PROLOGUE

I awoke in murky stages, the first being a nauseating sense of movement. The second was the realization that something was wrong. Horribly wrong. The third was the clearest and the most horrifying. My wrists were tied together as were my ankles.

I pulled at the bindings, and a low groan vibrated in my throat. Despite the persistent throb at my temples, I focused on the misty recollections; the wafting fog on the highway, the beam of a flashlight, the splintering sound of glass.

Forcing my eyes open, I met total blackness. My cheek rested against the floor of what I assumed was a van, and a putrid smell burned my nose, an odorous mixture of mildew and bleach. The van bounced over uneven ground, and I held my breath, my ribs hitting the floor hard with each lurch.

*What the heck happened?*

My heart beat out of control as I tried to remember, but I drew a blank. I couldn't recall anything beyond a blinding light and an explosion of pain...then nothing.

"Don't panic," I chanted in a whisper as I tested the rope.

*Come on!* I slid my wrists back and forth, and the knot loosened the slightest bit as the van came to a violent stop. The engine shut off, and I didn't dare move or make a peep. A door creaked open before slamming with an echo. I ceased to breathe as footfalls drew closer, crunching on gravel with each step. I counted them.

*One, two, three, four, five...*

Keys jingled from the other side, and the handle squeaked and turned. The van dipped, and instantly, I knew who entered behind me. I wished I could see him, but I was lying on my stomach, completely vulnerable.

"Where am I?" It wasn't the question I wanted to ask, the one I could barely think of.

*What are you going to do to me?*

My body went rigid as he came near. He rolled me to my back with rough hands, and his silhouette loomed large, a dark shadow blocking the light of the waning moon. He shifted, causing the moon's beam to glint off the cigarette lighter in his hand.

"No..." My plea came out a squeak, an ineffectual cry for mercy. I was only an object to him, something to torture and kill for his perverse pleasure.

I squeezed my eyes shut and yanked at the rope, ignoring the pain biting into my wrists. Hysteria wouldn't help my situation, so I held it in. In fact, from what I knew of the Hangman, my cries and pleas would only heighten his pleasure...his arousal. Vomit burned in my throat, accompanying the rancid taste of fear, but I forced my eyes open anyway.

He sparked the lighter to life, and the flame illuminated his face. Malevolent eyes peered at me, two expressionless voids holding no remorse for what he'd done to all of those other women.

For what he was about to do to me.

His expression distorted into something unrecognizable, and it took a few seconds to realize who towered over me. I couldn't comprehend what I was seeing.

"Why?" My voice broke on the question, but he didn't answer. A tear slid down my cheek as acceptance nicked at my composure. I wasn't getting out of this. Aidan would find my body—I didn't know how I knew, but I did. The bastard would dangle my death in front of him like a trophy. A muffled sob escaped. *Not* panicking was impossible.

For all the times I'd witnessed the murders of other women in my dreams, I'd failed to see my own.

# CHAPTER ONE

**One month earlier**

The Watcher's Point gossip mill welcomed me to town by exposing my mom's secret. I bet if she'd known about my *special ability* she wouldn't have kept the truth hidden all these years. Kind of hard to keep a secret when your daughter dreams of unexplainable things.

Like how I'd known the sun's rays painted the hillside in copper tones at sunset, or how violent the ocean became during a storm, crashing over jagged rocks and sending bursts of seawater onto the highway. I'd seen the town many times in my dreams, had walked the streets and tasted the salt in the air, but my mom hadn't known about my virtual visits to her hometown. The place where I'd been conceived, or so I'd recently learned.

That was the thing about secrets—they have a way of unraveling, even after twenty-three years.

"You're doing it again."

I blinked and focused on Six, the only friend I'd made since moving. "Doing what?"

"Dwelling."

"Sorry," I mumbled.

"No downers allowed on this night." She wagged a finger at me. "Besides, you'll forget all about this chaos with your mom when you see what I've got." She pulled a dress from her closet, which was so overstuffed it practically spit the garment into her hands.

"You're nuts if you think I'm wearing that." I folded my arms and bit back a smile. "Nuts enough to call Cahoots."

"What the heck is Cahoots?"

"Loony bin transport."

"Ha-ha, very funny." Sticking her tongue out, she threw the scrap of fabric at me. "Try it on, Mac. You won't regret it."

I hated the nickname almost as much as skimpy dresses. "Uh-uh. No way."

"These too." A pair of strappy heels landed at my feet. "By the time I'm done," she said, placing a hand on her curvy hip, "you'll be hell on heels. *Sexy* hell on heels."

I didn't want to be sexy hell on anything, especially in those torturous pair of shoes. "I don't do sexy," I said, draping the dress across her bed.

"Are you kidding? That outfit will do wonders for those legs."

"What legs?" I glanced down at my freshly painted toenails. She wasn't kidding about the makeover. "I'm five-four, not exactly leggy."

"Hence, the dress and heels, silly." She grabbed my arm and pulled me into her closet-sized bathroom. "Chill out and let me work my magic." One sharp look silenced my grumbling. Why had I agreed to let her drag me out? And to a dance club of all places?

Oh, yeah. To *meet* people.

Giving up the fight, I collapsed onto the lid of the toilet. It was only one night. Besides, maybe Six was right. I'd end up in a mental ward if I didn't lighten up. So what if the upheaval of my life nipped at my feet like a Pomeranian?

What a freaking understatement.

I didn't belong here. I should be back home, experiencing the high of my senior year of college, and mastering my artistic technique. But here I was, on my own in a new town, making new friends, and pretending my heart was still in one piece.

"It's time you learned the meaning of the word *fun*," Six said as she pulled out a tray of colorful palettes and brushes. How ironic that her cosmetic kit resembled my art supplies in the apartment next door—the only tangible evidence I lived there. I hadn't been there long enough to leave a personal imprint; no pictures or decorative touches, just my drawings and the related paraphernalia scattered throughout the space.

I stifled a sigh as she put her skills to work, transforming my face into God knows what. Fun...I could do fun. "You're not gonna make me look like a Geisha, are you?"

She burst out laughing. "Don't tempt me. You wanna talk about insanity? Missing masquerade night at High Times is unheard of." She snapped open an eyeshadow compact. "Tonight's our night to get drunk. Lord knows we're gonna serve enough wasted dumbasses on Halloween."

Working on Halloween didn't bother me, though I didn't bother telling her that.

"Close your eyes," she said.

I complied, and the soft bristles of her brush feathered across my lids. Instantly, a mahogany gaze flashed in my mind. Intense and brooding—those eyes imparted such a strong sexual vibe, the mere thought of them warmed the space between my legs. I pressed my thighs together, but vanishing the mystery guy from my head wasn't the easiest thing to do. I'd seen him in my dreams too many times to count, had no idea if he even existed, but whoever he was, I knew better eye candy didn't exist.

"Are you done yet?" I mumbled.

"Don't move!"

"Yes, master."

"Mackenzie, you're impossible."

Holding back a smile, I let her finish her "art." With face goo done, she went to work on my hair, wielding a secret female weapon: the curling iron. "You've got ten minutes, then I'm outta here," I warned.

"Not a problem." Apparently, short hair came with advantages. She finished in five and stepped back. "Dress time."

I groaned. "Can't I just wear jeans?"

"Nope."

A few minutes later, after squirming into the tight dress, I stumbled in the three-inch heels to the mirror on her bathroom door. "I look like a hoochie momma!"

"That's the idea." She twirled a red curl around her finger and grinned at me.

The classic *little black dress* emphasized places I'd prefer to leave alone, though I had to give her props for the gunk on my face. My slate gray eyes hadn't looked so smoky since prom.

"I thought masquerades were supposed to be classy." I yanked the hem down. "I mean, what kind of bar puts on a masquerade party?"

"You've obviously never been to High Times." Of course, her brand of coercion wouldn't be complete without a sparkly masquerade mask. She held it out, a challenge in her eyes. "Quit stalling and put this on. The night's not getting any younger."

An hour later, I wondered if the night would ever end. Six started right in on her Mac-needs-to-meet-people campaign. She must have introduced me to a dozen men. Freakishly tall guys, chubby short guys, full-bearded tattooed guys, hunky gym guys. Even geeky tech guys. It was a smorgasbord of guys, and I was positive I wouldn't remember a single name. Masquerade night, I scoffed. More like operation let's-get-Mac-laid night.

Techno music blared from every speaker, and like most popular bars, breathing room was a luxury. A kaleidoscope of masked faces whirled around me as I inched through the sea of bodies, amazed at what some people called dancing.

Six was nowhere to be found. I hadn't seen her since she'd dragged a tattooed guy onto the dance floor fifteen minutes ago, already drunk on some blue concoction. Sweat and alcohol wafted in the air, a reminder of another night, one that amped my pulse and made me want to hide behind closed doors for the rest of my life. I balled my hands as the room blurred.

Coming here was a bad idea.

"Watch out!" someone yelled after I'd stepped on a foot.

Sweat trickled down my hairline, and I blinked rapidly as the walls imploded. Spotting the women's restroom a few feet away, I muttered an apology and scurried inside. The room was blessedly empty. I tore off my mask and stared into the dingy mirror, breath coming in shallow gasps as I willed my heartbeat to slow down. It still hadn't returned to normal when the door squeaked open behind me.

"Hey!" A woman stumbled in with a crash. "You fucked up my shoe. Sorry ain't gonna cut it."

I froze, recognizing Christie's reflection despite the mask she hid behind. Out of all the toes I could have crushed, they would have to be hers.

Christie's dark eyes widened. "Why haven't you slithered back to your hole yet?"

I straightened my spine and turned to confront her glare. "I told you I wasn't going anywhere."

She smirked. "You don't belong here. Everyone knows it." Her gaze traveled to my toes and back up again. "Dressing like me. Trying to *be* me." She tsked-tsked. "So pathetic."

"This isn't about you." I paused, trying to think of a way to make her understand. "I had no idea when I moved here. I didn't know."

Christie's face twisted, and her fingers bunched into fists. "He wasn't your father!"

"According to the whole damn town he was." I clamped my mouth shut and tried to step around her. Last thing I needed was another argument with Christie Beckmeyer. Who would've thought I'd discover a sister just to have her hate me?

She blocked my exit at the last second. "Your mom's a slut. My dad wasn't the only guy she fucked."

"Get out of my way," I said through clenched teeth, fingers curling around my mask, "unless one ruined shoe isn't enough for you." Just because I wasn't speaking to my mom didn't mean I'd let anyone else badmouth her. Christie must have seen something dangerous in my eyes because she moved to the side. I resisted the urge to throw something as I shoved through the door and worked my way through the crowd.

"There you are!" Six materialized in front of me, something blue sloshing over the rim of her cup. "Why'd you take off your mask?" She shoved her drink into my hands before refastening the mask over my eyes. "You rock the mysterious vibe. Now, bottoms up. You don't look like you're havin' fun."

"Six, I'm not really in the mood—"

"Oh, *noooo* you don't. You need to loosen up." She bounced away with a gesture for me to follow. "C'mon! There's someone I want you to meet."

My gaze wandered to the bathroom entrance, where Christie stood drilling me with her glacial stare. Wonderful. I gulped down the alcohol and hurried after Six. "Who? Haven't I met enough people tonight?"

"Darn, he disappeared," she said as she coaxed me into the center of twisting bodies. "But let me tell you, this guy is *hot*. And he's a newbie in town like you. Fresh meat."

We began dancing, or more accurately, Six danced. I two-stepped with the finesse of a Ping-Pong ball. "I'm not interested in dating," I hollered above the music.

"Who's talking about dating." She scrunched her nose. "You know what you need?"

I was afraid to ask. "What?"

"A hot, sweaty romp in the sack. No strings, no expectations..." She paused long enough to wiggle her eyebrows. "Just a little wrestling between the sheets. It's good exercise."

I needed that about as much as a tax audit, but I laughed despite myself. "You're horrible!" The alcohol infiltrated my bloodstream with amazing speed. I couldn't say how long we danced. Three songs? Four? Ten? By the time she pulled me to a less crowded corner of the bar, I'd gulped down another drink and my ability to walk straight worsened by ten degrees.

"What was in that stuff?" I asked her.

"What stuff?"

"The blue crap you gave me!"

"Wouldn't you like to know." She laughed. "There's a reason they named it Adiós Motherfuck—"

"Okay," I interrupted, "I get the idea." Suddenly, the ceiling whirled in a nauseating spin. "Oh, shit. Be right back." Pushing through the crowd, I covered my mouth and made a beeline for the restroom. In my haste to escape inside, I tripped over a boot. Two strong arms reached out and grabbed me, holding me against a muscular chest to steady me. And how did I thank my rescuer?

I barfed down the front of his brown leather jacket.

"Oh God, I am *so...*" Raising my eyes, I trailed off, initially surprised he wasn't wearing a mask like everyone else.

Then I gaped at him.

Familiar mahogany eyes pierced me, and the Earth halted, crashed into Jupiter for all I knew. In that moment nothing else existed.

*I must be dreaming.*

To test the theory, I dug my fingernails into my arm. Okay, not dreaming, but something wasn't right. The blue drink from hell must produce hallucinations because the guy I'd dreamed about for years had his arms around me, and I was very much awake.

He glanced down at his soiled jacket and winced.

I cleared my throat, preparing to apologize, but couldn't force a squeak out, let alone a word.

He lowered his arms, stepped back, and watched me carefully, as if he believed I might crumble to the floor. "You okay?"

"I'm okay," I mumbled. *Not okay. Not okay at all. I've finally succumbed to insanity.*

His gaze fell to his jacket again. "I'm gonna grab some paper towels. Don't go anywhere."

As soon as he disappeared into the men's restroom, I bolted.

# CHAPTER TWO

My dreams held me prisoner in fragmented horror. Sound bites of tortured pleas. A flash of waves trailing down the naked curve of a woman's back. Rope securing bloodied hands and feet, circling a slender throat. The click of a lighter, its flames licking exposed flesh.

I wasn't sure which turned my stomach more—the torture, or the endless screaming, reminiscent of a lobster boiled alive. The noose tightened around her neck, and she made a sickening gurgling sound, struggling for air, for life. I willed my eyes open, but the dream wouldn't let go. Another scene unfolded.

Masked faces crowding me, pushing and shoving. Not much different from masquerade night, yet different in so many ways. These faces displayed an array of paint, ugly rubber monster faces, and sexy personas.

In the middle of the funhouse chaos stood the guy I'd dreamed about countless times. He turned away, but not before I glimpsed something in his eyes that resonated at the center of my being. Pain. Hopelessness. I recognized the deadness inside him because I struggled with it too.

He staggered down the uneven sidewalk, heavy boots crunching over a layer of leaves as a blanket of fog surrounded us. The haze obscured the glow of the few jack o'lanterns that dotted the street, and I realized which night played out in my dream.

Halloween...still a week away.

He disappeared from sight, and I hastened my steps until I found him halfway down an alley, a dark figure looming over him. Blood spurted in gruesome vividness, spattering the canvas of my mind in crimson.

I jerked awake, heart pounding, sweat and tears dampening my face, and rolled over to face the clock. Six-fifteen. I searched through the haze of alcohol-influenced memories and retrieved that first shocking moment when I'd come face to face with him the night before. Part of me wondered if I'd imagined the whole thing.

The eerie silence of my bedroom unnerved me almost as much as the nightmares. I missed the familiar noises of home —sounds I hadn't realized were in the background until they were gone. The weekend party animals, laughing and occasionally singing or arguing, but always present every Friday and Saturday night. The early morning commuters humming along the highway. Anything to chase away the dreams.

They'd taken a frightening turn during the last few weeks. I didn't want to believe they held any significance, but my track record with the bizarre was hard to ignore.

Going back to sleep was futile at this point, so I kicked off the covers and pulled on a pair of sweats. As I pushed my feet into cold slippers, shouting filtered in from next door. I rushed outside and found Six standing in her doorway, a red satin sheet grasped to her chest.

"Get out of here!" She flung a shoe at her latest conquest. He ducked but didn't quite manage to escape the shoe's mate. "I mean it, Kevin!" A dark T-shirt joined the shoes.

"What's your problem?" Glaring at her, he pulled the shirt over his tousled head of brown hair. I recognized him from last night. He'd been with another guy, and I'd placed them both into the hunky gym category. "You think you can do better than this, babe?" Kevin stepped back and spread his arms.

"I'm not your *babe*."

"What you are is *not worth it*." Stomping toward Six, he pulled a condom from his pocket. "For your next fuck," he sneered, tossing it at her feet, "in case you find a willing moron."

"You're the moron!"

I hurried to Six's side just as a black Toyota pickup jerked to a stop in the driveway. The other guy from the hunky gym duo hopped out and joined the drama. "What's going on?" he asked.

"I need a ride. The chick went psycho."

Six growled. "I'll show you *psycho*, you sick fuc—"

"Calm down." I placed a hand on her arm and addressed Gym Guy. "You need to get your friend out of here."

A set of stunning blue eyes twinkled at me. "Sure thing." He flashed a wide grin as he pulled Kevin toward the truck. "See you around," he called out before hopping into the driver's seat. Kevin sent one last glare in our direction before they left the driveway.

"Are you okay?" I asked.

Six nodded. "How much of that did you see?"

I bit back a smile. "Enough. You sure know how to start a day."

"Sorry about that." She ran a shaky hand through her bedroom hair.

"Did he hurt you?"

"No, nothing like that. Kevin's a jerk." She paused, and an impish grin spread across her face. "But damn if that man can't use his tongue."

"Not a good mental picture, Six."

She laughed. "Sorry. Come in. Least I can do is make some coffee." She bent to retrieve the condom and the morning paper, then tossed them on the couch on her way to the bedroom.

The studio was dinky, though she'd gotten creative with the space. A tall row of bookshelves sectioned off where she slept from the sitting area. Splashes of red added color, from the filmy curtain on the window in the living room to the throw pillows on her futon. She reappeared a couple minutes later wearing a black dress that swished against her ankles.

"What happened to you last night?" She switched on the coffee pot.

"Do you want the long story or the short?" Picking up the newspaper, I joined her at the dinette.

"Start with the short. My attention span stinks before I've had coffee."

I fiddled with the paper's thin edges and thought about the previous night. "I kinda...puked all over this guy." *Not just any guy.*

"You didn't!"

"I did. Then I hightailed it out of there as soon as he went into the men's room." I pushed the paper aside and buried my face in my hands. "I am such an idiot."

"And a lightweight."

I lifted my head, indignant, but the teasing glint in her jade eyes pacified me.

"So what did he look like? Have you seen him at the Pour House?" she asked, referring to the tavern where we both worked as bartenders.

"No, never seen him before." Not in the flesh anyway. I glanced down at the front page, where the headline jumped out at me.


WOMAN FOUND HANGING NEAR DIAMOND LAKE

# CHAPTER THREE

The atmosphere at the Pour House remained unchanged, despite news of the murder. Customers ordered their usuals, laughed over a game of pool, and got obnoxious after drinking a few too many. The media hadn't released the name of the victim yet, but I couldn't help but dwell on her identity. I wondered if she'd had long and wavy hair like the woman in my dream. Had she been raped? Burned? The sick feeling in my stomach wouldn't abate.

"Anyone home in there?"

Startled, I met Six's speculative gaze. "Sorry. I'm zoning again, aren't I?"

"Wanna talk about it?" She wiped the counter, cleaning an already gleaming surface.

"No, I'm fine. Just tired."

Six nodded toward the front entrance. "Maybe Mr. Blond-and-Interested will perk you up." She winked in typical fashion and dashed away as Kevin's friend approached.

"I was hoping to find you here."

I stifled a groan. "Hi." His name escaped me, though his roving eye didn't.

"I'm Brad." He extended his hand. "You probably don't remember me from last night." His hand folded around mine, and an uncomfortable sensation settled over me.

"No, I remember," I said, resisting the urge to squirm. "I'm surprised to see you here. I figured High Times was more your scene." I moved a couple feet down the bar and picked up an abandoned glass. Ice cubes clinked together like wind chimes. Brad followed my every move.

"High Times is lacking in cute bartenders," he teased. "I thought I'd drop in and say hi. You didn't give me a chance last night, and after this morning, well...I didn't want to leave under such bad circumstances. Kevin can be an ass."

I couldn't help but wonder why someone so confident and good-looking would be interested in someone like me. Plain and boring. Damaged. I suddenly felt out of place, much too jaded for my age and swimming in a sea of older, more experienced and interesting people.

Like Six, who reappeared and leaned over the bar. She raked her eyes over Brad's body, and I had to smile. She never passed on an opportunity to ogle.

"Mac wouldn't give you a chance, huh? Don't feel bad— she didn't give any of the others the time of day either." Of course she'd been listening. When it came to the opposite sex, her ears operated on steroids. Or maybe it was my love life she couldn't resist sticking her nose into. I almost snorted. *What love life?*

"Mac? Is that what you go by?" he asked. "It suits you."

I shuddered. "No. *No way*. Six just has a death wish," I warned, shooting her a glare.

"Nah, never mind her." She waved off the threat. "Mac's too sweet to dish out payback."

Brad aimed a brilliant grin at me. "Sweet enough to say yes to dinner?"

"Of course," she answered before I could open my mouth. "Six!"

"She's just shy."

"I'm standing right here, guys. No need to talk over my head." I squared my shoulders and met Brad's blue eyes. "You seem like a decent guy, so I'm gonna give it to you straight. I don't date." No way would I put myself through that pain again. As it was, memories of Joe fed off my heart like a rabid animal. I needed time to heal, though I had to admit that serving time on the healing wagon sucked. Dating sucked even more.

"Won't give a guy a chance, huh?" Brad arched a brow.

I shrugged. "I'm sorry."

"Brutal," Six said under her breath.

I planted my hands on my hips. "The place isn't hopping yet, but I'm sure someone's waiting for a refill," I told her.

"A few weeks of working here and the bossy pants are already on." She softened her words with a smile. "Okay, I'll get lost." She treated Brad to another one of her stunning grins. "Don't be a stranger."

"Wouldn't dream of it," he said.

I shuffled my feet, unable to *not* squirm under his gaze. "Well, thanks for stopping by, but I should get back to work."

"Yeah, sure. *You* don't be a stranger now." He gave me a hopeful smile, and I wondered if he'd heard a word I'd said. "I'll see you later, Mac."

*Apparently not.*

I lifted my hand in a noncommittal wave. After Brad left, the hours ticked by and the customers multiplied. It was a typical Saturday night for any bar, even in the dead of October. I was in the middle of making a lemon drop when someone pulled the door open. I raised my head, about to greet the newcomer, but dropped the glass instead.

*Holy shit.*

The veil between reality and dreamland disappeared, and I gawked at the guy standing in the doorway. Wind blew his dark hair into those incredible eyes I couldn't erase from my mind. I dug my fingernails into my skin for the second time in twenty-four hours. Nope, still not dreaming, only this time I was completely sober.

# CHAPTER FOUR

I had my first psychic dream when I was nine. Psychic implied power, and powerful wasn't a word I'd use to describe myself. I couldn't foretell the future or conjure visions at will, but I couldn't think of a more fitting word to describe what I sometimes saw in my dreams. At nine the dream had been inconsequential, though it had been the first. Fourth grade had been half over when Joe walked into Mrs. Silverstein's class. For every ounce of shyness I possessed, he excelled at standing out. And for some unfathomable reason, he chose to stand out next to me.

I hadn't told anyone how I'd seen him coming. Joe and I were inseparable those first few weeks, and I finally broke down and fessed up about the dream. He'd laughed me off the playground. He hadn't meant to be mean. Looking back, I considered his reaction a favor because he'd been right. Such claims *were* crazy. Even at nine, I hadn't wanted to be termed a freak. Over the years, my dreams became more active and detailed, and for a while I grew apathetic toward them, convincing myself they weren't a big deal.

Now I was far from apathetic. It was like experiencing that first dream all over again—only times ten. The door swung shut with a bang, jolting me out of my stupor, and someone chose that moment to break a rack on the pool table. A new song started on the jukebox, the melody as languid as the spilt liquid slowly inching toward the cupboards underneath the counter. I stood frozen in my drenched sneakers, forgetting about the order that needed filled, heck, forgetting to *breathe*.

Height-wise, I put him around six feet. Thick, dark hair brushed his ears—the kind of hair I ached to sink my fingers into. He'd replaced the brown leather jacket with a black one, and I couldn't decide which color suited him better.

Suddenly, his gaze shot to mine. Panicking, I ducked behind the counter and used the mess at my feet as an excuse. Alarm bells went off in my head. *Shit, shit, shit!* Would he recognize me from last night? Was I destined to be remembered as the girl who'd puked on him in a bar?

"What happened?" Six bent down and helped me pick up the glass. "Are you okay?"

"No," I hissed. "It's *him*."

"Who?"

"The guy I puked on!"

Her eyes widened. "That's the guy?"

"Yeah." I stood and kept my back to the entrance as I dumped the glass into a trashcan. "I need to grab a mop," I said, already envisioning my escape through the swinging doors leading to the backroom. The thought of facing him terrified me, and I wasn't altogether sure why. I should be eager to talk to him, to find out who he was—find out why he'd lived in my dreams for so long.

Six grabbed my arm. "I'll do it. He's coming this way. Go talk to him." She gave me a mischievous grin.

"Six!"

"Remember the guy I wanted you to meet? The hot newbie?" She pushed me further away and blocked the path. "Well *that's* him," she explained upon my blank stare. "His name's Aidan. Now go talk to him."

"He'll recognize me."

"No he won't." Her attention darted behind me, and I assumed he'd arrived at the bar. She lowered her voice. "You had your mask on, right?"

I swallowed a groan and nodded. Once she vanished into the back, I turned around and tried to convince myself he was just an ordinary customer. Nothing special about him.

Right.

"I'll be right with you." *Coward. You can't even look him in the eye.* I told the voice in my head to shut up and went to mix another lemon drop. All the while his name became a mantra.

*Aidan.*

By the time I set the cocktail on the counter, barely registering the customer waiting impatiently in front of me, my hands were shaking. Aidan's presence blasted me with the force of desert heat, and it took everything I had to feign casual when I approached him. "What can I get you?" Was that my voice sounding so normal?

He looked up and seemed to search my face for an agonizing second, and my mouth went dry. *He recognizes you...*

"I'll have a Coke."

"Sure." I hurried away to fill his request. Six reappeared from the back and began cleaning up the sticky mess. Her eyes traveled between Aidan and me, as if to ask "did you talk to him?" I gave an imperceptible shake of my head and almost dropped another glass. When I returned to Aidan, I had a death grip on his soda.

"Thanks," he said as I set his drink on the counter. A hint of a smile graced his mouth, enough of a tease to indicate how devastating a full-fledged grin would be.

"No problem." I cleared my throat. "So...Six says you're new in town."

"Six?" His dark brows scrunched over eyes full of intensity.

"Yeah," I said, pointing to my friend. "Six." She kept her attention on the mop, though I knew she was listening to every word. "She said she recognized you from High Times." Better to put the focus on her. *She* hadn't spewed blue crap all over him.

"The redhead?" He briefly glanced at Six with something close to amusement. "Yeah, I remember her." His gaze never wavered from mine as he sipped from his glass. I lost my breath. What was it about this guy that twisted my insides into a pretzel? Why couldn't I be more like Six, who never had a problem talking to men?

"How long have you been in Watcher's Point?" I asked.

"Not long." His expression shuttered, telling me no more than his two-word reply.

"I moved here about a month ago," I said. "It's a nice town." *Lame-o. Why don't you bring up the weather and add "Loser" to your social resume?* Had I wasted so much time on Joe that I wasn't experienced enough to simply talk to a guy?

"I'm kind of passing through," he said after a beat, and I

wondered if he was bored, or maybe uncomfortable with small talk. "What do I owe you?" he asked.

"Excuse me?"

His mouth twitched, as if holding back a grin. "For the drink?"

"Sorry." I rolled my eyes to cover my mortification. "Don't worry about it."

He lifted a brow.

"It's only soda," I said with a shrug. It was the least I could do after ruining his jacket.

"Thanks."

"Just holler if you need anything else."

He nodded. "Will do."

I stepped away from him, and several customers came in at once, including Christie and her boyfriend Judd. I kept one eye trained on her as I mixed a whiskey sour, and just as I anticipated, she hopped onto the barstool next to Aidan. Couldn't say I blamed her, though she had guts to flirt with him in front of Judd.

Six saved me the trouble of facing her. She greeted them with a tight smile before taking their order. I watched Aidan's expression closely. He didn't appear interested in Christie. In fact, his gaze drifted, leaving no area of the bar untouched. The crowd was average for the Pour House—a mixture of college-aged kids, men chasing a clandestine liaison, and a couple of bums seeking refuge from the cold while loose change burned holes in their ratty pockets. He took the scene in without prejudice.

And while he was busy watching everyone else, I was busy watching him.

"I never thought I'd see the day." Six appeared at my side, jerking me back to awareness.

"What?"

"You've got it bad."

Her scrutiny burned my face. "I have no clue what you're talking about." I couldn't "have it bad" for any guy. Never again.

Her eyebrows rose in perfect symmetry. "You're not fooling me." Her smirk really grated. Deep down I knew she was right.

"He's too old for me, Six."

"He's not *that* old." She glanced in his direction. "He couldn't be older than thirty. Besides," she said, grinning, "older men know what they're doing in bed. Admit it, you've been drooling."

I shrugged, attempting a pathetic display of nonchalance. "Well, what can I say?" I should have switched my major to theatre instead of art; maybe I'd be a better liar. "I'm not brain-dead. The guy's a looker."

Her grin widened. "Glad to hear it. You had me worried there for a while. You're too hot to hide behind a nun's get-up." She patted me on the shoulder. "Good to know you're normal like the rest of us."

*Normal like the rest of us.*

She went off to help another customer, and her laughter lingered, as did her words. They repeated in my head like an annoying song I couldn't silence. If I were normal like everyone else I wouldn't have dreamed of Aidan before setting eyes on him. Some of the dreams had been erotic enough to serve as porn fodder. One in particular was my favorite, and my skin flushed as I thought of his tongue dipping into my belly button while his warm, firm hands gripped my hips to lock me in place. Then he kissed lower…

Something in my belly fluttered and caught fire.

*Get your mind outta the gutter.*

By the time last call rolled around, my mind had clawed its way to the gutter's edge. I approached the trio. Christie held Aidan hostage with her slurred conversation, while Judd shot daggers at his girlfriend's back. A strong whiff of alcohol hit me, and I wondered how much she'd had. Two shot glasses sat untouched in front of her. Judd wasn't in uniform, so I assumed he was off duty. Shame, I thought, biting back a grin. It'd be fun to watch the sheriff's son haul her out in a drunken stupor, uniform and all.

"You heard right," she told Aidan, grabbing his arm. "Wednesday is hump day."

Aidan raised an eyebrow, and he and Judd exchanged a glance. Seemed like a heavy glance to me.

"Lucky for us, today's Saturday," I said, earning a glare from Christie.

Ignoring me, she continued, "Thursday is so close to Friday, it's criminal not to drink." She snickered, as if she'd made the funniest joke since the creation of standup comedy. "'Course Friday is *Friday*. No need to explain that one—"

"Do I want to know what you're talking about?" I interrupted. Aidan's gaze flickered to mine, and a smile teased his lips. God help me, the guy had dimples. If anything was criminal, it was those dimples.

"If you don't drink on Saturday," she started again, "you've got shit for brains. Everybody knows you drink on Saturday 'cause everybody's still drunk from Friday." Christie paused long enough to down the shots. "As for Sunday, who the fuck wouldn't want a drink? Just the thought of Monday is enough reason to grab a bottle."

"What about Tuesday?" I asked, figuring she could find a way to justify drinking every day of the year if she tried.

"Cheap two-dollar Tuesday. Kind of like that shirt you're wearing." Her eyes narrowed as she took in my Walmart special.

Judd grabbed her shoulder. "Knock it off, Christie. You're drunk."

"Speaking of drinking," I began, wishing I could hide in the back and take over dish duty, "last call." I directed the words at Aidan.

"I'm fine, thanks."

I stood dumbstruck for a moment, running all the replies to that loaded statement through my head.

Christie arched a brow. "Hel-lo?" she said, waving her hand in front of my face. "Still sitting here."

I arched a brow right back at her. The idea of cutting her off was tempting.

"Well don't just stand there. Fill 'em up." She pushed the empty shot glasses in my direction but only succeeded in scattering them. One rolled down the bar and fell off, landing with a soft thud on the fatigue mat behind the counter.

Gritting my teeth, I picked it up. Christie hadn't exactly been the frontrunner of the welcome committee. She blamed my mom for her parents' divorce and therefore me by association. I got that. My patience, however, was running thin. "She okay for another round?" I asked Judd.

He gave her a withering look. "Sure, if she wants to spend the rest of the night in the John."

"I'd rather lick a toilet seat than suck face with you!" She jumped up, and her raven hair obscured eyes glassy from too much alcohol. The barstool toppled in her haste to put some distance between herself and Judd.

"Come on, babe," he soothed as he reached for her.

"Don't touch me! Go away."

Aidan stepped back. "That's my cue to leave."

"I'm sorry," I told him. "I promise this doesn't happen every night." *Just half of them.*

"Don't worry about it. Have a good night," he said before heading toward the front entrance. I bit my lip, on the verge of asking him if he'd be back, but he disappeared into the cold.

"What's going on?" Six wiped her soapy hands on her apron. "I heard shouting. Luckily the place is empty, or you'd have lava erupting from Mike's ears." Good thing Mike, our bar manager, had gone home an hour ago.

"We're leaving," Judd said. "Come on, babe. Let's get you home. I'd say you're a level past FUBARed."

Christie jerked from his grasp and stalked toward the exit on wobbly feet. I smothered a giggle but felt guilty for it when she tripped over her platform heels.

Judd sighed. "Next time, Christie, *I'm* getting wasted. I'm sick of getting puked on and passed out on."

Six and I shared a glance, and we both burst into laughter as soon as their bickering faded into the night. "What is that...the third time this week?" I asked.

She shook her head. "That girl's gotta slow down."

"She was telling Aidan why drinking every day of the week is a necessity. The poor girl's got a problem."

"I'll slip her a pamphlet the next time she's here."

I rounded up the empties on the bar. "Like that'll help."

"I can't believe you guys are related." Six wiped down the counter.

"Me neither."

"Enough about her. Now dish. Already on a first name basis, are we?"

I stared at her blankly.

"*Aidan*?"

"What else should I call him?" I shot back.

"How about Mr. Dark-and-Mysterious?"

Six had a way of being uncannily perceptive. "Suits him," I mumbled. He remained in my thoughts as we walked home that night. Sleep was an elusive commodity, but once I fell under its spell, I dreamed of him again. The same dream, and in the end I found him in a puddle of blood.

# CHAPTER FIVE

Aidan came in every night, taking "his" spot at the bar. His spot, because I couldn't look at that barstool and not think of him. I dreamed about him, thought about him, and unleashed my crazy infatuation into my drawings, which really pissed me off. As if I hadn't drawn and painted the likeness of him enough over the past few years. Now, like a victim of OCD, I couldn't stop.

The dreams took over my nights. If I didn't dream about him, I dreamed of things too horrible to put into words. The media released the name of the victim a few days after she was found, and the smiling face of Chloe Sanders was enough to make me cry. I instantly recognized her as the woman I'd seen in my dreams.

As Halloween arrived, speculation over Chloe's murder had settled down some. Most customers gossiping about it assumed she'd ended up in the wrong place at the wrong time. Apparently, she'd had a drug problem. More than one customer described her as a "wild child."

"Ooh! I *like* it!" Six said the instant I entered the Pour

House. She was dressed to impress in an eighties style teeny-bopper outfit. Her eyes traveled up and down my body, assessing my old-fashioned sweater and knee-length skirt. "But...what exactly are you supposed to be?"

"I'm Bonnie." She stared at me blankly, so I added, "Bonnie and Clyde? Or did the gun escape your notice?" I twirled the dollar store pistol in my hand. The maneuver worked for about three seconds until it slipped from my grasp and hit the floor with a clatter. "Guess the gun wasn't such a good idea."

"I thought Bonnie was blond."

"I guess I could've dyed my hair—"

"Don't you dare!" Six wrinkled her nose, and her mouth turned up in that playful grin I was starting to recognize. "So does this mean you're gonna find yourself a Clyde tonight? Maybe Mr. Dark-and-Mysterious will fill the role."

"That's doubtful. Besides, being single isn't against the law. This chick is Clyde-free."

She pouted. "You're no fun, Mac."

"Yeah, the last time we tried fun, I ended up ruining a perfectly good jacket."

"I bet the pecs under it were worth the trouble." Six winked before bouncing off in the direction of the packed bar.

Mike had lured in a huge crowd by advertising cheap drinks and no cover charge. People spilled through the front door in droves, clad in a variety of costumes. Angels and demons, ugly masks resembling the monsters kids swore lived under their beds, celebrity likenesses, and pirates and... cowboys? I laughed at the group of guys sporting dreadlocks, eyepatches, and cowboy boots. What a combination.

"That'll be three dollars," I said, setting a Coors Light in front of a guy wearing an Elmo costume. "Where's Big Bird?"

"I ate him for dinner." His blue eyes smiled at me through the holes in the red fur.

I couldn't help but grin. "Can I get you anything else?"

"No, thanks. Keep the change." Our fingers brushed together as he handed me a five-dollar bill. I gave Elmo an amused smile and turned to the next customer, which happened to be Christie and two of her sidekicks. She leaned forward, shelving her breasts on the bar, and cleavage spilled from her Pocahontas costume.

"We'll take three Long Islands," she shouted over the raucous beat of the band. The dance floor in front of the stage was full to capacity. Cobwebs hung from the ceiling, eerie flameless candles lit the counter and the wooden tables, and black lights created an atmosphere ideal for the holiday of ghouls and goblins. The lead singer, belting out Michael Jackson's "Thriller," wasn't half bad. The guy could sing, I'd give him that, but he didn't hold a candle to Michael's dance moves.

"Sure, be right back," I hollered at Christie. I maneuvered around Tony, the third bartender working the shift, and fetched the order. When I returned a few minutes later, I noticed Aidan's arrival. I swear he had a sixth sense when it came to my presence. Our gazes collided, freezing me to the spot. I should have looked away. I should have done anything but stand there like an idiot drinking in the sight of him. His five o'clock shadow seemed out of place, the cagey glint in his eyes more pronounced, but damn he wore disreputable well.

As my pulse thrummed at my throat, I forced my feet to

move and set the tray of drinks on the counter. "You opening a tab?" I asked Christie.

"You bet." She slipped me her plastic before rubbing against Aidan, drink in hand, as she slid by him. At least the hussy wasn't sticking to the counter like chewed gum. She and her friends no doubt had bigger fish to catch. I spotted Judd in the crowd, clad in uniform. If he wasn't on duty, he was as boring as calculus when it came to costume selection.

The pirate-cowboys waved at me from the other end of the bar. "We're dry over here, baby!" Tony had just approached Aidan, so I resigned myself to serving the men with the come-hither eyes.

A half hour later, after three rounds of drinks and a dozen lurid jokes, I extracted myself and was certain four pairs of lascivious eyes were glued to my ass.

Six grabbed my arm mid-stride and gestured toward Aidan. "Talk to him. It won't kill you, I promise."

The band went to break, and I kissed my excuse to duck and hide goodbye. Six gave me a final nudge in his direction.

"How's it going?" I asked, gripping the counter for support. His eyes answered for him. Troubled and drawn, they indicated a sleepless night. Two full shot glasses sat between his hands, and three empties had already been pushed aside.

This couldn't be a good sign.

I said the first thing that came to mind. "No costume tonight?"

"I'm not really in a festive mood." His eyes traveled the length of my body, and the corner of his mouth crept up in a lopsided smile. "Nice hat," he said, swaying in his seat, "but wasn't Bonnie blond?"

I shrugged, fingering a dark lock. "I don't play well with hair dye or wigs. It's a character flaw." What had gotten into me? Talking to the opposite sex had never come so easily, especially with a guy as hot as Aidan.

*Sexy. Gorgeous. Hmm...wonder what he really looks like underneath those clothes?*

I swallowed hard. Now who had lascivious eyes? Time to pour cement into my mind's gutter.

"You're right. I can't picture you blond." He swayed on the barstool again, and I figured he must have hit the bottle before arriving. "Where's Clyde hiding?"

"Bonnie's an independent woman. She's going solo."

"Maybe you'll get into less trouble that way." He downed the remaining two shots without warning. The last hit the counter with a racket. "Can you believe today is my birthday?" The scorn in his tone confused me. Most people didn't get so bent over a birthday.

I wasn't sure how to reply. Somehow I guessed *happy birthday* wasn't what he wanted to hear, so I silently waited, hoping he'd shed some light. Even in my dreams, where I learned of things I had no way of explaining to others, he remained a mystery.

"I'll take another round," he said, gesturing toward the empties. "Make them doubles."

I swallowed hard. "You sure? You've had a lot already."

He flashed that crooked smile again, and I wondered if he realized how disarming it was. "You're worried about me?" he asked.

I hesitated. "Yeah, I am." Way more than I wanted to admit. Tonight was Halloween, after all.

"Thanks for the concern, but I have a high tolerance for

alcohol. Besides, turning thirty should make me a big boy now."

"You're thirty?" Dang, Six was right on the money.

"I know, over-the-hill to someone like you, right? I bet you're barely twenty-one." Melancholy tinged his tone. "Things were simpler back then."

"I'm twenty-three." I leaned over the counter and locked my eyes on his. "And things are far from simple." After a heated moment, I pulled away and began stacking the empties. "Just so you know, I'm good at climbing hills."

Where had that come from? I felt my cheeks grow warm, but a commotion a few feet down the bar saved me from further embarrassment.

"Hey! You can't smoke in here," Six shouted.

A cigarette lighter flicked to life, and so did the images stored in my memory. I dropped the shot glasses and held onto the bar. Something akin to burning flesh almost made me gag, and I saw Chloe Sanders' terrified face so clearly that she could have been standing in front of me. I opened my eyes, only realizing then that I'd closed them. Judd escorted the smoker outside to the designated area, the guy grumbling about "Oregon's stupid smoking laws" the whole way.

Aidan watched me carefully. "You okay?"

I blinked. "No, I mean yes. The lighter..." I shuddered at the recollection of her scream, which seemed to go on forever as she writhed under the torturous flame of her assailant's lighter. "It uh, it reminded me of the woman who was murdered last week." I bent to retrieve the shot glasses, and when I returned my attention to Aidan, he looked thunderstruck.

"The lighter?" he asked.

My throat tightened. "How about those shots?" I rushed away before he could reply. I didn't know what information the authorities had made public, as I hadn't picked up a newspaper since they'd released her identity. I returned to Aidan, placed two fresh shots on the counter, and fervently prayed he'd forgotten my slip of tongue.

He handed me a couple of bills. "Keep the change. Who knows? With enough tips maybe you won't have to rob a bank."

"Excuse me?"

"You know," he began, gesturing toward my outfit, "though you look the part, I can't see you going through with the whole armed robbery thing."

"I'll keep that in mind." I bit back a smile. Was he *flirting* with me? Or had I taken the meaning of dense to a new level?

He held up a shot glass. "Here's to crime sprees coming to an end." Some unidentifiable emotion darkened his face. "I'd offer to share, but I doubt you're allowed to drink on the job." He picked up the remaining shot.

"I don't drink much anyway."

"We'll have to fix that sometime. Are you corruptible, Bonnie?"

I corrupted his leather jacket. Did that count? It was all I could do not to snicker.

"Ah, never mind. You don't seem the type." He grinned at me, a full-fledged, dimples-and-all kind of grin that made my belly simmer. "You don't know what you're missing." He tossed back the alcohol like it was no big deal.

Good God. He needed distracting. Or I did. "So," I began, "thirty today. You've got plenty of time before you reach over-the-hill status. At least another twenty years before mid-life crisis hits."

He didn't say anything at first, and I wondered if he'd heard me at all. "Crisis can rob you at any age," he said, his tone soft enough that I had to lean closer to hear him. "I should've been a father by now."

I wasn't sure what I'd expected him to say, but that definitely wasn't it.

He pushed the empty shot glasses in my direction. "Keep them coming, Bonnie. Birthdays only come around once a year, right?"

"That they do, and if you want to see another one, I think it's time you slowed down." Tonight was not the night for him to get wasted, though I feared he'd already passed that stage by the time I'd found him sitting there.

"You worry too much. Anyone ever tell you that?"

"All the time. I still can't serve you more alcohol tonight."

"Seriously? You'd do that to a man on his birthday?"

"Sorry." I shrugged, doing my best to appear nonchalant. In reality, I was sick with dread. It sat in my gut, gnawing on my insides like a piranha.

"And to think I was gonna add you to my Christmas card list." He stood on unsteady feet. "Thanks for nothing, Bonnie."

As I watched him go, something in my chest tightened. He'd gone from brooding, to playful, to angry in a matter of minutes. He stormed through the exit, bumping into a man dressed as Dick Tracey on his way out.

Without hesitation, I sprang into action, ignoring a customer who tried to get my attention by holding up his empty glass. Spotting Six, I grabbed her arm and halted her swift pace toward Elmo.

"I have to go. Cover for me?"

She frowned. "What are you talking about? You can't just take off."

"It's important. I'll explain later, I promise."

Her eyes strayed to the spot Aidan had vacated. "Go. I'll smooth things over with Mike."

"Thanks," I said, though Six didn't hear me. She was too busy asking Elmo if he knew of any after-parties.

The instant I stepped outside, my hair whipped around in the frigid wind. I sped down the sidewalk as fast as my feet allowed. The scene became familiar; the same masks and costumes, the same uneven sidewalk…why hadn't I recognized it earlier? Fog clung to the ground, a misty orange from the glow of several jack o'lanterns.

I spotted Aidan stumbling along the bumpy concrete about a block ahead of me. A crowd of people exited an old warehouse-turned-haunted house, and I wanted to scream. Their faces blocked my view of him for several moments, and when I finally got through, he was nowhere in sight.

What if I couldn't find him? Or what if I did find him and it was too late? I broke into a sprint, then skidded to a stop two blocks down the street. An alley veered off to the right. Instinct warned me away, reminded me how evil people lurked in the shadows. I stared into the darkness and listened. Absolute silence. Someone saner would have turned back.

I inched forward.

The quiet set my teeth on edge. No voices, no footsteps, not even an animal. Heck, I would have settled for the sound of a scampering rodent. Anything to assure me I wasn't alone. The thought had barely formed when I realized I wasn't. A soft grunt rent the air, and the shadow of two men materialized as my eyes adjusted to the darkness. One slumped to the ground.

I froze, terror choking me as the guy left standing pulled something from his pocket. The click of a switchblade echoed off the walls, and the blade glinted in his hand, sharp and lethal.

*Oh God...*

"Help!" An endless, high-pitched scream poured from my throat, and I didn't stop until he ran off in the opposite direction. My breath escaped in foggy bursts, and as footsteps sounded behind me, I finally forced my feet to move.

Aidan lay sprawled on the ground, knocked out cold as blood oozed from a gash in his forehead.

# CHAPTER SIX

Time ticked by so slowly I could watch a raindrop fall. One landed on my cheek, reminiscent of a tear. I wiped it away, wishing I could turn back the clock by thirty minutes, wishing I hadn't succumbed to biting my nails again. Judd stood in front of me, thin lips moving, his angular face bathed in the strobe lights atop the emergency vehicles.

Wait. Was he talking to me?

"...what happened?" he asked.

"Huh?" I barely remembered calling 9-1-1. My attention remained on the scene behind him where two paramedics worked over Aidan. He came to when they lifted him onto a stretcher, and a low groan escaped his colorless lips. My stomach turned as the contents of his spilled out.

"Easy..." The paramedic said more, but Judd's words drowned out the rest.

"I said did you see what happened?"

I shook my head as I watched the doors to the ambulance shut behind Aidan. "Which hospital are they taking him to?"

Judd gave me an *are-you-kidding-me?* look. "The only one in town. Watcher's Point General?" His eyes narrowed. "Are you all right?"

I nodded. "The attacker had a knife." I turned the words over in my head and wondered how they'd come out so calmly. I was a mess on the inside, partly afraid for Aidan, and partly afraid because finding myself alone in an alley with an armed man had been enough to bring back memories I didn't want to think about.

Judd studied me with eyes as dark as Aidan's. "Can you give me a description?"

"Not really." A chill went through me, and I folded my arms. "It was dark. I think he was wearing a hood."

"What brought you this way? Weren't you working?"

"I left early. Is Aidan gonna be okay?"

Judd ignored my question. "He was at the Pour House tonight, right? How much did he have to drink?"

"A few shots? I'm not sure." Guilt chewed at my gut. If only I hadn't served him those last two shots. Why hadn't I tried to talk him into staying? Forced coffee down his throat? I should have done *something*. Worry and regret burned my nose, threatened to spurt from my eyes.

One of the firefighters sauntered up just as the ambulance pulled away. "So what's the verdict?" he asked Judd.

"He'd been drinking. Witness says there was a man with a knife. Probably an attempted mugging," Judd said.

"Halloween makes people nuts, especially in this town. He got lucky to come out of it with only a bump to the head." The guy punched Judd on the shoulder. "Aren't you on duty a little early?"

"Wasn't supposed to be for another hour," Judd replied.

"The old man and Jameson are busy rounding up the usual suspects on Watcher's Island. I was close by anyway."

The other guy chuckled. "What's it this year? Haunting or buried treasure?"

"They broke into the lighthouse, so I'm putting my money on haunting."

"Gotta love Halloween. Well, we're outta here. Don't work too hard."

Judd smiled. "Things will settle down in a few hours." As soon as his friend left, he returned his attention to me. "Do you need a ride home?"

"No, thanks. My apartment isn't far." I resisted the urge to chomp on another nail. "Can I go now?"

Judd's radio squawked, indicating another incident he was needed at, and he waved me away. "Yeah, I guess."

Getting to the hospital didn't take long, though waiting for word on Aidan turned out to be a lesson in patience. Three hours had passed and they still hadn't told me anything. *Would* they tell me anything? So far the nurse I'd spoken to hadn't been helpful in that department.

I shifted in the chair for what seemed like the hundredth time when Aidan suddenly crashed into the lobby of the emergency room. He stumbled and knocked into the triage station, sending a stack of forms and a blood pressure kit careening to the floor. His bloodshot gaze landed on me, darted away, then returned to do a double take. I froze in shock.

"What are you doing here?" he asked.

"I found you," I explained. "I wanted to make sure you were okay."

The ER doctor appeared behind him. He pushed a pair of

wire-rimmed glasses onto a nose that was too small for his face. "Where are you going?" he asked, peering up at Aidan.

"Home. What does it look like?"

"At least let me prepare the discharge instructions first."

"And spend another hour waiting on some damn paperwork? I don't think so. I waited for the CT scan, now I'm outta here."

"You have a concussion." The doctor took a long-suffering breath. "Do you have a way home? Someone to look after you for the next twelve hours?"

Aidan's jaw twitched and his heavy stare settled on me. "Sure I do. My good Samaritan can take me, right?"

My heart thumped. "Sure. I can take you home."

"See, Doc, all taken care of. Now where the hell are my clothes?" He gestured toward the hospital gown that fell to his knees. "Or are you gonna make me leave here in this?"

"Your clothes are back in the exam room."

Aidan turned, and my jaw dropped as he headed through the door. His gown gaped in the back, exposing the sexiest ass known to man. My breath stalled, cheeks flushing, as that image burned trails in my mind. By the time he returned, fully dressed, I'd worked myself into a tight ball of lust and anxiety.

"Ready?" I asked, trying to gauge his mood. The white bandage over his left eye didn't detract from his good looks in the least; if anything it gave him more sex appeal.

"It looks worse than it is," he muttered. He gestured toward the sliding doors, now slick with rain, and took off without a backward glance.

I hurried after him. "I'm over there," I said, indicating my beat up Honda. I slid behind the wheel as he sank into the passenger seat.

"Thanks for the ride."

"No problem." The air crackled with awkward silence. I started the car and backed out, trying to come up with something to say to break the ice. His words went a long way toward the opposite.

"Why'd you freak out over a lighter?"

My hands tightened around the steering wheel. "What lighter?"

"And I'm the one with the concussion? You know what I'm talking about. That guy lit up and you lost it. You bolted the second you realized what you'd said."

"Where am I taking you?" I asked, easing up on the accelerator once we approached the first turn-off into town. "I don't know where you live."

"Keep going south. I'm on the outskirts."

I pressed down on the gas pedal and pushed the speed limit. The car hummed over the wet pavement. Neither of us said anything for a while, and just when I thought he'd let the subject drop, he spoke again.

"You know something, though I have no idea how or why." His arm brushed mine, causing my stomach to roll. He was too close, and the awareness was exhilarating and terrifying all at once.

"You've lost me, Aidan. What am I supposed to know?"

"Did McFayden tell you?"

McFayden? He was speaking in riddles. "Who?"

"The sheriff's son."

"Judd?" I asked in disbelief. Was he serious?

"The sheriff isn't stupid enough to let something like that slip. It had to be his son."

I burst out laughing—the kind of laughter one faked in order to hide something. Like the truth. "You think Judd and I talk? I don't even know him."

"He knows you." The weight of his stare heated my face. "I've seen him watch you. Makes his girlfriend bat-shit crazy."

"You're the one sounding crazy right now." I sneaked a peek at him. "What happened tonight?"

His sigh filtered through the car, his clothes rustling as he settled into the seat. "I don't remember."

I didn't believe him for a second, but noticing how he'd taken to massaging this temples, I let it drop for the moment. "Are you okay?"

He didn't answer at first. "Yeah." Another sigh. "Take a right at the next street." I followed his instructions, and he pointed straight ahead. "I'm all the way at the end."

His street was deserted, save for a few trees on either side. The pavement turned to gravel, and as we bumped over a pothole, I realized that if Aidan suspected me of knowing something, then there was something to know. And how did he know whatever that something was?

"What do you think the sheriff's son told me?" I glanced at him again. The idea that I'd dreamed of Chloe Sanders' murder in accurate detail sickened me.

He opened his mouth, as if to answer, but mashed his lips closed instead. "Never mind. Forget I mentioned anything." He pointed toward a beachfront home, gigantic in comparison to my own apartment. "This is me."

I pulled into the driveway and gazed at the house. A two-car garage took up part of the first floor, while a steep staircase led to the front door on the second. Did he take up all that space by himself? Or did he share it with someone? The thought brought me back to the doctor's words. "Do you live alone?" As soon as the question left my mouth, I realized how it could be interpreted. "I mean...is there someone here to keep an eye on you?"

Aidan gave me a speculative stare.

"I overheard the doctor. He sounded worried about your concussion," I explained, wishing I'd kept my mouth shut.

"Don't worry about me." He unfolded from the car, then popped his dark head back inside. "Thanks for the ride." He stood, and his body tilted like a six-foot Leaning Tower of Pisa.

I bolted from the driver's side and rounded the hood. "You're not *fine*! You're full of shit is what you are. You can't even stand straight."

"Then why don't you leave so I can go crash?"

"With a concussion? Aren't you supposed to avoid sleep or something?"

"Or something." He laughed, the sound a mockery of joy. "Listen, Bonnie, forget about tonight, okay?"

The name threw me for a loop until I remembered I was still wearing my costume. "Mackenzie," I corrected.

"Whatever. Like I said, I'm fine. You can go home with a clear conscience. You did cut me off—I'd probably be shit-faced right now if you hadn't."

"Maybe if I'd cut you off sooner, you wouldn't have ended up in the hospital."

"You should've left me there."

"At the hospital?"

"No," he choked out, "in that alley."

His words sucker punched me. "Why would you say something like that?" A chill broke out on my arms. "Do you have a death wish or something? You could've been stabbed..."

He blinked away the sudden brightness in his eyes. "Now we'll never know, will we?" He turned and stalked away, muttering "go home" as he climbed the stairs. I ignored the order and rushed to keep up with his long stride. He reached the top and whirled around. "I don't need you nosing around in my business!"

"Yeah, I get that," I said, clinging to the wooden rail to keep from falling. "I'm just trying to help."

"I don't want your help, and I sure as hell didn't ask for it."

"So you expect me to just forget what happened tonight?"

"I expect you to go home, but obviously you've got a good Samaritan complex getting in the way." He rummaged in his pocket and withdrew a key. "Just...butt out. Wipe tonight from your mind. Better yet, forget you met me." The lock clicked after three tries, and he swung the door open. My bathroom couldn't compete with the size of his foyer. I envisioned the space bathed in light as the sun's rays seeped through the skylight. A pair of oversized windows provided the main focus of the living room.

Aidan blocked the doorway, as if I was a psycho stalker threatening to force my way into his home. "Anything else?"

I crossed my arms. "No, I guess not."

"Then consider your good deed done for the day." He slammed the door in my face and turned the lock.

"I should puke on you again, you jerk!" I kicked the door for good measure. "And you're welcome!"

Shivering from a mixture of anger and predawn air, I stomped down the stairs. For the second time that night, I wished I had a coat to keep me warm. I figured the heaviest coat imaginable wouldn't ward off the inner chill I felt—a chill having nothing to do with the weather.

# CHAPTER SEVEN

It had already been one of *those* kinds of nights—the kind of night where every fourth customer had a complaint. I couldn't do anything without dropping something, breaking something, or pissing off someone, and it didn't help that Six had the night off. Lack of sleep didn't help my lousy mood either.

And neither did obsessing over Aidan.

Would he show tonight? Better yet, did I want him to? I held my breath every time someone walked through the entrance of the Pour House, reliving the moment when he'd slammed the door in my face. The more I thought about his behavior the previous night, the angrier I became. Irritation vied with my growing curiosity. I didn't know Aidan. Sure, his face was so familiar that I could draw his likeness in my sleep, but I knew next to nothing about him. Except that he had a temper. And he was hiding something; of this I had no doubt.

The door opened again, and like the last two dozen times, I glued my gaze to the entrance. Only the guy who walked through had blond hair and a cocky bounce to his step that was far from Aidan's style. I stifled a groan as Brad weaved a path through the scattered crowd. One of those nights, indeed.

"Hey," he said, leaning against the counter and settling those unnerving blue eyes on me. "I heard you had an exciting night last night."

Exciting? That's what people were calling it? The town's grapevine continued to amaze me.

"What can I get for you?" I asked, hoping to steer him away from that particular subject.

"I'll take a Coors Light." He plopped onto a barstool. "So, did the guy really have a knife?"

Popping the cap off his beer, I nodded. "He didn't get a chance to use it though. Aidan was lucky."

Brad raised a brow. "So you know the guy that was attacked?"

"Not really." I set the bottle down with a thud. "He's a customer."

The guy sitting three barstools down let out a snort. "Customer my ass. The guy's trouble."

I stilled at the guy's tone. He'd been a permanent fixture at the counter for the past two hours, but I'd given him a wide berth, sensing he wanted to be left alone. Now he had my full attention. "What do you know about Aidan?"

"I know he was sniffing around Chloe before she was killed." He looked up then, and his dark hair partially obscured his green eyes but failed to disguise the malevolence in them. He crossed his arms and his sleeves inched up to reveal the tattoos hiding underneath. "You should think twice before entering dark alleys. You never know when nosy girls might end up dead."

My body went cold. Brad jumped up before I could formulate a reply. "Are you threatening her?" He towered over the guy, who in turn appeared unfazed.

"I'm *suggesting* she mind her own damn business next time." He got to his feet and shoved Brad back by a few inches. "And so should you."

Brad returned the shove, and an instant later they were throwing punches and knocking over barstools. The guy grabbed a glass from the counter and broke it over Brad's head.

"Hey! Stop it!" I screamed.

Mike stormed out from the back. "Break it up!" He and another customer forced the two apart, and the guy who'd started the fight shrugged free before bolting.

"What the hell happened?" Mike asked. "Do I need to call the cops?"

"He threatened Mac," Brad explained, "then he thought he'd get tough with me."

"Are you okay?" Mike looked at me.

"I'm okay."

"I'll call it in." He picked up the phone and gestured toward Brad. "You might want to see to that cut."

My eyes widened at the sight of blood trickling from his hairline. "You're bleeding." I pulled the first-aid kit from underneath the register and rounded the bar.

"And you're shaking," Brad said.

I hadn't noticed how unsteady my hands were until he mentioned it, but they visibly shook as I opened a package of gauze. I soaked it with antiseptic and dabbed at his wound.

"Thanks." He pressed his fingers over mine, stilling my ministrations.

I withdrew my hand and put a few more inches of space between us. Glancing around the bar, I half expected the maniac to come charging at any moment. Most of the customers had gone back to their drinks and conversation, and a couple even danced to a grating hip-hop song playing on the jukebox. A few stragglers still aimed curious and sympathetic stares our way.

Mike hung up the phone. "Cops are on their way. You're too shaken. Go take a break while we wait."

I let Brad lead me to an isolated table in the corner of the room, where I collapsed into a chair.

"Are you sure you're all right?" he asked.

"I'm fine. Just shaken."

"It's understandable." He removed the gauze and winced at the sight of bright red blood. "That'll leave a mark."

"I'm sorry about that," I said, waving toward the counter.

"Are you serious? It wasn't your fault. The jerk was threatening you, Mac."

I recoiled from the nickname, but considering how he'd jumped to my defense, I let it slide.

"Still, I'm sorry you got hurt."

Brad shot me a sly grin. "How about you make it up to me? Have dinner with me tomorrow night."

His words made me tense up again. "I have to work," I said, taking the easy way out, though I figured he wouldn't give up so easily.

"Maybe Six can cover for you."

"She's on tomorrow too."

His gaze darted around the bar before settling on me again. "It's just dinner."

I lowered my head, and a different face entered my mind,

a face with the sexiest brown eyes imaginable. "Brad, I think you're a great guy, I just...can't."

"You can't eat?"

I let out a frustrated sigh. "I can't have dinner with you." Having dinner meant it was a date, and dates tended to be shrouded in expectation.

"I hear there's an art exhibit this weekend at City Hall. You draw, right?"

I stared at him, surprised. "Yeah, who told you?"

"I asked around. Small town," he said with a shrug. "People talk."

Right...the Watcher's Point grapevine. I wondered if he'd heard about my mom's supposed affairs and the speculation that William Beckmeyer was my father. Had it been the same small town rumors that caused her to leave town before I was born?

Now William Beckmeyer was dead, and Thomas Hill— the man I'd thought was my father—had died before I'd taken my first breath. If only I could get Christie to do a sibling DNA test, the results would give me indisputable proof.

"So whaddya say?" Brad's voice broke through my chaotic thoughts. "Wanna go this weekend?"

"I can't. I'm sorry."

His reply was lost to me as the front door creaked open, giving me hope that the police had arrived. The sooner they showed up, the sooner I could get back to work, safe behind the counter and from Brad's pressure tactics.

I froze when I saw Aidan. He stood inside the front entrance, suddenly just there. Like he belonged. Like being in the same room was the most natural thing in the world. His attention landed on me, and he closed the distance between us, causing my heart to flutter.

"Hi." He shifted his gaze between Brad and me. "I'm sorry, I'm probably interrupting."

Brad opened his mouth, but a quick shake of my head silenced him. "No," I said. "Actually, I need to talk to you."

"I should get going," Brad muttered, his chair scraping across the floor as he stood. He hesitated, eyes darting back and forth between Aidan and me. "Talk to you later, Mac." He walked away, and the bounce in his step was gone. Now his feet hit the floor in a way closer to stomping. I'd wager he wasn't used to being told no.

Aidan took the seat Brad had vacated. "He doesn't seem too happy."

"Don't mind him. He has this crazy idea that I'm datable."

"And you're not?"

I gritted my teeth, suddenly remembering why I was *supposed* to be furious with him. "No. I'm too jaded. Guys keep proving to me how they're big time jerks."

That earned me a wince. "Well, since you upchucked on me, I'm hoping we can call it even and declare a truce."

"I'm sorry about that," I said. "I should have fessed up and apologized."

"No, I'm the one who needs to apologize. I'd probably be dead if it weren't for you." He absently folded a napkin into a small triangle. "You went out of your way to help me, and I was a complete jackass. Really, I can't apologize enough." He pinned me under the weight of his stare, and for a second I was certain he saw right through me, as if he could tell by one glance how I dreamed about him. "Forgive me?"

My stomach clenched, and a voice in my head pointed

out that for a jerk, his presence still made my skin tingle. I should have paid more attention in chemistry—there had to be a reasonable, logical explanation for this Aidan-induced psychosis I kept experiencing. It was those damn dreams. That was it. Mystery solved.

A drift of cold air accompanied two deputies inside. "The police are here. They need to take my statement."

"The police?" Aidan knitted his eyebrows.

"Yeah...actually, that's kind of what I need to talk to you about." I rose to my feet. "Are you gonna stick around for a while?"

"Sure. I'll wait for you at the bar."

I moved toward the deputies and Mike. They were in mid-conversation, and I realized with dread that one of the deputies was Judd. Something about his attitude just rubbed me wrong.

He looked up from his notepad. "We've gotta stop meeting like this."

I couldn't agree more, though I kept my thoughts to myself.

"I'm beginning to think your middle name is Trouble, Ms. Hill." His partner and my boss both gave Judd a funny look. "Oh, we met last night on another call," he explained. "She's got a knack for getting caught up in other people's drama." He went back to his notepad, pen at the ready. "So tell us what happened this time."

It took everything I had to give my statement in a calm tone. Mike put his two cents in every so often, and ten minutes later the deputies left, promising to keep an eye out for the guy.

Mike went back to his duties, and I went back to mine. I

approached Aidan. His hair didn't quite cover the white bandage hiding the gouge I knew was there. "Can I get you something?"

*Something non-alcoholic.*

"Coke, hold the Jack," he replied.

I filled his soda and slid the glass into his waiting hands. "So, how much *do* you remember about last night?"

"Bits and pieces." He stared into the dark, bubbly liquid, seemingly lost in thought. I wished I could read minds instead of dream about things that didn't make sense until after they happened.

Dammit, this conversation wasn't going to happen if I chickened out. I gripped the counter and leaned toward him. "Aidan, a guy was in here tonight talking about what happened in that alley." I lowered my voice. "Did you know Chloe Sanders?"

Aidan flinched. "No. I ran into her a couple of times before she..." He ran a hand through his hair. "What'd the guy look like?"

"Dark brown hair, green eyes, on the husky side. He had tattoos on his arms."

"Sounds like her dirtbag boyfriend."

"Was he the one who attacked you?"

"Honestly, I don't remember. I wouldn't be surprised though."

"What's his name? I'll pass it on to Judd." I rolled my eyes. "I'm sure he'll be *so* happy to hear from me again."

"I think you should stay far away from this, Mackenzie."

I liked the way my name rolled off his tongue. "It's a little late for that. He threatened me—that's why Brad got involved. They exchanged a lot more than just words."

He cursed under his breath. "Let me handle this, okay?"

With a nod, I chewed on my lip. If I wanted to know the guy's name, I could find out on my own easily enough.

"I should get going." He got up but lingered, shuffling his feet. "Can I borrow a pen?"

"Sure." Wondering what he was up to, I grabbed a lottery pencil from near the register and handed it to him. Though our fingers only connected for a fleeting moment, the warmth of his skin seared down to the tips of my toes, and they nearly curled as my thoughts ran away into forbidden territory. I'd started the day angry with him, had grown more furious as the hours passed, but he somehow managed to defuse me as easily as a bomb squad dismantled an explosive.

*I'm in trouble.*

He wrote something down on a napkin. "Here's my number." He held my gaze longer than necessary, and as our fingers brushed together again, a shot of electricity zinged up my arm. I wondered if he felt it too.

"Be careful, okay?"

"Okay," I said, stunned that I held his number in my hand.

"I'm gonna take off and let you finish your shift in peace." He hesitated. "Thanks for being there last night."

"Yeah..." I watched him go, stuck to the spot until he disappeared through the door, then got back to work. The rest of my shift went by with such ease that I questioned every minute, waiting for the next chaotic moment to thrust itself upon me. On the way home, I tossed Aidan's words around in my mind.

*Be careful.*

What had he meant by that? Did he think I was in

danger? I shivered, suddenly getting the distinct feeling someone was watching me. I studied the empty road, the trees surrounding me with their colorful leaves, but as far as I could tell, no one was there. As I approached my apartment, I ran a hand along Six's car in the driveway and considered waking her to talk about my conversation with Aidan.

*Tomorrow.*

Surely Six would be able to decipher man-code. Tonight my bones ached for sleep. I stumbled into my apartment, double checked the locks on the door, and fell into bed.

And as the night morphed into dawn's early shades of gray, I dreamed of Six's murder.

# CHAPTER EIGHT

The woman screaming was me, yet it was also Six. Echoes of her death lingered in the shadows like vague memories; they haunted from every corner of the room, threatening to jump out and consume me. Fear clung to my clammy skin, ached in my throat, and every gasping breath brought the smell of dampened earth, wet leaves, and the undeniable scent of the sea.

I untangled from the bedding, jumped to my feet, and found yesterday's jeans on the floor before pulling them on. My front door banged against the wall as I charged into the early morning gray. I skidded to a stop and beat my fists on her door.

"Six! Open up!" A glance through the gap in her curtains revealed nothing but dark, empty space. I was starting to accept she wasn't home when the newspapers under my bare feet caught my attention. I bent down and picked them up—two of them. The morning's headline was as dismal as the sky:

. . .

## BOISE HANGMAN LINKED TO SANDERS' CASE

*Police are investigating a possible connection between the Sanders' case and the killer believed to be responsible for a string of murders in Idaho. The Watcher's Point Herald received an anonymous letter signed by the "Boise Hangman" in which the perpetrator claims responsibility for the murder of Chloe Sanders.*

*A spokesperson for the sheriff's department said the letter has produced new leads, and they are doing all they can to find the person responsible for Sanders' murder. Authorities would not comment when asked about the possibility of a copycat. Anyone with information is asked to contact the sheriff's department...*

The paper slid from my frozen fingers. Now was not the time for Six to go missing. I was *wrong*. The nightmare hadn't meant anything. We'd laugh about this in a couple of days, right after I chewed her out for scaring the life out of me.

I rushed into my apartment and dialed her cell, but it went straight to voicemail. After leaving a frantic message, I keyed in Mike's number then wedged sockless feet into my sneakers as we exchanged a few words. He hadn't seen her since Halloween. A call to Tony produced the same results. I even tried Christie, but all that got me was a barked "haven't seen her," followed by dead air after she hung up on me.

Filing a report with the police seemed the next step. The

sun's rays had brightened the gray by the time I walked into the sheriff's office. Of course, the only available deputy happened to be Judd. He looked up from the morning newspaper, and his mouth twisted into a scowl as he set the front page aside, knocking over his cardboard cup of java in the process.

"Shit!" He pushed his chair back and used the newspaper to sop up the spill. "You again, huh? What can I do for you this time?"

"I need to report someone missing."

He settled into his chair with a sigh. "Well, don't stand there all day. Have a seat." He nodded toward the only chair facing his desk. I sat and wrung my hands in my lap.

"Who's missing?" he asked.

"Six."

"Six is missing?"

I nodded. "She's not answering her cell. I called around and no one else has heard from her either."

Judd sat forward, resting his elbows on the desk. I took in the abandoned soft drink cups, burger wrappers, and scattered paperwork. A teenager's bedroom could compete with that mess. He followed my gaze, viewing the clutter with an air of nonchalance that told me he couldn't care less about the state of his workspace.

"Sorry, my cleaning lady's on vacation." He smirked from across the desk-turned-wasteland. "So when was the last time you saw her?"

"The night of Halloween."

He ran slender fingers through his wavy, brown hair. "Sorry to tell you this, but we can't file a report until forty-eight hours has gone by. Not without reasonable cause."

"Are you kidding me?"

Judd shook his head. "It's policy. I don't make the rules."

"I don't care about your policies. All I care about is Six." A vivid image broke through of Six, her face pale and terrified, her wrists and ankles bound as she squirmed in the back of a moving vehicle. There was no mistaking those fiery locks, singed at the ends from the flame of a lighter. She never gave her tormentor the satisfaction of begging; she'd unleashed a litany of profanities right up until the rope tightened around her throat. Six was in trouble—the kind I couldn't stand to think about.

"What is your definition of 'reasonable cause'?" I asked through gritted teeth.

He shrugged. "Signs of foul play." He reached for his coffee cup but pulled back with a grimace.

"I want to talk to the sheriff."

"He'll be in later this morning. The old man's up to his ears dealing with the press since the story about the Hangman broke. You're free to try back later."

"Don't you find Six's disappearance alarming, considering the headline this morning?" I bit my tongue before I said something I might regret, or not, depending on how one looked at it. Damn cop was acting like a buffoon.

He grabbed a pad of paper from underneath the sodden mess. "Okay," he said grudgingly. "Where was she last seen?"

"As far as I know, the Pour House."

Judd asked a few more questions, all the while scribbling unintelligible notes. "I'll see what I can do. Can't be too careful, I suppose, especially with the media frenzy going on right now." He paused long enough to set the pad down on the desk again. "She's probably recovering somewhere from a couple days of heavy partying. Seen it happen plenty of times. She'll turn up."

"And what if she doesn't? What then?"

Judd scooted his chair back and stood. "Look, I understand your worry, but our department is overloaded right now. We'll do what we can. If you haven't heard from her by tomorrow, come back and we'll file the report." He crossed the room and opened the door. It seemed to me the only thing overloading him was an inability to use a trashcan.

I brushed past him. "Your concern is touching, deputy."

"I'm sure she's okay. If you know Six, you know she's a wild one."

I nodded. "Sure, like Chloe Sanders was?" I didn't stop to see if my point hit the mark. Judd's unspoken message came through loud and clear: he was only placating me. He didn't believe Six was in trouble. Guess I was on my own.

# CHAPTER NINE

As soon as I returned home, I went straight to my laptop and typed in two words: *Boise Hangman*. The search results were overwhelming. On the first page alone, I found links to Wikipedia, several true crime sites, and a dozen or more articles published by the local media in Boise, the most popular of which was the *Idaho Statesman*. I wasn't sure where to begin—the information was massive. I would need a considerable amount of caffeine for this. I poured a strong-brewed cup of coffee and returned to my computer, mug in hand, and began digging.

The Boise Hangman had surfaced three years ago, named for the city he terrorized and his method of killing. His first victim had been a bartender named Colette James. She'd been in her mid-twenties and a native of Boise. They found her body two days after Valentine's Day. A month after Colette's murder police discovered a second victim, Desiree Hammond, who had been an exotic dancer. Several more women were found, and a steady pattern was established.

But then the killing had stopped about eight months ago. Until now.

Taking a sip of coffee that had gone tepid, I leaned back in my chair and processed what I'd learned. The killer had taunted the media, and one name had come up numerous times. A.J. Payne, a reporter for the *Idaho Statesman*, had written the majority of press concerning the Hangman. The bodies had piled high as law enforcement continued their efforts in bringing a killer to justice and calming the rising panic taking hold of Boise.

I swallowed hard as I thought of the victims—a list so long, I couldn't stomach the idea of branding my mind with so many names. They'd been found within a twenty-five mile radius of the city, and they'd all been brutally raped and hanged. I shuddered. To think Six could suffer the same fate, that maybe she already had, was too horrible to imagine.

What I couldn't reconcile was *why* a notorious serial killer would choose a tiny town like Watcher's Point to terrorize. He'd disappeared off the radar for months, and then suddenly he was killing again in another town and sending more taunting notes to the media?

What had motivated him to cross state lines?

The computer screen blurred before my eyes as I tried to come up with a valid explanation, though none was forthcoming. Exhaustion skewed my ability to think logically. I got up and stretched the stiffness from my muscles. I wouldn't sleep. Not yet. Not until Six was home safe.

I grabbed my library card and headed next door, grateful that my flighty friend never slowed long enough to lock the deadbolt. After a few swipes of the card, the door clicked open. I began my search in her living room, though I had no idea what I expected to find. Maybe some clue to her whereabouts? A flashing neon arrow pointing me in the right direction?

Snorting at the thought, I headed for her computer. Password protected. Damn. After several failed attempts, I gave up and went to search the desk drawers. A stack of mail, mostly bills, and the normal office stuff I'd expect to find. I stumbled onto a letter from her mother but couldn't find a phone number. At least the return address would be useful in tracking her down.

I moved on to Six's sleeping area, noticing on the way how her jacket hung over the arm of the futon. I almost tripped over a shoe; the other lay abandoned a few feet away. I felt completely out of my element as I rounded the tall bookshelves that separated her bed from the living room. I wasn't a detective. The police were supposed to do the clue-gathering. Unfortunately for Six, I was all she had right now, and I was a sorry excuse for a search and rescue effort.

Her bed appeared untouched, as if she hadn't been back since the night of Halloween, though I knew she had. I remembered those shoes on her living room floor—they'd completed her costume to perfection two nights ago. Other than the shoes and jacket, nothing else seemed out of place. The decorative pillows on her bed hadn't been moved, and the candles on her dresser still sat in a layer of dust. Everything was as it should be...everything but Six. She should be there sleeping in her bed, gearing up for another shift at the Pour House. Her absence filled the space so completely that I almost gave in and cried.

Something caught my eye—something that reminded me

of Six's hair, only brighter. It poked out from underneath the bed.

No, not hair. It was *Elmo.*

The head of the Sesame Street character grinned in an unsettling way, its eyeholes now void where a blue-eyed gaze had danced at me on the night of Halloween. I resisted the urge to touch it. Never mess with evidence—that much I knew. Instead, I pulled out my cell and started snapping pictures.

A draft suddenly hit my skin, and gooseflesh erupted just as the floorboards creaked. I whirled around and came face to face with Aidan.

# CHAPTER TEN

For the longest time we communicated with our eyes, neither of us saying a word as Aidan blocked the path to the living room.

"What are you doing here?" I asked, clutching my cell phone hard enough to whiten my knuckles.

"I could ask you the same question." He leaned against the wall and crossed his arms, never taking his gaze off me.

"Six lives here," I said, as if that explained everything. "And I asked you first." I imitated his stance.

"I saw you break in. Call me curious."

"You *saw* me?"

His attention landed on my cell. "What were you taking pictures of?"

The question brought me back to my reason for being there. Six gone, and Elmo leaving his imprint on her floor. "Six is missing."

Aidan uncrossed his arms and leaned toward me. "What do you mean missing? Since when?"

"Since Halloween. She's in trouble, Aidan." Would he

believe me? God, he had to. I needed someone's help. The last bit of strength I possessed seeped from my noodle-like legs, and I sat down on the bed before they gave out.

He crouched in front of me. "Did you go to the police?"

I let out a disgusted snort. "They think she partied hard and crashed somewhere. They won't file a missing persons report until tomorrow morning." I blinked back tears. "I saw today's paper. I'm worried he has her."

"The Hangman?" His careful tone didn't match his eyes; something formidable festered in them.

Wringing my hands, I nodded, and in the back of my mind I questioned why I wasn't more alarmed at his sudden presence.

"Did you contact her family? Friends?" he asked.

"No one from work has heard from her, and I couldn't find her mom's phone number."

His warn fingers curled around mine and squeezed. "Don't think the worst yet."

I wet my suddenly dry lips, trying not to let the simple touch of his hand distract me. "It's hard not to." The idea of divulging my dreams were terrifying, but how else could I get across how serious the situation was?

Wait...Elmo. My only tangible clue. I got up and pointed to the floor. "I found this."

"What is it?" I sensed him staring at the red fur from over my shoulder.

"Part of an Elmo costume. There was a guy at the Pour House wearing one just like this on Halloween." I tilted my head and found Aidan's face inches from mine, radiating the same heat the brush of his fingers had.

"This is what you were snapping pictures of?"

"Yeah."

"And you have no idea who he was?"

"No." I took a discreet step away, putting a few more inches between us. "I don't know," I amended. "It's possible I've seen him. He had blue eyes, but other than that..." I sighed. "What bothers me is that I saw Six flirting with him before I took off to—" I abruptly stopped, stricken by what I was about to say. "Well, before I left."

The way he studied me, brows slightly raised, told me he was aware of what I hadn't said. I let out a small breath of relief when he didn't pursue it.

"So the natural assumption is she brought this Elmo guy home."

"That's what I'm thinking. I also found her jacket and the shoes she was wearing that night. They're out there," I said, pointing in the direction of Six's living room.

"Let's take a look." He gestured for me to go first. The tight space made it impossible not to touch him. The contact, however, shouldn't have made me so dizzy. I sank onto the futon and put my head in my hands, closing my eyes to the spinning room.

"What's wrong?" He sat next to me.

"I have no idea. I just got so lightheaded..."

"Hey, look at me." I raised my head and found his gaze roving my face for answers. "When was the last time you slept? Or ate, for that matter?"

The first question was easy—I hadn't *really* slept in weeks. The second took longer to answer. "I think I ate yesterday before my shift."

"You *think*?" Shaking his head, he let out a sigh. "C'mon," he said, pulling me to my feet.

"Where are we going?"

"I'm taking you home." He shut Six's door and led me to my apartment without any input on my part, which should have alarmed me, but I was too tired to care. He pushed my door open and treated me to another long-suffering look. "Don't ever leave your door unlocked again, okay?"

"Okay." At his insistence, I reclined on my worn sofa.

"I'll go find something to cook up in the kitchen."

This take-charge side of Aidan was disconcerting. I was used to taking care of myself, though I realized with shame that I'd done a lousy job of it lately. Then another thought occurred to me, blocking out my exhaustion. The drawings, all of Aidan, were scattered in plain sight on my dinette.

I bolted from the couch just as he reappeared. My gaze fell to his hands where he clutched a sketch in each one. I opened my mouth but could find no explanation.

"You drew this?" He held up the drawing in question— the one I'd finished right before Halloween of masked faces and him lying on the ground.

"Yeah." I bit my lip and told myself not to panic.

He studied the scene, which was mostly black with various grays and a few splashes of red. "You're very talented," he said, but then he held up the other, and this time his expression wasn't so friendly. "Explain this one."

I gulped. I'd sketched the portrait a couple of years ago, using my dreams as inspiration. His hair was shorter, not so wild and unruly, and a wide expanse of bare chest tapered down into the unknown. The tantalizing image still burned in my memory.

I faced his stony expression, certain my face had turned several shades of red. "I'm an artist. You caught my eye, so I got creative. I draw a lot of people." Nonchalance wasn't easy to forge when faced with such incriminating evidence. What would I think if our positions were reversed? If he'd drawn me before I cut my hair a few months ago?

"The necklace," he said. "Who told you?"

A simple chain encircled his throat—the only thing he wore in the drawing. I tilted my head and frowned. What was he getting at? "No one told me anything."

He seemed transfixed by the drawing, or more accurately, the necklace adorning an earlier version of himself. The paper shook in his hands, and for a moment I thought he was going to crush it in his fist. "How is it possible you came up with this on your own?"

My only option was to play dumb. "I'm not sure what you mean. Do you have a similar necklace or something?"

His mouth hardened into a straight line. "Not anymore." Without warning he disappeared into the kitchen again.

I fell onto the couch and dropped my head into my hands. As I pulled myself together, taking a few deep breaths to steady my nerves, I heard the refrigerator door open, followed by the creak of cupboards, the slide of drawers.

"How about eggs, potatoes, and toast?" he asked from the other room.

Despite the nervous flutters in my stomach, I nearly salivated at the thought of a cooked meal, even one as simple as breakfast. I hoped he was better in the kitchen than I was. "Sounds perfect." I'd question later why it seemed natural to allow a virtual stranger to cook for me in my own apartment.

"How do you like your eggs?"

"Scrambled is fine." Another drawer opened and closed,

and I wondered at the speed in which he'd shifted gears. Something about the drawing disturbed him.

Disturbed him so much he'd let it drop?

More sounds echoed from the kitchen. "Need help finding something?" I asked.

"Nope, found it."

While he busied himself cooking, I thought of how little I knew about him. What *was* his story anyway? He'd literally walked out of my dreams and into the flesh just days before Six went missing.

"I did a little digging on the Internet today," I said, listening while he chopped what I assumed were potatoes.

"About what?"

"The Boise Hangman."

He didn't answer for several moments, though the sound of the knife hitting the cutting board ceased, so I figured he must have heard me. "What did you find?"

"He killed several women, mostly bartenders. The media was all over the case. Apparently, he sent scathing notes to the major newspapers." Silence stretched into minutes, and soon something sizzled from the next room, making my stomach rumble. I let out a yawn and lost the battle to keep my eyes open.

Sometime later, he startled me awake with a plate full of steaming food. How he was able to get it all done at the same time, I'd never understand. I'd eaten cold eggs on more than a few occasions. He set the plate down on the coffee table and added a glass of milk.

I scooted over, giving him room to sit. "You have no idea how much I appreciate this." Noting the single plate, I asked, "You're not hungry?"

"I already ate."

I took a bite of eggs. Damn, he could cook. When I scrambled eggs, they tasted like rubber.

"Do you work tonight?" he asked.

"Yeah…" I trailed off and swallowed hard. "Six is supposed to work too."

"You should get some rest then." He started to move, clearly intending to leave, but the drawings sat between us like a third person. So did something else.

"Don't go yet." I set the fork down. "I need to ask you something."

"All right."

"Why did you come to Watcher's Point? You said you're passing through, but I feel like there's another reason."

"What other reason is there?"

"I don't know. That's why I'm asking." I winced at the petulance in my tone.

A sly grin flitted across his mouth. Obviously, he found me amusing. "I'm housesitting."

"Housesitting?"

"Essentially." He tilted his head. "What are you doing here besides sketching…interesting drawings and breaking into your neighbor's apartment? Do you have skeletons rattling in your closet, Mackenzie?"

"Doesn't everybody?" How had this conversation turned to me?

"You can't answer a question with a question. That strategy won't work on me."

I hesitated. "My mom grew up here." That was about as vague of an answer as I could get. I figured it was wise to leave out how I'd dreamed of the town for weeks preceding my move—how I'd seen horrific images that had kept me up at night. Still, something had drawn me to the place, and I was beginning to think it was Aidan.

He leaned forward, invading my space in a way that unsettled yet left me tingling with awareness. "And?" he persisted.

"And...it was as good a place as any to get away to." I folded my arms as a sudden chill went through me. "I never imagined I'd find out my mom's been lying to me all my life." Effortlessly, the words tumbled out. I hadn't really talked to anyone—other than Six—about what I'd discovered, but talking to Aidan was becoming easier each time I saw him. "Turns out the man I thought was my father...wasn't."

"I'm sorry," he said. "You must've been stunned. Are you an only child?"

I shook my head. "I have two brothers and a sister." I paused and let out a burst of bitter laughter. "And believe it or not, turns out Christie is my sister."

His eyebrows shot up. "Are you talking about who I think you are?"

"Judd's girlfriend? Yeah, and she hates my guts."

"No doubt. She's spoiled, rich, and you've come into town poaching on her territory. So, Will Beckmeyer was your father?"

I regarded him closely. "So I've been told. You sound like you know the Beckmeyers."

"Sort of. I know of them. My mother is from here too."

That tidbit of information surprised me. "But you're just 'passing through'? You know, I recognize evasion when I see it. Why are you really in town? Because according to creepy tattooed guy from last night, you're trouble."

"That part he's right about." He brushed an errant strand of hair from my brow, and his touch completely unhinged me. "You should heed his warning."

I opened my mouth, breath stalling in my lungs, and my gaze fell to his lips. Tension coiled around us, the kind that made me want to lean in and find out if he tasted as good as he did in my dreams.

He suddenly rose, as if to head off the undeniable vibe between us. "You should eat and get some rest. Worrying about Six isn't going to help right now. If you want to find her, you need to take care of yourself."

I halfheartedly glanced at the breakfast. Thanks to our conversation, I'd lost my appetite. But he was right; I needed to eat. Besides, it had been sweet of him to cook for me. Not many strangers were so thoughtful.

Maybe that was my problem. Aidan was far from a stranger in my mind.

He headed for the door. "I'll come by later and walk you to work. If you don't mind," he added, making me think he'd picked up on my independent streak. "I want you to be safe is all."

"I don't mind."

The door creaked open, and he stood on the threshold for a few moments. Behind his silhouette, dark clouds roiled with a vengeance, a dreary canvas for the gangly trees swaying in the breeze.

"I should probably tell you..." He hesitated, sticking his hands into his pockets. "I followed you last night. I wanted to make sure you got home okay. What you told me about Chloe's boyfriend bugged me."

I recalled the eerie feeling I'd had the night before with a shiver. But knowing it was Aidan comforted me in a way I couldn't explain. "I don't know whether to thank you or run in the other direction."

"You can thank me by being more careful. You shouldn't be out walking the streets at night by yourself."

"What aren't you telling me?"

His jaw twitched. "Try not to worry about Six," he said, completely sidestepping my question. "We'll find her. I'll do what I can to help."

"Thank you."

"See you later," he said. "Don't forget to latch the dead-bolt." He turned the lock on the handle and pulled the door closed. I forked up another bite of cold eggs, and only then realized that he'd never explained how he just *happened* to see me break into Six's apartment.

Despite the endless questions I had, sleep came easily. So easily in fact that I passed out on my sofa and dreamed of Six's murder again. Unlike the first time, this dream was so detailed it played out like a horror film. The way he brutalized her body, how he dragged her through the woods naked, pulling her by the noose around her neck. Scene by scene, I watched my friend die. Worse was the realization that it was probably too late. Six had been missing for more than a day, and my dreams still hadn't revealed who'd taken her.

I jolted awake and found myself on the floor, arms flailing against a ghost attacker. With a cry of despair, I rolled over, pushed to my hands and knees, and stood on trembling legs. Vomit rose, and I sprinted to the bathroom, barely making it in time to throw up the breakfast Aidan had cooked me. I didn't know how long I lay on the floor, wasting precious, valuable time, alternating between bawling and puking. I finally pushed myself up from the linoleum, depleted of tears and the contents of my stomach.

The shadows had deepened by the time I re-entered the living room. Sifting through the details of my dream wasn't easy, but one part crystalized into a vivid image.

A rock structure high above the ocean.

I pulled my sneakers on, grabbed my keys, and almost forgot my purse. Hysteria chased me around the room, and I was close to tears again when a knock sounded.

I turned the knob, wedged the door open a crack, and Aidan greeted me from the other side. In the midst of despair, I'd forgotten he was coming. Without thinking, I blurted, "I think I know where Six is."

# CHAPTER ELEVEN

"You need to talk to me," Aidan said from the passenger seat. "Where do you think Six is?"

"Some sort of rock structure." As I jabbed the key into the ignition, I recalled the details from my dream. A rocky path winding through an archway of stone, muddied from rain. Blood dripping down Six's legs, pooling under her feet...

I jerked the door open and dry-heaved. "I'm too late. He's already killed her."

"You don't know that. We don't even know for sure if she's missing."

"You don't understand, Aidan." I pulled the door shut with a slam and pounded my fists on the steering wheel.

He grabbed my hands, and I met his eyes, imagining what I must look like to him.

Like a crazed lunatic.

"Take a deep breath," he said. I focused on his soothing touch and forced air into my lungs. "I can't help if you won't talk to me. What's going on? Why are you so certain she's in trouble?"

I'd give anything to have a tenth of his composure. "No time. We need to find that rock structure." I closed my eyes and let the images come again. Darkness. Cold. Stone and mud. Tall trees swaying in the wind. I inhaled the salt in the air, and I wanted to cover my ears against the roar of the sea. "Somewhere high above the ocean."

"A rock structure?" he asked, his confusion palpable.

"Yeah." I pulled out of the driveway. The inevitable questions would come now, but there simply wasn't time to answer them, even if I was willing. I steered the car into late evening traffic. A minute of thick silence filled the air as I drove toward HWY 101, and when we reached the main road, I came to a stop.

North or south?

"I don't know where I'm going."

"Pull over at that gas station," he instructed. "I'll ask the attendant if he knows of any rock structures."

I pulled over, and Aidan jumped from the car before we'd come to a complete stop. As I watched him interact with the pimple-faced guy working the pumps, I marveled at the fact that he was so willing to help, despite his obvious confusion over my hysterics. Doubt gnawed at me, about Aidan's intentions and even the validity of my dreams, yet the intense feeling of urgency in my heart pushed my reservations aside.

Act now, question later. Six's life might depend on it.

He returned a minute later. "There's a turnoff a few miles down the highway. He said to follow the road to the top, and we'll find a scenic area up there. He called it a rock shelter. Apparently, it's a bit of a hike."

"We're going to need flashlights."

Aidan exited the car again and rushed into the convenience store. When he came back, he held two flashlights and a package of batteries in his hands. "What makes you think Six is up there?" he asked once we were back on the road.

I winced at the question. Now was not the time to get into this particular conversation. "Can we talk about this later? I don't want to miss the turnoff."

Aidan busied himself with ripping open the package of batteries, and I sensed his questioning eyes on me every few seconds. A rising sense of urgency pushed me forward, but I slowed anyway, keeping an eye out for the turnoff. Had he not pointed to the sign, I might have missed it.

"Cape Pointe?" I glanced at him. "You sure this is the one?"

"That's what the kid at the gas station said."

The headlights lit the road, catching raindrops in the beams, and trees caged us in on either side, their branches reaching out like long, skinny claws. A chill traveled down my spine before taking residence somewhere in my stomach. I pushed the pedal at every twist and turn, and the last curve was especially sharp. As the tires spun on wet pavement, Aidan braced himself beside me. The top consisted of a circular drive that led to a small parking lot, a brown building I assumed was a restroom, and a few scattered picnic tables. I bolted from the car, and rain drenched me in a matter of seconds.

"You'll need this," he said, tossing me one of the flashlights.

"Thanks." I flipped the switch and aimed the beam at

each of the three trailheads, then turned to him in desperation. "This could take hours! We need to split up."

"Like hell we're splitting up. A psychopath is on the loose, and you expect me to let you tromp through the woods by yourself?"

When he put it like that, it did sound kind of nuts. "Fine, let's start here."

"Mackenzie, wait." He grabbed my hand. "Take a look at the signs."

He was right. Each trailhead had one. I kicked myself for not noticing them sooner. Aidan trained his light on the first, then the second. "Here, this one leads to the rock shelter."

We started down the path, our feet covering ground at a fast pace, and I stumbled over tree roots. Nothing but tall trees and black night surrounded us, and my anxiety rose as getting lost became a possibility. It would be so easy to wander off-trail and not even realize it. I slowed, listening carefully as my eyes darted through the trees. Wind rushed through the branches, as loud as a raging river, and I could barely discern the sound of the wind from the sea. My senses were on overdrive, heightened by the darkness.

I sped up again, registering Aidan's heavy footfalls behind me. We hurried over mud and leaves, and my stomach tensed as the scenery became familiar.

"I remember this." I was sure my words made no sense to him. As I sprinted past the spot where Six had fallen, slicing her knee open on a sharp rock, I knew we were on the right track. The rain hadn't let up, which made our trek through the woods more treacherous. The ground was pure mud in some spots, and the trail reminded me of a muddy Slip 'N Slide.

"Th-this way," I stuttered, shivering from more than just the frigid air. Fear pressed on me, weighing me down as heavily as my sodden clothing.

Aidan grabbed my hand, pulling me close, and I was struck with the seriousness of his expression. He swallowed hard. "If you think Six is out here...then I think we should call the authorities."

I shook my head. "That'll take too much time." As I pulled away, his face settled into a look of resignation.

*Please be alive.*

The silent plea had barely formed when I saw it. Aidan bumped into me, and I gripped the flashlight, staring at the stone structure a few feet away. Tendrils of fog obscured the shelter, and when we crept forward the mist shifted to reveal pale legs dangling in the archway.

"No..." Aidan choked out the plea, a guttural sound that echoed my thoughts exactly.

*No, no, no! Not Six.*

But it was Six. The brightness of her hair, incongruent with the setting, was a sharp disparity to the darkness of the night. A noose had squeezed the last breath from her, and her bloated face, a ghastly blue color, stared back unseeing.

Frozen, just like me.

A sob burst free, and when I turned away from the sight, Aidan's arms sheltered me. I squeezed my eyes shut and clutched the soft leather of his jacket. Unmindful of the grief racking my body, I shook in his embrace and prayed for numbness. I didn't want to think or feel. Relentless, the image burned behind my eyes, and I feared the sight of Six's battered body, left bare for discovery as she hung from the beam of the rock shelter, would forever haunt me.

# CHAPTER TWELVE

The scratchy texture of the blanket irritated my neck. I tried to recall who had placed it around my shoulders but drew a blank. The last half-hour had passed in a blessed blur. God had answered my prayers. I was numb. Emotionless. Someone had uttered the word "traumatized." I'd wanted to laugh at that—was shocked I hadn't cracked up like a freaking hyena.

I ignored the people combing the area for evidence, their flashlight beams bouncing around in the woods and illuminating the yellow tape they'd draped on the trees, as if they were laying streamers and we were all there for a party.

As if Six would suddenly jump into the center of things, like she normally would, and shout "surprise!"

"I think I'm gonna be sick." I jumped up and let the blanket fall to the ground as I heaved into the surrounding brush. Once the dry-heaves passed, Aidan rested trembling hands on my shoulders. I turned around and faced him. Would I be able to pull myself together? Questions were about to start flying in my direction—in our direction. It terrified me to think of what my answers would be. What if I told them the truth and they didn't believe me?

"Hey," he murmured, "come sit back down before you collapse." He picked up the blanket and wrapped it around my shoulders again, and we settled back onto the picnic bench.

A man looking to be in his late forties approached us. His dark hair, trimmed short and sprinkled with gray, belied the youthfulness of his face. Weariness rested in his deep brown eyes as he sized us up. His gaze shifted to Aidan and something flickered to life. "I shouldn't be surprised to see you here."

*They know each other...*

The thought barely had time to register before he introduced himself. "Sheriff Jeff McFayden." He offered his hand.

Judd's father. I couldn't remember meeting him until now. As we shook hands, I tried to make sense of what I'd just heard. How—and why—had Aidan met the sheriff?

"I understand the victim was your neighbor?"

I nodded, and my throat tightened in nervous anticipation. I didn't have a clue what I was going to tell him.

The sheriff's eyes softened. "Did you know Ms. Hunsaker well?"

"Six and I...we were good friends." I paused, blinking to hold back tears. "We worked together."

"And you reported her missing this morning, correct?"

"I *tried* to. The cop I spoke to—your son—wasn't much help. That's when I went snooping in Six's apartment."

*Ask me anything but how I knew where to find her.*

"You broke into the victim's apartment?"

"Yeah, I did." I refused to back down from his stare.

"What I found told me she came home the night of Halloween, but no one's seen her since."

"What did you find?"

I told him about the guy dressed as Elmo and the costume on Six's floor.

"Did you touch it?"

"Of course not. I touched her computer and her desk drawers but nothing else."

"Probably not the only Elmo costume around," he said.

Aidan's empty laugh startled me. "Sure, Sheriff. How many men have you seen lately dressed in Sesame Street style?"

"Besides," I added, hoping to defuse the situation, "Six flirted with this guy." For some reason, one I was more than curious about, Aidan didn't like the sheriff's line of questioning.

"Do you know him?" he asked me.

"No. I served him, but the costume hid his face."

"What about a description? Anything that could help us track down this guy?"

"Um...he had blue eyes, and he was a few inches taller than me. Sorry, that's all I remember. Except for his eyes, he was covered from head to toe in costume."

McFayden nodded and wrote something down on his notepad. The rain had settled into a drizzle, and the thicket of trees overhead offered some cover, though drops still found their way to the soggy ground. He followed with several more questions, the standard variety. I answered the best I could, but trying to describe the men who came and went from Six's life was difficult.

"How did you know where to find Ms. Hunsaker?"

The question came out of left field, almost as an afterthought, and I was just as unprepared to answer now as I'd been a half-hour ago. "Well..."

"I'm to blame," Aidan said, and my gaze shot to his.

Sheriff McFayden turned his piercing stare on Aidan. "I don't know why I'm surprised," he said. "So, you care to shed some light on this matter? How did you know where to find the victim?" His tone had changed. Something definitely simmered between the two of them.

"I talked her into going for a hike. Never imagined we'd find...what we found."

McFayden narrowed his eyes, his jaw hardening in disbelief. I lowered my head, unable to face him any longer. We weren't fooling him.

"Because the weather was so perfect, right? Hiking just seemed like the thing to do?"

"If you must know," Aidan began, "it was more about being adventuresome. You haven't fucked until you've done it in the woods."

My jaw nearly dropped, and I clenched my hands to keep from burying my face in them.

"You're not fooling me, son," McFayden said. "You blast into town asking questions and shoving your nose where it doesn't belong and now you just *happen* upon a body?"

"That about sums it up, yeah."

McFayden looked ready to explode. He took a deep breath, and I assumed he was gathering his last ounce of patience. "Come on. Just tell me how you knew where to find her. I know you want this bastard as much as I do. Tell me what you know, so we can do our job."

"There's nothing to tell."

"Dammit, Aidan!" McFayden jabbed a finger in his face. "I oughtta haul your ass in for obstruction! I told you to leave this alone. You shouldn't even be here, and you sure as shit shouldn't have dragged *her* into it." Everyone within sight stopped and stared at the scene unfolding. "You have zero objectivity on this. I mean it. Go home."

Somehow, I didn't think the sheriff meant Aidan's house on the beach. I looked at him with new interest, wondering how he was connected to what was going on in Watcher's Point.

Aidan remained still as stone, seemingly unaffected by the sheriff's outburst. "I'm glad we got that cleared up. Are we free to go now?"

"Sure, as soon as I talk to Ms. Hill alone."

Aidan took a step forward. "We've told you everything we know."

"Now I want to hear it from her." McFayden gestured for me to follow him, and I gulped, shooting Aidan a helpless look. As soon as we had a modicum of privacy, the sheriff lowered his voice. "Are you sure that's all of it? Anything else you'd like to tell me?"

"That's it," I said, focusing on his muddied shoes.

"So you guys came up here to fool around? Why didn't you stay in the car? It's wet and freezing out here."

I shrugged. "I wanted to see the rock shelter. I'd never been up here before."

"Aidan said he talked you into the hike."

"He didn't have to try hard."

His silence weighed heavily. Finally, he handed me a card. "Call if you change your mind. I'm sure you want justice for Ms. Hunsaker."

With a nod, I clutched the card then loosened my fingers so I wouldn't crush it. "I'll call you if I think of anything that'll help."

Sheriff McFayden led me back to where Aidan waited. "Go, but don't think I won't be keeping an eye on you." He waved us off, his mouth set in a hard line.

Aidan guided me toward the car. "Give me your keys. You're too shaken to drive."

And he wasn't?

Figuring silence was my best option, I handed him the keys before settling into the passenger seat. He started the engine and tore out of the parking lot with tires spinning. I gnawed on my lower lip, lulled into a zombie-like state as the car weaved toward the main road. Once we reached the highway, Aidan relaxed his grip on the steering wheel. Our eyes met as he let off the accelerator. All trace of anger was gone, but something even scarier lurked.

Curiosity.

He turned onto the highway and finally fractured the quiet. "Looks like we have a few things to discuss."

# CHAPTER THIRTEEN

Aidan drove straight to his house. I didn't remember discussing where we'd go to "discuss" things, but now I found myself on his doorstep. I might have objected, but the thought of going home, while Six's apartment sat next door like an empty shell, sliced too deep.

I shuffled my muddy sneakers as he unlocked the door. A scent that was distinctly Aidan—a mixture of cologne, soap, and something I couldn't put a name to—hit me as soon as I entered the foyer.

He took my jacket and hung it on the coat rack by the door, then rubbed some warmth into my shaking arms. "Shit, you're freezing." He stepped back, his gaze spanning my body. "And completely soaked."

"You are too." I clenched my jaw to keep my teeth from chattering. I'd just begun to warm up in the car when he'd pulled into the driveway. Now I was cold all over again—a chill so deep it penetrated my bones. My numbed state was dissipating, and the reality of Six's death seeped in. I blinked rapidly, wishing I was anywhere but here with Aidan. The last thing I wanted to do was fall apart in front of him again.

"I'll grab some towels." He shrugged off his coat and hung it next to mine. Rainwater dripped from his hair, sliding down his neck and vanishing into the collar of his shirt. "Make yourself at home. I'll be right back." He disappeared, heavy boots thumping down the staircase.

I wandered into the living room. Except for a navy T-shirt carelessly tossed over the arm of a brown sofa, the room was spotless and empty. The absence of personal items struck me as odd. No pictures or signs of hobbies and interests—just a couch, coffee table, and the large flat screen television mounted above the fireplace.

Two windows peered at me like bottomless eyes. I pressed against the glass and stared into the dark void where the lighthouse stood like a beacon, its beam tearing through the wall of fog creeping in off the Pacific. Maybe it was the despair grasping my insides, but I was suddenly reminded of the night Joe had packed his bags and left. I'd driven aimlessly before parking near the airport where I'd hypnotically watched the tower's light strobe the night. Planes had come and gone, and each one had reminded me of a star. I'd wanted to hop on one and fly away.

But running away was impossible. Memories were like wounds that scabbed over yet never completely healed. I squeezed my eyes shut at the thought of Six, and I knew the memory of finding her like we had tonight would never fade.

Aidan returned and draped a towel around my shoulders. "I turned up the heat. This should help too." He flipped a switch and the fireplace lit up. A push of a button and poof—instant heat. "I'm sorry about Six," he said.

"I failed her. She was so good to me, and I failed her." I pulled the towel tighter, as if I could wrap myself in a cocoon that would protect me from my guilt.

"You can't blame yourself. Trust me. It'll eat you up until there's nothing left."

I turned my head and met his eyes, instantly aware of how close we stood. Equal amounts of guilt and desire stormed through me, as swift as the wind and rain. I wanted to lean back and align my body with his, take comfort and strength from the intensity of his presence.

But he was a stranger, no matter how many times I'd seen him in my dreams, had touched him, tasted him, breathed in the musky scent of his skin. The last thing I should be thinking about after finding my friend murdered was how badly I wanted to wipe away the horror with a guy I barely knew.

With a rough swallow, he averted his gaze, as if he realized the pull he had on me. I hugged myself tighter and shivered.

"You're still freezing. Come on," he said, taking my hand. "I won't be responsible for you catching pneumonia."

"Where are we going?"

"You need a hot shower." My eyes grew wide as he escorted me downstairs. "I'll dry your clothes while you warm up. Shouldn't take too long." He flipped the light on in the hall, and as I followed him down the narrow corridor, I hoped my cheeks weren't as pink as they felt. The thought of being naked in his home was disconcerting. We halted at the door to what I guessed was his bedroom. It stood ajar, revealing a room cast in soft light from a lamp on the nightstand. A four-poster bed overwhelmed the space with its masculinity.

I pulled my hand from his, willing my mind away from the thought of what we could do in that bed together, skin to skin, sliding between the sheets. Oh God, this was shameful. I blinked several times, but my eyes wouldn't stop burning. The setting was too intimate, and I was too raw from Six's death.

"I'll leave you to it," he said. "Bathroom is at the end. You'll find everything you need in the cupboard." He cleared his throat. "Just set your clothes outside. I'll toss them in the dryer for you." He gave me one last lingering stare before entering his room and shutting the door.

Shadows deepened as I neared the end of the hall and gooseflesh erupted on my arms, though I blamed the chill on my soggy clothing. I pulled a door open and instantly realized it was the wrong one. A cavernous garage big enough to house two cars, though only one was parked inside, appeared to run the length of the hall. The sight rooted me to the spot. There was nothing extraordinary or out of place about the garage, except for the lone vehicle sitting there.

A silver BMW sporting Idaho plates.

I shut the door in a rush and snatched my hand back, as if I'd been caught sneaking into the cookie jar. The bathroom was across from the garage. I hurried inside and locked the door, and I could only think of one thing.

*Idaho...as in Boise. As in...the Boise Hangman.*

I recoiled from the thought with my entire being. I *knew* him. The feeling was irrational, but I'd put my life in his hands. Besides, he'd been in the emergency room the night Six disappeared. There was no way, yet...it was too coincidental. The sheriff's words came back to me, casting new light on my discovery.

*"You have zero objectivity on this. I mean it. Go home."*

As I undressed and tossed my clothes into the hallway, I tried to piece together the puzzle that was Aidan. The shower spray went a long way toward warming me up, but I still felt frozen on the inside. I leaned against the wall, palms flat against the cold tile, breaths coming in short gasps as I recalled how he'd hung around the Pour House every night, always quiet but observant, and how he'd magically shown up at Six's apartment. I wasn't sure how long I stood there in shock, my body steaming from the hot water, but when Aidan's knock sounded on the door sometime later, I about jumped out of my skin.

"Your clothes are dry. I'm leaving them on the floor," he called through the door. "I'll be upstairs."

I shut off the water, toweled off quickly, and my hands shook as I dressed. I straightened my shoulders and drew in a breath before leaving the bathroom. The hair on the back of my neck stood on end as I hurried down the hall. I bounded up the staircase and found him standing in front of the windows. He'd changed into a dry pair of jeans and a white T-shirt.

"Better?" he asked, turning to face me.

"I accidentally opened the door to the garage. I thought it was the bathroom."

"Sorry, I should've mentioned which door—" He cursed under his breath. "You saw my car."

"You're from Boise, aren't you?"

He looked everywhere but at me. "Yeah."

"What's going on, Aidan?"

His face became an impenetrable mask. "Nothing."

I crossed my arms. "Then I guess we're done talking."

His jaw twitched once, twice. "We're far from done. I covered for you tonight with the sheriff. How did you know where to find her?"

"Is that why you lied about us...*fooling* around out there?" My cheeks heated. There was no way in hell I could use the word he had earlier. "You wanted to be the one to question me?"

"You seemed terrified of talking to the sheriff, and yeah...I wanted the truth from you. I didn't think about it at the time." He moved toward me, his expression softening. "Stepping in seemed like the thing to do. Talk to me, Mackenzie. You've gotta start trusting someone."

"You'll think I'm crazy."

"Not crazy. Foolish maybe, but not crazy."

"I dreamed about it." I studied my feet, avoiding the moment when incredulity would flash across his face. A few seconds ticked by. "Say something," I pleaded.

His clothes rustled as he stepped closer, and his feet came into view. He lifted my chin with fingers as warm as sun-kissed skin, and I had no choice but to look at him.

"You dreamed about her murder?"

"Yeah."

Aidan's eyes widened. "What did you see?"

I blinked. He believed me...and I could barely believe it. "I saw what he did to her." My throat thickened, making it difficult to get the words out. "I saw him drag her through the woods. Saw the rock shelter."

"What did he look like? Did you recognize him?"

"I didn't see him. I mean, he was there, but the dream didn't reveal any details about him. I only saw his hands."

Disquiet settled over us. I never thought silence could be so loud. I tried to pull away, but he gripped my shoulders. His face was so close—close enough to notice the tiny golden flecks in his eyes. Something suspiciously close to grief lived in them.

"Doesn't help much, does it?" I said. "The dream came too late. Six is dead."

"It's not your fault. You did what you could."

I pulled away from him, and this time he let me go. "You're from Boise," I began, needing to get back to his role in all of this. "And you arrived in town around the same time the Hangman did. What's your connection to all of this? And don't tell me you're only housesitting."

"Technically, I *am* housesitting. My mother owns this place."

I just about lost it. "No, don't you do that. Not after everything I just told you."

"Do what?"

"Duck and evade." I advanced on him until we stood close enough to breathe the same air. "Six is *dead*. Murdered. This isn't a game."

"This has never been a game." His wounded expression nearly got to me, but I stood my ground. "In fact," he continued, "you should take what happened to her as a sign." He brought his hands up and framed my face, and I closed my eyes against the warmth of his skin, against the emotions boiling between us. "Leave town, before something happens to you too."

My eyes flew open. "Why do you care? Why are you even here?"

"The sheriff was right," he said, letting his hands drop. "I shouldn't have dragged you into this."

"What are you talking about? You didn't drag me into anything. I'm the one who dreamed about her murder. *I'm* the one who dragged you up to that rock shelter."

He was shaking his head before I finished speaking. "I should have kept my distance. I never should've gone back into that damn bar to apologize. Better you think I'm a complete ass."

"Don't worry, there's still hope for that." I folded my arms and glared at him. "First someone attacks you, then you slam the door in my face, and just this morning I found you in Six's apartment. Why can't you be straight with me?"

"Because you're better off not knowing!" His words ricocheted off the walls, though I felt the impact of his anger deep in my gut. "You don't want to know what goes through my head. It's nothing but baggage."

"I'll find out on my own then." I turned and stomped toward the door. Yanking my jacket from the rack, I groped the pockets. "Give me my keys." I whirled around and bumped into him, and my breath caught.

"You're the most infuriating woman I've ever met."

I retreated, but he matched my steps, body unyielding as he trapped me between him and the door, his strong arms braced on either side.

"If you have any sense at all, you'll get the hell out of Dodge and forget you ever met me."

"Maybe I'd consider getting out of Dodge if you'd tell me why."

"A serial killer on the loose isn't enough for you?"

It should have been, and maybe it would have been before my dreams turned horrifying—before I knew he existed. "I'm not leaving Watcher's Point."

"Why not?" Our breaths mingled, hot and moist, and my pulse tap-danced in my ears. His gaze fell to my mouth and lingered. Until that moment, I hadn't known for sure.

Now I did. He felt it too, a sizzling connection, though something held him back. Baggage, he'd said. I had a good amount of it too.

"There's nothing to go back to."

"Don't you have family and friends?" he asked.

"I've bared enough of my soul for one night, but you've remained a closed book." I gave him a considering look. "What's your story, Aidan?" For the first time in my life, I wanted to see something in my dreams. I wanted to see him.

"The bastard killed my wife." His expression solidified into granite. "And when I find him, he'll wish the devil himself had gotten to him first."

# Chapter Fourteen

Something inside me cracked right along with Aidan's composure. Everything he'd been hiding spilled from his eyes. I reached a hand up, aching to brush my fingers against his cheek, but he recoiled.

"I need a drink." He strode away, leaving me glued to the spot where he'd trapped me. A crash resounded from the kitchen, followed by splintering glass. I willed my feet to move, ignoring the little voice of reason pointing out that maybe I should leave him be for now.

He was sweeping broken glass into a dustpan when I walked in. "Are you okay?" Instantly, I wished I could cast a net and pull back the stupid, inconsiderate question. Of course he wasn't okay. "I'm sorry. I know you're not...okay."

"Don't worry about it. I know what you meant." He emptied the dustpan into the trashcan then opened a bottle of Jack, all the while refusing to meet my eyes.

"Mind sharing?" I asked. If there was ever a time for drinking, it was now.

"I thought you were beyond corruptible."

I recalled how he'd said something similar on Halloween. "You remember more about that night than you let on, don't you?"

He pulled two tumblers from a dark cherry wood cabinet. "I remember you, Bonnie." He tipped the bottle and amber liquid sloshed into both glasses. A moment later he closed the distance between us. "Straight up?" The question sounded like a challenge.

"Sure." I gulped down the whiskey, ignoring the burn as it slid down my throat. Heat ignited low in my belly, though whether from the alcohol or Aidan's scrutiny, I wasn't sure.

He leaned against the kitchen sink and finished off his own drink before pouring another. "I'm sorry I blew up on you. I didn't come here to make friends...to complicate things."

"I'm a complication?"

His laughter was empty, cold as a morgue. "You're about as complicated as they come."

I stared at the bottom of my glass. "Why's that?"

"You look at me as if you see right through me. It's unsettling."

"I don't mean to unsettle you."

"Consider me unsettled. Problem is, I think you're using more than eyesight." He finished the whiskey in one long gulp, his eyes never breaking contact with mine.

I gripped my glass. I'd rather have my teeth pulled than tell him how often I'd dreamed of him over the years. "Can I have another?"

He grabbed the bottle and moved toward me, and I saw him in my mind's eye as he'd been in the drawing. Bare chest, subtle muscles, a thin line of hair dragging my gaze below his belly button, to a place I'd shamelessly dreamed of exploring with my mouth. I stumbled back as he poured a refill.

"Thanks." The word nearly squeaked from my lips, giving away my nervousness. I upended the glass, and the smooth whiskey went down easier the second time.

"Did you dream about me too? Is that why you followed me on Halloween?"

I took another step back, but he advanced until the edge of the counter bit into my spine. "I didn't." The lie sounded weak, even to my own ears.

"I think you did. The way you looked at me, like you saw a ghost or something..." Brushing against me, he set his tumbler on the cool granite. "At first, I thought maybe you recognized me from somewhere, had seen the news reports—"

"No," I interrupted, my head spinning from the combination of alcohol and his close proximity. "You were imagining things."

"No, I wasn't." He gently pried the empty glass from my fingers and set it next to his. Nothing stood between us now, not even the last shred of my secret.

I held fast to it anyway, like a child unwilling to let go of a tattered teddy bear. "You can think whatever you want. Doesn't make it true."

"Doesn't make it *not* true." He gripped the counter, and his arms grazed my sides. "Did you see my wife's murder?"

I hated myself for giving him false hope, especially in the face of such unveiled desperation. It drove him, I realized. I feared what else drove him. Justice?

Or vengeance?

Unable to speak, I resorted to shaking my head.

"Mackenzie, I'm begging you. If you know something—" He broke off, screwing his eyes shut. "I found her a year ago... on my fucking birthday...just like we found Six tonight."

I gaped at him, horrified. No wonder he'd gotten shit-faced on Halloween. Tears dampened my face by the time he opened his eyes. "I'm sorry," I whispered. "I didn't see anything in my dreams about your wife."

He brought his hands up and cradled my cheeks, and his thumbs brushed away the sorrow bathing them. "But you saw *me*." Not a question but rather a confirmation of what I already suspected. He knew.

"Yeah, I saw you."

We stood inches from each other, lips parted and breaths growing shallow as the air shifted. My face veered up on its own, my body acting on pure instinct, and met him half way. His kiss was tentative at first, a soft tease that warmed my lips and made me ache, but then he groaned, and we fell into each other, mouths opening in greed. Sweeping his fingers into my hair, he plunged his tongue deep, and I'd never tasted such sweet whiskey.

"God, you taste good," he mumbled against my lips, as if my thoughts had traveled from my head to his by the merge of our mouths.

He hoisted me onto the counter, settled between my trembling legs, and the rigid length of his erection pressed against me *just right*. I whimpered, a moment away from either begging him to take me to bed, or pleading for him to let me go. The former won out, and I expressed the need in the battle of our tongues, in the low moan escaping my throat.

His touch, his kiss...every part of him spoke to me, unleashed something inside me that couldn't be caged. His hands fell to my hips, pulling me closer as he rocked into me. I clutched his shirt to keep from melting in his embrace the way the gentle sway of his hips melted my panties.

Like a slingshot, he jerked back, long before my craving could be satisfied. "I'm sorry," he breathed, his face still hovering close to mine.

"Don't be sorry." I wanted to chase his mouth, addicted to the taste of him, but his hooded gaze pinned me, and the realization that I'd put the spark of desire in those gorgeous eyes sent thrilling zaps to every nerve in my body. As our breathing slowed, we pressed our foreheads together, and I closed my eyes, wishing the moment would never end.

"But I am sorry," he said. "That was a dumb move." He pulled away completely, and the moment fizzled and died. Though a mere couple of feet separated us, I felt as if he'd distanced himself by miles. "You've been drinking, and you sure as hell don't need to be jerked around by a screw-up like me."

I blinked. My legs were jelly and my insides alive with want and need, but he seemed to be in retreat-mode. "I wanted it as much as you did."

"That's what scares me."

"Because you can't move on?" I dreaded the answer but waited for it anyway.

One never came. He cordoned himself off, and the moat between us widened, drawbridge lying in tattered pieces in the trenches.

"Allowing you to get caught up in my life is unforgivable," he said. "I only had one thing on my mind when I came here."

"Justice." The hard set of his jaw told me I'd used the wrong word.

"Finding him...it's all I've thought about for the past year." He drew in an uneven breath. "It's late, Mackenzie." He hesitated before entwining our fingers. Still unbearably hot between my thighs, I hopped down from the counter, and my pulse thundered in my ears. I wondered if he could feel it where our hands touched as he led me downstairs.

We passed his bedroom and stopped in front of another door. He pushed it open, revealing a second bedroom. "Stay tonight?"

I couldn't have denied him if I'd wanted to.

# CHAPTER FIFTEEN

I awoke the next morning to raised voices drifting down the staircase. Male voices. I dressed quickly and crept into the hall, pausing at the bottom of the stairs as their words grew louder.

"I already told you all I know. I thought we covered this last night," I heard Aidan say, a hint of impatience in his tone.

"From where I'm standing, we didn't cover much of anything." That sounded like the sheriff. "I read the file on your wife's murder. Did he send you another note? Is that how you found Ms. Hunsaker?"

"No, there wasn't a note."

"Aidan, if you're withholding evidence—"

"I turned everything I had over to the police in Boise, didn't I? And you were the first person I talked to when I arrived here in town. Do you really think I'd withhold evidence?"

"Yes, I think you would, if it suited your agenda."

"My only agenda is to find the asshole that killed Deb, a job your department has failed to do."

"So you're a cop now? Last I checked journalism was your field." Thick silence filled the air. After a moment I heard the sheriff add, "And according to your colleagues, you were a ticking time bomb after your wife's murder. Lost all objectivity, they said. Caused an uproar that reached all levels of law enforcement and the media."

"Get out."

"Your refusal to cooperate has left me no choice. You're coming in for questioning."

"Like hell I am!" Aidan's voice boomed down the stairwell, and I jumped when the front door banged against the wall. "Get out of my house!"

Without thinking, I rushed up the stairs and blurted, "Wait!" Both men stared—the sheriff with interest, and Aidan with surprise. I tore my eyes from his and gave McFayden my full attention. "*I'm* the one you should be interrogating. Aidan didn't know where to find Six. I did."

The sheriff tilted his head. "Okay, I'm listening."

"You don't have to tell him anything." Aidan stepped forward, his shoulders rigid. "We already told him what we know. He was just leaving."

I shook my head. "No, if it'll help them find Six's killer, then I need to do this." I closed my eyes, and the image of her tortured body knifed my heart. I needed to come clean, not only for Six, but for Aidan. If he found the Hangman before the police did...I couldn't bear to think of the outcome. "I saw it in a dream. That's how I knew where to find Six."

I expected the sheriff's incredulous expression, and he didn't disappoint. "I don't have time for this Silvia Browne-type of psychic babble, Ms. Hill. Now, we'll try this one more time before I drag both of you in."

"I never said I was psychic, and you don't have to drag me anywhere." I paused, distracted by the twitch in Aidan's jaw. "I'll cooperate, but I'm telling you the truth. I dreamed of the rock shelter, and I saw him take Six up there." I told McFayden all the gory details of the dream, and when I finished recounting how we'd found her hanging, I was on the verge of throwing up. I clutched my midsection, as if that could stop my belly from revolting.

"You can't give me a description of the guy? Nothing on the vehicle?" he asked.

I was shocked he appeared to believe me or at least considered I was telling the truth. "No."

"Why didn't you tell me this last night?"

"Would you have believed me?"

"Point taken, but you shouldn't have waited to tell me." The sheriff sighed. "You have my card. If you think of anything else—"

"I'll call you," I said.

"Can't say I buy in to this psychic stuff, but I'll keep an open mind. I think we've established how much we all want this monster off the streets." McFayden's attention returned to Aidan. "You've got quite the reputation as a damn good investigative reporter. I don't mind getting help from the public on cases, never have. What I do mind is personal investment." He pointed a finger at Aidan. "Don't do anything stupid, son. Last thing we need is for this guy to go free because of a technicality."

Aidan remained silent. I didn't think he had any intention of letting his wife's killer get away. I feared he wouldn't rest until the Hangman was bagged and tagged. The sheriff seemed to pick up on the same vibe.

"Keep your hands clean, Aidan." McFayden left, leaving the door open.

A cool breeze drifted in, and the azure sky was a cloudless canvas. What a freaking disparity from last night. The glaring sunshine was a slap in the face. I shut the door, unable to confront the blue sky any longer, and glanced at Aidan. Neither of us seemed inclined to move.

He stood massaging the back of his neck, all the while staring at me as if he wasn't sure what to say. "Sleep well?"

"Yes, thank you." Was this what we'd been reduced to? Clipped, meaningless conversation to fill the silence? "And thanks for the T-shirt." He'd loaned me one to sleep in, and the memory of how wonderful it smelled, soft against my skin, haunted me. Now, as the morning highlighted everything that had happened, our explosive kiss sat like the proverbial elephant in the room.

"Are you hungry?" he asked. "I was getting ready to fix something when McFayden showed up." His hair was damp from showering, and several runaway strands had ideas of their own, despite his obvious effort to comb them in place.

"I should get home, but thanks for the offer."

He sighed, and I figured he felt the awkwardness between us too. "Mackenzie, about last night—"

"If you're going to apologize again, I'd rather you didn't." I grabbed my jacket. "I get it, I do. You don't need complications."

He pulled out my keys and stepped closer. "I don't think you do get it. I might not *want* complications, but I can't control what's happened." Worry etched across his face. "I care about you. I don't want you to get hurt."

*Or worse.* He didn't have to say the words. I heard the

message loud and clear, and I'd be lying if I said I wasn't scared. "I'll be careful."

"What if careful isn't enough?"

"It'll have to be."

"Are you refusing to leave town because of me?"

I avoided his keen stare. Walking away from him now would be as impossible as shutting off my dreams, though I wasn't about to confess this to him. "I really should get going."

"At least let me see you home."

"How will you get back?" I halted. "Now that I think about it, how did you get to my apartment last night? Your car is sitting in the garage."

"I walked." He grabbed his jacket and ushered me through the door.

"Why?"

"Less questions that way. Idaho plates, remember?"

I did remember, and with startling clarity, I remembered something else. As we drove to my apartment, the sheriff's words jabbed at me. He'd said Aidan was a damn good investigative reporter. A reporter...from Boise. Another puzzle piece shifted, and I wondered if Aidan and the reporter I'd read about—A.J. Payne—were one and the same.

# CHAPTER SIXTEEN

I spent the next two days pretending the yellow tape next door didn't exist. Six would come barreling into my apartment any minute now, flaunting some outrageous outfit she wanted me to wear. She'd talk me into going out again, give another push toward Brad, probably tell me to make a play for Aidan.

But Six wasn't going to do any of those things. As each minute crept forward, she never appeared. Acceptance nagged me with relentless power. She was *gone*.

Dead.

Lying on a cold slab somewhere in the dark recesses of the morgue. The medical examiner had probably sliced her open for an autopsy already. I thought of all this with the same mechanical detachment I'd experienced a few weeks ago when I'd thrown my life down the garbage disposal.

I padded into the kitchen to make coffee. Her memorial service was a couple hours away, and I still had to find something suitably grievous to wear, as if wearing black could convey my grief.

As the coffee brewed, my drawings of Aidan called to me. To say he served as a distraction was an understatement. Once again my eyes lowered to the necklace he wore in the one sketch. What did the chain mean to him? He knew about my dreams now, but I wasn't about to bring up these drawings.

Maybe I could find answers another way. I sat down with my laptop and typed in a name, the one I suspected he'd used as a byline for the *Idaho Statesman*. The first article Google brought up confirmed my suspicions. The piece reported on his wife's murder and included a picture of them together. Unlike the other victims, she hadn't worked in a bar. She'd been a teacher, and a pretty one at that. Beautiful really. Enviably elegant. Somehow, I'd expected his type to be of the tall and blond variety—a cliché, I know—but that's what I thought of when I looked at him. His dark looks seemed to attract the type. I didn't *like* to think about him with anyone, but the thought had been there nonetheless.

Deborah Payne hadn't been blond. In fact, her hair hadn't been much lighter than my own ebony locks. She'd had blue eyes, a shade so light they were almost gray. I scanned the article, growing more distressed the further I read. She'd been raped and tortured. Just like Six. Hanged. Just like Six.

And Aidan had found her like that. His own wife, the woman he'd obviously loved very much. Now he was out for blood, and I didn't have to guess at or even dream of the vengeance he craved. The certainty of it sat in my gut.

A knock on the door startled me. Taking a deep breath to calm my nerves, I closed my laptop in case it was Aidan. He'd called to check on me, and I wouldn't be surprised if he showed up on my doorstep. Mom had also called, and unlike all the other times, I'd finally answered. I'd had a difficult time convincing her I was safe in Watcher's Point. She'd seen the latest news reports. Thank God she had no idea how close Six and I had been...or that I'd been the one to find her. She'd no doubt send Marcus and Micah to drag me back home, by the hair if necessary.

Pulling the door open, I tensed at the sight of Judd McFayden. "What can I do for you, Deputy?" The question came out with an icy edge. I couldn't get past his refusal to help me find Six.

"There's no need to be so formal. I'm not on duty." He gestured to the door I held in a death grip between us. "May I come in?"

Giving in to curiosity, I opened the door wide and allowed him to enter. His dark gaze roamed my tiny apartment, touching on the old couch, the small television, and the ancient coffee table that was beyond repair. The apartment had come with the sparse furnishings, and considering how desperate I'd been to find a place on such short notice, I didn't mind the less than stellar décor or furniture. Sure beat sitting on the floor.

"Would you like some coffee?" The promise of caffeine wafted in from the kitchen. No way could I face Six's memorial later without a large dose of my personal brand of lifeblood. Nightmares had ensured sleepless nights. No murders this time, just some creepy cabin I couldn't erase from my mind. I'd sketched it yesterday, again and again, never satisfied with the outcome. Something was off. I hadn't gotten the surrounding woods right, hadn't drawn the windows correctly. There was water nearby, though I couldn't see that clearly either.

"Coffee sounds good, thank you." Judd followed me into the kitchen, and as I poured two cups, adding cream and sugar to his upon instruction, I wondered why he'd come by. My heart lurched in fear and in hope. What if they'd found a lead on the killer? I handed him a mug, and we each took a mismatched seat at my kitchen table. My sketches of Aidan covered the surface, his gorgeous eyes peering up from the paper.

"Sorry, let me get these out of your way." *Out of the way of your prying eyes.*

"I heard you were an artist."

I almost snorted. "I'm sure you've heard your fair share of gossip about me, Deputy. Christie has no doubt filled you in."

"You can call me Judd."

I raised my brows but refrained from saying anything.

"I came to apologize. I should have done more. I should have taken your report seriously."

"You guys went to high school together, didn't you?" I asked.

"Yeah. I knew her back then, but we didn't hang out with the same people."

Uncomfortable silence settled over us. What did he want me to say? That it was okay? Six's murder would never be okay. Neither would his refusal to file something as simple as a missing persons report.

"I need to get ready for her memorial service. I appreciate you stopping by," I said, not entirely understanding my need to remain polite. He'd dropped the ball, and now my friend was dead. There was no sugarcoating that.

"Sure, no problem. Before I go though, I was wondering

about what you told my dad. You dreamed of where to find her?"

"I'm sure you have access to the report."

"Yes, I do." His eyes strayed to the spot where my drawings had been. "I just wanted you to know that I believe you, and if you think of anything else that might help, don't hesitate to call." He handed me a card, and his fingers stalled on mine for several seconds. "I'll listen next time. You can be sure of that."

# CHAPTER SEVENTEEN

"Kinda weird when you think about it," Mike said as I stared at the spread of food on the table. My stomach turned, because not a single thing looked appetizing.

"What's weird?" I tilted my head up and met his deep brown eyes.

"All of this," he said, gesturing toward the smorgasbord. "Like anyone is up to eating after..." Mouth pressed into a hard line, he shook his head. Mike was as vain as he was buff. Six and I had often joked about how he used enough gel to supply a cheerleading squad for a year. His dirty-blond hair fell flat against his forehead now, unspoiled by the usual goo, and the pallor of his skin made him look older than his thirty-five years.

"I know what you mean. I don't have much of an appetite." I forked a piece of ham anyway and dropped it onto my plate. Maybe going through the motions would get me through the reception. I glimpsed Six's mother across the room. Her sons—all five of them—surrounded her as she dabbed her red-rimmed eyes, and I remembered Six telling me how she'd gotten her name.

*I have five older brothers and a mom who thought trendy names were in.*

I scanned the rest of the room, surprised to spot Judd, Christie, and even Brad. The number of people who'd shown up was testament to Six's popularity. So why would anyone want to hurt her? I stiffened, shivering at the sudden idea that it could be anyone. Would her killer have the nerve to show his face here? There were so many strange faces it was impossible to tell if any were out of place.

"Are you sure you're ready to come back to work tonight? You still seem shaken."

"I need to do something other than sit in my apartment. Besides, I know how short staffed we've been, with me and... with me gone." Her name jammed in my throat. I swallowed hard and glanced at him. "It couldn't have been easy on you either, but you've gone into work every night."

"It's my job. I'm the manager." His tone was all business. Mike wasn't one to show weakness, but I suspected Six's death had hit him as hard as me. "And we haven't been overwhelmed with customers lately," he added. "The slow business gave me time to train the new guy."

"You found someone already?" My stomach clenched at the thought of someone filling her position so soon.

"Yeah, the guy doesn't have experience, but he's proven to be a quick study. My options weren't good. People aren't exactly jumping at the chance to work at the Pour House these days." He gave me a searching look. "Are you sure you're ready to come back?"

"I'm sure."

"If you're sure."

Sometime later, after a tearful conversation with Six's mother and all five of her brothers, Mike and I finally began the hour drive back to Watcher's Point. We arrived at the Pour House a few hours into our shift.

I stood immobile in the entrance, trying to wrap my mind around the sight before my eyes. The "new guy" Mike had hired was Aidan. He stood behind the counter mixing a drink and making easy conversation with a woman seated at the bar. It rankled that the woman was Christie. She must have come straight to the bar upon leaving Six's memorial.

"You hired *him*?" I stared at Mike with wide eyes. *This isn't happening. Oh my God, this isn't happening.*

He shrugged. "I was desperate." He rested his hand at my back and propelled me forward. "I'll cover the front. Maybe you should take a few and talk this out with him."

I approached the bar, gaze darting back and forth between Aidan and Christie. They caught sight of me about the same time, and she laughed at something he said, though what really bugged me was how she set her grabby hand on his arm. I gritted my teeth. Jealousy was such a petty emotion, but I was honest enough to call it for what it was. Honest enough to know it was ridiculous. I didn't hold claim on Aidan. So what if he'd kissed me deliriously hot on the cold slab of his kitchen counter?

I marched around the bar, ignoring the smirk Christie sent my way. "We need to talk," I said, grabbing his arm and pulling him into the back. As soon as we were alone, I let go of him.

"Something wrong?" he asked.

I raised my brows. "You tell me. You're the one moonlighting as a bartender." I paused, distracted by the black T-shirt he wore, hiding the muscles I knew were underneath. "At the bar where *I* just happen to work."

"Moonlighting?" With a grin, he leaned against the door of the walk-in cooler. "Doesn't the term 'moonlighting' imply a day job?"

"You know what I mean. You're a reporter, so what are you doing working *here*?"

"No, I *was* a reporter. Now I'm a bartender."

My simmering emotions boiled over, and I let the words fly without thinking. "Six was killed just a few days ago. How you're able to stand here and joke about taking her place is beyond me."

His amusement vanished. "I'm sorry. I'm not trying to hurt you, but you left me no choice. I told you to leave town."

"So...what? You're here to play bodyguard now?"

"I'm here to make sure you're safe."

"I'm a grown woman. I can take care of myself." I folded my arms and mimicked his words from the night of Halloween. "Twenty-three should make me a big girl now."

His gaze drifted down my body, straying a second too long on my breasts, before jerking back to my face. "Yeah, that's what I'm worried about." He pushed away from the cooler and narrowed the distance between us. "This maniac, Mackenzie...he's got something against me. He's always been one step ahead. I've drawn too much attention to you and finding Six the other night didn't help."

"So what are you saying? That he's gonna come after me next?"

"That's exactly what I'm saying."

I shook my head, even as intuition that he could be right

prickled the back of my neck. "That's crazy. Besides, I don't think the police leaked our names to the media. Six's mother didn't know we'd found her."

"I asked McFayden to keep your name out of it. He's worried about you too."

I tightened my arms around myself. "You've been busy talking to people about me, I see. What did you tell Mike?"

"The truth."

"You told him we found Six?"

"I told him everything."

My stomach plummeted. When he said everything, did he mean *everything*? "You didn't tell him about my dreams..."

"I needed him to hire me." He had the grace to look guilty. "He didn't buy the hiking story. I'm sorry."

My jaw unhinged, and disbelief caught in my throat, a strangled gasp. "I've told only one person besides you and the sheriff. *One person.* I told you because I trusted you, and believe me, trusting people isn't something I do lightly these days." I jabbed his chest with a finger. "And for good reason, you jerk!"

He grabbed my hand. "You wouldn't *listen* to me." His mouth parted, eyes stalling on my lips, and I knew he remembered too. The heat between us, the electric current of attraction fusing our tongues together. This was why I was so upset, I realized. He had a way of tipping the ground from under my feet, playing with my emotions with his push-and-pull tactics, but he was too stubborn to admit that *something* explosive spiraled around us with binding force.

"I did listen," I said, keenly aware of his fingers wrapped around mine. "Just because I didn't agree with you doesn't give you the right to talk to my boss behind my back."

"Someone's gotta watch out for you." He let out a rough breath. "And Mike doesn't have any connections to Boise. I checked before telling him anything. You work for him. *Six* worked for him. Considering what's happened, he should know how serious this is."

I yanked from his grasp, taking a page from his instruction manual on retreat-mode. "It wasn't your place to tell anyone."

"I know, but I had to make a call. I'm worried about you."

"I need to get to work." I whirled around and pushed through the doors. Christie still wasted perfectly good space at the bar, and Judd sat on the stool next to her. Judging from the glare Christie aimed at him, they were headed to *off-again* status.

"You good out here?" Mike asked.

I nodded without meeting his eyes. "Yeah, we've got it covered. Thanks."

"Holler if you need anything. I'll be in the back."

The place was next to empty. Two people chatted over the pool table, and another man sat in front of a video poker machine, feeding it twenties as if he had them to spare. Every few seconds he tugged at his collar.

I pasted a smile on my face and approached Judd and Christie. "Can I get you guys anything?"

"You can kick *him* out." Christie pursed her glossy lips and sneered in Judd's direction.

"Don't mind her," he slurred. "I still haven't figured out how to pull the stick from 'er ass."

*You and me both, buddy.*

The doors swished open behind me, and instinctively, I knew it was Aidan. "We're not done talking," he whispered into my ear. His breath tickled my neck, igniting an uncontrollable fire in my belly. His arm brushed mine, and I cursed my body's reaction to his proximity and considered quitting on the spot.

How could Mike expect me to work in such tight quarters with Aidan? My manager was a few marbles short of an Aggravation game, no doubt about it.

"Later," I said, suddenly distracted by Christie's murderous expression.

Aidan nodded. "Everything okay here?" Apparently, he'd picked up on the tension between Judd and his girlfriend too.

The deputy smelled like a brewery. "Everything's A-okay, right, Christie?"

"Go fuck yourself!" She hopped down from the barstool and stalked toward the door.

"Come on, baby. I said I was sorry!" Judd rolled his eyes and went after her.

The man sitting at the video poker machine glanced up, and the two playing pool paused long enough to watch Judd and his girlfriend disappear into the thickening fog. The door swooshed shut behind them, pushing a drift of frigid air into the bar. The pool players returned to their game, and the lone man buried his nose in the spinning reels of his machine. I still couldn't bring myself to face Aidan head on.

"Will you forgive me?" he asked.

I ignored him and began clearing the glasses Christie and Judd had abandoned.

"It's gonna be a long night," he muttered with a sigh.

I couldn't help but agree. The crowd at the Pour House was non-existent. Slower than slow. I wasn't surprised when Mike sent us home two hours before closing time.

Aidan waited for me while I gathered my purse and coat. "Did you drive to work?" he asked.

"I rode in with Mike after the memorial. What about you? I didn't see your car in the lot."

Aidan opened the door for me, and we stepped into the fog. "I walked."

"You must like walking."

"Does this mean you're talking to me again?"

I pulled my coat tighter and fought off a wave of nervousness. "Maybe." Staying mad at him was useless—about as useless as forgetting that damn kiss. "Thanks for walking me home." I finally looked at him. "What's that?" I asked, pointing at the brown paper bag he carried.

"Oh, this?" He lifted the bag. "I'll show you when we get to your apartment."

Silence stretched between us for a block. "Was it everything you'd dreamed of?" I asked.

"What?"

"Serving the drunken population of Watcher's Point."

His deep laugh tickled my insides in a funny way. "It exceeded my expectations. Of course, working alongside you helped."

My apartment came into view, and I hastened my stride to the doorstep. My hands, as cold as ice cubes, fumbled with the keys.

Aidan's fingers closed over mine, and our eyes met. We stared at each other for a beat, the moment laden with something significant, though neither of us were willing to put a name to it. "Let me. I want to check your apartment anyway." He took the keys and unlocked the door on the first try.

I followed him inside then pulled the door shut, warding

off the cold. I was glad I'd had the foresight to turn up the thermostat. I rubbed my hands together and waited for warmth to seep in. "Looking for the boogeyman?"

"The boogeyman is child's play." He turned on a lamp and started removing items from his mysterious bag.

"You gonna let me in on the secret now? What's all that?"

"Window alarms, sticks for the tracks, extra locks for your door." He upended the bag. "And two cans of mace. Keep one with you and the other on your nightstand."

A warm sense of safety spread through me. "Thank you." Those two words were insufficient at expressing what I wanted to say, at how his thoughtful concern chipped at the ice enclosing my heart.

"You're welcome. Do you know how to use a gun? I can get you one."

"That's not a good idea. I'd probably end up shooting myself." I gestured to the items he'd laid out. "It means a lot that you're doing this, but is this really necessary? I mean, what makes you think he'll come after me?"

"I'm not taking any chances." He grabbed several of the items. "And since you won't leave town...guess I'd better get started." He headed into the bedroom, and I followed suit. Stalling in the doorway, he searched for the light switch for a few seconds before flipping it on, then took a step forward before coming to an abrupt stop.

I bumped into his back. "What's wrong?"

When he didn't answer, I peeked around him...and wished I hadn't.

Someone had left a photo of a woman's naked, tortured body on my lavender comforter.

# CHAPTER EIGHTEEN

I was dreaming. Conscious people didn't suspend over someone like a balloon, pulled along for the ride like a silent spectator. It wasn't normal. Then again, normal people didn't see the stuff I did in my dreams. My momentum slowed, and I watched Aidan pull into the garage of a single-level stucco home. He closed the garage door, concealing his silver BMW as two preschool-aged kids approached his front stoop while their smiling mothers waited on the sidewalk. The sun dipped toward the horizon, its last rays painting the mountain range a stunning burnt orange. The kids were getting a head start on trick-or-treating. Raggedy Ann stood back as the brave-faced pirate rapped on the front door.

Aidan entered the house through the kitchen. His hair was shorter than the careless length he wore now, his eyes bloodshot and weary. He halted at the counter and stood unmoving, lifeless as a pillar at Stonehenge. The two trick-or-treaters knocked a second time but were either ignored or simply not heard.

In a fit of rage, he grabbed a plate from the sink and

hurled it at the wall. The rest of the dishes joined the first, and glass shattered and rained everywhere. He stared at the mess, as broken as the shards glinting on his floor.

"Aidan—" My voice cracked on his name.

Of course, he didn't hear me. He strode from the room, stomping through the house and kicking anything in sight as a slew of obscenities filled the air. He reached the bedroom only to come to an abrupt stop. The room was alight with candles, and a banner reading "Happy Birthday" hung above the four-poster bed.

On the comforter sat a note.

No, not a note...a birthday card.

Aidan picked it up, and a photo fell out. He gripped the image, knuckles turning white as he stared at a woman with tangled dark hair. In the photo, she was still alive, her wide eyes full of horror as she stared into the camera lens with tears streaming down her cheeks. Her hands were restrained, her naked breasts burned.

Aidan's eyes overflowed, drops of despair drenching his face, creeping past unshaven cheeks. He flipped the card open, read the words I wasn't able to decipher, and fled the house.

I flew overhead, my invisible string carrying me along as he sped down the highway. He must have been doing ninety, maybe more. The darkening foothills grew larger as we spanned the distance. He pulled off the road, came to a screeching stop, and left the door open in his haste to take off running. Every so often he halted long enough to glance at the birthday card. Whatever was written there must have led him here, to this place in the middle of nowhere.

By the time brush gave way to spotted trees, the sun had

disappeared from the sky. Aidan didn't have a flashlight, though it didn't slow him down. He kept moving, stepping over rocky terrain, climbing higher, lower, and higher still. I tasted his fear, almost choked on it. I wanted to pull him back and embrace him, tell him not to go any further.

I knew what he was going to find.

A lone tree came into view, its branches streaking the night like thick snakes reaching for heaven. My heart stopped. A slim figure hung from one of the lower limbs.

"Deb!" His scream ricocheted through every cell in my body. I reached for him as he struggled to cut the rope, ached to hold him when he fell to the ground under the weight of his wife's limp body.

I grasped nothing but air, existing in a state of helplessness, condemned to watch while he tried to breathe life back into her lungs, as if his love alone could bring about a miracle. He finally gave up and gathered her into his arms, buried his face in her hair, and cried for the longest time...

I shot up in bed with a choked gasp, my feet tangled in the sheets as sweat drenched my back. A figure stood in the doorway blocking the light from the hall. I didn't immediately recognize Aidan's guest bedroom. All at once the details of the previous night flooded back. Finding the picture of Aidan's wife on my bed, then the subsequent hours spent at the sheriff's station—it all blended with the echoes of my venture into his past. My gut insisted I'd witnessed the truth, history without embellishment. I'd wanted to see Aidan in my dreams, and now I had. How ironic that I'd give anything to erase the knowledge from my mind because his pain lanced as deeply as my own.

I peeked at him now as he entered the room. He crouched

in front of me, and I suddenly realized how exposed my pale legs were underneath my T-shirt. I clutched the blanket and covered myself.

"Are you okay?"

I nodded. "Just a nightmare."

"Did you...see something?"

I jerked my head back and forth, a too-quick denial, and clenched my fists to keep them from shaking. My gaze fell to my lap.

He wouldn't allow me to withdraw. "Talk to me," he coaxed, tilting my head up.

"What time is it?"

He opened his mouth then pressed his lips together, as if he'd wanted to push but decided not to. "Six-thirty." He stood and wandered to the window where he parted the curtains. "I couldn't sleep. When I heard your cries..." He swallowed. "I thought something was wrong. I thought he'd broken in somehow."

A chill traveled down my spine. I was officially terrified now, had been since finding the sicko's trophy on my bed. Spending two hours at the police station hadn't eased my fear. The sheriff's concern matched Aidan's, and they were adamant about my needing protection. Returning to my apartment was going to cause a huge argument, especially since Aidan had vowed not to let me out of his sight.

Not that I was anxious to go home, but I couldn't stay in his guest room forever, and going back home to Eugene...I liked that idea even less. The Boise Hangman had killed in two states.

What was to stop him from following me?

Maybe the real question was why me? Aidan said the

killer held a grudge. Was that why he murdered his wife? Was he now after me because of Aidan? Or because we'd found Six?

"I'll make breakfast. Come on up when you're ready, okay?"

"Okay." An instant later he was gone, and I listened to his footsteps on the stairs.

The first light of day peeked through the curtains, and my mind went to work crafting crazy ideas Aidan would swear made no sense, but somehow made all the sense in the world to me. No, he wasn't going to like the thoughts formulating in my head.

I pulled on my jeans underneath the soft T-shirt he'd loaned me to sleep in. A scent that was Aidan, something unique that no detergent or cologne could replicate, brought about conflicting emotions, and I almost changed. But temptation won, and the shirt remained where it belonged—snuggled around my body, a constant sensory reminder of Aidan. I finger-combed my short hair and headed for the stairs.

He was barefoot in the kitchen flipping pancakes on a griddle. God help me, but what a sight. The sweats he wore hugged his hips to the point of distraction. I was thankful he'd pulled on a shirt. I would have been as red as a tomato if he'd stood bare-chested doing something as domestic as cooking. I'd never considered the act of cooking so sexy until that moment.

He turned around and smiled at me, dimples and all. "I hope you like pancakes."

"I love them." I settled onto a barstool at the center island and ran my palm across the cold granite. "How did you become so good in the kitchen?"

"My wife was a great cook. I picked up a few things from her." He turned off the stove and carried two stacks of golden pancakes to the island. "Anything I make is like ramen noodles compared to what she could do in the kitchen." He took the barstool next to mine.

I buttered my stack and tried to keep my expression neutral. His words had taken me straight back into my dream. "She was a good teacher," I said between bites. "I can barely boil water."

His mouth twitched into an almost-smile. "You couldn't be that bad."

"No, it's true. I burn everything. My mom says there was no such thing as burnt water before I was born."

"Are you and your mother close?"

"I guess so." My stomach flip-flopped. I stared out the window at the lightening gray and shoveled another bite into my mouth. The weight of his stare heated my face, and I sensed the wheels turning in his head, trying to figure out if he should push for more information or let it drop.

"The deception about your father...is that why you feel you can't go home?"

"It's a lot of things." I hated the tremor in my voice, hated how allowing my thoughts to drift anywhere near *that night* still filled me with terror. I pushed my plate away. My mom wasn't the only problem.

"I'm sorry," he said. "I have no right to pry."

I faced him with a tentative smile. "Where does your family live?"

"Seattle."

"Do you visit them often?"

"No." He grabbed our plates, and I sensed him withdrawing again. Aidan did *not* like to talk about himself. The observation only heightened my curiosity.

I joined him at the sink. "Now I guess I'm the one doing the prying."

He rinsed the few dishes from breakfast before he spoke. "You're not prying. My family is just complicated. I haven't spoken to my father in years."

"I'm sorry. I had no idea." I wasn't sure what else to say. Every time I tried to get answers from him, I only ended up with more questions. "What about the rest of your family?"

"I keep in contact with my mother, and my brother and I are pretty close, all things considered." He gestured toward the living room. "The couch is more comfortable than those barstools."

I recognized a shift in conversation when I saw one. He ushered me into the living room, his hand feathering across the small of my back, and I sank into the cool leather of his couch. He claimed the cushion next to me. Silence blanketed the room as we both studied the gray scene outside. A seagull flew past, chased by its mate. Aidan lightly tapped his foot against the carpet.

"Do you want to talk about it?" he finally asked.

I didn't have to ask what he was referring to. Retelling the dream would only bring him pain, slice open old wounds, possibly even inflame the rage I feared lurked inside him.

"Is that what all of this chit-chat has been about? You trying to warm me up so you can interrogate me?" I prefaced the question with a teasing grin, but deep down, his need to pick apart my head unsettled me.

"Here I thought we were getting to know each other, and you go and accuse me of having ulterior motives."

"Don't you?"

"Yeah, I do. My motive is to keep you safe." He leaned forward, one hand pressing into the leather cushion, agonizingly close to my thigh. "Whatever you dreamed about this morning, it rattled you. Tell me what you saw."

I couldn't think straight with him so close, and the truth spilled out before I could stop it. "I saw the night you found your wife."

Dropping his head, he let out a breath. "You dreamed of Deb?"

"Yeah."

"Did you see him?" He scooted even closer, moving his hand to the back of the couch, and his knee bumped mine.

"No," I said quietly. "Just you. Your house, the candles in the bedroom, the birthday card and banner, the...the picture of her." I lowered my gaze because facing the grief etched in his expression tore me up. He was remembering that night right along with me. "I watched you find her."

"You saw everything as if you were there?"

"I didn't mean to see it." I felt like a voyeur, though I witnessed the morbid instead of people getting naked.

He shifted on the couch again, and I swallowed hard. "Look at me, Mackenzie."

Slowly, I raised my eyes to his.

"Don't ever apologize for your gift."

"It's not a gift. It's a curse."

"Nothing about you is cursed. It can't be easy, seeing what you do in your dreams."

"Can I ask you something?"

"Anything."

"What happened? Why did he...? I mean, from what I saw, it didn't seem random."

"It wasn't." Pinching the bridge of his nose, he closed his eyes for a moment. "He sent me on a wild goose chase. Deb had been missing for two days, and when I got home...well you saw it. It was personal. Not random at all."

"Do you have any idea why?"

He shook his head. "Sickos like him don't need reasons. He used to send letters to my paper. After a while he addressed them to me. Challenges, taunts. I got too involved with the case." His breath shuddered out. "No, that's an understatement. I was obsessed, and Deb paid the price for it."

"It's not your fault, Aidan."

He didn't agree with or deny it. Instead he sidestepped the subject of guilt entirely. "These dreams of yours, they might be the key to finding him."

"Yeah, about that...I have an idea."

He raised a brow. "I'm not going to like this idea, am I?"

"Why would you think that?"

"Because you have that look about you."

"What look? You don't know me well enough to know all of my 'looks' yet."

"I know trouble when I see it. What are you cooking up in that mind of yours?"

"Nothing. I thought we already went over this. My cooking skills are *nada*, remember?" I was stalling, and he knew it.

"Just spit it out."

"Okay, but hear me out first."

He shook his head, a wry quirk to his mouth. "I'm all ears, Mackenzie."

"Well...you believe he's after me next, right?"

"I pray that I'm wrong."

"What if you aren't? The guy got into my apartment. I think we can assume he's got his eye on me." I was surprised at how steady my voice was, considering we were talking about a serial killer breaking into my apartment. "We can use this to our advantage."

He groaned. "You're not beating around the bush, you're bludgeoning it to death. Just give it to me already. What's your idea?"

"I say we use me as bait."

"I say you've lost your mind."

"It could work...it could *really* work. We might be able to get the sheriff's department involved too. Once they catch him, Watcher's Point will be safe again. Six will have justice. Your wife will have justice."

"I don't care about justice!" He gripped my shoulders, and we were so close that his breath, laced with a hint of maple syrup, teased my lips. My body flushed, my heart pounding so hard, I was certain he heard it.

Aidan's gaze roamed over my face before stalling on my mouth. "I don't know whether to kiss you or lock you in a closet and guard the damn door."

My breath caught. I pressed my thighs together, but the images his words brought forth dampened my panties. "I vote for kissing, unless you plan to join me in the closet."

He pulled his anguished eyes back to mine. "You're killing me," he whispered, searching my face, and I wondered if he guessed at how often I thought about him. Like twenty-four seven.

"Aidan—"

"You need to get this idiotic idea out of your head right now. Over my dead body will you be the bait for a serial killer." He let go of my shoulders and inched back until we no longer touched.

Disappointment sliced me, sharp enough to cut through bone. In the back of my mind, I wondered if he'd done that on purpose—used the sexual tension between us to knock me off my axis.

"It's not an *idiotic* idea." I glared at him.

"What other term should I use? You're going to get yourself killed."

"Not if we work together. He's after me anyway. Why not use it?"

He raised his eyes toward the ceiling, as if pleading with a higher power for patience. "Do you have any clue what he's capable of? Do you really want to risk your life?"

"Of course I know what he's capable of!" I sprang up from the couch. "I've *seen* what he does to them. He burned Six, choked her until she passed out just so he could wake her up and do it all over again. He...he sodomized her, Aidan." My voice broke, hysteria taking over, and I could do nothing to stop it. "I don't want to dream anymore. I need it to stop. Make it stop."

Aidan's arms came around me tightly, swallowing me whole in the warmth of his embrace. "I'm sorry," he said, words muffled in my hair.

"No, I'm sorry." I buried my face in the curve of his shoulder, my tears wetting his skin. I parted my lips and struggled for a deep breath, but instead of pulling away, I gripped his soft T-shirt in my fists. "We need to catch him."

"I know. But using you as bait? Absolutely not. We'll find another way."

"How?"

"Finding this Elmo guy is a start. I asked around a couple days ago. Someone saw him at High Times on Halloween." He dropped his arms and backed away, breaking the hyper-aware state I'd fallen into. "One of the bartenders says she doesn't know who he is, but I think she's covering for him. I haven't had the chance to check back yet."

With a rough swallow, I nodded. "Okay, let's go tonight."

# CHAPTER NINETEEN

"I thought you were keeping the Batmobile hidden in your cave?" I said, making Aidan laugh as he opened the passenger door for me.

"You're calling my car the Batmobile?"

I settled into the seat and grinned up at him. "Well, the official Batmobile is black, but I suppose silver will do."

He closed the door, and his laughter filtered in as he went around to the driver's side. "We could take your car," he said, sliding in beside me, "but it's parked in your driveway."

Last night, after discovering my apartment had been broken into, we'd ridden with the sheriff to the police station to give our statements. Afterward, he'd taken us straight to Aidan's.

"Seriously though," I said. "I got the impression you were keeping the Idaho plates under house-arrest."

"I was trying to keep a low profile."

"Now you're not?"

He shrugged. "People know I'm in town. The Hangman sure as hell does." A frown darkened his face, erasing any speck of humor. "He wouldn't have left Deb's picture in your apartment otherwise."

When we pulled into the parking lot of High Times, I could hardly believe how busy the place was. You'd think after two murders, not to mention all the media hype, that people would get a clue. But Aidan had to drive around to the back in order to find a parking spot.

"Crazy," he muttered, as if he'd read my mind.

"Sure is. If the Pour House is half as busy, then Mike really did us a favor by giving us the night off, especially on such short notice."

Aidan activated the car alarm, and we headed toward the entrance. "He's an understanding guy. I'm sure he wants Six's killer caught as much as we do."

Loud music blasted my ears the instant we stepped inside High Times. Aidan grabbed my hand and pulled me along behind him, weaving a path between the bodies crowding every nook and cranny of the bar. I gaped at the number of people. Not unusual for a Saturday night, but it seemed wrong to be out partying so soon after Six's murder. No one seemed to care. They drank, they danced, they damn near fornicated in public. To be fair, I had to stop and recall how I'd been almost as detached before Six went missing.

We approached the busy bar, and Aidan let go of my hand. Two bartenders kept rapid pace mixing and blending drinks. He wedged in next to a group of young guys as the four women next to them broke out in laughter before slamming another round of shots. Techno music blared from two speakers overhead, and Aidan had to yell to get the attention of the brunette working behind the counter. Her height nearly matched his. Deep cherry-glossed lips parted in a wide smile as soon as her eyes settled on him. Intuition told me she'd seen him before tonight.

"Gimme a minute here," she shouted above the music. She leaned over the bar, green eyes alight with flirtatious intent. "I'll meet you in the back. Same place as the other night."

I already hated her.

Aidan gestured for me to follow him. The monotonous techno beat receded as we made our way to the back. He led me past one of the walk-in coolers and into a tiny office.

"You seem to know your way around."

"Delilah was working the other night when I came in. She remembered a guy dressed as Elmo, but she said she didn't know who was behind the costume. I think she knows more than she's letting on."

"You think you can get her to fess up?" I asked, taking a mental detour from the thought of him and that smiling Amazon woman. Her height was the only thing I could find to pick at. I was pathetic.

Aidan shrugged. "I hope so. I got the feeling Dee wanted to help me the other night, but something held her back, so we'll see."

*Dee?*

The woman in question sauntered in and shut the door. I plastered a smile on my face as she gave me a once-over. Her dismissal stung. Guess she didn't see me as worthy competition.

"I'm glad you came back," she told Aidan, moving toward him like a lethal feline eying its prey. She stood close to him. Too close.

"I was hoping we could talk again." His mannerisms had

undergone a transformation. He leaned toward her, his voice lowering to a sexy timbre, and when he smiled he did it in a way that made my teeth hurt.

"I didn't expect you to bring someone." Her eyes darted in my direction.

"This is Mackenzie. Six was a friend of hers."

"I'm so sorry," she said, and I couldn't fault her sincerity. She shifted her attention to Aidan again. "Look, I want to help you..." She wavered, her gaze jumping between him and me. "It must have been awful to lose your wife like that, but I already told you everything I know."

A lump formed in my throat. Aidan had told her about his past? I'd had to twist his arm to get him to open up to me. Even worse, I'd witnessed what he'd gone through firsthand in my dream.

His eyes met mine, and I couldn't ignore the uncomfortable glint in them, as if he knew exactly what I was thinking. "Do you mind giving us a few minutes?" he asked me.

I swallowed hard. "Sure, I'll wait outside." I left the room, closed the door behind me, and waited a few seconds to see if he'd change his mind. I knew he wouldn't. He was too desperate to find his wife's murderer, would do anything, use anyone, if it suited his agenda.

A new song pulsed through the speakers as I re-entered the crowded bar. Several couples wrapped themselves around each other in what could loosely be called slow-dancing. I hadn't taken two steps before a familiar, well-built body blocked my path. I lifted my head and met a pair of striking blue eyes.

Brad grinned. "Dance with me. I wanna talk to you." He grabbed my hand and yanked, ignoring my protests as he dragged me to the dance floor. I started to step out of reach, but his words stopped me.

"I'm sorry about Six." A second ago he'd been his happy-go-lucky self, but now his eyes were heavy with sadness. I was a little surprised. He hadn't known Six, other than the few times they'd spoken at High Times or at the Pour House.

Or had he? It occurred to me that maybe he'd known her really well.

"I didn't realize you guys were so close." Another song started, the undertones of the beat slow and haunting.

Brad's muscular arms suddenly encircled my waist, pulling me flush against him. "We weren't close. Not like this, Mac."

I broke out in a cold sweat. "No!" I yelled, shoving him, though pushing against his chest was like trying to move concrete.

"Oh, come on. This song is awesome." Before two more beats could pass, his hot mouth was on mine, slimy tongue pushing between my lips and transporting me back in time to another situation...to another man.

To the nauseating stench of tequila. To the memory of rough hands shoving me to the mattress, smothering my muffled cries as my dress bunched around my thighs. The cold pads of fingertips on my skin, dragging my panties below my ass, and the moment that hit me night after night for weeks beyond, when I'd struggled to catch my breath at 3 a.m. from just thinking about it.

The instant he forced himself inside me, forever changing my life.

But the tequila, God the tequila. I tasted it now on Brad's

tongue and gagged as the memories fisted my throat. My plea for him to stop came out in a strangled squeak.

Frantic, I pounded against his chest until his hold loosened, and I barely registered his incredulous expression as I stumbled back a few steps. Stumbled into something solid. I whirled around and came face to face with Aidan. His jaw hardened, on the verge of cracking, and his attention fell on Brad, eyes alight with dangerous fury.

He had Brad down on the floor before I could blink.

The music cut off mid-lyric, Delilah screamed at them to stop, and two men pulled Aidan off Brad. I stood in a fog, arms wrapped around myself to keep from shaking apart, seeing but not quite believing what had just happened.

"Break it up!" one of the men ordered. It was Judd. The other man seemed familiar, and it took a moment to place him. I'd seen him at the Pour House playing video poker.

What a crazy thing to recall at a time like this.

Aidan shook free, and the video poker guy helped Brad to his feet.

"I want him arrested for assault!" Brad yelled as he jabbed a finger in Aidan's direction. Someone handed him a bunch of napkins, and he pressed them to his nose to stop the flow of blood.

Aidan took a step forward. "Better assault than murder. Go ahead. Tell the deputy what you were wearing on Halloween. I'm sure the Elmo costume was just a coincidence, right?"

Brad's eyes widened. "What does that have to do with you attacking me?" He turned to Judd, who observed the scene with crossed arms and an air of nonchalance. "Mac and I were dancing, and this idiot came flying in, throwing his fists around." He smirked at Aidan. "Clearly he's jealous."

"Jealous? Are you fucking kidding me?" Aidan's shoulders tensed, and I grabbed his hand before he could launch himself at Brad again.

"So let me get this straight," Judd began, attention back on Aidan. "Are you saying Brad is the guy we're looking for? How did you come across this information?"

"It doesn't matter. It's true. Ask him."

"He didn't kill anyone." Delilah said. "Brad was with me, okay? He didn't do it."

Judd let out a long sigh then radioed in for backup. As soon as the static *squawk* of his walkie-talkie fell silent, he gestured toward Brad, Delilah and me. "You're all coming down to the station for questioning." He pulled a set of hand-cuffs from his belt, his eyes on Aidan. "I'm placing you under arrest for assault."

"This is bullshit!" Aidan said, fingers slipping from mine as Judd grabbed him. "You should be arresting *him*." He nodded toward Brad as the cuffs fastened around his wrists.

Judd ignored his rant and read him his rights. "Come on, people, move it."

I opened my mouth to back Aidan up, to tell Judd how Brad attacked me, but the words stalled in my throat, the idea of talking about it forcing me into silence. My eyes clashed with Aidan's as Judd herded the four of us through the crowd of gawking bystanders.

Just what I wanted—another night spent at the police station.

# Chapter Twenty

Twiddling my thumbs for three hours hadn't erased the memory of Brad's assault or Aidan's familiarity with Delilah. After being questioned, I'd had plenty of time to stew over the events of the evening while I waited for him to be released.

Now, as we headed north on HWY 101, a deafening silence stole over us. I watched the black night fly by and tried to keep the gate to my past firmly shut. I wanted to scream at Brad for opening it after all these months. "Where are we going?" I finally asked.

"For a drive." Something was clearly eating at him.

I kept my gaze glued to the passenger window, remaining silent. My own emotions simmered just under the surface. The night had been a disaster. Even discovering the identity of Elmo had been a let-down. Brad had gone to Six's apartment the night she disappeared, but the police didn't have enough to hold him. Delilah had provided him with a tight alibi.

Aidan pulled the car off the highway and killed the

engine. The neon glow from the stereo, turned down low to a rock station, cast the interior in a bluish tint. Outside, the lighthouse beam cut through the dark every few seconds, and the windshield became a canvas for the splattering of raindrops.

"What are we doing here?" My heart thundered in my ears and awareness crackled in the darkness. I stole a look at him from the corner of my eye.

"Thinking." His eyes strayed to the rearview mirror, and he silenced the radio.

"About what?"

"About how you ended up on the dance floor with Brad." There was a slight edge to his tone. "And how he thought it was okay to put his hands all over you."

Sweat broke out on my skin, despite the comfortable temperature in the car. "I'd rather forget about it, if you don't mind." The words came out sharper than intended. I wanted to put the nightmare behind me, though I realized now how futile a possibility that was. I'd been trying to put nightmares of all varieties behind me for a long time.

"Is that why you didn't turn him in? You'd rather forget about what he did to you?"

"I don't want to talk about it, Aidan. *Please*. You were there to stop it. That's all that matters."

He didn't say anything for a while. I settled into my seat, oddly comforted by the quiet. Or maybe it was Aidan. Something about him made me feel safe, which was contradictory to the way he made me feel emotionally. My stomach burned as I thought about the way he reacted to Dee's presence, and I folded my arms around myself.

"Are you okay?" he asked, his tone softening to a whisper.

Something about Brad forcing himself on me pricked at the layers Aidan hid under. Had the incident brought back the memory of what his wife had endured?

Or was it something more?

"Did you kiss me the other night because you wanted information from me?" I had to know, hated that I felt the need to push him now, but the question was out and I couldn't draw it back.

"Why would you think that?"

I bit my lip and listened to the increasing pitter-patter of rain on the roof. A loud swooshing sound indicated the wind had picked up. "You got real cozy with Dee tonight."

"I'm not interested in Dee," he said, a little too harshly. He softened his tone. "I'm sorry if asking you to leave upset you, but I needed her to talk."

"I know. You'd do anything to find your wife's killer."

He shifted in his seat. "Look at me," he ordered.

I turned toward his voice.

"You're right. At first it was all about finding him. I wasn't looking for justice. I wanted to rip his fucking heart out and shove it down his throat." He slid a warm palm along my cheek, and I closed my eyes, trembling from his touch. "I wanted to drown my pain by causing his. But then you happened. I have no explanation for this *thing* between us, Mackenzie. I only know that the thought of you getting hurt makes me crazy." He moved even closer, his breath warm on my lips. "You have no reason to be jealous. You're all I think about."

His words found the bulls-eye of my heart and patched over the hurt that had lived there for so long. I opened my eyes and saw my longing mirrored in his. I couldn't speak. I wouldn't know what to say anyway. I did the only thing I could think of.

The only thing that felt right.

I kissed him.

Without reservation, without inhibition. Without giving thought to anything but his mouth on mine. With a moan, I sank my fingers into his hair, and like a match to kindling, my body ignited to the core.

"C'mere," he murmured against my lips. I climbed over the center console, and he pulled me onto his lap, my knees straddling his thighs. He pushed the seat back as far as it would go. "Comfortable?"

"Yeah," I whispered. My hair fell forward, tickling his cheeks, and I ran my palms over the stubble on his jaw. And for a few heavy moments, we just stared at each other. I pressed down on his lap, my hips rocking me into the hard length of him behind his zipper. My lips parted, and a small gasp escaped.

"I can't fight this anymore, Mackenzie."

"I don't want you to."

His fingers curled around my waist, holding me immobile against the gentle tilt of his hips. He raised his mouth to mine, and we were kissing again, a tangle of tongues and limbs and fingers darting through silky strands. I unraveled in his arms, was lost and spiraling into the unknown, and nothing and no one had the power to pull me back. I leaned into him until every inch of our bodies pressed together and his heart beat to the cadence of mine. His fingers crept underneath my shirt, searing bare skin, and every part of me came alive under his hands. There was only him—under me, enveloping me, branding the center of my being with his touch.

He broke away with a groan.

"God, Aidan, if you're gonna hold back, kill me now."

"No one's dying tonight," he said as our chests heaved together. "Though not for lack of trying on your part." He reached up and held my face between his hands. "I can't stop thinking about you in my bed. If you want to be there, I want you there."

I brought my lips to his, almost touching but not quite. "What are you waiting for?"

# CHAPTER TWENTY-ONE

I settled into the passenger seat, my flushed body nestling into cool leather as Aidan drove back onto the highway. Then he touched me, and my heartbeat started galloping all over again.

His hand rested on my thigh, radiating warmth through the thick denim of my jeans. As the road rushed underneath us, reality trickled in, like a slow invading force I couldn't stop. The first hint of doubt pricked at me, threatening to ruin everything, and I swallowed the lump in my throat. I hadn't been intimate with anyone...in a while. Kissing, fully clothed, was one thing, but what if...

What if I couldn't handle it?

"Shit!"

I jumped, and my gaze flew to his face. His attention was riveted to the rearview mirror. "What's wrong?" I asked.

"I think we're being followed."

"What? Why do you think that?"

"Looks like the same headlights from earlier." He withdrew his hand and gripped the steering wheel.

"Wait a second...you thought someone was tailing us?"

"Possibly."

"Why didn't you say anything? I figured you were angry and needed to let loose on the open road or something."

"I *was* angry, but I didn't want to alarm you."

He was alarming me now. The car flew over the road, increasing speed by the second. I turned around in my seat and squinted at the headlights behind us. Whoever he was, he kept a safe distance. "Do you think it's him?" I shivered at the thought of the Hangman stalking us.

"No," Aidan said, pausing to focus on the rearview mirror again, "it's not his style. I don't know who this idiot is, but I'm gonna find out." He reached across my legs, opened the glove compartment, and my jaw dropped at the sight of the gun. He handled the weapon as if he knew how to use it.

"Aidan...don't!" I stared at the gun in horror. "I don't have a good feeling about this. What if you get hurt?" *Or worse.*

"You don't need to worry about me."

Was he serious? "When you stop worrying about me, we've got a deal."

"Point taken." He pulled onto the side of the road and calmly watched as the other vehicle slowed for a few breath-stalling seconds then passed. Wondering how he could be so calm, I jumped as he jerked the car back onto the highway.

"What are you doing?" I cried, grabbing the "oh shit" handle above my window.

"Trying to see the license plate."

"You need a gun for that?"

"Hopefully not."

*Oh, Lord.*

We gained on the black sedan, and Aidan pulled up until the front fender of his car almost touched the bumper.

"Oregon plates." He focused on the letters and numbers for a few seconds, and I figured he was committing them to memory.

The black car sped up, lengthening the distance by a few feet. Aidan let off the gas pedal and wheeled the vehicle around. I loosened my grip on the handle as we headed in the opposite direction. His gaze darted between the road and the rearview mirror every so often, but the road behind us remained empty.

"Who do you think it was?" I asked as he put the gun back inside the glove compartment.

"I don't have a clue, but I know someone who'll run the plate for me. We should be able to find out in a couple of days." He enfolded my hand in his. "You okay?"

I nodded. "Now that you've put the gun away, I'm great."

He squeezed my fingers. The remainder of the drive to his house passed in silence, which gave the nervous flutters in my stomach plenty of time to resurface. He pulled into the garage and shut off the ignition, but neither of us moved.

"I'm sorry I scared you. The gun...it's a precaution."

"Is that all it is?"

His fingers flexed around mine. "You want the honest answer?"

"Always."

"I never planned to shoot him. I'd planned much worse."

I envisioned all sorts of scenarios. Chopped limbs, pools of blood, amputation of...a certain male organ. The sicko deserved that and more. Still, the thought made me ill.

"I can only imagine what you're thinking," he said. "I'm

not a violent person. Except when I think of him, or like tonight, when I saw Brad..." His hand slid from mine and the click of his door handle sounded. I squinted against the sudden brightness of the dome light. He rounded the car and helped me from the passenger side, and moments later we entered the blackened hallway. He brushed against me, so lightly I might have imagined his touch. All my senses were amplified as I sensed him reaching for the light switch.

"Leave the light off." I didn't second-guess myself, didn't allow the reality of the moment to intrude. I reached for his face, thumbs grazing the roughness of his cheeks, and sought his mouth in the darkness.

Aidan's fingers tangled in my hair, a grip of desperation that mirrored my own. He expelled a soft sigh against my lips but didn't grant me what I wanted—his mouth on mine. "Are you cold? You're shaking."

"I'm not cold."

"Scared?"

Terrified, but I'd never wanted anyone more. "Aidan... kiss me."

And he did. Good Lord, did he kiss me. My mouth opened under the press of his lips, and we stumbled a few steps until my back hit the wall. A groan strangled free of his throat, and his hands slid down my body, gripped my ass, and lifted. I wrapped my legs around him, and we became one, locking together perfectly like two connecting pieces of the same puzzle.

He carried me down the hall, wedged open a door, and our frenzied fingers peeled away jackets and shirts. The first touch of his bare chest on mine knocked the breath from my lungs. He laid me on the bed and settled over me, his hands twisting in my hair, elbows depressing the mattress on either side of my head.

His heavy breathing blasted me, tore through me like a memory waging war in my veins. Instantly, my vision filled with nothing but static as the shadow of his face distorted into a monster. Panic clawed to the surface, and though his hands caressed, thumbs swiping the sensitive skin underneath my ears, I could only remember violence.

Wrists restrained in a large fist.

Face pushed into the mattress.

Legs forced apart, and the burn of dry intrusion...

Oh God. I couldn't breathe, couldn't move, but I must have made some pathetic, pleading sound because he sprang away and turned on the light.

I got up on shaky limbs and fell to the floor. "I'm sorry," I said, hugging myself, ashamed of my half-naked state.

Averting his gaze, he crouched in front of me and held out my shirt. I quickly pulled it on, thankful for his discretion. Choppy breathing filled the room. His. Mine. The sound nearly drowned out the thunderous roar in my head, the baritone voice that had taunted me for so long. The one I thought I'd chased away by sheer force of will.

Not even a new town could do that.

I screwed my eyes shut and let the memories liquefy down my cheeks.

"Mackenzie, please...look at me."

"I didn't...I mean...I haven't been with anyone since..." I choked out the disjointed words, and when I finally brought my eyes to his, the intensity of his expression leveled me. I didn't deserve his empathy, not after leading him on and freaking out on him. "It happened months ago. I thought I'd moved past it. I'm so sorry."

"You have *nothing* to apologize for." He settled next to me at the foot of the bed, and his arm brushed mine. "You don't have to talk about it, but I'm here for you. I'm here in any way you need me."

I reached for his hand, and he silently laced our fingers together. "I was okay until we got to the bed." I stared at our hands for the longest time, amazed how something as simple as handholding had the power to bring such comfort. I felt connected to him in a way I'd never experienced with anyone, not even Joe. The quiet stretched out, and I sensed him waiting, giving me the space, the freedom, to unload on him when I was ready.

"He was waiting for me when I got home." Each word wanted to stick in my aching throat, but I forced them out anyway. I'd never talked about it, had never wanted to until now. "I don't even know how he got in. It was dark and I was tipsy. I never drink...why did I do it that night? Why did I go *out* that night?" I relaxed my fingers, only realizing now that I was crushing his in a vise grip. "He reeked of *tequila*—" My voice cracked, and I couldn't bring myself to continue.

He squeezed my hand. "You're safe with me."

"I know." I hesitated, thinking of the one thing I wanted. The only thing I needed. "Will you hold me?"

He let out a breath. "God yes. C'mere." He folded me in his arms, and I buried my face in the crook of his shoulder. His skin was warm against my cheek, his scent calmingly familiar. I'd breathed him in countless times in my dreams, but now he just smelled like home.

"For months I tried to forget. When I moved here, I

stopped thinking about it all the time." I didn't think about it *at all* anymore.

"Something like that is never completely forgotten." He combed his fingers through my hair. "Who hurt you?"

"It doesn't matter."

"It matters to me."

But he didn't press the issue. We sat in that position for a long time, his chest moving in rhythm with mine. I welcomed the silence, interrupted only by the soft showering of rain against the bedroom window.

There was no kissing, no shedding of clothes—it was just the two of us holding on as if the alternative was unthinkable. Time ceased to exist. We could have stayed frozen like that forever and it still wouldn't have been long enough.

My eyes drifted shut eventually. I vaguely remembered him carrying me to bed, recalled reaching for him when he tried to leave. He settled behind me, wrapping me in the safety of his arms, and for the first time in what seemed like forever, the dreams were absent. And I slept.

# CHAPTER TWENTY-TWO

I hadn't realized how much I missed awaking in someone's arms. The room was chilly, but there was only warmth where our bodies touched, chest to chest. I didn't want to wake up yet, didn't want the mortification of last night to encroach upon this perfectly serene moment.

"Sleep well?" Aidan's voice, thick with sleep, sent shivers through me. Nothing had ever sounded so sexy.

Stretching my legs, I nodded. I wasn't brave enough to meet his eyes yet. "I can't remember the last time I slept so well."

He trailed a hand down my spine and splayed his fingers across my lower back. "You talked in your sleep once."

"What did I say?"

"You said 'Joe.'"

After all these months, hurt still ricocheted at the mention of his name. "I don't remember."

"Is he the one...?"

"It wasn't Joe."

Aidan's silence bothered me. I lifted my head and didn't

like what I saw. It was the same look he got when he talked about finding the Hangman.

"You can't rid the world of every monster, Aidan."

"Not all of them. Maybe just a couple."

"It won't bring her back." I lowered my gaze, horrified by what I'd said. "I'm sorry."

"You spend too much time apologizing." He twirled a lock of my hair around his finger. "If anything, I'm the one who needs to apologize. I shouldn't have let things go so far last night."

I never thought an apology could hurt so much. "I understand. It was a crazy night, with you getting arrested and being followed"—oh God, was that my voice cracking?—"just a heat of the moment thing."

He let out a heavy sigh and rolled us until we faced each other. "There's heat all right, but it was more than a 'thing.' I'm glad we stopped because I don't have any protection."

"Oh." This was beyond awkward.

"Yeah..." He trailed off, and I guessed the conversation was just as awkward for him. "There hasn't been anyone since Deb. Sex hasn't...really been an issue."

Until now, or it would have been if I hadn't freaked out on him. How I wished I could go back and change the outcome of last night.

"I'm on birth control." So much for avoiding mortification. "Not for *that* reason."

"I'm not sure you want to tell me that," he said, his hand on my back pulling me a little closer, "considering where we are right now."

"What if I do want to tell you that?"

He opened his mouth, but then he shook his head, seemingly at war with himself. "We did the right thing. You barely know me."

And yet here we lie...in bed together talking about sex. The irony didn't escape me. How could I explain something to him that I barely understood myself? That I felt as if I'd known him for years. The way he'd held me all night, with no expectations or ulterior motives, cemented what my heart had already figured out. I could trust him.

"I know you, Aidan." I placed my palm on his chest, over the steady *thump-thump* of his heartbeat. "I've dreamed about you more than I want to admit."

He grabbed my hand and threaded our fingers together. "Are you saying you saw me in your dreams before we met?"

"That drawing—the one showing a lot of skin?" I bowed my head to hide my embarrassment. "I sketched it over two years ago."

"I'm not sure what to say." He sounded stunned. "Wait. How much of me did you see?" A hint of mischief entered his tone, and I peeked up to find his mouth creeping into a smile.

"A lot." I ached to taste his mouth again. It would be so easy, just a few inches closer and my lips would be on his.

"I think there's an unbalance in fairness here." He arched a brow. "I've only seen half of you."

"We can fix that."

He shook his head, his expression hardening. "Getting involved is the last thing we should do right now. Last night, I let what I feel for you take over, but we don't need to rush this."

I gave him a teasing grin. "You feel something for me?"

He rolled his eyes. "Do you really have to ask?"

I suppose a part of me did. Although I'd seen plenty of

him in my dreams, so much about him still remained a mystery. "What does the necklace mean to you?"

He flinched, and I thought he was about to withdraw, so his next words surprised me. "Deb gave it to me on our first anniversary, the night we decided to start a family."

No words would lessen his grief, so I said nothing.

"I buried it with her." He rolled onto his back and stared at the ceiling, and for several seconds we watched a spider crawl above our heads.

"I'll destroy the drawing. I'm sorry I drew it."

"No, keep it." He flexed his fingers around mine. "I've learned the hard way that memories can't be buried."

We had that in common. I slid my hand from his and sat up, figuring we both needed a little space. "Mind if I take a shower?"

He propped himself up on his elbows. "Of course not. We need to stop by your apartment today. You're gonna need clothes."

"I shouldn't stay here." I stood, and my bare feet sank into the plush carpet as I padded to the door.

"Did I say something wrong?"

"No, but staying with you...it's not a good idea." Not when all I could think about was how amazing it felt to kiss him. How, despite everything, I wanted to crawl back into bed with him and finish what we'd started last night.

But I couldn't do that.

I was too conflicted, too confused, to know what the hell I wanted. One minute I wanted to be as close as humanly possible, and the next I was panicking when I got my wish.

No wonder he'd put on the brakes.

"He broke into your apartment, Mackenzie. You can't go

back home, and you refuse to leave town, so that leaves you staying with me." I heard his sigh from across the room. "This is my fault. He's targeting you because of me."

And there it was—the one thing that bothered me most. I didn't want to be an obligation to him. He said he had feelings for me, but I couldn't help but wonder how much of what he felt stemmed from guilt.

"I'll think about it." I grabbed the doorknob and hesitated. "I know you better than you think." I left the room, wondering how he'd react if he knew how close I was to giving him what was left of my heart.

# CHAPTER TWENTY-THREE

Despite my misgivings, I temporarily moved into Aidan's guest bedroom. It wasn't that I didn't want to stay with him, and I didn't lack common sense either—I understood the danger I faced. No, the part I hated was how he considered protecting me his duty, as if keeping me alive would assuage his misplaced guilt. I wanted him to want me around because he just...did.

"What am I missing?" He crossed his arms and perused the mess of newspapers, records, and printouts arranged in slapdash fashion on the table. He'd turned the dining room into what I called "Operation Find Psychopath."

"No luck?" I slid a pile of tax records out of the way and made room for his cup of coffee.

He absently picked up the mug and gestured to the table. "Real estate records turned up zilch. No one else has come here from Boise in the past few months."

"What about family members?" I fiddled with a notepad, the kind important people like lawyers used. Details of my dreams barely filled the first sheet, and my drawings—more useless sketches of the same cabin, of images that didn't make sense—mocked me from underneath. "Maybe he has family here. If he's staying with someone, I doubt you'd find any real estate records."

"I thought about that." He picked up the morning's newspaper, which claimed the sheriff's department was following all leads, blah, blah, blah. The only good thing about the front page was the absence of another murder headline. "It's more than just the lack of evidence. There's no logic. Why come here? Why kill in Watcher's Point? My mother is the only connection I have to this town."

"You think the murders might have something to do with her?"

He threw the paper on the table. "I have no idea. I'm at a loss. This makes no fucking sense." He sipped from his mug, and as I watched the steam snake upward, an idea occurred to me.

"What if he didn't relocate here? What if he's been here all along?"

Aidan stilled. "You mean like a copycat?"

"I guess."

"Impossible. He left a picture of Deb in your apartment."

He had a point. But what if... "What if the Hangman didn't kill your wife?"

"What? How did you come up with that theory?"

"I don't know, but maybe you can't find anyone with a connection to Boise because there isn't one."

"No." His mouth flattened into a stubborn line. "It was him. Classic Hangman M.O."

"Except your wife was a teacher." I averted my eyes,

uncomfortable with discussing her murder. "All of the other victims worked in bars or clubs."

"Did your dreams tell you that?"

The grandfather clock announced the hour, unleashing its haunting melodic strains. I jumped every time the darn thing went off. Twelve chimes completed the ritual. We'd been going over the case since breakfast.

"No, the Internet did."

Aidan's curious gaze followed me around the table. I lingered at the window and pressed close, my breath fogging the glass as I peered down at the rhythmic tide. Waves frothed over the rocks, reaching a furious crescendo as seawater spouted through the cracks.

"After Six went missing, I googled the Hangman. The name A.J. Payne popped up, and the sheriff said you were a reporter, so I wanted to know if you were him."

"All you had to do was ask."

"Right," I said, arching a brow as I faced him, "because you've been a fountain of information since I met you?"

He folded his arms defensively. "I didn't want to involve you."

"Well, now I'm involved, and I'm asking. Is it possible a copycat was responsible?"

"Anything's possible. The police looked into it because of Deb's profession and the set-up in our bedroom." He refocused on the disorganized mess that separated us. "But they didn't find anything. They thought it was a personal attack aimed at me."

I leaned against the windowsill and recalled what I'd read about the Hangman. "He disappeared a few months later, right? Only resurfacing in Watcher's Point a couple of weeks ago?"

"Yeah, there was another victim after Deb, and then poof—he was gone. I don't know what brought him here, but he made sure I had a front row seat." Aidan rubbed the bridge of his nose, and I was struck with how exhausted he looked. My nightmares had woken him the past two nights, even though we slept in separate bedrooms.

"Why do you say that?" I asked.

"I received a letter three weeks ago. Whoever sent it claimed that Chloe Sanders had information about Deb's murder. If I hadn't been so desperate for a lead, I would've written it off as a prank."

But then Chloe turned up dead, and that had pretty much ensured he was on the right path. The night of Halloween, when I'd followed Aidan, came to mind. "So it *was* Chloe's boyfriend who attacked you, wasn't it? He must have assumed you had something to do with her death."

"That's my guess. Can't prove it, though. My memory of that night is sketchy."

"Okay, let's forget about the copycat angle for now. What about a connection? There's gotta be a reason he's targeting you."

"Trust me, I've wondered the same thing. I checked out every person I could think of—people I've pissed off, people I've sent to jail. Digging into my past didn't turn up anything." He reached for a thin newspaper clipping, ragged around the edges from too much handling. Ragged, just like Aidan. He stared down at the smiling face of his wife. "Whatever the reason, it got Deb killed."

"How is blaming yourself gonna help?"

He set aside the clipping. "Let's go over your dream again. Tell me about this van you saw last night."

"Aidan," I began, unable to mask my frustration. He wore his guilt like armor. Evidently, he had no intention of letting me talk him out of it. "I already told you. It was a white utility van." I moved around the table and sifted through my sketches until I found the one I'd drawn this morning.

He frowned. "What about lettering on the sides? Dents, or cracks in the windshield?"

I screwed my eyes shut and visualized what I'd seen in my dream. He remained quiet, and the silence buzzed in my ears, morphed into the roar of the ocean. A wave of dizziness threatened to pull me under. Blindly, I reached for the edge of the table. Memories stuttered like movie clips behind my eyelids. Foamy waves and jagged rocks, milky sprays of seawater, and the moon—a perfect circle to illuminate the night. The last thing I saw was a white van speeding toward a tunnel.

"No windows," I said, pausing, "and no lettering either. I'm not sure about damage, but there's a tunnel. Gotta be Highway 101." Upon returning to the here and now, I found that he'd inched closer. "There was a full moon."

Aidan moved over to his laptop. A calendar of November popped up, and I realized instantly what he was looking for. Lunar cycles.

"There's a full moon this Sunday."

I slumped into a chair as the magnitude of the situation hit me. "If I'm right..." *Another woman is going to die...* "then we don't have much time."

He pulled up a chair and sat facing me. "What about the

victim? Can you remember anything? Hair or eye color? Height?"

"I'm not sure...brown hair? God, Aidan, I can't see who she is. He's gonna kill again, and I can't do shit about it because I can't see what I need to see."

He leaned forward, sliding his hands into my hair, and I froze. His warm fingers held me steady, his gaze dipping to my mouth before meeting my eyes again. We'd been tiptoeing around each other ever since our heavy talk about sex, and how, apparently, we'd come to the conclusion it didn't need to be rushed.

Now I waited, barely breathing. When he finally brought his lips to mine, the pent up sexual frustration of the last two days poured from him. He gripped my hair in a painful clutch, angled my head back, and forced my mouth open under his desperate need for connection. A moan escaped my throat, and reality faded for a few delirious moments as the world narrowed to only him.

We broke apart, breaths coming in heavy puffs, our eyes dazed. "What was that for?" I asked. "I mean, you barely touch me for two days, and now you're kissing me?"

"You were having a meltdown."

"Now I'm having a different kind of meltdown."

He pressed his forehead against mine and groaned. "I know the feeling. I can't keep my head on straight when I'm around you, which makes touching you a *really* bad idea."

But then he was kissing me again.

I weaved my fingers through his silky strands. He needed a haircut, though the thought of shortening the length made my fingers ache. I loved his hair.

"We'd better stop," he murmured, words ghosting across my mouth, "or we're gonna end up in bed."

"And that's a bad thing?"

"Mmm-hmm. When I think of a reason, I'll let you know."

His phone vibrated on the table, shattering the moment. He reached for it and stared at the display. "Finally."

"Who is it?" I asked when what I really wanted to do was strangle whoever had interrupted us.

"My brother." He answered the call with, "What did you find?" and got up to pace the floor. "You want me to come to Portland? Why?" A pause, and then, "No, that's okay. I'm on my way."

"Did you find out who was following us?" I asked after he'd slipped the phone into his pocket.

He nodded. "The plate traced back to a private investigator."

"The car belonged to a PI?"

"So it seems, and for some reason Logan wants to talk to me in person." He stopped pacing. "Feel like going to Portland?"

Didn't he know I'd follow him to the gates of Hell by now?

# Chapter Twenty-Four

Three and a half hours later we arrived in the "City of Roses." Portland was possibly the most gorgeous city in the US, even if a sheet of rain obscured the view. Several bridges connected eastern and western Portland over the Willamette River, and high-rise buildings towered amongst a thicket of greenery.

Aidan steered the car off I-5 and headed into the heart of the city.

"I'm surprised Mike gave us the night off, especially after what happened Saturday." I strained to catch a glimpse of the skyscrapers through the passenger window.

"Maybe he's taking bets on whether or not I'll get arrested again."

"Can I get in on this bet?"

The corner of his mouth turned up. "When I told him how Brad accosted you on the dance floor, he said I should have knocked out a couple of teeth while I was at it."

I smiled despite myself. "I can't believe you got yourself arrested."

"Wouldn't be the first time."

"You're kidding." My attention shifted to him, tall buildings and riverfront scenery forgotten.

"When I was a reporter, I didn't always play by the rules."

"What did you get arrested for?"

"Breaking and entering, mostly. I wasn't about to let a little thing like a locked door keep me from landing a story." He shot me a dimpled grin. "Though one time I got arrested for jaywalking."

"*Jaywalking?*"

"The cop was an ass. He said I had an attitude." He steered the car onto SW River Parkway. "I suppose ripping the ticket to shreds didn't help my case."

"Probably not." I tried to hide a smile but failed as he pulled into the underground parking garage of one of downtown's riverfront high-rise buildings. "This is it?" I asked.

"Yeah." He armed the car alarm, and we headed toward the lobby where a doorman greeted us.

"Good afternoon, Mr. Payne."

Aidan nodded his acknowledgement before escorting me into the swankiest elevator I'd ever seen. Dark wood and marble surrounded us, and a cushioned bench, tucked against a wall, invited people to relax and enjoy the ride. He pressed the button marked with "P."

"Your brother lives in the penthouse?"

"Yeah." As the mirrored doors closed, he averted his gaze.

The name of the building, carved into seashell marble, drew my notice. Payne-Davis Riverscape.

"Payne-Davis...as in the *corporation*?"

*As in the largest conglomerate in the Pacific Northwest?*

He must have been fascinated by the doors of the elevator; his attention never strayed from them as we continued to climb. With forty floors to travel, we still had a ways to go.

I stared at his reflection, slack-jawed. Payne-Davis did business in everything from weaponry to pharmaceuticals. "You're one of *those* Paynes?"

"Hamilton Payne is my father," he finally admitted as we passed the twenty-eighth floor.

The CEO was his *father*?

I realized then how little I knew about him. I knew what was in his heart, of this I was certain, but the rest of his life remained a blank canvas, smudged only with the horror of his wife's murder. The elevator dinged and the heavy doors slid open. Rendered speechless, I followed him down the hallway, my feet gliding along polished tile. Two doors faced each other across the hall.

The one on the right swung open before Aidan had a chance to knock. "Long time, no see." A guy, shorter and stockier than Aidan, pulled him into a bear hug. "How've you been? I heard you quit the paper."

"I wouldn't say I quit...exactly," Aidan said. "More like forced into a leave of absence."

"Come on in." His brother ushered us into a living space that put the word "opulent" to shame. Immaculate hardwood floors, granite surfaces, and accents of chrome and crystal made my apartment ghetto-worthy. A wall of glass spanned one corner of the room, presenting a spectacular view. We were elevated high enough to see the treetops as the Willamette River journeyed through them.

"This is Mackenzie," Aidan said.

"Nice to meet you. I'm Logan." He took my hand. "My brother always did have excellent taste in women."

Aidan rolled his eyes. "Cut it out, Logan. It's not what you think."

Logan's grin disappeared. "Yeah, neither is this get-together, I'm afraid." He gave his brother a wary look. "Don't blow up, okay?"

Aidan stiffened. "I know that look. Dad's here, isn't he?"

"In the library. He wants to talk to you."

# Chapter Twenty-Five

A smile was the only feature Logan Payne shared with his brother. He flashed that familiar grin now and said, "I hope they don't kill each other in there."

"Are you sure we shouldn't be worried?" I couldn't make out the muffled words filtering through the library door, but I doubted Aidan and his father were exchanging pleasantries.

"Nah. Their roars are bigger than their bites." He pocketed his hands and stood in front of the fireplace. Artificial flames danced, casting him in a warm glow that brought out the highlights in his dirty blond hair. How odd that there were no pictures on the mantel. Like Aidan's place on the beach, the penthouse had a shell-of-a-real-home feel to it.

"Would you like something to drink?" he asked.

"No, thanks." Drifting to the windows, I tried to pinpoint why Logan Payne unsettled me so. The never-ending gray had deepened, and I craned my neck to glimpse a portion of the skyline. Skyscrapers twinkled in the emerging twilight north of Ross Island Bridge. "You've got an amazing view."

"Thank you. I guess I've been here long enough to take it

for granted." He joined me at the windows. "So, how did you and my brother meet?"

Who knew such a simple question could be so loaded. I could tell him about the night of Halloween, or the night we found Six, or—

"It's okay, you don't have to tell me."

I tilted my head and peeked at him. "It's complicated."

"Usually is."

I smiled at that because he was right. When was it *not* complicated? "We met in a bar," I said, holding back a snicker at the cliché answer.

Logan failed to see the humor. "He's been drinking again, hasn't he?"

That got my attention, and I wondered what land mine I'd stumbled upon. "Not really." Not if you didn't count the anniversary of his wife's murder, or the night we shared our first whiskey-induced kiss.

Logan sighed. "What you're not saying is coming through loud and clear." He leaned against the glass and leveled me with his scrutiny. I was wrong. A smile wasn't the only trait they had in common. They also shared the same intensity. "Seriously...is he okay?" He punctuated the question with a note of hesitancy, as if he wasn't sure he should be asking me about his brother's well-being.

"I don't know. We haven't known each other long."

"But you know about his wife." It wasn't a question. "He must have told you, or you wouldn't be so worried about him."

His insight gave me pause, and I had to dig deep to uncover the truth. I worried about Aidan more than I wanted to admit. I brought my fingers to the window and traced the raindrops as they squiggled down the glass, all the while remembering his bipolar behavior on Halloween. Consumed with guilt and grief, he hadn't cared if he lived or died. I shivered, unable to conceive a world without him.

"You love him."

My heart stuttered. The way Logan said it—with absolute certainty—stole my breath. How could he be so sure of something I wasn't even sure of? Where was he coming up with this? He'd just met me.

The library door flung open, and Aidan stormed in. "You should've told me he was going to be here." He shot his brother an accusing glare.

"Hey!" Logan threw his hands up and stepped back. "You know how he is. He insisted."

"Oh, knock it off," an older man snapped as he entered the room. "I'm still your father, whether you like it or not. If you'd answer your damn phone, I wouldn't have to resort to such tactics."

Aidan jerked around to face him. "I've been busy."

"No, you've been foolish." His steely gaze swooped over me before landing on his son again. "Is she the one who got you arrested?"

I gaped at him, my eyes ping-ponging between him and Aidan.

"Leave her out of this. And while you're at it, stay out of my damn business."

"You're my son, a fact which makes this my *business*." He stood a few inches shy of Aidan's six feet, though his imposing presence made up for the deficit. His expensive charcoal suit didn't hurt either.

Aidan folded his arms. "Sounds to me like you're the one who hired the tail."

"Don't be ridiculous. I don't employ incompetent fools."

"Well you've obviously been talking to someone."

"Damn right I did! I hear my son's got a PI on his ass, you bet I checked into it. What are you hoping to accomplish in that wretched town?"

"You shouldn't have a problem figuring it out."

"Going after him won't bring her back. Deb is *dead*."

Aidan lurched forward. "Don't you dare say her name," he warned, hands balling at his sides.

"Dad!" Logan jumped between them. "A little harsh, don't you think?"

"Stay out of this." Aidan shoved his brother out of the way and stood face to face with his father. "You wanted this little get-together, well you've got it." He jabbed a finger in his face. "You never liked her, a fact you made abundantly clear when you didn't show at her memorial."

I held my breath, certain he was about to pummel his father.

"Dad..." Logan shook his head, his face saturated with guilt. "You need to go."

"I own this building," their father snapped. "I'll go when I'm good and ready."

Logan wedged between them. "You might own the place, but it's my apartment and I'm asking you to leave."

Hamilton's face turned to stone. "Fine," he said through tight lips, "but don't come running to me when your brother ends up in jail." He threw one last hardened glance at Aidan before storming from the penthouse. The door slammed in his wake, his ire echoing off the walls. Now the three of us stood motionless, fearful of aftershocks.

Logan broke the silence first. "I'm sorry about the ambush. I used Payne-Davis resources to find the info you wanted, and Dad caught wind of it. He froze me out, wouldn't tell me who hired the PI."

"So you and Dad are best buds now, huh?"

"Hardly." Logan let out a dry snort. "I try to keep contact with the ole Payne-in-the-ass to a minimum. Why do you think I jumped at the chance to work in the Portland office?"

"But you guys must have talked about me."

"He mentioned that you disappeared from Boise a couple of weeks ago. I guess Mom's so worried, she's got her panties in a bunch—his words, not mine."

Aidan dragged a hand through his hair. "I should call her."

"Probably." Logan stuffed his hands into the pockets of his khakis. "What were you thinking, leaving in the middle of rehab like that without saying a word to anyone?"

My gaze flew to Aidan's, but he looked away. "What do you think?" he asked.

Logan walked to the granite bar that sectioned off the kitchen. He grabbed a newspaper. "It's been all over the news. So it's not a copycat?"

"I don't think so," Aidan said. "He left a picture of Deb in Mackenzie's apartment. It's him. No doubt about it."

"Dad's not completely in the wrong here, you know. Do you really wanna end up in jail?" Logan's contemplative gaze darted between Aidan and me. "The best thing you can do is move on. Get your life back."

"I just want him caught."

"No." Logan shook his head. "You know better than to lie to me. It's rolling off of you in waves."

"Don't go there, Logan."

"Trust me, I try not to." He stared at the paper for a moment before tossing it back onto the counter. "Did Dad at least tell you who hired the PI?"

"Yeah." Aidan's jaw twitched. "He said it was the sheriff."

# CHAPTER TWENTY-SIX

Trying to get out of Portland during rush hour was a nightmare. Bumper-to-bumper traffic congested I-5 for miles, and an accident ahead worsened the chaos. The emergency lights flooded the night in whirling color.

Aidan's silence was more stifling than the heat coming through the vents. He hadn't said two words since leaving the penthouse. I stole a look at him and wondered what was going through his head, wondered if he was as mystified as I was at discovering the sheriff had hired the PI. In fact, I had enough questions to fill a page.

He caught me staring, and some of the tension melted from his shoulders. "I'm sorry you had to witness the Payne family freak show."

"It's okay."

"No," he said with a burst of dry laughter, "it's not. My dad and I...we've never meshed."

"How come?"

It was a simple question, though from the way he

frowned as he turned down the heater, I guessed his father and the word "simple" didn't mesh either. "It's complicated."

*Usually is.*

Irony played at the corner of my lips. "We have time." I gestured to the road in front of us.

"I guess we do." Traffic inched forward a few feet and then stopped as an ambulance came onto the scene.

"Well, I won't twist your arm," I said, "but if you want to unload it's not like I'm going anywhere for a while."

"If I don't tell you, you'll probably just dream about it anyway." He shot me a teasing grin.

"Always a possibility." Especially when it came to him.

He eased onto the gas pedal, and we rolled forward at a snail's pace. "I guess it all came to a head in high school. My father already had my future mapped out for me. Harvard, a degree in business, a job at Payne-Davis."

"I take it you had other ideas?"

"I didn't know what the hell I wanted. I just knew I didn't want *his* life." Aidan stomped on the brake to avoid rear-ending the Escalade in front of us. "Jeez, I forgot how crazy traffic gets up here." He let out a breath and tightened his hold on the steering wheel.

Gripping the leather seat, I waited for him to continue.

"He cheated on my mom constantly, was never home..." Rain splashed the windshield, making visibility difficult. The wipers flapped back and forth to keep up. "And when he was home he made certain we all knew who was in charge. Bastard could've used a cattle prod and it wouldn't have been enough for him."

I didn't know what to say. He looked so lost in the memories of his past. Lines of hurt crisscrossed his face. I could have sketched them in charcoal.

"My junior year of high school, I met Deb." He paused, and his face relaxed in the memory of his wife. "It was something else to see her so focused on her dreams. She knew exactly what she wanted, right down to the school she wanted to teach in. I had a habit of editing her essays, and one day she told me to join the school paper so I'd stop torturing her."

A lump formed in my throat. His wife might be gone, but his love for her wasn't. A part of me ached for him—for his pain, for what he'd lost. The other part ached for me. How could a ghost inspire such jealousy?

"So I did it," he went on, "and I never expected to like it so much. Dad flipped when I told him I wanted to go into journalism. Said he'd yank my college fund if I didn't follow his plan."

"From what I saw of your father today, I can imagine."

"Yeah, those weren't happy times, not that there were a lot of them anyway. Mom supported me, but he's always had her stringed like Pinocchio. I refused to back down." His expression turned impish. "Got a scholarship and shoved it in his face."

We passed the scene of the accident then. A pickup truck had pinned a sports car to the median. What was left of it. I cringed. The path of life was much too tenuous for my liking. The flow of traffic picked up, and I steered the conversation to more recent events.

"Why would the sheriff hire a private investigator?"

Aidan shook his head. "I don't know. I've thought about it, but something's off. My father said he looked into the guy. Turns out he's a personal friend of McFayden's."

"But he's a PI?"

"Yep."

"Maybe he's worried you're gonna do something stupid."

"I already got the third degree from Logan." A hint of warning crept into his tone.

"Yeah, about that. He asked me if you've been drinking."

"What'd you tell him?"

"I didn't tell him anything. Aidan...you were in rehab?"

Muttering something about his brother's "big mouth," he nodded. "I didn't handle Deb's murder very well. Took to drinking for a while. Logan, he's just worried."

"Should I be worried too?" As if I wasn't already.

"No."

I wasn't sure I believed him, and it was clear his bother didn't either. In fact, Logan's insights set me on edge. "Speaking of your brother, what is up with him?"

"What do you mean?"

"Well, he's...I don't know how else to put it, but he's kinda odd."

Aidan laughed. "He'd be heartbroken to hear that, I'm sure. What else did he say to you?"

No way would I admit how he'd guessed, with matter-of-fact certainty, the extent of my feelings for Aidan, so I settled for a vague answer. "He just had an uncanny way of getting into my head. It was disturbing."

He seemed to consider his words carefully. "I guess you could say he's special like you."

"How do you mean?"

"Well, the rest of us call him exceptionally perceptive, but

—and I can't believe I'm telling you this—Logan has always called himself an empath."

"An empath?"

Aidan nodded. "Someone who can sense people's emotions. Can feel them even. Supposedly the Payne side of our family tree is full of ancestors with 'odd quirks,' as Mom likes to call them."

"You're pulling my leg, right?"

He laughed. "It's all legend, but my dad and Logan believe it."

"What about you? Do you *believe*?" My voice dropped on the last word, and I gave him a wide-eyed look. I wasn't being fair, but I couldn't help myself. For someone who possessed an "odd quirk" of my own, what right did I have to mock other people's claims? When had I become so jaded?

He shrugged. "I never put much stock into it, but then I met you. Who knows?"

"What's your super power?" I bumped my shoulder against his. "You must share the legacy, right?"

He rolled his eyes. "I knew telling you was a bad idea."

"Oh, come on, I'm only teasing. So what is it? Do you have super hearing?" I eyed his hands. "You don't launch spider webs, do you?" Or even worse... "Tell me you don't read minds."

He arched a brow. "What if I did read minds? Would that worry you?"

My mouth fell open. "Not funny, Aidan."

Apparently, he disagreed. He laughed and said, "Sorry to disappoint, but I'm ordinary. Although my mom's compared me to the Hulk on occasion." He took my hand, and his skin warmed mine as our fingers locked together. "It's all tall tales,

Mackenzie. Though Logan does seem to know things he shouldn't, just as you do."

The comfort of his touch, along with the lull of the road, cast me into a light slumber. Somewhere along the way I sank deeper, to a place where comfort was nonexistent, where dreams weren't an inconsequential product of the subconscious, but a vision of the future.

A man masked in shadow nudged a body with his boot. He bent and slipped a noose around her neck.

"No," she cried, struggling on the ground, her arms straining against the rope binding her hands at her back. "Why are you doing this?"

"Headlines, sweetheart." He tossed the rope over a branch and tested it for strength.

"Oh God! No! Plea—" Her cries cut-off as he strung her up, and her feet scissored above the ground. Behind her the ocean lit up like snow under the full moon.

"Mackenzie!"

I awoke gasping for air. Slowly, Aidan's garage came into focus. The low rumble of the engine was absent. His hands cradled my cheeks, his worried face hovering close to mine.

"He wants headlines."

"What?"

"She asked him why he was doing it. He said 'headlines, sweetheart.'" I closed my eyes. "I still can't see who she is, or who he is, but I saw the full moon again."

"Shh." His breath whispered across my face before he pressed a kiss to my forehead. "First thing in the morning, we're gonna pay the sheriff a visit. We'll tell him about your dream and hopefully get some damn answers."

# CHAPTER TWENTY-SEVEN

"I suppose you're here about the PI?" Sheriff McFayden didn't bother to look up from the file in his hand.

"Gee, you think?" Aidan closed the door behind us, and we settled into the chairs facing his desk.

The sheriff snapped the folder shut. "I already got an earful from your father, so let me have it—give me your best shot." He folded his hands and waited with the air of a patient man.

"First off, I'm not my father." Aidan's expression turned sour, as if the thought of Hamilton Payne left a bad taste in his mouth. "I didn't come here to argue with you. I came here to find out why you hired a private investigator to tail me."

"How do you know I didn't put the tail on Ms. Hill?"

"If you had, my father wouldn't have jumped your shit."

"Fair enough." He leaned back and crossed his arms. "Is this off the record?"

Aidan rolled his eyes, and I had to smile. The gesture seemed so un-Aidan-like. "I'm not a journalist anymore."

"And this won't get back to your father?"

He straightened at the sheriff's words. I did too. "No, we don't talk, if I can help it."

McFayden didn't seem surprised by his reply. "I'm only telling you this because I figure you'll find out on your own anyway, and I need to keep this between us."

"Okay, I'm listening."

The sheriff sat forward and refolded his hands, and I was struck with how nervous he suddenly appeared. "Your mother and I went to high school together. She contacted me."

Aidan looked stunned. "You knew my mom?"

"It was a long time ago." McFayden shrugged. "She only contacted me because I'm the sheriff, and she's worried about you." His mouth twisted into a scowl. "You might try staying in touch with her once in a while. Couldn't hurt."

Aidan didn't say anything, and they seemed to come to an impasse.

"Can I help you with anything else?"

"Maybe." Aidan didn't elaborate, and I wondered if he was being purposefully vague in order to goad the sheriff.

"Well, let's have it."

"Mackenzie's had some tough nights lately."

"More dreams?"

"Mostly vague," I said, "but I did see a white van."

The sheriff propped his chin on his knuckles. "No shit?"

I blinked at his reaction. Was he making fun of me, or was he genuinely surprised?

"Someone else mention a white van?" Aidan asked.

The sheriff hesitated. "A witness reported seeing a van outside Ms. Hunsaker's apartment on the night she was murdered. Didn't see anyone in it though, so no description of a suspect."

"Who's the witness?"

"You know better than to ask that."

"It was Brad, wasn't it? I mean, we know he was there."

"He has an alibi." He grabbed a notepad. "Anything else you can tell me, Ms. Hill?"

Aidan let out a sigh. Clearly, the sheriff wasn't going to give an inch.

"It was a utility type of van with no windows. I saw it on Highway 101 heading toward a tunnel. There was a full moon."

He took a few more notes.

"In case you're wondering," Aidan said, shifting in his seat, "there's a full moon Sunday night."

"*Perfect*." The sheriff threw down his pen. "That's only three days from now." His frustrated gaze landed on me. "We've checked DMV records for all the white vans registered in the area, but nothing yet. Do you have any idea who the next victim might be?"

"I didn't see her clearly, but she's a brunette. Last night I heard him say he's after headlines. Sorry, I know it's not much."

"It's a start." Setting aside the paper, he scrunched his brows. "I'll see if I can round up an extra deputy to patrol the highway, though with Jameson out on vacation that might pose a problem." He closed his eyes and pinched the bridge of his nose. "I'll put Judd on it. Maybe the state troopers can help too."

He was either desperate for a lead, or he believed me. Maybe it was a little of both. He stood, and we followed suit.

"Don't go putting yourself in the middle of this now," he warned. "Let us handle it."

Though Aidan nodded, I knew him well enough by now to guess at what he was thinking.

*When hell freezes over.*

"That's probably too much to ask, isn't it?" the sheriff asked. Apparently, Aidan's reputation as a rule-breaker had traveled all the way to Watcher's Point. Aidan remained silent, so McFayden's attention fell on me. "Let's hope you're wrong about this."

I hoped I was wrong too.

# CHAPTER TWENTY-EIGHT

A freakish November thunderstorm ushered in the evening, and a sense of excitement infused the Pour House. The crowd of customers was surprisingly large for mid-week. Of course, Christie and her cohorts were in the thick of it.

"Word is you're shacking up with your coworker." She sat alone at the bar while the other two men-prowlers she'd come with were busy rubbing against a couple of guys at the other end. "So tell me"—she perched an elbow on the counter and smirked at me, chin in hand—"is he good in bed?"

I set another shot down in front of her, the sixth or seventh of the night. "Not that it's any of your business, but Aidan offered me his guest room because someone broke into my apartment." Thunder boomed, causing the lights to flicker.

"Whatever," she said, though her nasty expression contradicted her indifferent tone. She demolished the shot.

"Look, Christie, I know today was your dad's birthday." I

was taking a stab in the dark on this one, but she seemed off tonight, like something was eating at her. Otherwise she would have joined the girls-gone-wild group a few feet away. Christie didn't normally do the alone thing.

"What do you know about his birthday? You don't know shit about my dad."

"You're right, but I wish I had known him. I grew up without a father, and to learn that maybe I could have changed that—" I clamped my mouth shut. My anger over the situation wouldn't help her right now. "I'm sorry. I guess I'm just trying to say—"

"Oh stuff the 'poor me' speech." She got up on wobbly feet, and her dark hair swung in her face. "Not everything is about you." She stumbled away and joined her friends.

I gave her a wide berth for a while, until she started waving at me. "We're dry over here, honey! Stop cooling your heels and load us up."

Filling a tray with another round, I approached them. Christie let out an obnoxious laugh as the blonde to her left made a pyramid out of the empties. Blondie threw her head back and joined in the laughter.

"It's not *that* funny," said the woman on Christie's right, a near replica of Christie herself. "Let's see you walk twenty blocks in fuck-me boots."

Blondie arched an eyebrow. "Sounds like the only thing that got fucked were your feet."

"And my pride. Remember Elmo? Well he ditched me. Can you believe that?"

Christie laughed again. "Wish I'd stuck around for that one."

"Hey!" she cried. "Don't be hatin'. He turned out to be a

jerk anyways. I saw him arguing with some girl." She folded her arms. "I can't believe you left me on my own."

As their words sank in, I narrowed my eyes. If they were talking about Elmo...that meant they were talking about Brad.

Had he been arguing with Six?

I turned around and bumped into Aidan. God, he had a way of sneaking up on people. He trained his attention on the three drunken women. "You heard that?"

"Yeah." He leaned down and spoke into my ear. "I'll see what I can find out."

I focused on the next customer, but I couldn't help trying to decipher Aidan's conversation with Christie and Company. He poured them another round of shots, a wide smile on his face as he made eye contact with the brunette who'd seen Elmo.

I took a stack of dishes into the back, and when I returned, Aidan was still situated in front of them, chatting and flirting. Lightning brightened the night outside the windows. I blamed my nerves on the storm and not on the fact that he was deep in conversation with three gorgeous women who wouldn't hesitate to eat him alive.

Keeping busy, I did my best to avoid watching him, and sometime later he blocked my path.

"What in the world is a Habu Sake shot?" he asked.

I laughed. "You haven't been initiated yet, have you?"

"This doesn't sound good."

"Be right back." I disappeared into the back long enough to grab the Japanese-labeled bottle. A long Pit Viper snake coiled at the bottom. I remembered the first time I'd seen the ugly thing. Six had gotten a lot of amusement out of my reaction.

Now it was my turn.

I pushed through the doors and found Aidan waiting. "This," I said, presenting the bottle so the snake's gaping mouth faced him, as if poised for attack, "is Habu Sake, also known as 'snake juice.'"

"Are you shitting me?" He took a step back. "People actually drink that stuff?"

I grinned. "A few of the regulars do." I held out the bottle. "Go ahead, pour your first shot."

"Not a chance."

"You aren't scared of a little dead snake, are you?"

"I don't like snakes, and they don't like me. Wait, I take that back. They like to bite me. Rattlers have gotten me twice now." He nodded toward the bottle. "You're on your own."

"You must be pretty tough to withstand two snake bites. Sure you don't wanna pour? You'll never live it down."

"No, thanks."

Still grinning, I poured the shot. "The person who serves the snake juice gets out of dish duty, just so you know."

"Not a problem. In fact, I hear the dishes calling my name right now." He disappeared into the back as I served the snake juice, and then I moved down the bar and froze. Brad stood on the other side, just a couple feet away.

"Let me say this before you kick me out."

I sent him a hard stare—the only reaction I felt he deserved.

"I'm sorry."

"That's it?" I raised my brows. "That's all you came up with? 'I'm sorry'?"

"No, it's just...I was drunk, and I know it's no excuse, but I'm sorry. I've thought about it and I probably would've punched me too, had I been in his shoes. I've dropped the charges."

"Yeah, I know. The DA already told him." I wiped down the counter and kept my face neutral, hoping he'd notice how unimpressed I was with his little speech. The lights flickered again and then went out. Voices drifted through the air, hushed excited chatter, as if the darkness demanded whispering. I jumped at the rumble of thunder that followed.

"It's pitch dark in here, Mac."

Chills traveled the length of my body. Brad's voice sounded much closer, and just as I was about to panic, another bolt of lightning zigzagged outside the windows. The bar lit up long enough for me to spot the flashlight underneath the register. I grabbed it and aimed the beam at his face, my heart pounding as loudly as the thunder.

"Crazy weather, huh?" he said.

The doors to the back flung open, and my hands shook as I looked over my shoulder. Aidan joined me and rested his hand on the small of my back.

"You have a lot of nerve coming in here," he told Brad.

"Since when do you work here?"

"Since when is it any of your business?"

Brad threw up his hands. "Chill out. I just came to apologize."

Aidan curled his fingers around my side. "Did he apologize?"

"Yeah."

"Mission accomplished," he told Brad. "Now get the fuck out."

"Yeah, forget it. I'm outta here." Brad turned to go, but Aidan's voice stopped him.

"One more thing, Brad." Once he had Brad's attention, he continued, "I hope you told the sheriff about your argument with Six. You can bet I'll mention it."

"I told the cops everything I know."

"What were you arguing about?" I asked.

"Maybe your boyfriend can figure it out." He stomped from the bar without another word.

I let out a breath and sank against Aidan. He embraced me from behind, hands rubbing the gooseflesh from my arms.

"You okay?"

"Yeah."

"You're shaking."

"I don't like the dark."

His fingers slid over mine and loosened my death grip on the flashlight. He held it up and aimed the light at the area underneath the register. "There's gotta be some candles around here. Didn't you guys have those flameless ones on Halloween?"

With a hard swallow, I nodded and directed him to the cabinet he was searching for. Once the eerie fake flickers lit up the place, we tended to the customers while we waited for Mike, who showed up ten minutes later.

"I called the power company. The good news is they're working on it."

"And the bad news?" Aidan asked.

"The bad news is they don't know how long it'll take. Might as well close down." He commanded the attention of the customers and told them we were closing as soon as they finished their drinks.

We got through our closing duties the best we could without power and exited through the back where Aidan's car was parked. The downpour soaked us before we could get inside.

"Do you think he did it?"

"Brad?" Aidan glanced at me as he steered the car onto the highway. "I doubt it, but he knows something. Whatever it is, I'm guessing the sheriff knows about it too."

The drive to his house seemed longer than usual with the wind battling the windows. He pulled in front of his house and shifted into park, then dashed into the rain to manually open the garage door. Without power, an ominous chill permeated the night. By the time he returned, his hair was plastered to his forehead. He rolled inside, and we plunged into blackness the instant he shut off the engine.

"I can't see a thing," I said, my jittery voice giving away my fear.

He leaned toward me, and I heard the glove compartment pop open before a light switched on.

I breathed a sigh of relief. "You must have been a boy scout. Flashlights, guns. Though I doubt they'd approve of the gun."

"Me neither."

"So what did you find out from Christie and her friends?"

"Pretty much what I told Brad. The brunette saw him and Six shouting in her driveway. She didn't stick around to hear what they were arguing about, but she did notice a white van." Aidan squeezed my hand. "Your dreams are right on the money, Mackenzie. I don't know what to do about this weekend, but we've gotta find a way to stop him." He handed me the flashlight, and we both exited the car. Even with the beam lighting the way, the hall was suffocatingly dark.

"I guess there isn't much we can do tonight," I said, "except go to bed." I didn't like the thought of going into that room alone. I wasn't in the habit of sleeping with a nightlight, but the knowledge that I couldn't turn one on thickened the air with anxiety.

"Yeah." We paused in front of the guest room. "You keep the flashlight." He leaned toward me the slightest bit, and I wasn't sure if he was going to kiss me or say something else, but whatever his intentions, he changed his mind. "Goodnight, Mackenzie."

"Goodnight." I almost pleaded for him to stay, if only to hold me through the night, but I couldn't bring myself to say the words. He headed down the hall, and I didn't open the door until he vanished into his room.

Every part of my body felt cold. I would have given anything to take a long hot shower, but I wasn't about to venture down that dark hallway. I changed quickly and snuggled under the covers. The storm grew distant after a while, and I fell into a dreamless sleep until the thunder came back, until the noise morphed into the worst kind of nightmare.

I sprang up in bed, and my sobs mingled with an explosion of thunder. Without a second thought, I went to Aidan's bedroom.

# CHAPTER TWENTY-NINE

I inched toward his bed and stopped when the edge of the mattress connected with my thighs. A streak of lightning lit up his room, and for a second I watched him sleep, focusing my watery gaze on the movement of his chest. Only then did I allow myself to breathe. Relief flooded me, but then my dream hit me all over again and I choked back more sobs. I wrapped my arms around myself and let the tears fall.

It had seemed so real. Then again, most of my dreams did.

After a while my eyes adjusted to the darkness. The outline of his body moved, and he sat up, as if he sensed me standing there. "What's wrong?"

My lower lip trembled. "I need you to hold me."

He reached for me without hesitation, and I fell into his arms. "Another dream?"

I nodded but didn't trust myself to speak. Fear was a formidable foe—it choked me as surely as the Hangman would if given the chance. I clung to him, my fingers biting into his skin, afraid he might slip through them if I let go. I still saw him falling, replayed the horrible moment over and over again.

"What did you see?" His unfailing acceptance of my dreams amazed me.

I shook my head, as if denying anything was wrong would make it so. Denial wouldn't save me from the vision of his dark eyes, lifeless in the doppelgänger of a face I loved more than anything. "Aidan," I said, my voice cracking. I could say no more. Do no more. Except kiss him.

There was no panic this time as our mouths came together. He held me against him, wrapping me in his protective power, and I'd never felt so safe or wanted. I gripped his face and slid my tongue deeper. Despite my protest, he pulled away.

"Mackenzie, talk to me."

"No."

Our legs tangled as he pressed his body against mine. He thumbed away my tears, and I was suddenly conscious of the scant clothing between us. His boxers. My tank top and shorts. I sucked in a breath, hyper aware of his erection taunting me from beneath the thin layers.

"I can't stand it when you cry. Tell me what's wrong."

"You were dead." I wished I could erase the words, paranoid that speaking them would make them true.

A bolt of lightning brightened the room again, and his expressive eyes met mine an instant before he dropped his head. "I'm right here," he said, his breath teasing my ear. "I'm not going anywhere."

Though we didn't voice it, the fear was there stifling the air. He couldn't guarantee his safety any more than I could mine, and the fact that I'd dreamed of his death was something I suspected neither of us wanted to face.

"There was a boom, like a gunshot, and you were falling. And your eyes"—I jerked at the crack of thunder that sounded overhead—"they were yours, but your face seemed different, like someone else's."

"It was just a dream, probably from the storm." His words ghosted across my skin, making me shiver all the way to my toes. He nibbled the curve of my neck, and his teeth scraped over my shoulder as he pulled down a spaghetti strap.

"Tell me if you're scared," he said.

I clung to his broad shoulders. Despite the chilly temperature in the room, his skin was hot to the touch. "I'm only scared you'll stop."

"In an instant if you want me to."

"I don't want you to stop. I just want you."

"You've got me." He edged one side of my top down, over my breast, and dipped his head, lips hovering achingly close. "I want to kiss every part of you, if you'll let me."

My breathing quickened, and my arms flopped to the mattress because the thought of his mouth all over me stole my strength. "Don't stop," I pleaded.

He darted his tongue out, tasting, teasing, then finally sucked my nipple into his mouth. I almost came undone, arching into him with a swift intake of breath, body straining, about to turn to cinder.

And he'd barely touched me.

He got to his knees, settling at the juncture of my thighs, and slipped my top over my head. Planting his hands on either side of my face, he lowered his mouth and explored my breasts again, and the heat of his knees seared through my damp panties.

I twisted the sheets in my hands, squeezed my eyes shut, and just *felt*.

Felt his tongue dipping between my breasts, lower...lower still until he reached my belly button. His hands clamped down on my hips, holding me in place while he thoroughly explored my navel with his tongue. He cherished me with his kiss, held me steady in his capable hands, and I'd never experienced such vulnerability, such complete openness, as I did then.

And he didn't even have me fully naked yet.

As if we were on the same wavelength, he pulled on my shorts and panties, and slowly inched them down my thighs, knuckles grazing my skin as his mouth followed suit. He kissed my hipbone, traveled the expanse of thigh, always a breath away from the raging heat between my legs.

Legs that quivered in his hands. His strong hands that lifted my limbs and pulled my clothing free.

Then he spread me wide open, his fingers curling around my thighs, thumbs pressing near the spot that was already dripping for him.

Oh, God.

Lightening lit the room again, and in that mere second, our eyes met. What a sight he was in that moment, sitting on his haunches between my thighs, his chest moving as rapidly as mine.

Beautiful. I could find no other word to describe him.

He shifted on the bed again, gripped my hips, and lowered his head between my thighs. My body jackknifed off the mattress, his name bleeding from my lips. I'd never known what it meant to be tortured with pleasure until then. He took me to the edge only to pull me back, again and again, until the edge shot higher with every whirl of his tongue, with every dip of his fingers, and he pushed me into the longest free fall of my life.

Arching. I couldn't stop arching, couldn't stop digging my heels into the mattress, toes curling as I clawed at the sheets with desperate fingers.

"Aidan!" I sobbed his name as a full body shudder tore through me. I wanted more of him, every inch of him. I didn't know how long I lay there, trembling and gasping for air, my hands balling around the bedding, but when I opened my eyes, the outline of his face hovered over mine. He cradled my cheeks, his breath drifting against my skin as he kissed away my tears. I hadn't realized I was crying until then.

"You okay?" His voice, a hoarse timbre from his own need, ignited me all over again.

"Better than okay." I wrapped my legs around him and rubbed against his raging hard-on, unobscured by boxers.

He exhaled on a groan. "I'd give anything to see you right now." He lowered his forehead to mine. "Are you sure?"

"Aidan, I'm gonna combust in about five seconds if you're not inside me."

He let out a curse and pushed into me. I cried out, overwhelmed by the sensation of being joined. It felt so right, being with him this way.

"Am I hurting you?"

"No...you feel incredible."

"So do you," he whispered.

Our bodies moved like the tide, slowly at first, then with increasing tempo as raw need took over. Oh God...nothing had ever felt so good. I would never tire of this, would never get enough of him. His hair brushed the sweat on my brow, and his breath was like a drug to my senses. I claimed his mouth and smothered a moan.

His thrusts intensified, the chase for release taking over, and he jerked deep before going still. "Shit. I can't hold back," he ground out.

"It's okay. Let it go."

A long groan rumbled from his chest, and he pushed even deeper as he buried his face in my hair. My name was a sigh on his lips, a breathy vow that whispered through my heart and awakened it. I laced our fingers and held on, and as we plunged into surrender, our echoing cries outmatched the thunder.

# CHAPTER THIRTY

idan's spot was empty. I sensed his absence before I opened my eyes. Footsteps moved around in the kitchen upstairs, and the aroma of coffee teased my nose. He must have been up a while.

Smiling, I stretched, enjoying the way my body ached in places I'd forgotten about. I hadn't slept so well since the first night he'd held me in his arms. There'd been no more dreams, just the sexiest man alive wrapped around me. The scent of him still lingered on my skin. I'd bottle it if I could.

I searched for my clothes and pulled on my tank top and shorts once I found them on opposite sides of the bed. Nerves set in as I trekked upstairs. Would we become victim to the awkward "morning after" syndrome? I hoped not. After everything we'd been through together, the idea seemed silly.

My body flushed the instant I saw him. He wore nothing but a pair of sweatpants. Standing in front of the stove with his back to me, he flipped an omelet with ease. My mouth watered, though it had nothing to do with the wafting smell of breakfast. He turned off the burner and transferred the omelet onto a plate and, almost as if he'd sensed my presence, turned around. A reassuring smile stretched across his face.

Something about the way he stood there, shirtless and barefoot with a spatula in his hand, drove me across the room. I reached for him, reliving the amazing moment when he first thrust inside me, and pulled his mouth down on mine. The spatula clattered to the floor, and his arms came around me, pulling until I couldn't discern where he ended and I began.

He lifted me onto the center island and settled between my legs. "Food's gonna get cold," he breathed between kisses.

"I want you for breakfast."

"I don't taste as good."

I nipped at his ear. "Omelets have nothing on you."

He groaned against my shoulder. "What are we doing, Mackenzie?"

"Having breakfast?"

"I'm serious," he said, but then he slid his hands under my shirt and yanked it above my breasts.

"So am I."

"If we end up back in bed, we're never gonna leave it." He bent down and sucked a nipple into his mouth. Eyes drifting shut, my head fell back, and I thrust my fingers into his hair, only realizing now that he must have taken a shower already, since the strands were damp.

"Who says we need a bed?"

I guessed the idea appealed to him because he tugged at my shorts next.

By the time our bodies cooled, so had the omelets. A quick reheat took care of that problem, and we sat down at the bar, keeping a good three feet between us for the sake of fueling ourselves with something besides each other.

I took a sip of coffee and sighed. "Caffeine should have its own food group."

Aidan gestured toward my mug with his fork. "You live off that stuff, don't you? I don't think you'd eat if I didn't feed you." To prove his point, he fed me a bite of omelet.

I laughed as a string of cheese trailed down my chin. "Mmm, that's pretty good too."

"No more nightmares last night?"

I scooped in another bite and shook my head, but the reminder of the first dream dampened my Aidan-induced high. Before I was able to dwell on it, my cell went off, vibrating on the counter. I gave him a puzzled look.

"I put it on the charger for you earlier. Figured you wouldn't want a dead phone."

"Thanks." I stole a kiss before moving across the kitchen. The call was from an unknown number. I answered with a bit of caution, and the voice on the other end sent a shiver through me.

"Don't hang up," he begged.

The months melted away, and his voice was still as familiar as my own.

"I'm *sorry*, Mac," his voice broke, and so did my composure. I dropped the phone back on the counter and recoiled when he called back.

Aidan's arms came around me from behind. "Who is it?"

"No one."

"No one must be someone, or you wouldn't be going to pieces right now." He reached for my cell before I could stop him.

"Come on, Aidan," I said, turning around and trying to pry it from him. "Give it back." My fingers slipped, and he wedged the phone between his back and the counter.

"Not until you talk to me."

Giving in to him was inevitable. "It's Joe."

"The guy you mentioned in your sleep? Who is he?"

"My ex-boyfriend." This was not happening. How had we gone from breaking in his kitchen island to talking about my ex?

He gave me a suspicious look. "You said he didn't—"

I shook my head. "I wouldn't lie to you, Aidan. Not about that." My gaze fell to his feet, which were suddenly fascinating. I knew what was coming next. He wasn't about to let this go.

"Who raped you?"

The screeching ring of my cell fell quiet. A few seconds of heavy silence passed before Joe tried again.

"His father."

Aidan immediately enfolded me in his arms. "Does Joe know?"

I nodded and experienced shame all over again, heard the accusations in my head. Joe's warm and familiar eyes had gone cold like a stranger's. "He didn't believe me." A fact I still had trouble reconciling. After all the years we'd known each other, how could he think I'd lie to him? Especially about something so serious.

"What an ass." Aidan tightened his arms around me. "I'm so sorry."

It still hurt. Time apart hadn't erased the memory of Joe turning away when I'd needed him most. "We grew up together," I said, finding comfort in his embrace.

"But he took his father's side?"

"He couldn't believe his dad would do something like that. He thought I made it up."

"He really didn't know you, did he?"

I raised my eyes and noticed a hint of sorrow and anger in his. "I thought he did."

"You're honest, Mackenzie. If there's one thing I've learned about you, it's that."

The phone went off again, and Aidan hesitated before handing it to me. "You should rip him a new one, though I'd be glad to do it for you."

I let out a breath. "It's not him. It's my mom."

"Oh." He leaned down and brushed his lips across mine. "I'll be in the living room if you need me."

I watched him go, already needing him more than he realized. My mom's call couldn't be a coincidence. She'd always had a soft spot for Joe.

"Hi, Mom."

"How come you haven't been answering your phone?"

"Joe called you, I take it?"

"That boy is a mess, Kenz."

"I can't believe you gave him my number."

"Whatever issues you have with him, you need to set them aside right now." She huffed in a way that only my mom could. "Some girl accused his father of rape. They arrested him yesterday."

I almost dropped the phone. "Th-they did?"

"Yes!" she said, loud enough to make my ear ache. "Can you believe it? Of course the little bitch is lying. Professor Keely would never..."

I closed my eyes and tightened my fist, and her voice

became a muffled screech. I couldn't deal with this now. Not with everything going on.

"Mom," I interrupted her, mid-tirade, "I've gotta go."

"What? Have you listened to a word I've said?"

"Yes, I've just...got an appointment I'm late for."

"I can tell when you're lying."

"That makes one of us," I snapped. If lying was a skill, then she'd mastered it.

"You'll never let it go, will you?"

I was *not* having this conversation with her now. "I'll call him."

"I've never seen him this way. Just talk to him, okay?"

"I will."

"Promise?"

"Yes."

"Good, I..." Her voice wavered. "Everyone's gathering here for Thanksgiving. I...*we*...were hoping you could make it."

"I don't know, Mom."

"How long are you going to punish me? What about your family, Mackenzie? How long are you going to let this drive you away?"

"I'll think about it."

A sigh drifted through the receiver. "We'll save a spot for you."

"Save two," I said suddenly.

"Oh? Is this a male friend?"

"*Mom*," I groaned, rolling my eyes. "I've really gotta go. I'll talk to you soon." I hung up before she could object and joined Aidan in the living room. He stood in front of the windows looking at the overcast sky, arms folded.

"She wants me to go home for Thanksgiving."

"What about Joe's call?"

"She said his father was arrested yesterday." I wandered to his side. "Another girl came forward."

He reached for my hand. "But you never did, did you?"

I shook my head. "He's a popular professor at the university. I figured if my own boyfriend didn't believe me, who would?"

"I believe you."

"I know, and that means everything to me."

"Are you gonna go?" he asked.

I studied him from the corner of my eye, getting the feeling he wasn't referring to Thanksgiving. "You think I should come forward too, don't you?"

"Yes, I think you should. Maybe this isn't what you want to hear, but you have a chance to help put this guy away so he can't hurt anyone else." He tugged me against him. "He should pay for what he did to you."

"Will you go with me?"

"Of course I will. Where else would I go?"

# CHAPTER THIRTY-ONE

I could have throttled Mike. In an effort to bring in more customers, he'd hired a KJ. Karaoke was supposed to be fun, he'd said, though he hadn't been able to keep a straight face as he uttered those words. I winced as Christie hit a particularly high note. She demanded attention by screeching her wrath with the appropriately named song "I Hate Everything About You." Judd was absent, but I'd wager he was the recipient of her public rant.

"I wouldn't want to get on her bad side," a guy at the bar said. Ignoring his comment, I set a rum and Coke in front of him. Kevin was his name. I recalled his argument with Six the morning after masquerade night.

He tore his eyes from Christie. "So you're the chic Brad can't stop talking about," he said with a smirk. "He's never been able to stay away from the ones he can't have."

"Tell him if he comes back, my..." My *what*, exactly? Was Aidan my boyfriend? A friend...with benefits? I didn't like that idea, even if the benefits were damn good. "My coworker will toss him out on his ass," I finally finished.

Kevin chuckled. "Chill out. Brad's harmless. Besides, I'm pretty sure he got the clue last time."

I wasn't so sure Brad was harmless, but hopefully his friend was right about the last part. Christie stepped down from the stage as someone else took her place. She hopped onto the stool next to Kevin and aimed a flirty smile his way. "Haven't seen you in a while. How've you been, Kevin?"

I tuned out their chatter. Mike had three women captivated by his juggling talent at the other end of the counter. His smile disappeared when the sheriff strolled in. McFayden towered over most in the bar; in fact, his height rivaled Aidan's. He moved in an easy gait toward Mike, whose expression was less than welcoming. They exchanged a few words before the two of them disappeared into the back.

My gut tingled with an ominous sensation, and as ten minutes bled into thirty, the feeling intensified. Something was up.

"Something bugging you?" Christie's voice intruded upon my inner turmoil. I considered thanking her for the distraction until I noticed her poisonous gaze. Kevin had disappeared. "Did you finally bore that sexy coworker of yours into quitting?" she asked.

"No, he's here." I gave her the sweetest smile I could muster. "He's in the back doing the beer order. Now that I think about it, he disappeared when you walked in."

She scowled. "Ooh, clever. I bet you practiced that one." She got up and stumbled in typical Christie fashion. "Tell him I said 'hi.'"

I clenched my teeth. The woman had a way of getting under my skin, and the thought of shoving a certain viper up her ass gave me more pleasure than it should. Without another word, she stomped over and joined two men playing pool.

The backdoors flung open and McFayden strode toward the exit, his face a blank mask. I was still trying to figure out what that was all about when Mike entered a few minutes later.

"Tony's on his way." He set a tray of clean glasses on the counter. "I'm taking off. Go ahead and take your break. I'll cover the front until he gets here." He popped a piece of gum into his mouth, but the mint didn't mask the scent of tobacco. Six had once told me that he'd quit smoking a few years ago.

"What's going on, Mike?"

He slammed a glass onto the counter. "I don't want to talk about it." The edge in his tone warned me to tread carefully.

"Is Aidan finished with the beer order yet?" I asked.

"I don't know."

Mike's tight expression was still bothering me when I found Aidan in the cooler. I crossed my arms to ward off the chill from the controlled temperature.

"I take it the sheriff left?" he asked.

"Yeah, and Mike is *not* happy. I think he's about to lose it. He called Tony in to cover."

Aidan set aside the clipboard. "Come here," he said, opening his arms. "You'll freeze in here without a jacket."

"We don't have to stay in the cooler, you know," I teased as his arms came around me. "We can take a five-minute break elsewhere."

"I want to talk to you, and I'd rather not be overheard."

"Sounds serious."

"Did I ever tell you that breaking and entering isn't my only talent?"

I tilted my head and grinned at him. "You're preaching to the choir. You're a man of many talents. Especially with your hands."

He tickled the nape of my neck. "My hands just happen to like you."

"As much as I love snuggling with you instead of working, it is kinda cold in here. What did you wanna talk about?"

"I overheard the sheriff's conversation with Mike."

My eyes widened. "You *are* handy to have around."

His mouth twitched at the corners, but he didn't smile. "I found out what Brad and Six were arguing about that night. Or rather *who*."

"Mike?"

He nodded. "Turns out they were involved. He interrupted Brad and Six, and apparently, there was a huge blowup. They pulled Mike in for questioning a couple of days ago." He paused long enough to give me a careful look. "He submitted to a DNA test."

"You're not saying..."

"The semen they collected matched Mike's."

I shook my head, unable to grasp it. "But that doesn't mean he killed her."

"No, but it does mean that Brad might not have been the last one to see her alive."

I thought about my manager and tried to picture him doing unthinkable things to Six, pictured him hanging her. My head told me it was possible, but my gut insisted otherwise. "He couldn't have done this."

"I agree, especially since the Hangman doesn't leave a trail of DNA. You gotta admit though, things aren't looking good for Mike."

"Six never told me." I shivered and nuzzled even closer to him.

"Makes sense they'd keep it secret. Sleeping with the boss is taboo."

"What about coworkers? Is that acceptable?"

"Better be," he said before settling his mouth over mine, which did a lot to warm me up all on its own. I could have stood there for another hour kissing him.

"I'm almost finished here," he said. "You should go before you lose your toes."

"Don't take too long." I nibbled on his lower lip before backing toward the door. From out of nowhere, spots flickered in my vision. A dozen miniature camera flashes exploded, and I was no longer in the cooler—instead I stood high above the ocean on a rocky ledge. Watcher's Island darkened the horizon, and the dancing spots coalesced into a blinding beam; every few seconds it cut through the blackness.

My knees buckled, and I slumped to the floor.

I came to in Aidan's arms, his fingers tapping a Morse code rhythm against my cheek. "Shit, you scared me. Are you okay?"

I blinked a few times and looked up at him once my vision cleared. "That's never happened before."

"You mean you don't faint every day?" Underneath the sarcasm, I sensed how shaken he was. It was evident in the firm set of his jaw, in the way he tightened his hold on me.

"No, I meant I was awake this time."

"You had a vision?" His eyes widened. "What did you see?"

"I'm not sure. It was freezing...there was a light—" I gasped. "The lighthouse!"

Aidan pulled me to my feet. "Come on, you're gonna turn into a popsicle in here." He ushered me into Mike's office, where he rubbed some warmth into my arms. "Are you sure you're okay?"

I nodded, but then I gave up the facade as another wave of dizziness set the room spinning. I collapsed into a chair just as the bright beam hit me in the face again. "Wherever he's going to hang her, the lighthouse is close by."

"I'm taking you home." Aidan crouched in front of me, looking worried enough to drag me to the hospital, and equally determined to do it by force if he thought it was necessary.

"No, I'm okay. I probably got too cold."

"Don't bullshit me." He brushed his knuckles against my cheek. "I'm tempted to say something dirty just to put some color back in your cheeks."

That got a smile out of me. "I'm tempted to let you." I pulled him close and planted a kiss on his lips. "I'm okay. The dizziness is gone."

His brows narrowed over eyes sharp enough to slice through the BS of the best of liars—which I was most definitely not. "You're way past dizzy. You fainted. Sit tight. I'm gonna see if Tony's here yet. Maybe he can close without us."

"That's not necces—"

"Yes, it is." He moved toward the door. "I'm serious, stay put for a second."

Resigned, I leaned my head against the chair and waited. I wouldn't admit it to Aidan, but having a vision like that had shaken me. I rubbed my sweaty palms on my jeans and counted to ten, but my heart still stuttered. A heavy, sick feeling turned in my stomach. By classifying the visions as dreams, I'd been able to sidestep the word "psychic" to some extent, if only to myself. Now I wondered what had changed. Why was this happening to me?

Aidan re-entered the room. "Mike's gone, but Tony said he can close on his own since the karaoke is winding down." He grabbed my hand and pulled me to my feet. "Let's get you out of here."

Despite my moaning and groaning, he drove me home and immediately tucked me into bed, and the only thing that pacified me was the fact that he tucked himself in beside me, sans-clothing.

# CHAPTER THIRTY-TWO

A idan and I had a colossal disagreement the following morning. The fact that we did so in bed, wearing nothing but each other, would have been amusing if he weren't so damn stubborn.

"You can't go back to your apartment," he said. "Besides, staying here makes more sense. Bigger bed." He flashed a grin as he teased me with his morning hard-on, just enough to make me insane with wanting him. He was an expert at fighting dirty, as if lying on top of him, his erection nestled between my thighs, wasn't disarming enough.

"You're missing the point," I said, trapping his hands on either side of his face because their tendency to wander all over me wasn't helping my distracted state. "We can't spend twenty-four-seven with each other."

"Until he's caught, we sure as hell can." Before I had time to blink, he rolled over and pinned me to the bed, and his fingers tightened around mine. A week ago I would have panicked, but now all I could think about was how I loved the feel of his body pressed against me.

"We have a real chance of catching him tonight," he said. "I can't focus on that and keep you safe if you're not with me." My face must have given away my fear, because he halted, eyes narrowing in suspicion. "Why are you in such a hurry to go home?"

"I'm not." A layer of black powder still covered my apartment from when the police had dusted for prints, and the sight of my bed was enough to make me sick. I'd only dangled the idea of going home as a means of distracting him. Apparently, he wasn't in the market to buy bullshit.

"What's this really about?" he asked.

"What do you mean?"

He let go of my hands. "Spill it. I've told you ninety-nine percent of my secrets."

I almost smiled. "Only ninety-nine percent?"

He groaned. "Quit avoiding the question. Why are you trying to get rid of me?" He nibbled the spot along my neck—the one that never failed to drive me to distraction. He really was playing dirty.

"I don't want to get rid of you..." My eyes drifted shut as the heat of his tongue seared my skin. "That's the problem."

"I fail to see a problem here."

I pushed him back so I could think straight. "I had another dream last night. I..." Swallowing my fear, I forged ahead, "I saw you die again. If you go after him tonight—"

"I'll be fine."

"You can't pick and choose what to believe, Aidan. If you believe my dreams about the full moon, then you have to believe—"

"I can't sit on the sidelines on this one."

I pushed him away and scooted to the edge of the

mattress. "I won't watch you die," I choked out. "And don't tell me you'll be okay because you can't guarantee that."

The mattress shifted, and I registered his nearness before he touched me. His fingers slid along my jaw, a gentle caress that coaxed me to look at him. "You're right. I can't give you guarantees."

Not what I wanted to hear. His words had a double-edged effect, as I hadn't realized until then how being with him made my insecurities rise to the surface. I was terrified of him being killed, but I was also scared of him walking away in the end. I averted my eyes and asked the question I was afraid to hear the answer to. "Aidan, what are we?"

"What do you mean?"

"I mean...what is this? You and me. Us."

He didn't answer right away, which only heightened my anxiety. "What do you want us to be?"

"Uh-uh, I asked you first."

"I care about you..."

I shrugged away from him, and what he didn't say settled between us like an impenetrable wall.

He got to the floor and kneeled in front of me, leaving me no choice but to face him. "This isn't just about your dreams, is it?"

He had a knack for asking the tough questions—the ones I didn't want to answer. "No," I said, avoiding his gaze.

"What's it about then?"

Where should I start? Maybe with how I ached for him, in every sense of the word, yet the best he could do was offer a generic "I care about you" speech? Or the part where he'd go back to Boise eventually, assuming he didn't get himself killed in his pursuit of vengeance? I drew my knees to my chest and hugged them. "I can't believe I was stupid enough to fall in love with you."

His silence invaded the room, leaving me suspended like an acrobat without a safety net.

"Say something," I pleaded.

"Loving me could get you killed."

My heart thumped painfully in my chest. "Loving you could break my heart."

"I'm not looking to break your heart, Mackenzie."

"Then don't."

"I can't sit by and do nothing while he goes free." He hesitated, his expression pensive. "And I can't make you promises. Not until I know how this ends. When I first came here..." He trailed off, shaking his head. "I expected to either end up dead or in jail, and it didn't really matter to me either way."

I curled my fingers around his shoulders. "Don't go after him. Aidan, he's gonna kill you! I saw it again, just like the night the power went out. I don't know how it's gonna happen—"

"It won't—"

"You don't know that!" Scrambling away, I put some much needed distance between us. "Don't be glib about this. You hold everything that's important to me in your hands."

He opened his mouth but said nothing.

"I can't do this." I crawled to the other side of the bed and got to my feet. "We're just...getting too close, and...and maybe we do need some space." I gathered my clothes and clutched them to my chest. "Maybe going home is for the best." Every part of me railed against the idea.

"I can give you space without leaving you vulnerable to a madman." He pulled on a pair of jeans, followed by a T-shirt.

"If you go back to your apartment, I'll just live on your doorstep. You wouldn't make me do that, would you? It's cold out there."

I shook my head. "You're so stubborn."

"Only when it comes to one thing, and no one's gonna make me budge on this." His jaw formed an indomitable line that backed up his words. "He'll have to kill me before he gets anywhere near you."

The memory of his lifeless face flashed in my mind. "How can you say that to me? After I just spilled my heart out to you?" Blinking back tears, I focused on the squiggly pattern on the rumpled comforter.

"Because it's true. If that doesn't tell you how much I care about you, then I don't know what will." A quiet tension infiltrated the room. "Don't leave." The low plea in his voice was unmistakable, and it pulled at me in a way I couldn't ignore. "You need some space? You've got it. Just...don't go."

I couldn't walk away from him if I tried. When I lifted my head to tell him so, he was gone.

# CHAPTER THIRTY-THREE

The moon had never seemed so full or bright. Every time I spotted it, my stomach tightened. I knew in my gut this was the night—the night the Hangman would strike again. The night Aidan would die.

Never before had I wanted to be wrong about something so badly. I snuck a glance at him. We'd barely spoken all day, both of us too raw from our blow up that morning. In the end, he won. I wasn't about to let him go alone, and if I stayed behind, he'd only resent me for it.

"Are you positive the cliff you saw was directly off the highway?" His voice was clearly laced with frustration. We'd been combing the highway for the past four hours, checking every turnoff, campground, and park we could find. We'd spotted a state trooper, a semi, and had passed Judd twice. At least the sheriff had come through with extra manpower to patrol the highway. Traffic was next to non-existent, which wasn't surprising considering it was one o'clock in the morning on a chilly November night.

"As positive as I can be. Maybe we should go back to the tunnel. There has to be a reason I saw it in my dream."

He turned the car around and pressed down on the gas, and we picked up speed once the road went into a slight downslope through the tunnel.

"Wait!" I cried as soon as we came through the other end. "Stop!"

Aidan stomped on the brake, and I braced myself as we screeched to a sudden halt. "What is it?" he asked.

"I...I don't know." I bolted from the car and ran to the side of the road. Wind whipped my hair into a tangled mess as I looked over the steep cliff. The sea was at high tide, and we were elevated by at least two hundred feet, at level with the lighthouse, which stood tall on the northern bluff of Watcher's Island. It was a beacon of light, even under the full moon. The lighthouse's beam sliced through a patch of fog, and suddenly Aidan's house flashed in my mind. I experienced the same kind of dizziness, the same disorientation as the previous night. With a moan, I dropped my head into my hands as images streamed into my consciousness.

"What's wrong?" Aidan's voice cut into my confusion, and I felt his hands on my shoulders.

"He's at your house," I shouted above the wind. "We're in the wrong place. He's gonna do it in front of your house."

Moving quickly, Aidan ushered me back to the car. I settled into my seat, and he slammed the door before rounding the hood to the driver's side. As soon as he slid behind the wheel, he turned around and sped toward his beach house. His street was dark and cloaked in fog, and his house stood isolated at the end. Through the haze, the headlights of a white van met us head-on.

"Holy shit!" Aidan slammed on the brakes and lunged for his gun.

"What are you gonna do?" I cried.

"Whatever I have to. Call McFayden."

I pulled my cell out and dropped it twice before punching in the number. The van jerked into motion, and Aidan angled the car in a way that blocked the exit. The van sped toward us anyway, showing no signs of slowing.

"He's gonna hit us, Aidan!" I screamed just as McFayden's voice came over the line.

Aidan swerved to the side at the last second. "Damn!" He locked his jaw and began to wheel around, preparing to give chase.

"Wait!" Ignoring the sheriff's frantic questions, I grabbed Aidan's arm. "Look!" I said, pointing to a tree at the end of the drive. Its contorted branches reached over the rocky incline, and the branches weren't the only things suspended above the sea. A woman dangled from a thick limb, her naked body unmoving.

He cursed, and sending one last glance at the van's tail-lights, stomped on the gas pedal. We jerked to a stop, his front fender almost smashing into the tree. "Use this if he comes back." He pushed the gun into my hand, and I dropped it, startled by the heavy feel of metal in my palm. "And stay in the car!" He was out and running toward the woman before I could utter a word.

Like hell I was staying in the car. I rushed after him, my footsteps pounding the pavement in perfect sync with the thunderous beat of my heart. Aidan stepped onto the rocky ledge, and I skidded to a stop, paralyzed with terror.

"Talk to me!" McFayden's voice went off in my ear. "What the hell is going on?"

"We found another victim."

"Where are you guys?"

"At Aidan's house." I hadn't realized I was near hyperventilation until the sheriff told me to take a breath.

"I'm on my way," he said. I heard a door slam in the background, followed by the turn of an ignition. "Are you safe?"

A tremor tore through me, and I kept my eyes glued to Aidan. He cut through the rope with a pocketknife, then swayed under the woman's weight. He pushed her to safety just as the rock crumbled under his feet.

"Aidan!" The scream tore from my throat, and I watched in horror as he slid from sight. The phone fell from my fingers. I lunged for the ledge and leaned over as far as I dared, terrified at the thought of what I might find.

"Stay back!" he shouted. Several gnarled tree roots protruded from the side of the cliff. One had broken his fall. "The rock isn't steady."

"Don't you *dare* fall!" My dream hitting me with full force, I swiped at my eyes and gave him one last glance before sprinting to the car. He shouted something unintelligible, but I was too focused on what I had to do. I pressed the button to open the garage and hurried inside before the door had finished its slow rise to the top. Tearing through drawers and shelves, I tossed stuff everywhere until I found a thick coil of rope.

I returned, and his furious shout was nearly lost to the roar of the ocean. "What are you doing? Get back in the car!"

"I'm not leaving you out here." I brushed my hair from my eyes and estimated the distance between him and me. The rope wasn't long enough. "Can you tie yourself to that?" I asked, pointing to the tree root he was clinging to.

He lost his grip and slid down a few more feet.

"Aidan!"

"I'm okay," he called up. "Toss me the rope, then get back in the car! You're not safe!" I threw the rope into his waiting hand but didn't budge from his sight. He wrapped it around his waist and anchored himself to a tree root. "Dammit, go!"

My eyes darted between the car and Aidan before settling on the crumpled body of the woman he'd cut down. She wasn't moving. Her skin gleamed stark against the night, burned and bloodied from the torture she'd endured. Her dark hair twisted down her back in a mess of tangles. I was about to check on her when two headlights beamed from the other end of the drive.

What if he'd come back? I was such an idiot! I'd left the gun in the car. I reached into my coat pocket for the mace but remembered it was in my purse...also in the car. The vehicle neared, and I stood paralyzed, my limbs wanting to quake but unable to as the headlights blinded me. He'd come back for me, I was sure of it.

"Mackenzie, get back in the car!"

Aidan's panicked shout pierced my ears just as the vehicle screeched to a stop. I exhaled in relief at the sight of the gray Chevy pickup.

"It's okay," I called down to him. "The sheriff's here."

"What happened?" McFayden barked as he exited the truck. "Where's Aidan?"

I pointed over the ledge.

His eyes widened, and he rushed to my side and swept

the scene with a single glance. "You okay?" he hollered down to Aidan.

"I'm fine. Is she alive?"

The sheriff frowned. "Backup is on the way. Sit tight and I'll check on her." He crouched next to the woman and pressed his fingers to her neck. His eyes shot to mine. "She's alive."

*Thank God.*

The state troopers were the first to arrive, followed by Judd and the fire department. The firefighters tended to the victim while the others worked to pull Aidan to safety. They hauled him up just as the paramedics pulled onto the street. He engulfed me in his arms.

"When I saw you go over..." I clutched him, my knuckles turning white, and buried my face against his shoulder. "I was sure I'd lost you."

"You okay, son?" McFayden asked.

"I'm okay. What about Dee? Did we get to her in time?"

*Dee?*

I regretted every bad thought I'd had about the bartender who'd helped Aidan a week ago.

"She's in bad shape, but she's alive," the sheriff replied. I peeked up in time to see him rest a hand on Aidan's shoulder. "Thanks to you guys."

# CHAPTER THIRTY-FOUR

I shot up in bed and immediately reached for Aidan, but his side was cold. We hadn't spoken since returning from the sheriff's station. Vocal communication wasn't required. As soon as we'd entered the dark hall, he'd taken my hand and led me to bed, where we'd clung to each other until sleep claimed us.

Now I squinted in the darkness, listening for any sounds that might indicate where he'd gone. Gooseflesh pebbled on my arms, and I gulped at the absolute quiet that penetrated the room. Where was he?

"I'm over here." His voice floated from the other side of the bedroom.

"What are you doing?" I asked, rubbing the chill from my skin.

"Does it matter?" A sloshing sound followed.

My eyes adjusted, and I was able to make out the outline of his body. I heard it again, like liquid swishing against glass. Was he drinking? Noiselessly, I slid out of bed and crossed the room. The bottom of my favorite sleep shirt—the one I'd stolen from him—tickled my thighs. He sat on the floor with his forearms resting on his knees. I zeroed in on the bottle of Jack in his hands.

"How long have you been sitting there?"

"Long enough. Sun should be up soon." He lifted the half-empty bottle to his lips.

I lowered to my knees. "You don't need this," I said, coaxing the bottle from his vise-like grip.

"I need you." He thumped his head against the wall, as if frustrated with himself for needing anyone.

"I'm right here." I set the bottle aside and scooted between his legs.

"Nuh-uh. I don't wanna need you."

"Tough shit. You're stuck with me."

"Deb was pregnant." His glassy eyes pierced through me. "We tried for two years. Thought it wasn't gonna happen... then it happened." A smile ghosted at the corners of his mouth, faint like the memory of happiness.

Disarmed by his vulnerability, I leaned forward and wound my arms around him, holding him as tight as I could, but it would never be enough.

"It could've been you tonight." He shuddered, burrowing his face in the hollow of my shoulder, and his breath dampened my skin. "He's getting more brutal, and I'm scared. I'm really scared I'm gonna lose you."

I wanted to tell him everything would be okay, but the platitude somehow seemed like a slap in the face after what we'd been through together. All I could do was hold on to him. "Dee is alive because of you," I said.

"No, she's alive because of you. God, you're amazing. I dragged you into this mess, and you're sitting here comforting me." He laughed, a dry and bitter testament of his grief. "I wish the 'Hangman' was a fucking word game to you. I'd turn back time if I could. Make sure you never met me."

"Are you *trying* to rip my heart out?"

He pulled back and held my face in his hands. "I'm an ass. A drunk, stupid ass." He brushed the tears from my cheeks with gentle patience. "I wish you'd never laid eyes on me, never came to Watcher's Point. I love you enough to want that for you."

My heart stumbled. "Don't say those words unless you mean them."

"I mean them." His whiskey-flavored breath fanned across my face, evoking the memory of our first kiss. Like the scent of pine was reminiscent of Christmas, the smell of whiskey would always remind me of him.

And it reminded me of how he shouldn't be drinking at all.

"You can't keep doing this to yourself. Alcohol isn't—"

He shut me up with his mouth, his kiss frantic. Fire ignited in my belly, spreading lower until it burned between my thighs. I crawled onto his lap and straddled him.

"You make me crazy," he said.

"Is that good or bad?"

"Bad"—he removed my T-shirt in one fluid motion—"good. All of the above." His hands warmed my breasts, thumbs whisking across sensitive peaks, and my breath came quicker, escaping in small bursts. I rose on my knees, reached down, and freed his erection from his boxers before closing my fingers around him.

"Definitely good," he moaned.

He was silky smooth against my palm, and as I slid my

hand up and down his length, my gaze pinned to his, his desire leaked all over my fist.

He covered my hand with his. "Stop. I want inside you." He hooked a finger along the edge of my panties, sweeping them aside, and pushed in with a groan. His hands commanded my hips, drawing me closer and guiding the pace as we started our dance. I was drowning, completely possessed as he strengthened his hold on my heart.

Arching my spine, I flung my head back and purred as his mouth left a wet trail down my throat. My pulse throbbed under the heat of his tongue, and I held on tighter as every part of him speared through me like lightning.

"Aidan…" I buried my face in his hair, inhaling as I dug my fingers into my dampened shoulders. My hips took on the rhythm of desperation. "Aidan!"

Anything I might've said after that became inaudible cries. I thrust down hard on his lap, impaling myself to the hilt, and his ragged breathing drowned out the beat of my heart. I cried out again as he swept me up in the tide of intoxication that had nothing to do with whiskey and everything to do with the man.

# Chapter Thirty-Five

A search of Aidan's kitchen produced three bottles of whiskey. I upended the last one into the sink and stared as it splashed down the drain. I was so entranced by the swirling amber that I failed to hear him enter. He wrapped his arms around me from behind.

"I missed you in bed."

I nibbled on my lip. "I couldn't sleep." That wasn't entirely true. I'd fallen asleep after we'd made love, but then a dream had awakened me, and I'd tossed and turned next to him for an hour. "Are you mad?" I asked, holding onto his arms. Not that it would change anything. I still would have poured the alcohol down the drain.

"No." He held me tighter, almost crushing me in his embrace. "I'm still a little drunk, probably headed for a wicked hangover, but all I want is to sleep with you by my side." He exhaled against my neck. "Safe by my side. Thanks for dumping it, but you can come back to bed now."

I turned in his arms, and every memory from the night

before assaulted me. The good and the bad. "Promise me you won't drink anymore."

"I promise." He kissed along my jaw, feathery teases until his mouth captured mine. I sighed, loving the simple act of kissing him too much. Loving *him* too much.

"You're too agreeable," I moaned against his lips. "I'm serious. Please...promise me and mean it. Don't drink anymore."

"I'll try." He kissed me again, and when we finally broke apart, he gave me a perplexed look. "Do I smell food?" His eyes veered toward the stove.

I hid a smile. "I figured it was my turn. It's nothing complicated, just eggs and toast." I ran my fingers down his chest toward the waistband of his sweats, enjoying how his stomach muscles tightened under my touch. "I couldn't remember where you kept your plates."

"Well, if you're cooking, I can't go back to bed now. Have a seat. I'll dish up."

I sat at the center island and thumbed through my sketchbook.

"Drawing again?" he asked.

"I had another dream about the cabin."

"Anything new?"

"No, but I can see it more clearly now. I don't know what it means, or even if it's important." I drew a few lines and smudged the charcoal with my thumb. "Maybe it doesn't exist."

He pulled down two plates from the cupboard next to where I'd found his stash of Jack. "It exists."

He didn't need to explain his certainty. I knew what he was getting at. I'd dreamed of this strange cabin for the last couple of weeks, and the dreams had only intensified. If I was dreaming about it, then it was out there somewhere, foundation and wood, surrounded by trees and water.

Oregon had a lot of lakes.

Growing restless, I slid from the stool. "I'm gonna grab the paper." I wondered what the media had to say about Dee's attempted murder. I'd called the sheriff earlier that morning and learned that she was in a coma. Would she come out of it and name her kidnapper?

The sky was its usual dreary gray when I pulled the door open. Nothing seemed out of place except for the Bible that accompanied the newspaper on his porch. It wasn't your everyday standard Bible. Not like the ones the Gideons distributed. This particular tome had been handled frequently, the brown leather cover worn and the gold-tipped pages faded to dull brass.

What really caught my attention was the bookmark placed between the pages. I reached for the book and opened it to the marked spot. As I skimmed the text, noting the highlighted bits, my instincts screamed that something was off. The story, a timeless tale of ultimate betrayal, was a familiar one; the story of Cain and Abel. Good brother killed by bad brother. Bad brother banished for his crime.

How odd. Didn't church people usually leave pamphlets or knock on the door? They didn't leave Bibles with bookmarks in them. A chill traveled down my arms and legs as my fingers brushed over the worn leather. I bent down and picked up the paper before returning to the kitchen. "Someone left a Bible on your porch."

He dropped the spoon, paying no attention to the eggs that covered the counter. "Let me see." He set the newspaper aside and flipped through the Bible, his expression growing tense. "We need to tell the sheriff about this."

I gulped. "You think the killer left it?"

"I don't think, I *know*. He left a Bible once before, right after Deb was killed." His brows narrowed. "Though this one has obviously been handled a lot."

I shivered at the thought that the Hangman had been on the other side of the door, just a few feet from me while Aidan slept downstairs. "Was it bookmarked too?"

"Yeah, the same story of Cain and Abel."

"What about the other victims in Boise? Did he leave a Bible in those cases too?"

Aidan's expression was grim. "No."

His answer only reinforced my earlier theory that a copycat was responsible for his wife's murder, as well as the murders in Watcher's Point.

"What do you think it means?" I asked, shaking my head. "I mean...what would the story of Cain and Abel have to do with you, with these murders? Is he a religious nut or some-thing?" I began pacing, as if I could simply walk away the feeling of being stalked. I turned and bumped into Aidan. "He was right on the other side of that door. He could've... could've..."

"He didn't." He folded his arms around me, and we both held on. "He didn't. I won't let him hurt you."

I wanted to melt into him, hide from the world and all the turmoil in it. The threat of the Hangman, the impending visit with my mom.

"He won't get anywhere near you, Mackenzie."

# CHAPTER THIRTY-SIX

The days leading up to Thanksgiving passed in a state of madness. The Feds sent agent Victoria Kipp to town shortly after Aidan and I found the Bible on his doorstep. She'd subjected us both to a long line of questioning. Aidan especially, since he'd talked to Chloe Sanders the day before she was murdered.

Of course, a chaotic week wouldn't be complete without several calls from Joe. He'd called every day, but so far I'd been too chickenshit to answer. Mom had also called, freaking out as only a mother could when reports of Dee's kidnapping and attempted murder hit the news. Third victim in three weeks, and the media was having a field day with speculation.

"Pumpkin is done." Aidan set the pie on the counter to cool. "I'm gonna make another one. What do you think? Chocolate or banana?"

He'd been up since the crack of dawn acting utterly domestic and pretending to need my help with baking pies—

from scratch, of course—because going to my mother's house empty handed on Thanksgiving would be a travesty.

"Doesn't matter. Either is fine."

We'd spent endless days running errands and doing simple things like laundry, not to mention the slow shifts we shared at work—shifts he found ways to fill with busy work, despite a lack of customers.

Anything to keep me so preoccupied that I wouldn't dwell on seeing my mom again. The day loomed in front of me like an emotional root canal. I wasn't looking forward to facing the past, but not going meant Aidan would continue this absurd state of normalcy. As if anything was normal. Dee had come out of her coma, but she didn't remember a thing about the night the Hangman had taken her. Somewhere in her subconscious lay the answer to the killer's identity, and I couldn't decide if I wanted her to remember or not. Who'd want to live with that kind of horrific experience coloring their every step?

"I changed my mind."

"About what?" He grabbed a saucepan and began pouring sugar and cocoa into it.

"About going." I wandered to the counter and peeked at the cooling pumpkin pie before ambling to Aidan's side again. "I don't want to deal with my mom right now."

"It'll be good to get away." He added a can of evaporated milk to the mix, and the sight of him doing something as simple as making a pie ebbed at my irritation.

"Do you have any idea how sexy you are when you do that?"

He arched a dark brow. "Are you trying to distract me?"

I laughed. "The only distraction in this kitchen is you." I

eyed the stovetop and caught a whiff of what he was cooking. "And maybe the smell of that."

He grinned as he cracked open an egg. "No more distractions. So why the one-eighty?"

Shit. His ability to exude nonchalance before striking at the heart of the matter was annoying. "I've barely talked to my mom since I moved here." I tapped my fingernails on the granite countertop. "I never told her what Joe's dad did. I guess in the back of my mind, I'm worried she won't believe me."

Though Aidan didn't say anything at first, I didn't miss the tick in his jaw. If he ever came face to face with my rapist, I knew he'd lose it and probably take another trip to jail while he was at it. I wondered how many "get out of jail free" cards he had left.

"Of course she'll believe you. She's your mother." He lifted the spoon and blew on the filling before bringing it to my lips. "Try this."

I rolled my eyes but complied. Damn, he was good.

"You're not gonna let two perfectly good pies go to waste, are you?" he asked, all innocence.

I was an idiot to think he'd let me get away with changing my mind. "No, that would be criminal."

"Good." He set the spoon down and pulled me against him. One hand cradled the back of my head as he brought his mouth down on mine in a lingering union that ignited a fire in my veins.

"Now who's being a distraction?" I breathed between kisses.

"Mmm, you definitely are." He buried his face in my hair.

"That cherry-vanilla weapon you call shampoo gets me every time."

Pressed so close to him, I'd have to be brain-dead not to get his meaning. "Want me to stop using it?"

"Don't you dare." His words whispered against my ear. "Don't let this rift ruin your relationship with your mother. Take it from someone who's lived with a lot of regret."

I tilted my head. "Was this your intention all along? Fluster me with your sex appeal and then hit me with a dose of reasonable Aidan?"

"I'm feeling far from reasonable." He hoisted me up, and I wrapped my legs around his waist. "I'm thinking we have enough time to use the counter for something other than cooking."

"Well by all means, don't let me stop you."

He was definitely unstoppable. It didn't matter when or where, but whenever we came together, I never failed to lose myself. Raindrops drummed against the dining room window, and when we moved to the couch, falling onto it in a tumble of limbs, time ceased to exist as I screamed his name, my nails gouging his skin.

We left for my mother's house shortly after, and the storm was in full swing. Aidan slowed the car to ten under the speed limit due to the curtain of rain that pounded the road. During the two-hour drive to Eugene, my insecurities rose to the surface again.

"You're obsessing." His voice broke the thick silence.

"We should have stayed home."

"It's Thanksgiving. Leave the past at the door and spend some time with your family. It'll be fun."

The closer we got to my childhood home, the more the

edgy feeling intensified. Aidan turned into the driveway, tires crunching over gravel, and parked behind my brother's minivan.

"Nice place," he said. "Hard to believe we're so close to town." The yellow farmhouse was the only house in sight; acres of farmland separated neighboring homes.

"That's what I loved most about growing up here. It's close enough to town, but we never had to worry about privacy."

"You've got two eager fans waiting to greet you." He gestured behind me.

I turned around and found my nephews staring at me from the other side of the passenger window, their faces pressed against the glass. Both were drenched from the downpour, though neither seemed to care.

"My nephews, Michael and Mason." I grabbed the two pies Aidan had baked that morning and gently eased the door open. They pounced the minute I was out of the car.

"You brought pie!" Two identical voices screeched at me.

Aidan came around the hood. "They're twins." Water dripped from his hair and into the collar of his jacket as he swerved his gaze back and forth between the boys. Other than their clothes, there was little difference in appearance. Both had the same curly, dark hair and blue eyes. A newcomer like Aidan would have a hard time telling them apart.

"Identical," I said. "And they have energy in spades." I smiled as the boys jumped up and down, paying no attention to the rain. "Come on, guys. We're getting soaked." The boys scurried to the wraparound porch before Aidan and I had taken three steps. They disappeared into the house, and an instant later my mom appeared in the doorway. She engulfed me in a hug.

"I'm so glad you're here, Kenz."

I laughed as some of the hurt disappeared. I hadn't realized how much I missed her. "Hi, Mom. Don't smash the pies."

She pulled away and eyed them. "They look homemade," she said, throwing me a suspicious look as she ushered us inside.

I bit back a grin. "That's because they are. Aidan made them."

She took the pies from me and scrutinized Aidan with a tight smile. "I'm Jane. You must be the friend Mackenzie mentioned."

"It's nice to meet you. I'm Aidan." Even in the face of her less-than-welcoming smile, his never wavered. I could have kissed him for the way he handled my prickly mother. Hopefully she'd warm up to him by the time we left, though considering her bias for Joe, I wasn't about to hold my breath.

"Kenz!" I barely had time to prepare for another hug, this one bone-crushing. "I'm so glad you made it. Mom wasn't sure you would." My sister gave me a once-over. "You look great." Her eyes landed on Aidan, and she lowered her voice. "He looks even better. Who's the hottie?"

I stifled a groan. Leaving my mom's house sans-embarrassment wasn't going to happen. "Aidan, this is my sister Mackayla."

The following half hour was filled with more introductions, more questions. How did I like my job? When was I coming home? How long had I known Aidan? I was grateful when my brother Micah saved him from a brewing inquisition from my oldest brother Marcus. I cringed to think of what my mom had in store for him.

"I like him," Micah said, pulling me into a one-armed hug. "Any guy who can talk football like that has my vote. It's about time Joe had some competition."

Marcus disappeared into the kitchen, and my mom reappeared a moment later. Her hair, nearly as dark as my own, fell below her ears in the simple bob she'd worn for the past decade. All four of us kids had inherited her smoky gray eyes.

"Dinner will be done soon, but we need more Cool Whip." She glanced down at the brown turtleneck she wore and picked off a piece of lint. "Aidan, would you mind driving Micah into town? I'm afraid he's already hit the beer."

"I'll go with him," I said, reaching for my jacket.

"Actually, Kenz, I could use your help in the kitchen, if you wouldn't mind." She disappeared into the other room before I had a chance to reply.

"It's okay. I'll go." Aidan leaned down and kissed my cheek. "We've got everyone blocked in anyway. I'm sure your mom wants a moment to grill you without me around." His eyes twinkled as he pulled away. "Good luck."

I grabbed him by the shirt and yanked him down for a real kiss. "Don't be gone long."

"I won't." He and Micah left, keeping their heads bowed against the continuous downpour.

"Don't worry," Mackayla said as she closed the door behind them, "I'll play mediator so Mom won't steamroll you."

I laughed. "Thanks, I appreciate that." Delaying the inevitable confrontation with my mom, I wandered around the living room, and Mackayla followed. The room hadn't changed much over the years. Same fireplace in the corner, same well-used leather furniture. Only the pictures above the mantle had morphed with time. Weddings and graduations replaced the photos of adolescence, and the twins' portraits were now accompanied by their baby sister's in the montage. I ran my finger along my graduation photo, unsurprised to find it free of dust. "Where's Alicia?" I asked, referring to Marcus's wife.

"I think she's napping with the baby."

"I haven't seen her yet. How old is she now?"

"Four months."

I folded my arms. I'd been raped four months ago, which was why I hadn't gone to Salem to meet my new niece.

*Leave the past at the door.*

The past always had a way of knocking. The doorbell rang, and Mom materialized from the kitchen. She sent a furtive glance in my direction as she headed for the foyer.

Oh shit. I recognized that look. It was her I'm-meddling-and-you-won't-like-it look. Maybe it was someone she was dating. Yeah, fat chance. I knew who was on the other side. I followed, rounding the corner as she turned the knob. She pulled the door open, and there stood Joe, looking so calm it was irritating. His blue eyes zeroed in on me.

"Hi, Mac."

What had Aidan said about this day being fun? How could I leave the past behind when it literally walked through the front door?

# Chapter Thirty-Seven

"What is he doing here?" I asked my mom, barely keeping the accusation out of my tone. She didn't display an ounce of guilt as she glanced at me in her typical stubborn manner, her only answer a shrug.

"Come on," Joe said. "You had to know I'd show up here. You won't answer my calls. How else was I supposed to talk to you?"

"You wanna talk? Fine, let's talk." I headed toward the kitchen, sending my mom an accusatory glare on the way, and didn't bother to check if he followed. I knew he would. I busied myself with washing the few dishes that littered the counter. "You have five minutes," I said, sensing his presence behind me. I finished rinsing a mixing bowl and picked up a casserole dish.

"Can you stop for a minute and talk to me?"

"No." I hated how my voice shook, how my heart tripped and my body grew warm. Too warm.

"Mac, please..."

"Don't call me that."

"What?" He sounded surprised. "I've been calling you that for years."

I dropped the dish and whirled around. "So did your dad."

He looked broken, there was no other word for it. "I messed up bad. I just...I need you to know how sorry I am."

"*You* need? What about what I needed?" I blinked, holding back a range of emotion varying from despair to rage.

His expression cracked. "Don't cry, I didn't mean to...I'm so sorry."

He reached for me, but I held up my hands. "Don't," I said, firming my resolve. Falling apart because he'd had a change of heart was pointless. "Now you know he did it. Still doesn't change anything between us."

His blue eyes took on that familiar determined glint. "It changes everything. I know I messed up. I should have trusted you." He moved toward me, lifting a hand to touch my face, but let his arm fall instead. "I've missed you so much."

"I stopped missing you weeks ago." I faced the sink again and picked up the forgotten dish, putting all my energy into scrubbing away the last remnants of crusty yams. If only I could make the hole he'd left in my heart disappear so easily. It had grown smaller over the last few weeks, but it was still there, and my hurt whistled through it now. He was clueless if he thought an apology could resurrect the ashes of our relationship. "My mom obviously wanted you here. Why don't you go mingle with her for a while? I'm sure she's missed you."

"That's cold, Mac."

"That's how I feel when it comes to you. Cold." It was

true. The guy I'd experienced my first taste of love with, the man who'd promised me forever, had shattered my love for him so completely that only dust remained. "You hurt me more than he did."

He sucked in a breath. "I still love you."

"Your five minutes are up." I left the kitchen and grabbed my jacket, ignoring the curious stares of my family as I slammed through the door. I didn't allow thought or emotion in, didn't do anything but focus on putting one foot in front of the other. The wind tore through the branches above me, whipping my ebony locks into my eyes, but I didn't slow down.

"Mac!" Joe's footsteps pounded the gravel behind me.

"Leave me alone!" I hastened my stride and turned onto the main road, paying no attention to the raindrops sluicing in rivulets down my cheeks. He kept pace with every furious step.

"I'm sorry!" He pushed his dirty blond hair out of his eyes. "I hate myself for what I put you through. Please...please let me make this right."

"You can't," I cried. "You ripped my fucking heart out! No one...*no one* has ever hurt me the way you did." I wiped the moisture from my cheeks, not entirely certain it was only rain at this point. "An apology can't erase the past, Joe."

He grabbed my arm and pulled me to a stop. "I know it can't."

I kicked at a rock on the muddied ground. A nightcrawler inched away, working hard to escape the threat of danger. "I wanted to hate you." I still wanted to. So, so much. Hate was easier to hang on to than hurt, easier to get through. Hate had kept me going. I buried my face in my hands and wished it would all go away, wished he would go away. He brought his arms around me, and I stiffened until the familiarity of his embrace crumbled a little piece of the wall I'd erected.

"I hate you! I hate you so much." I pounded my fists against his chest. He took every blow without a wince. Finally spent, I slumped in his arms and sobbed. After all these months, everything finally poured out; the emotions I'd buried deep...but not deep enough.

"I'm sorry. I'm so sorry," he murmured those words over and over again, his breath exhaling in gasps against my neck as he held me tight, one arm bracing my back while the other tangled in my hair. "I want to kill him for what he did to you."

It was tragic, because after all this time, most of which I'd spent alternating between hatred and intense longing to be where I was now, all I could think of was how these were the wrong arms.

This was Joe. The kid who'd pushed me on the swings during recess, the guy who'd used my math homework as a cheat sheet for his own. The guy who'd snuck into my bedroom in the middle of the night when he was sixteen, heartbroken over his parents' divorce.

I had no doubt that I'd loved him. But it wasn't enough. I gently untangled from his hold and stumbled back a few steps. Joe's gaze darted behind me, and when I turned around, I found Aidan and Micah parked on the side of the road. Micah peered through the passenger window, his face a blanket of curiosity. Aidan stood on the other side, and only now did I register the annoying ding that indicated he'd left the door open with the keys still in the ignition.

"You okay?" he asked, his gaze moving between Joe and me.

I quickly wiped my eyes and nodded. His face was tense with what I recognized as worry. If I wasn't so forlorn, I would have smiled. That was Aidan, my perpetual worrier. When it came to me, he had the role of protector down to an art.

Joe flung an arm around my shoulders. "Who's the guy?"

I ducked out of reach, and before I could reply, Aidan beat me to it. "I'm her boyfriend. Who are you?"

My eyes collided with Aidan's, and his mouth twitched at the corners, as if we shared a secret. "Come on," he said, "get in the car. You're both drenched." He looked at Joe, his expression hardening. "You know how to drive?"

Joe scoffed. "Of course."

Aidan rounded the car and grabbed my hand. "Keys are in the ignition," he told my ex before opening the back door for me. He slid in after me, and I snuggled against him as Joe settled into the driver's seat, where he slammed the door shut, making his displeasure at this new development known.

"You're so warm," I mumbled.

"You're freezing." Aidan engulfed me in his arms and brought his lips to my ear. "What were you thinking?" He inched away and peered into my eyes. "I saw a white van parked a couple blocks down the street."

I shuddered. "I-I wasn't thinking. I was upset." I closed my eyes as the implications hit me. White vans weren't exactly rare, but...what if?

"We can't afford to be reckless, Mackenzie."

"I know."

Joe pulled into the driveway and killed the engine.

"Can you guys give us a minute?" I asked.

His blue eyes met mine in the rearview mirror for a few

heavy seconds. Then he barreled out of the car and slammed the door in his wake.

Micah turned to face us, brows raised. "Thanksgiving's are never dull. See you guys inside." He grabbed the Cool Whip and went after Joe.

Raindrops pelted the roof of Aidan's car. In that moment, sitting next to him surrounded by the howl of the wind and the pattering of rain, a surreal peacefulness settled over me. I burst out laughing, as if a pressure valve had been released.

Aidan arched a brow. "Are you sure you're okay?"

"I just realized you let my ex drive your car. You must really love me." Grasping a handful of his jacket, I pulled him down with me onto the backseat, and all traces of laughter died.

"How much of that scene back there did you see?"

"Well," he began, brushing a lock of stray hair from my eyes, "when I pulled over it looked like you were beating the shit out of him."

"I don't know what came over me. I was just so...angry."

"And hurt." Aidan frowned. "Do you still love him?"

I gnawed on my lower lip and searched for an honest answer. "He'll always hold a small piece of my heart, Aidan." I slid my fingers into his hair and pulled him closer. "But I am so in love with you, it's ridiculous."

He let out a breath. "If we weren't parked in your mother's driveway, I'd have no problem steaming up these windows."

"I think we can steal a minute," I said before tugging his mouth down on mine.

# CHAPTER THIRTY-EIGHT

Joe reminded me of a wounded puppy. He spent some time chatting with my mom, but once she disappeared into the kitchen to finish dinner, he was left with nothing to do but stare at me. He finally gave up and left.

Mackayla grabbed my hand and pulled me up from the couch. "C'mon."

I sent Aidan a pleading look, but he and Micah were in the middle of an intense discussion about college football. He shot me an infuriatingly wide grin as my sister dragged me away. He wasn't about to save me from my family.

"Tell me all about him," Mackayla demanded once we were out of earshot of the living room. "Is he good in the sack?"

"Mackayla!"

She waved away my indignation. "I heard about the hell you went through after you and Joe split. I'm just glad to see a sappy smile on your face."

"Can we not talk about Joe?"

Michael ran past, followed by Mason. They were in the middle of a heated game of tag.

"Who's talking about Joe?" Mackayla asked once the coast was clear. "I thought we were talking about Aidan and how good he is in the sack?" She wiggled her eyebrows, and I was suddenly reminded of Six. I'd never realized how much the two of them were alike—had been alike.

A mixer buzzed to life. I peeked into the kitchen and saw Mom busy at work with a gigantic bowl of mashed potatoes. Satisfied our conversation wouldn't be overheard, I turned back to my sister. "He's amazing. I've never felt this way before."

"You're in love with him."

"Crazy in love with him," I agreed. "He makes me happy."

"You look happy, but I wish you'd come home. Talk about a bad time to move to Mom's hometown. We're worried about you."

"Aidan doesn't let me out of his sight. You have nothing to worry about." I couldn't quite meet her gaze. My family had no idea how close the Hangman had zeroed in on me, and I wanted to keep it that way.

The mixer shut off in the kitchen. "Dinner's almost done," Mom announced.

"Need some help?" I asked.

She smiled. "Sure. I want to talk to you anyway."

*And here it comes.*

Mackayla gave me a sympathetic pat on the back before I entered the kitchen. "What is it, Mom?"

"I wanted to talk to you about Joe." She kept her eyes on the gravy she was stirring.

I crossed my arms. "I didn't come here to talk about him."

I hadn't come here to see him either, but that hadn't stopped her.

"I don't get you," she began. "You guys have always been so close, and he's going through a lot right now with his dad—"

"Mom," I interrupted. "Joe and I aren't getting back together."

"I didn't raise you to turn your back on the people who care about you."

"I didn't turn my back. He did."

"What are you talking about?"

"It doesn't matter." I was not getting into this with my mother on Thanksgiving. "Do you want me to put the rolls in the oven?"

Pursing her lips, she picked up two packages and handed them to me, and I began arranging them on baking sheets.

"What's going on with you, Kenz? You left so suddenly, and now you come home a few weeks later with a man you barely know?"

"Aidan has stuck by me through a lot. You have no idea."

"Joe has stuck by you. I don't understand how you can cast him aside when he needs you most." Her voice shook. "He doesn't deserve—"

"I didn't deserve to be lied to my entire life, but that didn't stop you." I dropped the rolls into the oven and slammed the door shut.

"I did it to protect you."

"From William Beckmeyer? That's great, Mom. I could've had a father, but there's no chance of that happening now, is there? Why didn't you tell me?"

"Because it was for the best."

"Did he...did he not want me? Is that why you didn't tell me?"

She turned around and grabbed the counter, and her shoulders slumped. "After your father"—she shook her head —"I mean after Tom died, I lost myself, did some stupid things. It was one time, one mistake, but I don't regret it because it brought me you. I never told anyone who he was. Everyone believed what they wanted to, and it was easier to let them."

Something cold fisted my heart. "What are you trying to say?"

"Will wasn't your father."

My jaw dropped. "What?"

"People assumed he was because we'd been high school sweethearts back in the day, and he was a good friend to me after Tom died. But the rumors destroyed his marriage, and I just...left like a coward before you were born."

She went to the stove and removed the vegetables from the burner. I was struck speechless. Marcus entered the kitchen before I could question her further.

"I'll carve the turkey." He lifted the platter and disappeared through the door leading into the dining room. One by one, everyone trickled in and carried the varying dishes to the table.

Mom pulled me into a quick hug. "We'll talk more later."

I was still in a fog when we all sat down at the huge oak table in the dining room. When it was my turn to say what I was thankful for, Aidan laced his fingers with mine to bring me out of my stupor.

His brows furrowed. "Everything okay?"

I smiled. "I'm thankful for new beginnings."

Everyone fell into comfortable conversation after that. Alicia talked about the baby, Marcus mentioned his work in the state's capital, Micah had us in stitches over some funny stories involving his EMT coworkers, and Mackayla complained about the restaurant she worked at and how mean her boss was. Mom was still miserable but making decent money at the law firm where she worked as a paralegal.

Halfway through dinner, as the twins were giggling and using their straws to blow bubbles in their drinks, Mom engaged Aidan in the lets-get-to-know-each-other conversation I'd been dreading. "What do you do for a living, Aidan?"

"At the moment, I work with Mackenzie. I'm kind of on a prolonged leave from the paper I worked for in Boise."

Marcus, sitting directly across from me, took a sudden interest. "Did you cover the Hangman stories?"

I jumped in, wanting to distract from that particular subject. "What is this, an interrogation?" I joked.

"I'm certainly not interrogating your boyfriend, Kenz. I just find it interesting that he lived in Boise, considering what's happened in Watcher's Point recently." Forks scraped against plates, and someone had a heavy hand when they set a glass down on the table.

Aidan swallowed hard. "Yeah, I covered the Hangman."

"You have any theories?" Marcus persisted. "Exactly how much has the media left out?"

"I wouldn't know. I no longer report the news."

"Then why are you in Watcher's Point?"

"Marcus..." I gave my brother a smoldering glare.

"Stop badgering our guest," Mom warned him before

refocusing her attention on Aidan. "Do you have family in Watcher's Point?"

"Not anymore. My grandfather passed a couple of years ago. You might have known my mother, though. She was born and raised there."

"How interesting. What's her name?" She picked up her glass and brought it to her lips.

"Lila Payne, but you probably would've known her as Lila Davis. She married my father right out of high school."

The glass slipped from her fingers, and though it didn't break, water pooled around her half-eaten plate of food. Appearing stricken, she scooted her chair back and stood.

"What's wrong, Mom?" I asked, wondering if something she'd eaten had made her sick.

"Can you come into the kitchen with me?" she directed the request at me.

I scrambled to my feet and followed her into the adjacent room. She closed the door behind us, and it was eerily quiet.

She grabbed my shoulders. "Tell me you haven't slept with him."

My eyes widened. "What?"

"Tell me it hasn't gone that far."

I shrugged her hands off. "I am not talking about sex with you!"

All the color drained from her face. "Oh God. You have, haven't you?"

"Mom! It's none of your—" I broke off and shook my head. "If this has to do with Joe—"

"This isn't about Joe." She grabbed my hands. "Promise me you'll end it, Mackenzie. You and Aidan can't be together."

*What the hell?*

I jerked my hands from her grasp. "You need to under-stand something, Mom. I'm in love with him, and that isn't going to change." I couldn't believe we'd interrupted Thanks-giving dinner to have this conversation.

"Oh my God..." She propped herself against the counter, as if she couldn't bear to stand on her own. Something in my gut tightened in response, and the same bad feeling I'd had on the way to Eugene resurfaced.

"Mom?"

"This is my fault. I should have told you."

"Told me what?"

"Hamilton Payne is your father."

# CHAPTER THIRTY-NINE

*Hamilton Payne is your father.* My mom's words roared through my head like the ocean during a storm: deafening, brutal, and unpredictable—similar to a sneaker wave that tumbled from her lips and caught me off-guard.

I stumbled back and bumped into the center island. Aidan and me...sharing the same father. Sharing DNA. Siblings didn't feel this way about each other. It was unnatural, absurd. The room spiraled out of control as I whirled in memories that crushed me—his skin on mine, our mouths colliding, bodies moving in tandem.

Vomit burned my throat. "It's not true."

"I know I've given you no reason to trust—"

"Shut up," I cut her off, and the slight tremble of her lips only infuriated me more. "How could you sink so low? What do you have against Aidan that you'd try to sabotage us?"

Tears hung on her lashes, big drops of truth I didn't want to acknowledge. "I-I'm not lying. He's your brother."

"Yes you are!" My voice bounced off the walls. Everyone at

the table probably heard every shouted word, but I didn't care. This wasn't real. I'd wake up any moment, heart thudding too fast, body drenched in sweat and twisted in my sheets, and I'd shake off this ridiculous nightmare. "I don't believe you."

"Kenz, please..."

"Is this about Joe? Is that it? He must be desperate if he's got you going to bat for him like this."

"It's not about Joe."

I ignored her denial. "You wanna know why I turned my back on him? His dad raped me. There, I said it." My chest heaved, and I blinked, trying to hold it in. Hysteria bubbled up anyway, gushed from me like a dam bursting. I hadn't spoken that word once—not once since it happened.

Horror coursed from her eyes, and she opened her mouth, working to speak.

I beat her to it. "He didn't believe me, Mom. He didn't... didn't..." I shrank back when she reached for me. "Just... don't."

I ignored her pleas and stalked into the dining room, wiping my face as I went. Everyone stared at me, their expressions identical masks of curiosity. Relief hit me as I realized they hadn't overheard what I'd told my mom.

Aidan sprang up and took a step in my direction, and instinctively, I moved back. Every touch, every inch of closeness, took on new meaning in light of what my mom claimed.

*It's not true...*

"Get me out of here, please."

"What's wrong?"

My eyes would overflow again at any moment, and once I started, I feared I wouldn't be able to stop. "Can we just go?"

He rested his hand at the small of my back, and something in me shattered. I barely registered the perplexed faces crowding around me, didn't feel their arms as they hugged me goodbye. Didn't answer the questions they wanted to ask.

*Glad you made it, sis. Sorry you're leaving so soon.*

That was Micah.

*Stay safe.*

That was my sister.

Marcus also said goodbye, but I wasn't in the mood to deal with his disapproval. I wasn't in the mood to deal with anything. I hurried toward the door, the exit just a few feet away.

My mom was suddenly in front of me, face tense, her lips moving in desperation to get through to me. "Please...don't leave like this." She blocked my escape into the storm, and her gaze fell on Aidan. "Let's sit down and talk about this. I-I didn't know, Kenz..."

"There's nothing to talk about." I shoved past her, and as I took my first step across the threshold, she grabbed my jacket.

"I have something for you. Just...wait here." She disappeared from sight, leaving me alone with Aidan.

"What's going on, Mackenzie?"

I shook my head, a rapid denial, and focused on his shoes. They blurred in my vision, but I refused to let the tears fall. I craved his arms, his smell, the way the essence of him surrounded me and made me feel protected. I hated my mom for making me doubt that feeling, for making me doubt the unstoppable connection I felt with this man.

This amazing man...who was *not* my brother.

He must have sensed my need for him. Without a word,

he drew me to his chest. My head fit perfectly under his chin. "Talk to me when you're ready. I'm here."

My breath hitched, and I held it, as if doing so would contain the chaos threatening to explode from me. I tightened my grip on him. "I will."

I would have to, eventually. When I could make sense of what she'd told me. When I could find the words to repeat her absurd revelation. When I was strong enough to face the possibility that she was telling the truth.

We'd inched together too closely, like a magnet to metal that couldn't fight the pull. My mom returned to the foyer, and I untangled from his arms. She slid an envelope into my hand before embracing my limp body. "I hope you'll read it. I'm so sorry," she whispered. "Forgive me."

I couldn't reply past the thickness in my throat. I avoided her eyes as we left through the door, and I'd never experienced such relief upon leaving my childhood home. The weather had worsened since our arrival, and the driveway was now a huge puddle of rainwater. We tiptoed on the outskirts of the small pond, navigating around the tree branches that littered the ground in haphazard patterns. A gust of wind carried us to the car.

Aidan backed out of the driveway, and too many thoughts vied for space on the raceway of my mind. Words, fragments...razor sharp truth. Yet questioning that truth kept me from total insanity. This had to be someone's idea of a sordid joke. A mistake. A misunderstanding of epic proportions.

The word "brother" didn't belong in the same sentence as Aidan. Not in relation to me. Mustard and chocolate made more sense. Snow in the tropics. Santa and Satan. I could find logic in any of those. But not this. Her letter burned a metaphorical hole in my coat pocket, but the idea of pulling it out, of opening the envelope and discovering whatever was hidden inside, terrified me. Paper was tangible—not as easy to set aside as spoken words.

"What happened back there?" Aidan's voice was quiet compared to the anguish in my head.

"I don't want to talk about it right now." I never wanted to talk about it, but I knew I'd have to. I kept my unseeing eyes fastened on the passenger window. My mom's face materialized in my mind, her horrified expression when Aidan told her who his mother was. Dread squeezed my heart, and I finally asked myself the question I'd been avoiding.

*What if it's true?*

I wiped the thought from my mind. *No, no, no.*

"We've got a lot of time between here and Watcher's Point." I felt his gaze on me, sensed him waiting for me to give in. I always gave in to him. But not this time.

Not yet. Not while he was driving in this weather.

"Did you ever visit Watcher's Point as a kid?" The question slipped out before I could weigh the wisdom of voicing it. If my mom was telling the truth, then his father was in Watcher's point when Aidan was about six.

He raised a brow at the change of subject. "A few times."

I swallowed hard. "Did your whole family go?"

His mouth turned downward. "Yeah, why?"

Why, indeed.

Why was I going there now? "No reason. I'm just curious, I guess."

He gave me an assessing look. "We saw my grandparents a few times."

Silence filled the space for several minutes until Aidan broke it. "What were you guys fighting about?"

"Nothing new," I mumbled. *God, please let it drop. I'm not ready to deal with this yet.*

"Sounded pretty intense. Reminded me of some of the fights I've had with my father."

The temperature grew chillier. I reached for the dial of the heater. "Your temper is gonna get you in trouble some-day." My warning wouldn't do a bit of good. Did he get that quick temper from his father?

I gulped. My father?

The weight of my mom's words pressed on me a little more with each mile. If Hamilton Payne was my father, then what traits had I inherited? Aidan's words came back to me, spoken only two weeks ago.

*"Supposedly the Payne side of our family tree is full of ances-tors with 'odd quirks,' as mom likes to call them."*

"Pull over. I'm gonna throw up."

Easing off the gas pedal, he edged the car onto the shoul-der. I pushed the door open before the wheels came to a complete stop, and his warm hands held my hair back as I lost my dinner and my pride.

"Sorry." I took a deep breath to curb another bout of nausea. "I don't think I messed up your car."

"I don't care about the damn car." He dabbed at my mouth with a napkin, and the gesture was so gentle, so Aidan-like, that I wanted to cry. "Was it something you ate?"

"I don't know, maybe."

He brushed the hair from my face then pulled away, and I let him. His touch, always so quick to comfort, to arouse, was now taboo. I leaned against the window, and once we were on the road again, I allowed the hum of the engine to lull me into numbness.

I had to get to the bottom of this. But first I had to figure out how to tell Aidan. And if it turned out to be true...I knew walking away from him would be the hardest thing I ever did.

# CHAPTER FORTY

"Can we stop at my apartment?" I sat up straight as Watcher's Point came into view. Aidan shot me a questioning look.

"You need to grab something?"

"Yeah." I had to grab something, all right. Courage. And being on my own turf when I ripped both of our hearts out had to count for something.

He pulled in next to my beat up Honda and parked in what had been Six's spot. Twigs and branches littered the area, and wind whipped soggy strands of hair into my eyes, making it difficult to find the keys to my apartment. Getting inside wasn't much easier. And what a dismal sight it was. Aidan followed me in and shut the door.

"We'll have to get someone out here to clean up," he said, indicating the layer of black dust the police had left behind. I wondered how long I'd feel the need to watch my back in fear. Until months had passed...years? Until the Hangman was caught?

The place felt colder than usual, or maybe it was just me.

I turned on the heat. "I'll clean it up," I said, flicking on the small lamp on the end table. The soft glow chased the shadows away but did little to dispel my unease.

I wanted nothing more than to go back to Aidan's place and curl up beside him in bed, clinging to his body for warmth, but I couldn't do that. I couldn't touch him until I knew for sure.

Coming to a standstill in the middle of my living room, I warred with myself. Sure, my mom was a better liar than I'd ever realized, but something about her expression tonight haunted me. If I didn't have good reason to believe she could be lying, I would have sworn she was telling the truth. I jumped when his hand settled at my back.

"Ready to talk yet?"

I didn't answer. His heavy footsteps followed me into the kitchen. I didn't know what I was doing.

Stalling.

"Not yet, no." I circled the kitchen before going back into the living room, as if some tiny corner of my apartment would give me the courage to say the words.

*Aidan, you might be my brother.*

"You seem like you're mad at me, though I have no idea why."

I collapsed onto the couch and folded my arms around myself. "I'm not mad at you. I'm...I'm..."

*Shattered into a million pieces.*

He sat next to me. "Were you guys fighting over me? I can't help if you won't tell me."

"You can't fix this, Aidan." I wished he could, but there was only one thing that would fix this and that was for it not to be true.

"You're right, I can't, especially since I don't know what 'this' is."

The thought of telling him made me physically ill. I couldn't do it...oh my God, I couldn't do it. I dropped my head into my hands. "Just leave me alone for a while." The words were a muffled plea against my sweaty palms.

"Is this a space issue again? Is it Joe? God, Mackenzie, just tell me what's wrong. You're scaring the shit out of me."

Wiping my eyes, I looked up and faced him. "I will tell you. I need to tell you. But right now I can't. Please...I need to be alone."

"I'm not about to leave you here alone, if that's what you're expecting." He reached for me, and his eyes widened when I recoiled from his touch. "What's got you so spooked?"

"You and me...we're a mistake."

"Why are you doing this?" he asked, almost a whisper, and I'd never seen him so ashen. "How can you tell me we're a mistake?"

"It's true." I stared at the floor, knowing I had to do better than this. I needed time to process and that wasn't going to happen if I couldn't get him out of my apartment. "You even said it yourself. You wished we'd never met."

"I also said I loved you." He grabbed my shoulders and forced me to look at him. Those eyes told me so much. His hurt mirrored my own, and anger and confusion mixed with it, all warring in the depths of his gaze.

"Let me go." Pushing against him was pointless. He wouldn't budge.

"Not until you tell me what happened back there."

"You're such a bully!" I shouted. "So quick to intimidate to get what you want." I wasn't sure who was more shocked by my outburst, but I didn't take back the words.

He instantly let go of my shoulders. "You know me better than that. I'd never hurt you. I just want an explanation. Don't you think I deserve that much?"

An explanation? Was that all it would take to get him to leave? "I'm still in love with Joe," I said, the lie born of desperation.

"That's bullshit." His mouth came down on mine, igniting heat instantaneously, and for a blessed moment, his kiss obliterated realty.

"No!" My mom's words screeched in my head, bringing me back to earth. "I said no." I shoved him away and put all my weight into it, hoping he'd mistake my self-disgust for repulsion. "No one will ever ignore that word from me again." I'd meant to maim, and that's exactly what I did.

His expression broke, and his mouth hung open in disbelief. "I guess that says it all. I'll get out of your way then." He rose and stalked to the door, wrenched it open, and halted. He didn't say anything at first, though the heaving of his chest and the rigid set of his jaw painted the picture of a man struggling for control.

"You know where to find me if you need me," he said, his voice calmer than I'd expect. The door slammed shut, followed by silence so heavy, so final, that for one insane moment I considered going after him.

Except I couldn't.

Moving like a robot, I latched all the locks and realized how ineffectual they were. The killer had gotten into my apartment once already, and a few locks weren't going to keep him out. I shrugged my coat off and flung it across the room as if the fabric had the power to burn. The stupid thing landed on the couch, and its mere presence challenged me.

Dammit. Ignoring the envelope wouldn't make it go away. I stomped across the room and yanked it out of my coat pocket, and with trembling hands, I pulled out the contents.

*Mackenzie,*

*I don't know if you'll ever read these words, but I need to get them out. Ever since you moved away and learned the truth about your father, I've been haunted by my past. Grief can make people do stupid things. I let a good man take the blame for my mistake, and even now I'm still perpetrating the lie. You think William Beck-meyer is your father, but he's not. I loved him once, not like I did Tom, but enough to fall back on his friendship when Tom died.*

*Will and I were close, and he was my rock during a time when I needed someone to lean on. But it never went beyond anything platonic. He loved his wife and daughter and wouldn't have done anything to jeopardize that.*

*I was a coward. People thought you were his, and I didn't deny it. Denying it would open questions, and questions could possibly lead to who your real father is. My silence destroyed my friendship with Will. I'm ashamed that it also destroyed his marriage.*

*But your real father is a nasty man, Mackenzie. I was scared he'd find out—I still am. I kept the truth hidden all these years to make sure he never knew about you. I did it to protect you. If you ever learn the truth, I pray you'll heed my words and stay away from him...*

. . .

I read the letter several times, only stopping after the words blurred across the page, words that only added to my confusion. She wanted me to stay away, but she never mentioned why.

The ringing of my cell jolted me, and glancing at the display, I saw it was my mom. I sent her to voicemail and returned to the letter. There was only one person I wanted to talk to—one person who was going to give me answers—and I was determined to get them, even if I had to show up on Hamilton Payne's doorstep in Seattle.

# CHAPTER FORTY-ONE

The light of day hadn't improved my outlook. Whoever came up with that bogus idea hadn't been told they were in love with their own flesh and blood. I shoved another shirt into my duffle before zipping it shut. My apartment, now entirely clean of the black powder the police had left in their wake, no longer felt like home.

I stopped cold as it hit me. I couldn't think of a single place—other than by Aidan's side—that felt like home. What in the hell was I supposed to do about this? Somewhere deep inside, I'd come to accept my mom's words as truth, otherwise I wouldn't be thinking like this.

I grabbed my bag and ventured outside. The storm had dissipated overnight, and now the sun shone down on the destruction the high winds had left behind. Tree branches covered the ground, and a utility crew was working on a downed telephone line nearby.

None of it surprised me as much as seeing Aidan and Joe standing a foot apart in my driveway, faces tense and hands clenched at their sides.

"Hey! What's going on here?"

Two pairs of eyes swerved in my direction. Aidan retreated to his car and leaned against the door, arms crossed over his chest. Joe didn't move, but his hands unclenched. Neither bothered to answer my question.

"What are you doing here, Joe?" Glancing between the two of them, I added, "In fact, what are both of you doing here?"

Joe got in the first word. "Your mom's worried sick about you. She got your address out of Mackayla. Gotta say, Mac, your whole family is freaking out after the way you left yesterday." He threw a dark look at Aidan. "Wasn't expecting to find him staking out your driveway."

"Someone needs to make sure she doesn't get herself killed." Aidan returned Joe's glare. "The Hangman broke into her apartment once already."

Joe backed down from his tomcat stance. "What's he talking about?"

"Nothing you need to worry about." I brushed him off and focused on Aidan again, taking in his rumpled clothes—the same dark button-down shirt and jeans he'd put on yesterday morning, right after we'd broken in his couch. A lump formed in my throat.

"Were you out here all night?" I considered the idea and realized it made perfect sense. I should have known. Truth was I'd been too scared to even peek out my curtains. I hated the fear the Hangman had instilled in me.

"Just because you've lost all sense of rationality doesn't mean I have."

He was talking about my safety, but I didn't miss the undercurrent of his words. The first thing I'd thought of this morning, after grabbing a fitful hour of sleep, was how I should have told him about my mother's revelation. I needed some time though. I closed the distance between us and lowered my voice. "I'm sorry about last night." Keeping my back to Joe, I tried not to think about him listening to every word. "I know you'd never hurt me."

The anger leaked from his expression. "I did a lot of thinking," he said as Joe let out an impatient sigh behind me, "and it finally dawned on me."

"What dawned on you?"

"You have a habit of running when things get tough. I wish you'd tell me why you're doing it again."

I forced a laugh as I switched the duffel to my other shoulder. I'd have a hard time convincing him otherwise with a packed bag in my hand. Might as well not even try.

His gaze fell on the bag. "Going somewhere?"

"Yeah."

"Where?"

"I don't know. Just somewhere. Anywhere. I don't want to push you away, Aidan, but I meant what I said. I need some time to think about things."

"What do you need to think about? If you're having doubts about us, just say so. Don't put yourself in danger over it."

"I'm not having doubts." I lowered my gaze to the ground. "My mom dropped a bombshell on me yesterday...I'm not ready to talk about it yet. I just need to get away for a while."

"Don't go alone," he pleaded. "I know I wanted you to leave town, but not like this. Not when he's so close."

"She's not going alone," Joe spoke up. "I'm going with her."

I whirled around. "You're what?"

"You've done a real good job at keeping us in the dark, Mac. You didn't say anything about him breaking into your apartment." Joe twirled his cell phone in his hand. "Your mom's gonna shit psychedelic Twinkies when she finds out about all of this."

"No," I said through gritted teeth, "she won't because you're not going to tell her."

"Fine. I won't tell her, but I'm going with you. He's right. Someone's gotta keep you safe."

Aidan's rancorous laugh brought me back around. I felt like a damn yo-yo. "That's just great, coming from the guy who sided with his rapist father."

Heavy footsteps and the swishing-sound of denim brought Joe to my side. He radiated a territorial vibe from every pore. "You don't know shit about me and Mac. You're just some rebound guy she hooked up with."

"I know you're not good enough for her."

"Knock it off," I cried. "This isn't high school. And just so we're clear, I'm going alone."

"No you're not!" they shouted in unison.

Ignoring them both, I stalked to my car and tossed my bag in the trunk. Joe was hot on my heels. "Come on, I'm going with you, unless you'd rather I tell your mom?"

"I don't care what you do."

"Good, then it's settled." He got into the passenger seat and slammed the door.

Wonderful. If I didn't get out of there quick, Aidan would jump into the back and this trip would turn into a nightmarish *Three for the Road* remake. "Don't worry about me. I'll be fine," I said, forcing the words past the thickness in my throat. This felt like goodbye. The I'm-never-gonna-see-you-again kind of goodbye.

"You're asking the impossible." He took a step toward me, and I wished he would engulf me in his arms. Just one more time.

*This is wrong. So wrong.*

I squeezed my eyes shut against the sting of tears.

"Look at me."

I complied and found him standing a few inches away. It would be so easy to reach out, to draw comfort from the one person on this planet who could give it. The only person I wanted anything from.

He tugged me against him, and the world ceased to turn. The birds silenced their chirping song, the gentle morning breeze failed to stir, and I wasn't aware of anything but him. I didn't dare breath because I needed his touch more than my next breath. I snaked my arms inside his jacket and held on tight. Somehow, I needed to find the strength to get in that car and drive away from him.

"What are you running from?" he asked.

"The truth." I bit my lip. "It's probably a good thing Joe is coming. We need some time to work through everything." I felt like the lowest form of pond scum, but if he thought I was trying to work things out with my ex, maybe he'd let me go without a fight.

He inched back, and his gaze darted behind me. The flash of hurt I saw on his face told me all I needed to know. He believed the lie...believed I'd chosen Joe over him. He drew me close again and whispered some unintelligible plea against my hair. My car horn blasted in a series of irritating spurts, but I didn't pull away from him.

"I'm sorry," I choked out.

"How can you trust him?"

"I've known him since the fourth grade."

His sigh blew a few strands of hair into my eyes. "Let me go with you. I don't know why you're pushing me away, but it's killing me."

"I'll call you when I get back," I said, stepping out of reach. I hurried around to the driver's side and slid in, and I kept my eyes fastened on the rearview mirror as I backed out of the driveway.

# CHAPTER FORTY-TWO

"Come on, Mac. Let me drive." Joe's insistent tone unleashed an exasperated sigh from my mouth. I'd lost count of how many times he'd bugged me about the issue.

Yes, I was tired...okay, exhausted...but I wasn't ready to relinquish control of anything to him. Not even the steering wheel of my car.

Maybe it was my tired and heartbroken state of mind that caused my next words to slip out. "I guess you do take after your dad. He couldn't take no for an answer either."

Joe didn't say anything for a moment, though the wound I'd inflicted came off him in painful waves. A sliver of guilt burrowed underneath the surface, but I ignored it.

"You're never going to forgive me, are you?" he asked.

"I don't know. Maybe I can get past it eventually." I risked a glance in his direction. "You really tore my heart out, and you did it at the worst time." I reverted my attention to the road. "You have no idea what I've been through."

"Then tell me. I'm not a mind reader."

My defenses lowered, and the words poured out. I told him about the murders I'd seen in my dreams, about Six, about how Aidan and I had managed to save Dee. But I held back plenty; details about my relationship with Aidan and the issue of Hamilton Payne were two subjects I refused to bring up.

He rubbed his hands down his face. "You were going through all of that, and I wasn't there for you. I'm an idiot, Mac."

"Don't call me that."

"I've been calling you that since you were in pigtails. I can't not call you that. You're my Mac."

"Not anymore."

"I know you still love me. You can deny it all you want, but I know it's true."

"I won't deny it. But it's not the same."

"We can fix this, baby." He settled his hand over mine and caressed my skin.

I retreated from the contact. "Since when do you call me baby?"

"Since now. Since I can't call you that...other unmentionable name."

"Don't make a joke out of this. All you're doing is pissing me off."

From the corner of my eye I saw him grin. "I've missed you so much," he said.

What he wanted—for us to exchange endearments and sweet words of love—wasn't possible. I couldn't do it. "It's been months." I paused and contemplated my next words carefully, because the last thing I wanted was to rip his heart out the way he had mine. I guess I really had moved beyond our relationship. "If you're looking for more than friendship," I said quietly, "I can't give it to you."

"It's him, isn't it? He's really got you wrapped."

I peeked at him and saw him scrunch his brows together.

"I didn't figure it out right away," he said, "but something about him bothered me. I mean, other than the fact he was with you." He tapped his fingers against the passenger window. "He's the one you've been drawing all these years."

I didn't answer him. What could I say anyway?

"I used to get so damn jealous over a drawing. I knew you saw him in your dreams, but I kept telling myself it didn't mean anything since he didn't exist. Man was I wrong." His bitter laugh infiltrated the car. "I make the biggest mistake of my life and there he is to pick up the pieces. Perfect fucking timing. So why isn't he here with you now?"

"Just drop it." I hated how my voice cracked. Hated how Joe knew me too well.

"I don't know what you're not telling me, but I'm not blind. I saw the way he looked at you. That didn't bother me nearly as much as the way you looked back." He squirmed in the passenger seat until he was no longer slouching. "Come on, as much as it'll kill me, tell me what's wrong."

A yawn escaped, and I figured this was the perfect time to give Joe something he wanted. "Okay, you're right. I am too exhausted to drive." I pulled the car onto the shoulder and shifted into park. "Take over for me?"

"Don't think for a nanosecond I don't know what you're doing," he grumbled, but he pushed his door open. We switched sides, and as soon as the road rumbled underneath us again, sleep pulled at my consciousness.

"Where are we going?"

"Seattle."

How hard could it be to track down Hamilton Payne?

# CHAPTER FORTY-THREE

"Can you pull off at the next rest stop?" I grabbed my cell from the center console and was shocked to see all the missed calls. My gaze flew to Joe's. "Did you turn my ringer off?"

His guilty expression answered for him.

"What the hell, Joe?"

"Hey!" he started, "don't get mad at me. I didn't want to wake you."

The majority of the calls had been from Aidan. "You had no right. Why would you do that?"

"You were asleep, okay?" He gave me a sidelong glance. "And he was following us. When I lost him in Salem, he started calling."

Of course Aidan had tried to follow me. If I'd had my head screwed on straight, I would have noticed, or at least considered the possibility. "Jeez, Joe. You should've told me." I immediately recognized the hypocrisy of my words. What Joe had kept from me didn't compare to what I'd kept from Aidan. "Just pull over, okay?"

He didn't look happy about it, but he drove into the next rest stop. "I'm gonna take a leak and stretch my legs. That should give you enough time to get lover boy on the phone."

I rolled my eyes. "Can you be any more juvenile?"

His resulting grin only inflamed my exasperation. "It's your fault. When we're together I just can't help myself." He stole a kiss, so unexpectedly that I went still. "I've missed being with you," he said, his playfulness turning into something more serious. His lingering look haunted me as he left the car and disappeared into the men's restroom.

I found my voice and called information to get the number for Payne-Davis headquarters. Getting Hamilton Payne's receptionist to put me through to him was another matter though. I finally resorted to dangling Aidan's name to get his attention. He agreed to meet me in two hours at a Starbucks near his office.

Joe exited the men's room, but instead of coming back to the car, he stopped in front of the vending machines. I took the opportunity to call Aidan. He answered on the second ring, and I nearly melted at the sound of his voice.

"Where are you?"

"At a rest stop."

"Are you okay?"

Physically? "I'm fine." A white utility van pulled into the next space, and without thinking, I locked the doors. An older man, his graying hair matching the color of his uniform, got out and headed toward the restrooms. The black lettering on the side advertised Phil's plumbing. My breath shuddered out, and I ordered myself to get a grip.

"You don't sound fine," he said. A beat of silence passed. "Ever since I lost you guys, I've been going crazy."

"I'm sorry I worried you. Joe told me what happened. He turned my phone off while I was asleep."

"You can't take off on me like that. Shit, I was so desperate I called your mother."

"You called my mom?" I cringed at the alarm in my voice.

"Yeah, I did, and trust me...what she told me didn't make me feel any better."

"What did she say?" I managed to squeak out.

"Well, she doesn't want me near you, I gathered that much. She said I should leave you alone and let you work things out with Joe."

I exhaled in relief. "Aidan...we need to talk. As soon as I get back."

"I wasn't even sure you were coming back." The dejection in his tone made me ache.

"There's nothing going on between Joe and me." Damn. I couldn't give him hope. It wasn't fair.

"When will you be back?"

Joe knocked on the window, and I jumped, my heart thudding painfully. I unlocked the doors and told Aidan we wouldn't be back until after midnight, unless we ended up stopping for the night.

"Be careful," he said as Joe slid behind the wheel. "And call me the minute you get back. I don't care how late it is." The warmth in his voice traveled to my toes.

"I will." We said our goodbyes and ended the call. "You need me to drive?" I asked Joe, ignoring his tight expression. "You've been driving since this morning."

"No, I'm good." He stared straight ahead, refusing to even glance in my direction.

"Okay." I waited until we'd been on the road a while

before bringing up what was sure to be a difficult conversation. "I meant what I said earlier."

"You said a lot of stuff earlier."

"About us being friends. I can't give you more than that." I scooted in my seat and faced him. "Friends don't kiss each other."

"We're not just friends, Mac. We've never been *just friends*. We shared an apartment for fuck sake."

"And you moved out of that apartment, remember? Right after you accused me of lying." At the reminder, the familiar ache in my chest returned. Would it ever stop hurting?

"I didn't want to believe you," he said quietly. "I wanted it to be a lie. So bad. I still do." He swerved onto the shoulder and jerked to a stop, his fingers tightening around the steering wheel. "The thought of anyone doing that to you..." He blinked several times, keeping time to the cars whirring past us. "I should've been there...should've never gone camping that weekend."

We fell silent, and a strangely peaceful aura settled over me as we sat on the side of the road. His regret was tangible, and it knocked down another little piece of my wall.

"Aidan thinks I should come forward."

"Well that's one thing we can agree on." He turned in his seat and met my eyes. "I'll support you one-hundred percent." His hand rose, hesitantly, and he brushed his thumb across my lips. The familiarity of that gesture flooded me with warmth. A small part of me still hadn't let go of him, still hung onto the years we'd had together.

I'd always assumed I'd marry him one day. How frightening to think that things could change so irrevocably in the space of five minutes. Three-hundred seconds—the time it took to check the mail or run into the store for a gallon of milk—that was all it had taken for his father to steal forever from us.

I pushed his hand away. "We broke up."

"Doesn't mean it's set in stone."

"In my mind it is. You need to accept that, and you need to respect me when I tell you no."

That single word settled between us like a wall—a wall made of bulletproof glass that could neither break nor dent. The pain on his face told me he got the message. "Fine," he muttered. He pulled onto the highway again, and the last leg of our trip passed in stop-and-go traffic. Eventually, the Seattle skyline came into view.

"So where to? I swear, Mac, you're taking me on a joyride here."

I entered the address into my phone's GPS and gave him directions, and fifteen minutes later he parked across the street from the bustling Starbucks where I was due to meet Hamilton Payne.

"You gotta give me some answers." His fingers tapped a frustrated beat against the steering wheel. "You've had seven hours to come clean about all this." His gesture encompassed the busy street and sidewalks. "Why are we here?"

"You didn't have to come along," I reminded him. "I didn't ask you to."

Joe sighed and dropped back against the headrest.

Sitting still was impossible. My foot bounced against the floorboard as I stared across the street. The chaotic atmosphere surrounding the coffee shop was no doubt the result of Black Friday. People cluttered the sidewalks, bumping into each other as they entered and exited the neighboring shops, most struggling to carry their packages.

A black Mercedes pulled into a space across from where we'd parked. I recognized Hamilton instantly. His tall, imposing build wasn't easy to forget.

*This is a mistake. I shouldn't have come.*

I got out of the car before I chickened out. "Stay here." I slammed the door, silencing Joe's protests, and took my time crossing the street. A breeze disrupted my hair, and I pulled my jacket tighter. Trees lined the sidewalk, their sparse leaves glittering like spun gold in the sun's last rays of light.

I welcomed the warmth of the coffee shop and rubbed my hands together as I searched the interior for Hamilton. I found him seated at a small table in the far corner away from the other customers. Needing something to keep my hands busy, I ordered a mocha and then forced my feet in his direction.

His expression was unreadable as I slid in across from him. He took a sip from his cup and pierced me with cool, hazel eyes. "You said you needed to talk to me about Aidan?"

"I only said that to get you here."

He clenched his jaw. "Of course you did. Well I'm here. What do you want?"

"Do you remember a woman named Jane Hill?"

He blinked. "Can't say I do."

I took a sip of my mocha and swallowed, despite the scalding temperature. "She grew up in Watcher's Point." I paused for a beat. "She's my mom."

He tapped his fingers against the tabletop. "What does this have to do with me?"

"According to my mom, everything. Please, it's important.

Do you know her? Her name's Jane Hill," I repeated. "You would have crossed paths with her in 1989. Her husband had just passed, and she had three kids back then."

He rubbed his chin. "The real question here is why are you harassing me about her?"

"She said...she claims you're my father."

He actually laughed. "You should have come up with something more original. You're not the first 'kid' to come knocking on my wallet."

"This isn't about money." I swallowed and prayed my hyperactive emotions wouldn't make an appearance.

Hamilton rose and, casting a furtive glance around us, schooled his features into a neutral mask. For the first time since arriving, I noticed the audience we'd attracted. "Find someone else to scam, and if you know what's good for you, you'll stay away from my son." He turned his back to me, and I felt as insignificant as a fly.

"Hamilton." My voice splintered on his name. He turned and regarded me with an air of annoyance, and something inside me snapped. I grabbed the cup he'd left and dumped black coffee down the front of his immaculate suit.

He took a threatening step toward me, eyes narrowed. "Do you know who you're dealing with?"

I held back tears as I stepped around him. "Yes, I think I do. No wonder Aidan can't stand you." I went to move toward the door, but his hand shot out and stopped me. I whirled, about to demand he remove his hand, but his stunned expression paralyzed me.

He opened his mouth and worked his jaw, but instead of speaking, he yanked me closer. His fist enclosed my wrist, and a long moment snuck by as he gaped at me.

"You see things," he said, his voice low enough to avoid being overheard.

"Excuse me?"

"Your power. I can feel it."

I tried to pull away, but he only tightened his grip.

"Have you told Aidan about this? About what your mother claims?"

I gulped. "N-no. Is...is it true?"

*Say no. Say this is a fluke. A morbid joke. Anything. Just say—*

"You have power. I'd recognize it anywhere. We need a DNA test to be certain."

I jerked from his grasp and my heart stopped. The glint in his eyes had changed. I no longer annoyed him; I intrigued him.

"No..." I shook my head helplessly. "It's not true." I heard him call after me as I bolted from the coffee shop, bumping into faceless people as I ran. I didn't stop or look back until I threw myself into the passenger seat of my car. Hamilton stood across the street, searching the crowd of shoppers for me.

"What's going on?" Joe asked.

I shook my head and sank low in my seat. "Just go. Get me out of here now."

# CHAPTER FORTY-FOUR

"You're freaking me out, Mac." I was freaking *myself* out. I couldn't stop crying and was almost hyperventilating as the truth crashed over me.

*OhGodohGodohGod...*

I'd slept with my brother. I was in love with my brother.

"Come on. Tell me what's going on."

"Not now," I said on a hiccup. Curling into a ball, I turned my back to him and let the sobs consume me. He pulled onto the shoulder of the highway and gathered me against him. His arms wound around me, unrelenting yet strangely comforting. I clung to that comfort, afraid I'd break if I didn't have something to hold on to.

"Mac, please."

I couldn't speak and after a while he gave up trying to pry it from me. By the time my tears dried, the temperature had dropped inside the car, and a deep chill crawled underneath my skin.

He rubbed the goose bumps from my arms. "I was

thinking about stopping to get something to eat. Are you hungry?" His voice dropped, and I knew him well enough to know what he was doing. Trying to pull me out of my despair. Trying to distract me.

"I'm not hungry." My stomach flopped at the thought.

Without another word, he steered the car back onto the highway. The road disappeared underneath us, and I practically heard the wheels in his head spinning from where I sat. He took the next exit and pulled into a Burger King drive-thru.

"You haven't eaten much today. You've gotta be hungry," he said.

"I'm not hungry."

"Wanna talk about it?"

"Just order your food." I winced at my short tone. "I'll think about it."

The idea of unloading on someone was tempting. Heat flooded my cheeks at the thought of telling him the entire truth. No way could I tell my ex that I'd slept with my brother.

"That smells disgusting," I complained, cracking my window and allowing the crisp air in. "I'll never figure out how you can eat and drive without wearing at least half of it."

He greeted me with a boyish grin. "What can I say? I'm the shit." When he failed to get a response from me, he added, "Okay, Mac. What's going on? Lay it on me. You'll feel better."

"Thomas Hill wasn't my father." The words escaped and hung in the air.

He wadded up the burger wrapper and tossed it in the bag. "What do you mean?"

"My mom lied to me."

"Oh, man." His shocked, blue-eyed gaze met mine. "So that's the reason for this trip?"

I nodded. "I met my...my father."

He raised a brow. "And it didn't go well?"

"No." I gnawed on my lower lip and watched as Tacoma sped by.

"What did he tell you? Did he deny it?"

"No." I leaned against my window and closed my eyes, concentrating only on the hum of the road. Hamilton had known about my ability. A simple touch and he'd known. I still couldn't grasp it, and I didn't want to think about what it meant.

Joe fell silent. I wasn't sure if he was giving me space to process, or if he didn't know what else to say, but conversation was non-existent after that. I was too upset to let sleep take me so I gladly took over the wheel in Portland. He immediately fell asleep in the passenger seat, and the quiet wasn't so disturbing with his soft snores filling the air.

All I could think of was Aidan. Nausea hit me, becoming more intense the closer we got to Watcher's Point. I mentally rehearsed what I'd say and tried to think of the right words to use. Nothing sounded right. How would I ever face him again once he knew the truth? I'd have to tell him everything and leave Watcher's Point permanently. Move on. Never look back.

As the thought percolated through my head, I glanced into the rearview mirror at the blinding headlights following too closely. "What is up with this idiot?" I let out a curse and stepped on the gas, but the car kept pace.

"What's going on?" Joe asked, stirring in his seat.

"This guy won't get off my tail."

He sat up straight and cranked his neck to see. "Where are we?"

"About ten miles outside of Watcher's Point."

"I'd slow down just to piss him off."

I laughed. "I know you would. I've lost count of how many tailgaters you've driven mad." The car behind us swerved into the oncoming lane and sped past, and only then did I realize a cop had been tailing us.

"Unbelievable!" Joe exclaimed. "That's exactly why I don't like cops. They think they own the road."

We reached my apartment a few minutes after midnight. "Thanks for tagging along," I said wryly, thinking of how he'd wormed his way into my car. Part of me was glad he'd come. The drive would have been long and lonely without someone along for the ride.

Joe gave me a funny look when I failed to shut off the ignition. "You're going to see him, aren't you?"

I nodded.

"I'll follow you in my car."

"No." Absolutely not. No way did I want him knowing where Aidan lived. He was being much too pushy as it was. "I'll be fine."

"You can't go by yourself, Mac."

"Well that's the beauty of us no longer being together— you don't get a say in what I do. Go home."

"Why do you have to be so stubborn?"

I inhaled and counted to ten. "His place isn't far. I just need a few minutes alone."

His expression softened, and I knew he was going to relent. "Are you sure?" he asked.

"Yeah."

"Fine," he said as he opened the door, "but I'm calling you in a few minutes to make sure you get there okay. You better answer."

"I will. Tell my mom I'm okay, will you?"

"Sure, but we're not done. I'll talk to you soon."

I waited until he backed down the driveway before calling Aidan, but he didn't answer. A chill went through me, and suddenly, I couldn't wait to see him.

As I drove toward HWY 101, I realized how weird being alone was. Other than last night, the majority of which I'd spent in my apartment alternating between crying and scrubbing away the black grime, this was the first time in weeks I'd had to myself.

Bright, colorful lights flashed in the rearview mirror. I checked my speed, but going five over the limit didn't normally catch the police's radar. Just my luck. I'd probably caught the attention of a cop who needed to fill his quota.

I let off the accelerator and steered the car onto the shoulder. Fog drifted on the highway, and the lights atop the patrol car turned the scene into a misty kaleidoscope of color. My cell phone vibrated on the console, the display lighting the darkness with its soft glow. I switched off the ignition and answered the call.

"I just got pulled over. I'll have to call you back."

"Speeding to get to lover boy, huh?" Joe let out a derisive laugh, and I knew he was using sarcasm to hide his hurt.

The officer approached the driver's side, his flashlight bouncing with his steps. "I've gotta go. I'll call you when I get there."

I raised my gaze to the window, but the beam blinded me.

The window shattered before anything else registered. A scream tore from my throat, and the last thing I remembered was Joe's frantic voice in my ear as the pain in my head pulled me under.

# CHAPTER FORTY-FIVE

I awoke in murky stages, the first being a nauseating sense of movement. The second was the realization that something was wrong. Horribly wrong. The third was the clearest and the most horrifying. My wrists were tied together as were my ankles.

I pulled at the bindings, and a low groan vibrated in my throat. Despite the persistent throb at my temples, I focused on the misty recollections; the wafting fog on the highway, the beam of a flashlight, the splintering sound of glass.

Forcing my eyes open, I met total blackness. My cheek rested against the floor of what I assumed was a van, and a putrid smell burned my nose, an odorous mixture of mildew and bleach. The van bounced over uneven ground, and I held my breath, my ribs hitting the floor hard with each lurch.

*What the heck happened?*

The floodgates opened, and the memory of flashing lights hit me like a cold fist.

*A cop...oh my God.*

My heart beat out of control as I tried to remember more,

but I drew a blank. There was only Joe's voice in my ear. Or had I imagined that? No. I remembered answering the phone, remembered a blinding light and an explosion of pain in my head...then nothing.

"Don't panic," I chanted in a whisper as I tested the rope. *Come on!* I slid my wrists back and forth, and the knot loosened the slightest bit as the van came to a violent stop. The engine shut off, and I didn't dare move or make a peep. A door creaked open before slamming with an echo. I ceased to breathe as footfalls drew closer, crunching on gravel with each step. I counted them.

*One, two, three, four, five...*

Keys jingled from the other side, and the handle squeaked and turned. The van dipped, and instantly, I knew who entered behind me. I wished I could see him, but I was lying on my stomach, completely vulnerable.

"Where am I?" It wasn't the question I wanted to ask—the one I could barely think of.

*What are you going to do to me?*

My body went rigid as he came near. He rolled me to my back with rough hands, and his silhouette loomed large, a dark shadow blocking the light of the waning moon. He shifted, causing the moon's beam to glint off the cigarette lighter in his hand.

"No..." My plea came out a squeak, an ineffectual cry for mercy. I was only an object to him, something to torture and kill for his perverse pleasure.

I squeezed my eyes shut and yanked at the rope, ignoring the pain biting into my wrists. Hysteria wouldn't help my situation, so I held it in. In fact, from what I knew of the Hangman, my cries and pleas would only heighten his pleasure…his arousal. Vomit burned in my throat, accompanying the rancid taste of fear, but I forced my eyes open anyway.

He sparked the lighter to life, and the flame illuminated his face. Malevolent eyes peered at me, two expressionless voids holding no remorse for what he'd done to all of those other women.

For what he was about to do to me.

His expression distorted into something unrecognizable, and it took a few seconds to realize who towered over me. I couldn't comprehend what I was seeing.

Judd McFayden. The sheriff's son.

"Why?" My voice broke on the question, but he didn't answer. A tear slid down my cheek as acceptance nicked at my composure. I wasn't getting out of this. Aidan would find my body—just like we'd found Six. Just like he'd found his wife. I didn't know how I knew, but I did. Judd would dangle my death in front of him like a trophy. A muffled sob escaped. *Not* panicking was impossible.

For all the times I'd witnessed the murders of other women in my dreams, I'd failed to see my own.

"Here's what we're gonna do," he said, coming closer and letting the flame of his lighter lick my cheek. I shrank away with a whimper. "I'm gonna untie your feet and you're gonna get out. And don't even think about testing me." He exited the van and released my ankles. "Get out slowly."

Slow was the only speed I could go with my hands tied behind my back. My legs shook as I touched ground, and they buckled. Sharp rocks bit into my knees.

*No. Don't give up. Fight, dammit!*

He wrenched me up by the hair, and I struck without thinking, digging my knee into his groin with as much force as I could manage. He let go, and as he spat a litany of obscenities, I ran for the trees, kicking up dust and rock in my wake. I heard him coming after me, his heavy steps pounding the earth. Thick fog blanketed the trees, and I prayed it would be enough to cover me. I tripped over a rock and tumbled to the ground.

"There's nowhere to go, sweetheart!" he shouted.

*Oh God...get up! Go, go, go!*

No matter how fast I ran, it wasn't fast enough. I struggled against the rope, trying to free my hands as I stumbled over rocks and tree roots. Hot tears blinded me, but I kept going, ignoring the twigs and branches that scratched my face.

The shoreline of the lake came into view. I skidded to a stop against a tree, unwilling to leave the cover of fog, and sucked in lungfuls of air. His footsteps were gone.

*Don't panic. Think! Need to find help.*

I pulled at the rope again, but after several minutes of trying to get free without success, I went limp against the tree. That was when a small structure in the distance, maybe a quarter mile down the lake, beckoned me with a single porch light leading the way. I blinked several times to make sure I wasn't seeing an apparition. Pushing away from the tree, I took off for it. Leaves crunched behind me, and I whirled, hoping to find glowing eyes, a burly bear; heck, I'd settle for a mountain lion at this point. Anything but him. A raccoon skittered from the brush and raced behind a tree.

I sucked in a breath...then had the air knocked from me as I hit the ground hard. Dirt entered my mouth as I fought against the hands grabbing me. I spit it out and screamed at the top of my lungs, hoping to get the attention of the occupants in that house. So close, but so far away.

He dug a knee into my spine, yanked my head back, and slipped a loop of thick rope around my neck. I retched into the dirt, and in that moment the only person I thought of was Aidan. My despair gushed down my cheeks in salty tracks. I tasted them on my tongue as Aidan's face flashed behind tightly-closed lids.

"I've been waiting for this," he said, his tone oddly normal, "much too long to let you get away." He didn't talk like a villain in a movie; there was no sinister undertone. He sounded no less menacing than the guy who bagged my groceries. "Just wasn't counting on all the complications."

"Why are you doing this?" Instinct took over, and I rolled and kicked, but all I managed to do was attack air.

He laughed. "I do enjoy the feisty ones." He grabbed the rope and pulled, and I gagged as he hauled me along the water's edge. He stopped long enough to push me into the lake with a muddy boot. I surfaced, sputtering water as I coughed.

"Get up," he ordered. Before I could so much as move, he tugged me up by the other end of the noose. I swayed and blinked away the stars in my vision. "You can walk, or I can drag you the rest of the way. Makes no difference to me." His expression contradicted his words. He relished the thought of a fight.

"I'll walk," I bit out through chattering teeth. He turned and yanked on the rope, and I stumbled behind him on shaky legs.

*This is it.*

The closer we got to the van, the closer I faced my death. I stalled when we reached the clearing. He tugged on the rope and propelled me across the gravel driveway, and I realized how isolated the location was. Trees cordoned off the area from the outside world, and through the thicket, I spotted a sliver of the glimmering lake.

We approached a small cabin, and I panicked all over again. Not only did I recognize it from my dreams, but I knew with certainty that I'd never get out of there alive. I'd rather he strangle me now. He stopped to open the door, and I struck with my feet—the only means of self-defense he'd left me.

His fist connected with my cheek bone. "You stupid bitches never learn." He forced me inside, kicking and screaming the whole way, and the rope became a vise around my throat. I struggled for air as bright light flooded the cabin. I recognized the rustic architecture from my dreams— dreams that were worthless in hindsight. They hadn't saved Six, and they weren't going to save me now.

He dragged me to a bedroom where I fell to my knees. "Get your ass on the bed."

"No," I choked out. I'd fight him with everything I had.

He jerked me up and pushed me to the mattress. I screamed again, squirming and kicking until something sparked and buzzed from the corner of my eye. Intense pain pulsed through every nerve in my body, and I howled in agony, louder than I thought possible until I couldn't even do that anymore. Muscle spasms rendered me incapable of moving, of fighting him. He prodded me with the Taser again and again, and I was left disoriented and tied to the bed, spread-eagle and facedown after the last shock lanced through me.

*He sodomized Six.*

It was my only thought. I spewed bile onto the scratchy blanket against my cheek as the bed dipped under his weight.

"Don't hurt me, Judd." My voice sounded odd, as if a small child was the one doing the begging. I squeezed my eyes shut and cried into my vomit. Fabric ripped through the air, echoing in my ears. I bit into my lip and drew blood as he tore the last article of clothing from me.

"I'm going to do more than hurt you, sweetheart. Foreplay first." He brushed latex-covered fingers down my spine.

My head spun with dizziness, and like the time I'd seen Aidan's past, I now floated above a room I didn't recognize, staring down at people I'd never seen.

Except...the little boy, maybe eight or nine years old, looked familiar. He cowered at the feet of a balding man. Risking a glance up, his eyes pooled with tears. I recognized him as a younger version of Judd.

"I'm sorry. I tried not to be bad."

I gasped when the man backhanded him.

Rather than cry, the boy glared at him. "My daddy will kill you!"

"You're daddy isn't around, is he? Even he didn't want you." The man clenched his hands. "Who would want a sinful, nasty little boy?"

In a display of courage, the boy stood and hardened his gaze. "He'll come back for me."

His tormentor laughed. "Stupid kid. Your old man isn't coming back, and your mom can't help you either. Now repent for your sins." He unbuttoned the front of his jeans, and I sobbed upon witnessing what happened next. The boy begged for his mother, and when she failed to come, he began to pray. I couldn't stomach it. I crashed back into the present as Judd sparked a lighter to life.

"I'm sorry he did that to you."

I felt him go still. "What are you talking about?"

"You were just a boy." My voice cracked, and even though he had me bound and was about to kill me, a part of me hurt for the younger version of him...the little boy who had no one to rescue him. "I saw what happened to you as a child."

The flame went out. "You what?"

"Just now. I saw what he did."

"You didn't see shit!" He tossed the lighter aside, and it hit the wall before dropping to the floor. "You're just trying to stall, hoping to buy time so your knight in shining armor will rush in." He laughed. "I've got news for you. He's not coming. I made sure of that."

My body went numb. "What did you do to Aidan?"

"Nothing you need to worry about. By the time they find him, this pretty little head of yours will be hanging." He yanked my head back by the hair.

I sobbed, overwhelmed with grief at the thought of him hurting Aidan. "Why are you doing this? What do you have against him?" The rope tightened around my throat. "Please—"

"What's that? Sounds like you're beggin' for something."

I shook my head and ignored the blinking lights in my vision. "Just...wanna...talk."

"No pillow talk tonight, baby. I'm gonna fuck you like a real man."

He shifted, and I heard the sound of a belt unbuckling...a zipper lowering. I coughed and fought for breath. The room spun, and I focused on the bright light coming through the window.

Judd cursed and tightened the noose. I thrashed, my lungs burning for air as the weight of his body disappeared. A crash came from the other room, followed by another.

"Where is she?" someone screamed. It sounded like Aidan, but that was impossible. I had to be hallucinating. More voices...the sound of breaking glass...then the promise of nothingness as the shadows infiltrated further, smothering the last speck of light. Finally, as my heart thumped to a slow drumbeat, I welcomed the darkness calling.

# CHAPTER FORTY-SIX

I was weightless, like an untethered kite soaring through the sky. I drifted upward, bounced on a cottony cloud, and dipped down to sit on it. An onyx void existed below, incongruent with the luminescence above. I was either having the most bizarre dream of my life—and that was saying a lot—or I was dead. The idea ricocheted through my mind, propelling me into motion. Avoiding the glaring brightness seemed of utmost importance. I reached for the darkness and forged through the pain that rippled through me.

Pain was good. Pain meant I could still feel. I became more aware of it the further I descended, and I wanted to scream, except I couldn't get a sound past the crushing weight around my throat. My heartbeat pulsed in my ears, slowing with each passing second, and my will to cling to the darkness waned. I floated upward again, distancing myself from the agony even as cold fingers pried the vise from around my neck. An anguished voice called out, "Breathe!" It was Aidan. I'd know his voice anywhere.

"Mac, wake up!" Was that Joe?

The pain receded and the voices became garbled background noise until they disappeared altogether. The scene shifted as I floated toward the light, and I found myself staring down into my own slate gray eyes. Sweat dripped down my face, and my complexion was as white as the sheet covering the table beneath me. Aidan stood to my side, though something was different about him. Contentment softened his face, drove the pain from his eyes. I jumped when my lips parted to expel a long, animalistic sound—a cross between a grunt and a scream.

Oh my God! What the heck was going on?

My doppelgänger gripped Aidan's hand, using such incredible strength that her knuckles turned ash-white. Another scream tore through the air, and I was so transfixed that I failed to notice the doctor that rushed into the room until his bulky form blocked my view. Time shifted, appeared to matter no longer. More agonizing cries, growing louder... louder still. I squeezed my eyes shut and plugged my ears to block out the terrifying sound.

When I opened my eyes, the scene below didn't make any sense. The doctor laid a slippery newborn onto the stomach of the mother...me. The baby wailed; a symphony compared to the screams I'd heard just minutes ago. Tears brightened Aidan's eyes as he gazed at the baby, and I was stunned when he leaned over and kissed the woman who looked so much like me but couldn't possibly be me. Brothers and sisters didn't have babies together.

The vision faded as I crashed into inky blackness, and I wondered at the strange sensation of air rushing into my lungs.

"Come on, dammit! Please, baby—" Aidan's voice broke, and I felt another rush of air. "Breathe!"

I coughed and gasped.

"That's it," he murmured. "Come back to me."

"Is she breathing?" Joe's voice was abnormally high, like he was a moment away from losing it.

"She's breathing," he said. I wanted to reach for him when he pulled away, but I couldn't get my arms to move. "Bastard's gonna pay for this."

"Aidan!" shouted a third voice. "No!"

Sirens blared, growing rapidly closer, and tires turned and slowed over gravel as footsteps pounded the ground outside. The third voice—the one I hadn't been able to place —barked orders in quick spurts. "I'm going after them," he announced.

"No, we'll handle this," someone else said with authority.

"My son's out there!"

"My point exactly. You're too close to this."

Footsteps scurried around me. I coughed again and opened my eyes. Joe's face swam above, and everything else blurred. People crowded the space as two of them loaded me onto a stretcher. They wheeled me into the chilly night, and the strobing lights of the emergency vehicles lit up the surrounding trees.

I shut my eyes as the doors of the ambulance slammed, and the only thing that penetrated my consciousness was the blast echoing in the distance—as startling as a mortar on the Fourth of July.

# CHAPTER FORTY-SEVEN

I recalled my rescue in snippets, like vague, disjointed fragments from a long ago dream. Joe's face, Aidan's voice...more voices...sirens, flashing lights, and fireworks. Wait...fireworks?

Obviously, my mind was as disorganized as my memories. "Ms. Hill?"

My eyes fluttered open and landed on the woman the voice belonged to. She couldn't have been much older than me. Her long, honey locks were pulled into a tight ponytail, and the white of her uniform was as blindingly bright as the light overhead. "Welcome back."

"How long have I been here?" Wherever here was. The room resembled a hospital room, yet the décor was warmer than I'd expect. Pictures of the ocean and the lighthouse hung on walls painted a deep crème.

"You were moved up here about an hour ago. You became agitated in the ER, so they gave you a sedative. You don't remember any of it?"

"No," I whispered, trying to keep my emotions under control.

She patted my hand. "Try not to worry." She took my blood pressure and frowned. "Can I get you anything?"

I shook my head.

"The doctor will be in shortly." She handed me a control attached to a thick wire. "Press the call button if you need anything." I was grateful when she dimmed the lights on her way out.

Yet the darkness brought a new onslaught of memories. Rope tightening around my neck as hands ripped the clothes from my body, and my panic at being unable to breathe. I swallowed a sob as I recalled the moment I'd given up—the moment I'd accepted death.

Staring into the vacant hall through watery eyes, I imagined Judd strolling through the open doorway—imagined him finishing what he'd started. A bone deep chill went through me until every part of my body shook. Being alone was probably the last thing I needed right now.

But where was everyone? Where was Aidan? I reached for the call button just as a doctor entered.

"I'm Dr. Armstrong. How are you feeling?"

"Confused...scared." I wiped the moisture from my face.

"It's no wonder after the ordeal you went through." She glanced at the chart in her hands. "With your consent, I'd like to start a rape kit."

My eyes widened. "I wasn't...he didn't..."

Her expression softened. "Are you sure? You were unconscious when they found you, and the paramedics worried you might have been."

"I-I don't remember being raped..."

"Let's collect some samples just in case, okay?"

"Okay." I raised my eyes to hers. "Can I see Aidan first? Aidan Payne? Where is he?" My heart pounded as I waited for an answer.

She didn't give one. She placed her hand on my arm and asked, "Are you up to speaking with Agent Kipp? She's been waiting to get your statement."

"No," I said without hesitation. The last thing I wanted was to deal with the FBI.

"I'll tell her to come back later then. I'm going to put in the order for the rape kit. In the meantime, someone's been antsy to see you. Want me to send him in?"

I nodded, eager to see Aidan's face.

"I'll be back shortly." She left, and a few moments later my visitor hurried in. But it was Joe, not Aidan, who stepped to my bedside.

"Hey," he said softly.

"Where's Aidan?"

His face fell, though he recovered quickly enough. He collapsed into the chair next to my bed. "They wouldn't tell me anything. I've been pacing the halls for the past hour." He ran both of his hands through his hair. "Mac...I've never been so scared in my life. When we found you—"

"How did you find me? And where's Aidan? Judd told me..."

*"I've got news for you. He's not coming. I made sure of that."*

But he did come. I remembered hearing his voice. "What happened, Joe?"

"I heard you screaming on the phone, so I went to the police. I followed the sheriff to Aidan's place and we found him unconscious."

"But I *heard* him."

"He came to, and that's when the sheriff found your drawing. He recognized the cabin. If not for that, we probably
wouldn't have found you in time. Shit, Mac, they found a
tracking device on your car. Sicko was just waiting for the
perfect opportunity to get at you." He grew uncomfortable
and avoided my gaze. He was holding back something. I was
sure of it.

"Just tell me." A burning sting ignited behind my eyelids.
"He'd be here if he could..." I inhaled sharply. "Please, Joe...
oh God! Where is he?"

"He went after Judd."

A loud blast echoed in my mind, a vague recollection of
something I didn't want to remember. "What happened?" I
studied his expression and tried to keep mine from shattering. When he failed to answer, I pushed back the blankets
and hopped from bed. The room spun around me, and I
promptly fell into his arms and clung to him.

"Tell me," I pleaded. "Tell me he's okay."

"He's in surgery right now," he said, his voice so low I
could tell he didn't want to continue. "He tried to stop Judd
from running, and he got shot."

I untangled from his arms and fell to the bed. Curling
into the fetal position, I sobbed into my pillow. He was going
to die, just like in my dreams. Joe's voice rattled off more
words, but I couldn't hear him. He gripped my shoulders and
gave me a shake.

"Mac! The doctors are optimistic he'll pull through."

"Go," I moaned. He was worried about me enough to say
anything if he thought it would help. I wouldn't believe Aidan
was okay until I saw it for myself.

"Mac, please."

"I want to be alone."

I heard him shuffle away. "Your mom should be here soon. I heard Aidan's parents are on their way too."

Hamilton. The thought of him angered me. I welcomed anger—it was easier to deal with than despair. "Joe?"

He was back by my side in an instant. "What is it?"

"Let me know when he gets out of surgery."

"Of course."

"Will you tell the nurses I don't want to see Hamilton Payne?" I risked a glance up and took in the perplexed line of his mouth.

"Okay," he said slowly, nodding as if he understood when clearly he didn't.

I turned my back to him and hugged my pillow. He remained silent for a few moments before his quiet steps took him into the hall.

I was emotionless by the time Dr. Armstrong returned, accompanied by the nurse who'd greeted me when I'd awakened. She pushed a cart in and closed the door, and I couldn't bring myself to look at all the supplies on the tray. Instead, I kept my gaze fastened on the ceiling and prepared myself for what was to come.

After it was over, I waited—for news about Aidan, for the doctor to tell me I hadn't blocked Judd doing the unthinkable. She returned at dawn, and I pounced before she reached the side of my bed.

"Is Aidan out of surgery yet?"

"Not yet. I'll let you know as soon as I hear something." She took a seat and offered me a reassuring smile. "From what I could tell, you weren't raped." She glanced at the chart in her hands. "And there's no sign of miscarriage, so that's good."

My world stopped. "Wh-what?"

She tilted her head. "You weren't aware of your pregnancy?"

"No!" I cried, horrified.

"You're not very far along, so I'm not surprised you didn't notice a missed period."

"This doesn't make any sense. I'm on birth control."

"Birth control isn't one hundred percent effective."

"I know, but..." I brought a fist to my mouth and calculated the time Aidan and I had spent together. It couldn't have been more than two weeks since our first time. I lowered my face into my hands and fell apart.

"Is there anything I can get you? Anyone I can call?"

"I just want out of here."

"Soon. Eat breakfast first, then I'll prepare your discharge papers."

I folded my arms, more of a defensive gesture than anything else, and avoided the sympathy in her expression. Or maybe it was more in line with pity. I hated pity.

"If you need someone to talk to, I can get you a referral. You've been through a lot."

I shook my head. "I'd rather not."

She looked as if she wanted to press the issue, and I was thankful when she didn't.

"Agent Kipp is here again," she said. "Should I send her in?"

I shook my head. "I want to talk to Sheriff McFayden."

"He's here too, but we thought you might be more comfortable with a woman."

"I need to talk to him."

"I'll let him know. Are you sure you don't need anything?" She brushed chestnut colored bangs from her eyes as she waited for my answer.

"I'm sure." I could have used a painkiller for the throbbing in my temples, though the strongest painkiller on Earth wouldn't take away the deep ache in my heart.

# CHAPTER FORTY-EIGHT

"You wanted to see me?" The voice made me jump, and I was surprised to find Sheriff McFayden standing in the doorway holding a tray in his hands.

"Breakfast," he said, as if I'd asked for an explanation. "I told the nurse I'd bring it in since I was headed in here anyway." He set the tray on a table, and I willed my pulse to return to normal. I expected him to lower into the chair at my bedside, but he focused on the window instead. The blinds were drawn, though a bit of light leaked through. I'd lost all sense of time. The whole night had gone by in a surreal blur.

"Is Aidan out of surgery yet?"

He nodded. "The bullet grazed his liver, and he lost a lot of blood, but he's okay. He's in recovery."

His words caused a dam to burst in me. I clutched my stomach as the most intense form of relief I'd ever experienced rushed through me. "When can I see him?"

"He'll be in recovery for a while." McFayden pointed toward my cooling breakfast. "You should try and eat something."

I grabbed a banana nut muffin and picked at it. "Why did Judd do it, Sheriff?"

He dropped his head, and the haggard lines on his face reminded me of Aidan on the night of Halloween; it was the image of devastation. "I don't know, Ms. Hill." He wouldn't meet my eyes as he lowered his tall frame into a chair.

"I had a vision about him."

His eyes widened. "About Judd?"

I played with the edge of my blanket and avoided eye contact. Suddenly, I wondered if he was aware of what his son had endured while growing up. "I saw him as a child."

"I wasn't around when he was young," he said, and the regret in his tone made me lift my head. He swallowed hard. "His mother wasn't...right in the head. She took off with him shortly after we divorced. I didn't see him for years."

I shivered, remembering how utterly abandoned Judd had felt. "Did you know he was abused?"

"I suspected. His mother committed suicide when he was twelve, and he went to therapy when he came to live with me, but it was hard to know if it helped. No one could get him to open up."

Obviously, it hadn't helped or he wouldn't have turned into such a psycho. He blinked several times, and I looked away, giving him a few moments to collect himself.

"His childhood was rough, but that doesn't excuse him for what he's done." He sighed. "I shouldn't even be talking to you about any of this."

"Other than Judd, you're the only one who can give me answers."

"I wish I could give you answers." He appeared to have aged ten years overnight, and that was never more apparent than when he raised his head and looked at me with tired, red-rimmed eyes. "I want you to feel one-hundred percent safe, so I've upped the security here. He won't get near you." He pinched the bridge of his nose. "I can't begin to apologize for what he's done."

I gripped the blankets as I tried to process the apology, but I was stuck on one thing—the fact that McFayden was talking as if... "But he's in jail."

He ran a hand through his graying hair. "Aidan tried to stop him. By the time I found him he'd been *shot*,"—his voice cracked, and he struggled to continue—"and Judd was gone."

He was still out there somewhere. The reality of it hit me in the chest, and I sucked in several breaths before speaking again. "But you're gonna find him, right? You *have* to find him!"

"We're doing everything we can." He stood. "Agent Kipp needs to get your statement. Is it okay if I send her in?"

I nodded, unable to find my voice.

He never did offer an explanation, or even a guess, as to why his son had done what he'd done. Maybe he was as clueless as the rest of us, though instinct told me differently. The agent appeared in my doorway almost immediately upon his exit, and retelling what had happened in minute detail left me mentally drained.

I'd grown numb by the time my mom arrived. She brought me a change of clothes, and I hadn't protested when she pulled me into her arms and held on for what seemed like forever.

As promised, Dr. Armstrong discharged me after breakfast.

Now we waited, Mom, Joe, and me. Aidan was unconscious and still in recovery, and I didn't know if that was normal or not after surgery; the nurse hadn't elaborated.

My mom paced the hall outside the family lounge as she talked on the phone. She returned a few minutes later and plopped into a chair. "That was Mackayla. She and Micah are on their way. They're calling Marcus too."

"Call them back. I'm not ready to see everyone yet."

"Come on, Kenz, don't be ridiculous."

I loved my family, but I didn't feel up to putting on a brave front for them now. It was bad enough Joe refused to leave my side, especially since he knew me too well. "I'm not ready yet. Please, Mom."

She got up with a sigh and dialed, and I noticed the stress on her face as she stepped into the hall again.

I bounced my foot against the floor as if I'd consumed a pot of coffee, though I'd had none. Knowledge of my pregnancy changed everything, and I already found myself thinking in small, protective ways.

Every so often I'd spot a deputy combing the halls. His presence made me nervous, as it was a constant reminder of Judd and the fact that he was still free...free to try again. I got up and started pacing, and Joe gave me a worried glance. So what if I was a nervous wreck and unable to sit still? Didn't mean he had to look at me as if I were about to break. Who knew, maybe I was.

Maybe I'd already broken in half and this was all some weird dream. Bizarre nightmare was more like it. If only I could wake up, preferably next to Aidan in a world where he wasn't my brother...in a world where I wasn't pregnant with his child and we didn't have to worry about the threat of a madman. Somewhere in a small corner of my mind the full impact of what we'd inadvertently done festered, but the rest of me wouldn't accept it yet—the shame was too much to handle.

Vomit rose in my throat. I sprinted for the restroom, registering my mom's alarmed look on the way, and barely made it to a stall in time. A couple minutes later, as disgusting brown swirled down the toilet, I sensed her behind me.

"Are you okay?"

I cranked my head. "No." I stared at her for a few seconds and debated on whether I should utter the words, but she'd find out eventually. Better to get it over with now. "I'm pregnant."

She blanched, and I wondered if she was going to be sick herself. "Tell me it's not Aidan's..."

"I just found out—" I covered my mouth and squeezed my eyes shut, as if doing so would block out the horror of the situation. "It's his."

"Didn't you use birth control? You barely know him, Kenz!"

Was she serious? "Of course I used birth control!" I jumped to my feet and glared at her. "Don't you dare put this on me. You should have told me the truth." My words sliced through her like I'd meant them to. The two sides of me went to battle—the scared girl who needed her, and the grown woman who was knocked up by her own flesh and blood and wanted to hurt her.

Badly.

I pushed past her and moved to the sink to wash my hands. "I love him. If the situation weren't so sick and twisted, I'd be ecstatic to have his child."

"You're too young—"

"Don't go there." She'd had Marcus a year after graduating high school. "Can you take Joe and get something to eat or...something? I need to be alone for a while."

"I'm not leaving you alone."

"*Please*. You guys are smothering me!"

"Okay," she said, raising her hands and stepping back. "I suppose we could grab some coffee." She'd always been the strong-willed one, accustomed to getting her way, so the speed in which she relented surprised me. The door shut with a whoosh, and I waited a few minutes after she left before heading toward the waiting area.

Watcher's Point General still had that new smell to it—in the paint on the walls, in the wood used to construct the building. The place was only a few months old, and I knew the scent of fresh paint would always bring me back to this day—to the waiting that seemed endless, spent boxed in the tiny lounge with too many magazines cluttering the tables and no real desire to open them much less flip the pages. Waiting, for news about Aidan, for someone to say, "he's awake and wants to see you."

I entered the lounge and smacked into a wall of a chest. A cry escaped me, and I stumbled back, a moment away from screaming for help.

But it was Hamilton Payne—not a monster in human form—who reached out and steadied me. My heart jackhammered, and I brought a hand up to my chest. Relief seeped into my bones until he tightened his grip. His eyes widened, and the way he studied me, as if I were a science experiment, caused fear to course through me again. I didn't like this connection I sensed, as if he were stripping me, layer by layer, until he saw through me. Was this how Aidan felt under my scrutiny?

He guided me to one of the leather couches and urged me onto the cushion. "Are you okay? Do you need a doctor?"

I raised my brows, stunned by the lines of concern in his forehead. "I'm fine."

He settled beside me and relaxed. "They tell me Aidan is in recovery?"

My voice was in full mutiny, so I nodded. We sat in silence for a while, and I was trying hard not to freak out. I didn't know what to say to him, didn't know how to handle his presence.

"Is...is Aidan's mother here too?"

*Does she know about me?*

"She's talking to the doctor."

I hunched forward and rested my elbows on my thighs.

"We need a DNA test," he said, so out of the blue it startled me. "Though I'm positive you're mine."

The way he said "mine," with a possessive undertone, alarmed me, and I wondered if I should have listened to my mom. Maybe confronting him really had been a bad idea. What if I'd opened Pandora's Box?

Only I was clueless about what was inside.

"How can you be so sure I'm your daughter?" I knew how he knew, but I wanted to hear him say it anyway. Maybe the truth would penetrate and stick.

"You're able to see things, past and future, I suspect. Well, I'm able to sense when someone is...special. There's a certain feeling when it's blood related. I felt it with Logan, and now with you."

"Aidan told me about Logan." I glanced at him and noticed the downturned set of his mouth.

"Logan fights who he is." He shifted in his seat. "We can do the test now. I can arrange it in a matter of minutes."

"Why are you so anxious about this? When I told you what my mom claimed, you wanted nothing to do with me." Not until he'd touched me. "What do you want from me?"

"I want to know my daughter. Your mother had no right to keep this from us."

"She really created a mess," I mumbled.

"What was that?"

"Nothing."

He tilted his head. "How close are you to my son?"

My silence answered for me. I was afraid to look at him, afraid I'd find contempt on his face. Deep down, that's how I felt. Never mind the fact that Aidan and I hadn't known—what we'd done was plain wrong.

"We need to handle this situation with a certain amount of discretion. I think it's best if you and Aidan put some distance between the two of you. Why don't you come visit Seattle for a while?"

"It's not that simple."

"I'll make it simple. You can even work for me. After all you've been through, I think it'll be good for you to get away."

"I can't just up and leave. My life is here."

"I'll set up a trust for you, so you won't have to worry about a thing."

I blinked. "What?"

"I take care of what's mine."

I jumped up. "I'm not *yours*. Just yesterday you accused me of being a scammer after money, and now you're wanting to give me a trust fund and a job?" I folded my arms. "I don't want your money."

"Of course you do. I can open doors for you, give you opportunities."

My body went cold. I was certain he had an ulterior motive, though I had no idea what it was. "What do you get out this?"

He stood, rising to his full height, and looked down on me. I took a step back. If not for the hard glint in his eyes, his irritation might have gone unnoticed. He was about to argue the issue, I could already tell, but a nurse interrupted us.

"Ms. Hill? Aidan's awake. He's asking for you."

# CHAPTER FORTY-NINE

*alm down.* I closed my eyes for a brief second before peeking inside Aidan's room. The door was ajar, and I saw a woman holding his hand as she wiped the tears from her face.

"I'm fine, Mom." His voice was foreign to my ears, a weak and raspy sound that contradicted everything I knew about him. He spotted me, so I stepped over the threshold.

Upon my presence, his mother stood. She looked younger than her age, though I knew she had to be pushing fifty. Her deep auburn hair tumbled to the middle of her back, and she came across as tiny and fragile despite the inner strength I sensed within her.

"You must be Mackenzie." She wiped the last trace of tears from her cheeks and gave me a weak smile. "I'm Lila."

"It's nice to meet you," I said, though every part of me screamed how she'd hate my guts once she found out the truth. Surely she didn't know—she wouldn't be this polite if she did.

"Mom, would you mind giving us a moment?" Aidan asked.

She wiped her cheeks again and nodded. "I need to call your brother anyway." Her expression tensed when she glanced behind me, and I turned to find Hamilton waiting in the hall. She brushed past and closed the door on her way out.

I returned my attention to Aidan. His hooded gaze traveled up and down my body before he stopped to linger on the bruises circling my neck. He jolted into a sitting position, yanking on the various tubes and wires attached to his body, and then fell back against the pillows with a groan.

"Sonofabitch," he said. Sweat beaded on his forehead, and the pasty hue of his skin made the dark hair sweeping his left brow more striking. The monitors went haywire. "Remind me not to move." He squeezed his eyes shut and hissed a breath between clenched teeth.

I wanted to go to him, but my legs had other ideas. There was so much left unsaid between us, so much I hadn't told him, and I couldn't fathom telling him now. This wasn't the time.

"I'm gonna kill him," he said, his gaze settling on my neck again.

Without thinking, I brought my hand up to my throat. I didn't mention he'd have to find him first, but knowing Aidan, he wouldn't rest until he did. "It looks worse than it is."

"Don't do that."

"Do what?" I finally willed my feet to move and lowered into the seat next to his bed. I took in the IV attached to his hand and listened to the rhythmic beeping of the machines that monitored his vitals.

"Don't put on a brave front for me," he said. "After what he put you through..." Barely contained rage laced his words, though his eyes told a different story. Self-inflicted blame. "All I wanted was to keep you safe—"

"It's my fault." Everything was my fault. If I'd been honest with him from the beginning, maybe Judd wouldn't have had the opportunity to kidnap me, and Aidan wouldn't be in the hospital torturing himself with more unnecessary guilt.

"How the hell is this your fault?"

"It just is."

"Did he...did he *rape* you?" His strangled question cut through me, and I could tell his mind had gone back to finding me in that cabin, naked and bound and unconscious.

"No." I laid my hand on his arm. "You got to me in time." The warmth of his skin seeped into my palm, and I jerked my hand back, mortified by the instant reaction I had to touching him. "How are you doing?"

"I'll live. I want to know about you. Are you sure you're okay?"

Of course his first concern was for me. He operated on autopilot. I flattened my lips to keep them from trembling. "I'm fine."

"I don't believe that for a second." He grabbed my hand and weaved his fingers with mine, refusing to let go when I tried to pull away. "Why are you blaming yourself?"

*Don't break down now.*

I blew out a nervous breath. "We have a lot to talk about, Aidan."

"Now *that* I believe." He pulled away and grabbed a magazine from the table beside his bed. "Starting with this." He held up a tabloid and on the cover was a photo of Hamilton and me after I'd thrown the coffee on him. The headline claimed I was "Payne-Davis CEO's latest mistress."

"Logan gave my mother a heads-up about this. She didn't want me to see it from someone else. What were you doing with my father?"

My cheeks flushed with mortification. "I can only imagine what your mom must think of me." Now her polite greeting really confused me.

"I told her it wasn't true, told her there has to be a good explanation. Of course, I'm sure my father has his own twisted version of the truth." The intensity of his stare paralyzed me. "I don't trust him to be honest, Mackenzie. But you...you're not a liar. I want to hear it from you."

"But I did lie to you." The words came out barely audible —the initial crack in the dam that would spring a flood of truth.

"Then be straight with me now."

"I want to, but the timing sucks." I gave the machines surrounding his bed a pointed look. "You were shot." The blanket had fallen to his lap, and a line of blood dotted the front of his hospital gown. I jumped to my feet. "You're bleeding."

He glanced down and winced. "The nurse was in a little while ago to check the wound."

"Or maybe you shouldn't try jumping out of bed. You're still recovering from surgery."

"You know what? Fuck the surgery and fuck explanations. I almost lost you." He scooted over, clenching his jaw with the movement. "C'mere. I want you in my arms, and I don't give a shit how much it hurts to hold you."

My gaze fell on his forearm, on the IV going into the back of his hand, and I remembered how amazing his fingers felt against my skin. "I need your arms more than you know." A tear dropped onto my shirt.

"What's stopping you?"

"DNA." The answer slipped out before I could stop it.

"I'm not following."

The words wouldn't come. I shook my head as helplessness stole over me. "I don't know how to tell you this."

"Whatever it is, just tell me. I can take it."

"I went to Seattle because my mom said that Hamilton is..." Finding the right words was a struggle; there wasn't any *right* way to say this. "He's my f-father."

The thundering beat of my heart blocked out everything, even the beeping of the machines. When I finally found the courage to meet his eyes, I wished I hadn't. Clearly, in his book, I'd lost my marbles. If only that were true. Awkward silence ensued, and when I could stand it no longer, I pleaded with him to say something.

"Okay," he said. "How about *this is insane*? You and I... there's no way we're related. Your mother is either crazy, mistaken, or full of shit."

"Your father confirmed it. He touched me and knew instantly that I...see things."

He shook his head. "No..."

"There's more," I added, my voice unusually high.

"Just tell me. It couldn't possibly get any worse."

"The doctor did a rape kit, and she found out that I'm...

I'm..." This was going to kill him. I placed a hand over my stomach as tears of shame drenched my cheeks.

"Aw shit," he whispered. He dragged both hands down his face. "This is...*crazy.*" He shook his head again, apparently at a loss for words. A former journalist at a loss for words. This was too much for even Aidan to handle.

I stumbled back a few steps. "If you need some time alone..."

"Where do you think you're going? C'mere," he said again, his voice thick and raw. He patted the space next to him. "We'll get a DNA test, but for now I want to hold you while I still can."

I couldn't argue with him. How could I argue against the one thing I wanted most, especially in light of nearly losing him? I climbed onto the bed and nestled against him, careful to keep my distance from the wound in the right side of his abdomen.

His fingers tunneled through my hair in calming familiarity. "We'll deal with it when the time comes. At the very least, we need to know for sure, without any doubts. God...a baby."

"I know." My fingers curled around his shoulder, and I clung to him, inhaling his scent and branding my mind with this moment, the memory of which might have to last a lifetime. "I've missed you so much."

"You should've told me."

"I didn't know how."

He reached for his cell phone. "The sooner we know, the quicker we can put it behind us...or face it if we need to."

"What are you doing?"

"Arranging a DNA test."

"Your father said he was going to."

"I don't trust him. I want my own results." He dialed and talked with someone about making the arrangements.

"Don't we need a sample from Hamilton?"

"Not necessarily, but it couldn't hurt. I'll get it from him."

I rested my head on his shoulder. "You don't seem too worried."

"I'm scared shitless."

Silence stretched out between us, and as I closed my eyes and allowed sleep to tickle my consciousness, I wondered how I'd survive never being with him again...if the news was bad.

"I've missed you too," he whispered sometime later, and I wasn't sure if his words warmed my heart or squeezed it so tight it bled.

# CHAPTER FIFTY

*Oh God.* He was so close. His feet hit the ground behind me, each step bringing him horrifyingly closer. I forced my legs to go faster despite the uneven path, and everything moved in slow motion. Gigantic trees stood tall on either side, their skinny branches unmoving in the breezeless night, and I felt as if I were forging through thick mud, each hard-won step taking me nowhere.

His hands grabbed at me, pulled...pulled some more until he dragged me into the darkness where I suffocated.

"No!" My eyes flew open as a hoarse cry tore from my throat. Slowly, the dreary walls of the hospital room came into focus and I remembered where I was.

"It's okay. No one's gonna hurt you." Aidan embraced me from behind, and his hands locked around my wrists to still them. Our position had to be painful for him, pressed against me the way he was, but he seemed more concerned for me than for himself.

I gulped in a breath. "Don't let go."

"Never." He drew the covers over us, and his arms tightened around me again. We were so close we could have been one.

"This is so wrong," he said. "Holding you shouldn't make me feel this dirty." His voice sounded ragged, though from emotion or the narcotics they were feeding into his veins, I couldn't be sure.

My heartbeat had begun its slow decent to normal. "I don't care. I need you right now."

"I'm here."

But he wouldn't always be. Eventually, after Judd was caught, I'd have to move on.

"There's no way you came from that man," he said. "You're too good."

"Not that good. I lied to you. If I hadn't—"

"Stop. I know where you're going with this, and I understand why you didn't tell me at first. It was a lot to take in." He expelled a deep sigh. "Shit, it still is."

"But I should've told you."

"And I shouldn't have treated you like shit the night you drove me home from the hospital, but you forgave me. Let it go, Mackenzie. People make mistakes."

Gradually, I relaxed in his arms. "You came from him, and I think you're pretty amazing," I said.

"See what I'm talking about? You choose to see the good in people, but there's nothing good about my father. I don't want you getting sucked in by him."

"What would he want with me? I'm nobody."

"That's where you're wrong. He's power hungry. Logan is a mess because of him."

"How's your wound?" I asked, needing to change the subject.

"I'm okay." He slid a palm beneath my shirt and settled over the spot where our baby grew.

We fell silent for a while, and the weight of his touch brought my pregnancy to the forefront of my mind. I hated my mom for the sick feeling that twisted in my gut anytime I let my thoughts drift there. "What are we going to do about this, Aidan?"

"Absolutely nothing until we know for sure."

"We should prepare for the worst. At least talk about options."

His arms stiffened around me. "What options? What are you talking about?"

"Genetic counseling...abortion." A ball of guilt formed in my stomach at the thought, and Aidan's silence only made it worse. I blinked back tears. "You must hate me for even thinking it."

"Of course I don't hate you." He let out a breath that feathered against my cheek. "Could you really abort our baby?"

"I don't know," I choked out. A vague recollection of a dream flitted through my mind. Aidan kissing me, a look of pure joy on his face while our newborn cried on my chest. The scene faded almost as quickly as it had come, leaving behind another ache in my heart. "But if we're related..." I didn't want to consider what kind of birth defects our child could end up with.

"We don't have to talk about this right now." His voice was laced with sleep, and I wouldn't be surprised if he was having a hard time keeping his eyes open.

"I'm so scared."

"I know." He swept the hair from my cheek and brushed a kiss there. "I could kill our parents right now."

"Me too."

We remained wrapped in each other like we had so many times before, though this time was different. This time each touch was a shameful, stolen moment, and only the reality of how we'd have to part for good kept the guilt at bay. His breathing evened out, and after a while his soft snores tickled my ear.

How had we gotten to this place—this crazy place where DNA hung over our heads as a serial killer ran loose?

I must have dozed off again because I awoke sometime later, startled by the lullaby that played over the hospital's intercom every time a baby was born. Once the melody fell silent, low voices filtered into the room.

Blinking sleep from my eyes, I came fully awake and glanced at Aidan to find that he was still out. The tense exchange in the hall propelled me from bed. I recognized my mom's voice immediately, and I had a good guess at who the other belonged to. I tiptoed toward the open doorway.

"You can't keep me from her." Hamilton's tone was low, and something about it sent a shiver through me. "If I'd known about her before, there would be no contest, Jane."

"I guess it's a good thing you didn't then."

"You selfish"—Hamilton dropped his voice—"*woman.* Your silence denied her so much. She could have gone to the best of colleges. She wouldn't be in this God-awful town serving drunks all night long!"

"Don't presume to think you know anything about her life."

"She's *my* daughter, and she's going to know who she is."

"She knows who she is, and no amount of DNA will—" My mom cut off, and when I peeked around the corner, I noticed Joe standing a few feet away.

I closed my eyes for a moment before making my presence known in the doorway.

Joe held up the same tabloid magazine Aidan had confronted me with earlier. "Someone want to explain this to me?" Everyone fell eerily quiet, and even the normal background noise seemed to be missing.

"Can we not do this here?" I asked.

Hamilton cleared his throat. "Jane, a word in private?"

"Fine," she snapped. She looked anywhere but at me. They disappeared down the hall together, and I tried not to dwell on what they were arguing about.

Joe studied the picture of Hamilton and me. "Tell me this isn't what I think it is."

My stomach dropped. "Where did you get that?"

"Gift shop. Never expected to find you on the cover of one of these rags. What's going on, Mac?"

I peered into Aidan's room one last time, then gestured in the direction of the lounge. "Come on."

The waiting area was thankfully empty, and Joe wasted no time in throwing his questions at me. "Am I going nuts, or is your father the CEO of Payne-Davis?" He glanced at the front page again. "I mean, you said you met your dad in Seattle, and that was him just now with your mom, right?"

"Yes."

"But isn't Payne Aidan's last name?"

Avoiding his eyes, I nodded.

"Shit, Mac! So that's why you freaked out?"

I didn't have the strength to convince him he was wrong. Fighting a sudden bout of nausea, I sank onto the couch. "I didn't know he was my father. Not until Thanksgiving."

"But at least you and Aidan didn't...?"

I lifted my head. "I'm not talking about this with you. It's none of your business."

"You slept with him? So you make me wait *two* years but jump into bed with the first guy you meet after we break up?"

I got to my feet and jabbed a finger at the door. "Get out," I said through clenched teeth. "I don't need this from you."

"Look, I know you've been through hell, but there's nothing here for you." He rubbed his hands down his face. "I mean shit, he's your...your...what? Your cousin or something? That's just *wrong*."

I folded my arms, not about to correct his assumption that Aidan and I were only cousins. That would be a step up from the truth. "Wrong or not, it's reality. I have to deal with it, and he has to deal with it, but you don't. I'm grateful you were there last night, but you need to go home now."

"Of course I was there for you! I love you." He took a step toward me, and I recognized the resolution in his eyes. "Come with me. We can disappear for a while—you always wanted to get in the car and just drive. Let's do it. Mac, *please*."

"I can't."

"You can't be serious! Staying here is only going to hurt you, not to mention put you in more danger. You can't be with him."

"I'm aware of that." I hugged myself and widened the space between us. Why couldn't he just leave? "Go home, and take my mom with you. There's no point in you guys hanging around."

"How can you be so cold? She's your *mother*."

I couldn't answer him. Maybe I was being a bitch, but everything was piling up fast, and I could hardly breathe.

"If anyone should be pushed out of your life," he said, "it's him. He almost got you killed."

"It's not his fault."

"He seems to think it is. He couldn't stop blaming himself last night when we found you."

I hesitated, debating on what to tell him. "His wife was one of the victims in Boise." Judd's victims. I gulped. "He's been through a lot too."

He raised his brows. "I don't give a shit what he's been through. I almost lost you because of him."

"I'm the one who chose the wrong time to go on a road trip. I shouldn't have left."

He shook his head. "Water it down however you like. He's trouble."

"That's not fair. He isn't to blame."

"You aren't either." He spanned the distance between us and brought his body much too close.

"Look at me."

Stubbornly, I kept my gaze on his sneakers.

"What happened *isn't* your fault. Any of it." He tilted my chin up, and his blue eyes lowered to my mouth. I went perfectly still, fearful of what he'd do. "I made the mistake of walking away once already. I won't do it again."

"You don't have a choice." I pushed on his chest until he got the hint. "Just because we've known each other forever doesn't mean you can stick your nose in my business."

"You will always be my business," he said, inching closer still.

"I'm pregnant, Joe." I winced because I hadn't planned on telling him, but the sight of his gaping mouth indicated my words had the desired effect. "You need to go home. This *doesn't* involve you."

He was struck speechless, so I took the opportunity to slip from the lounge. When I reached Aidan's room, I stalled in the doorway.

Logan stood next to the bed, and I watched as he handed Aidan a plastic bag with a cardboard cup inside. "Now will you tell me why you sent me after Dad's trash?"

# CHAPTER FIFTY-ONE

I t was weird how time crawled when you wanted it to speed up. I was beginning to think hospitals had a way of slowing time so those dying would have longer to live. Longer to say goodbye. No matter the reason, three days shouldn't feel like a decade.

But they did. Three long days waiting for the DNA ball to drop.

I turned on the restroom faucet and splashed my face with water, and my tired eyes stared at me from the mirror. The term "morning sickness" was an evil, misleading myth. I'd been vomiting so much Aidan's mother had noticed, though I'd convinced her I had a stomach bug. I left the restroom and returned to Aidan's room, finding it empty of visitors. Hamilton and Lila weren't in sight, and my mom and Joe had thankfully left already.

So had Logan. He'd taken the news of our possible relation in stride—unnervingly so. Aidan later told me Logan had become an expert at suppressing his emotions in order to cope with the empathy overload of others.

At one point I overheard him muttering about the grief in the place. He'd returned to Portland shortly after that. I couldn't deny he intrigued me, and the fact that he was likely my brother made it more so. Logan knew what it was like to be different, and I'd never met anyone who could relate in such a way.

"You okay?" Aidan asked, snapping me back to the present.

"Define 'okay.'" My eyes zeroed in on the large envelope in his hands; he clutched it as if it held the secrets of the universe.

Maybe it did.

"Is that...?"

"Yeah." He scooted into a sitting position. "I'm scared to open it."

I wanted to go to him. I wanted it so badly, but we'd been careful not to touch since we'd fallen asleep together the day he'd awakened after surgery.

He patted the spot beside him. "Come here. Let's do this together."

"Okay." I settled next to him, and we both stared at the envelope. Inside contained the power to either grind the last pieces of my heart into dust...or meld them back together again. "Just do it."

He inhaled quickly, then tore into the envelope. The next few seconds seemed longer than any span of time I'd ever held my breath through.

"What does it say?"

His jaw slackened, and my heart shattered all over again at the disbelief on his face. It wasn't a joyous or even relieved expression.

"Aidan, just tell me."

"He's your father."

The room spun, and for a few moments nothing registered. I wasn't sure why I was so stunned—deep down I'd known. I finally found my voice and began to cry, and that's when I noticed his hands on my shoulders, shaking me.

"Mackenzie!"

I raised my head. "God, this isn't happening."

"Listen to me. He's your father, but he's not mine."

"What?" I blinked, expecting to wake up at any moment. No way had I heard him correctly.

"According to this, you and I aren't related, and he's not my biological father."

His words burrowed into my consciousness, and with a cry of joy, I launched myself into his arms. The breath whooshed from him as we fell to the mattress. I could only imagine what this revelation meant to him, to us, but I was too selfish to think about it just then. "Oh God...oh God!" Tears bathed my face as I held onto him. "Tell me this is real."

He cradled my head, his fingers tangling in my hair, and then we were kissing. Our mouths fed off each other, devouring in unashamed abandon. We rolled, him with a groan of pain, and me with a whimper of desperation.

He broke away a few seconds later and dropped his forehead against mine. "I've never been so relieved in my life."

I couldn't fight the smile that spread across my face. "I can't believe I'm free to love you."

"I would've loved you anyway." He closed his eyes, or I closed mine—maybe we both did—but the moment held us captive in a state of temporary reprieve; he wasn't wounded and in pain, our mothers weren't liars, and Judd wasn't free.

For the sixty seconds that we breathed each other in, I almost convinced myself it was true.

"I need to find my mother," he said. My eyes flew open when he pulled away. He stood, his body swaying for a moment, and reached for the bag that contained a change of clothes.

I jumped to my feet. "What are you doing?"

"Getting dressed."

"Don't you dare. Get back in bed." This was not a new argument. He was the worst kind of patient. Just yesterday he'd tried to talk the doctor into releasing him early. I hated to think of what he'd do if he knew Judd was still out there somewhere. "You're still recovering."

His mouth flattened into a line, and his eyes lowered to my abdomen. "You actually talked about abortion. I wanted to protect her from his affairs, but I can't keep quiet about this. She's got some explaining to do."

"I agree, but it can wait."

"No, it can't." He reached behind his back to unsnap the hospital gown and tried to hide a wince.

"You're so stubborn," I said, stepping behind him to undo the snaps. I helped him dress so he wouldn't hurt himself. He took off through the door, and for someone who'd been shot a few days ago, he didn't have any problem storming down the hallway. I hurried to keep up with his long stride.

Lila couldn't have gone far. She and Hamilton had checked into a hotel, but she spent every waking moment in the hospital. Last I'd heard she'd gone to get something to eat. He swung a door open, and we found the cafeteria empty save for his mother. It was late, and the dinner crowd had cleared out a while ago. Lila sat in the corner of the room, picking at a salad that looked as if it had come from one of the vending machines.

Aidan charged across the room and flung the DNA results on the table.

"What's wrong?" she asked as she rose to her feet, eyes wide. She glanced around, as if someone were about to strike. She wasn't far from the truth, though I doubted she expected the strike to come from Aidan.

"You tell me, Mom."

She blinked, clearly alarmed by his tone. "I don't know what you're getting at." She gestured toward the papers. "What's this?"

"A paternity test."

That got her attention. She snatched up the results, and her gaze quickly roamed the text. After a few moments, she faced Aidan, still holding the papers in her shaking hands. "Why would you do this?"

"I wanted to protect you from this, but it turns out Dad isn't the only one who's untrustworthy." Aidan leaned against the table before sinking into a chair. Perspiration dripped down the side of his temple, and his face had gone pale. "Dad had an affair with Mackenzie's mother. She's his daughter."

Lila set the results down. "This has to be a mistake." Her non-reaction stunned me.

"There's no mistake."

Her gaze swerved between Aidan and me. I wrung my hands, recalling my devastation upon hearing my mom's bombshell. "Did you know?" I asked. "My mom told me on Thanksgiving."

"I heard the rumors involving Will Beckmeyer, but this has to be a mistake."

"We can't afford mistakes." I locked my eyes with hers. "I don't have the stomach flu. I'm pregnant."

"Wh-what?"

Aidan rose again, his full height towering over her and the table, despite her standing up straight. He placed his palms flat against the surface. "The last three days have been hell. We thought we were related—even talked about abortion—all because no one can tell the damn truth around here!"

I flinched, glad I wasn't on the receiving end of his anger.

"Aidan, you don't understand."

"Then make me understand. Who's my father?"

"There are things you don't know..." She clutched the back of her chair. "Things I never wanted you to know about your father."

"Which one are we talking about, Mom?"

"I'm talking about Hamilton. Does he know about this?" She brought a shaking hand to her mouth, concealing the tremble of her lips, and I realized the difference between her reaction and my mom's when confronted with the truth. Whereas my mom had been riddled with guilt, Lila seemed terrified.

I grabbed Aidan's arm before he went off on her again. "Lila, are you scared of Hamilton?"

Instead of answering, she picked up her purse. "I have to go. I'm sorry."

My mouth hung open as she scurried from the cafeteria. Aidan watched her go, and only after she'd disappeared from sight did he move. Without warning, his foot struck out and he kicked over a chair. "Dammit!"

I jumped but said nothing. He wouldn't have heard me

anyway. He grabbed at his hair with both hands and stared through the empty doorway, as if he could will his mom to come back and give him answers.

"I'm sorry," I whispered, completely understanding how he felt. I slid my palms along his sides, keeping clear of his wound, and waited for him to come back to me.

Eventually, he dropped his arms and folded me inside them. "Things keep getting crazier, don't they?" he said, burying his nose in my hair.

Afraid of hurting him, I inched back. "Tell me it gets better."

"God, I hope so." He laced our fingers and tugged me into the hall, and when we reached his room again, we found Hamilton pacing, cell phone to his ear.

"No! How many times do I need to tell you? He's not the man you need to talk to—Stevens is." He paused, noticed Aidan and me, and held up a finger. "I don't care what you have to do. I want it done or you're fired." He ended the call and turned his attention on us. "Why are you dressed and running around the hospital like you weren't shot three days ago? I know damn well the doctor didn't release you yet."

Aidan ignored the question and threw the test results at him. "Did you know?"

"Know what?" He grabbed the papers but didn't look at them.

"That I'm not your son."

Hamilton's stature shrank, and I never would have thought it possible. He quickly scanned the papers. "Where did you get this? We're still awaiting the results."

Aidan gripped my hand tighter, and I wondered if he did

it to keep from hitting his father. "You weren't going to tell us, were you?"

Hamilton opened his mouth, but Aidan raised a hand. "You know what? Forget it." He pulled me back into the hall, refusing to acknowledge Hamilton when he called after us.

"What are we doing?" I asked.

"Getting out of here."

"You can't leave yet."

"Yes, I can. Anywhere's gotta be less toxic than this place."

Hadn't I had the same sentiment a few days ago? I swallowed hard. We all knew how that turned out.

"Wait," I said, yanking on his hand. If he was going to walk through those doors, then I couldn't put off telling him about Judd any longer. "There's something you need to know." I chewed on my lip, dreading each word I was about to say. "Judd got away. He's still out there somewhere."

"What?" His fingers flexed around mine. "Why didn't anyone tell me?"

"Because of this right here. You need time to recover. We didn't want you flipping out and trying to leave."

"He killed Deb...he almost killed *you*. Damn right I'm flipping out." He let go of my hand, and I ran to catch up with him.

"Aidan, let it go. Let the police deal with him."

"Yeah, that worked well the first time."

It took him a while to get ahold of his doctor, but he grudgingly agreed to release him. Aidan called for a taxi, and we waited in the lobby. Disquiet ate away at my nerves. Ten minutes passed, then twenty, and I was hoping the cab wouldn't show. Hoping Aidan would change his mind.

No such luck. A green sedan with a glowing "Watcher's

Taxi" sign on top pulled in front of the lobby's entrance, and Aidan opened the back passenger door. He gestured for me to get inside before sliding in next to me.

"Where are we going?" I studied him closely, sensing an urgency in him that scared me.

He gave the cabbie his address. "We're picking up my car, then I'm taking you to Logan's."

My eyes widened. "What do you mean you're *taking me*?"

He wouldn't look at me. "Just what it sounds like."

"What are you gonna do, Aidan?" My voice rose, and I glanced at the driver to see his reaction to our conversation.

"I don't know yet, but I want you safe until he's found."

"You're not leaving me anywhere."

"We'll talk about this later."

The cabbie pulled up to Aidan's house, and we rushed up the staircase after he paid the fare. The skies opened again, drenching us before we entered the foyer. The door had barely swung shut when his cell rang.

He took one glance at the display and answered with a clipped "Yeah?"

I rubbed my arms, chilled since the house was ice cold. Nothing but blackness greeted us beyond the windows.

Aidan did a walk-through of the kitchen and living room, pausing long enough to switch on the fireplace. "You had a chance to explain, Mom. Instead you took off."

I followed him as he headed for the stairs. "I'm not at the hospital. I'm at home." He sighed. "*Fine*." He hung up in irritation. "My mother's on her way. She says she needs to explain."

A breath of relief escaped me. Maybe she could talk some sense into him.

"Go pack a few things," he said, his shoes thumping down the stairs. "I'm gonna get my gun out of the safe."

"No!" I catapulted the last step and rushed around him, blocking his path. "No guns." I shook my head, hating how helpless I felt. How helpless he felt. I saw it in his eyes. "I almost lost you once. Let him go." I rested my palm on my stomach. "We have one more to think about now. Our baby needs a father. Don't do this. Please, Aidan. *Please*."

My heart twisted when he dashed away a tear. I'd only seen him cry once before and that was when I'd dreamed of the night he found his wife. "You and the baby—that's why I'm doing this." He moved past me and headed toward the garage. I went to follow, but a hand shot out of the bedroom and fisted my hair.

I screamed, and Aidan whirled, eyes wide in terror as Judd pressed the barrel of a gun to my temple.

# CHAPTER FIFTY-TWO

"Looking for your gun?" Judd asked, his taunting voice too loud in my ears. Aidan went still, his body wired tight enough to spring into motion at any second.

"Let her go."

"Look at him. So pathetic. He actually thinks he has a say in this." Judd pushed me to my knees, and I squeezed my eyes shut as he jabbed the barrel hard against my scalp. "I could pull the trigger now, blow her fucking brains all over these walls, and there isn't a damn thing you can do to stop me."

"Don't do this," Aidan pleaded, his voice an octave away from breaking. "Whatever you have against me, I'm begging you, don't take it out on her."

I blinked, and my tears spilled over as he tossed a set of handcuffs at Aidan's feet. "Cuff your hands behind your back."

Aidan bent in tiny degrees, never taking his eyes off me. I expected him to fight, but he didn't hesitate to do as he was told, which spoke volumes on how hopeless the situation was.

"You won't get away with this," he said as he clicked the cuffs in place. "Everyone's looking for you."

"Shut the fuck up!" Judd yanked me to my feet. "Don't you think I know that? This isn't ending well for any of us. I have nothing to go back to, thanks to the two of you." The gun shook against my head, and I felt his body tremble as he dragged me back a few steps.

*Stall him. Keep him talking.*

"What did we ever do to you?" I asked.

"You messed everything up! You and your stupid dreams. I had it all mapped out." He pointed the gun at Aidan. "He practically set himself up by coming in to see you. He'd go down for your murder—he'd go down for them all." His voice dropped. "Six took your place that night, you know."

My body went cold. He'd completely unhinged, even more so than before. "You don't have to do this. Killing us won't get rid of the pain."

"No, but it'll be satisfying as fuck." He tightened his hold on me and gestured toward Aidan. "Get in the bedroom."

"You're gonna kill us anyway," Aidan said, his jaw twitching as he assessed the situation. "Why draw it out?"

Judd shoved the barrel into my mouth, and I nearly threw up. "Do *not* test me."

"No!" Aidan cried. "I'll do whatever you want. Don't hurt her." He moved into the bedroom slowly, his face ash-white.

Judd pushed me in after him and indicated a chair in the corner. "Sit down," he ordered Aidan.

"What do you want from us?" he asked as he lowered into the chair. "Why are you doing this? I don't even know you."

"You don't know shit. You're fucking clueless." Judd pulled the barrel from between my lips, and I broke down crying as he shoved me toward Aidan. "Use the rope at his feet and tie him to the chair. Either of you gets any funny ideas, and you're dead, sweetheart."

I knelt, reaching for the rope, and dropped it three times due to my shaking hands. Finally, I secured one ankle to the chair leg and then raised my head.

"It's okay," Aidan said. "We'll get out of this."

I didn't believe him. Even worse, *he* didn't believe himself. My heart squeezed painfully as I saw something in him die, and that scared me as much as the threat of Judd. He was giving up, right before my eyes, and I could do nothing to stop it.

"If you get the chance, run. Don't worry about me."

"I'm not leaving you," I said as I finished tying the last knot.

"Quiet! You guys can forget whatever you're whispering about. No one's going anywhere." I stood slowly, and Judd nodded toward the bed. "Climb up."

Automatically, I shook my head, self-preservation dictating my reaction. Pleading with him wouldn't help, and running wouldn't help—he was blocking the way to the bedroom door—but I couldn't *not* try. "Don't do this—"

"Do I need to use the Taser again?"

I gulped, placing my palm over my stomach. "No."

He ignored Aidan's threats and grinned, and his eyes fell to my hand. "I'm going to enjoy this."

Reality faded, and I let my mind drift in a fog. None of this was happening. As he tied me down, I didn't think, didn't feel. I wasn't real. This wasn't real. This was another nightmare, and I was still at the hospital with Aidan, warm beside him in bed.

Except that Aidan was screaming, and that alone was enough to jolt me back to reality. "Don't you touch her! Sonofabitch, I'll kill you!"

I lifted my head as Judd stalked over to him. "You had it all. Illustrious career, a shitload of money, hot wife." He smiled, a thin-lipped grin that chilled my blood. "But I did something about that, didn't I? Now I'm going to do something about her." His gaze swerved in my direction. "Only this time you're going to watch every fucking moment."

My muscles tensed as he neared.

"Kill me!" Aidan pleaded. "Kill me, not her!" His torment lanced through me, and in that moment I wished Judd *would* kill him first. I didn't want him to see this. We were both dead anyway. Better he go first, never having to witness what was about to happen.

Judd rounded the bed and halted on the left side. "I've already seen her naked. She's got a great body, but you know that, don't you?"

"Don't hurt her." The tears in Aidan's voice seared me, as did the hopelessness on his face as he fought against the bindings. I prayed my knots were loose enough for him to get free, though I had no idea how he'd get out of the cuffs.

"Why are you doing this?" I asked. I felt like a broken record, but if he was going to kill me, I wanted to know why.

"No, sweetheart." He grabbed at the front of his pants. "Enough stalling. I'm in the mood to play." He crawled onto the bed, and I sank into a surreal state. The shadows in the bedroom deepened, and I didn't hear Aidan yelling, didn't hear the roar of my own heartbeat...failed to notice the doorbell sounding until Judd jumped from the bed.

"Who the hell is that?" he demanded.

My gaze clashed with Aidan's, and I knew we remembered at the same time. His mother.

"No one knows we're here. Just ignore it," Aidan said, though his panicked tone gave him away.

Judd narrowed his eyes, flexed his fingers around the gun, and disappeared into the hall.

Aidan let out a curse as hysteria finally bubbled from my chest, erupting from me like a volcano. "We're gonna die."

"No, baby. Look at me." The chair leg thumped.

I lifted my head again.

He'd freed one leg and was now rocking the chair to free the other. "Everything's gonna be okay." Rocking some more, he nearly fell sideways at one point, but managed to break free. He rushed to the side of the bed. "I can't untie you, but you might be able to reach my cell. It's in my coat." He leaned toward my bound hand, and I strained to reach into his pocket.

"If that's your mom..." My fingers barely touched the phone, so I reached further.

"I can't think about that right now. The only way any of us are getting out of here is if we get help." He leaned his body more heavily on the mattress. "Hurry."

"I'm trying!" I finally got a good hold and pulled the phone from his pocket.

"Call 9-1-1. Shit! Hurry, he's coming."

Aidan sprinted back to his chair as I tried to key in the numbers. The rope kept my hand at an odd angle, and I was scared Judd would return before I had a chance to get help.

*Come on! Don't give up.*

I hit the correct buttons as footsteps sounded in the hall.

"9-1-1, what's your emergency?"

"Help us!" I cried, keeping my voice low. "He's holding us at gunpoint." I rattled off the address and then gasped. The phone slipped from my fingers and dropped to the floor as Lila and the sheriff appeared in the doorway. They entered the room, Judd behind them, his gun at the ready between his hands.

"Look who crashed our party."

"Let them go," The sheriff said. "This is between you and me. Let's talk about this."

"Sure, let's talk. This is turning out to be a nice little family get-together, isn't it?" Judd snickered. "We've got Aidan here, the golden child, and his fine piece of ass. Oh, and we have mommy here too. This should be interesting." He grabbed Lila and pressed the weapon against her head. "He doesn't know, does he, Dad?"

Thick silence ensued, and the sheriff slowly put his hands in the air. "You know." It was a statement—one he and Judd understood perfectly. Aidan and I were left in the dark, and Lila seemed too terrified to make a sound.

"Shitty way to find out you have a brother," Judd said.

Aidan's eyes widened as understanding dawned.

The sheriff dropped his head. "How'd you find out?"

"I overheard you guys talking when *she* came here for her dad's funeral."

Lila yelped as Judd shoved her forward. She fell into the sheriff's arms and came apart, her body shaking as she clung to him.

"I don't understand," McFayden began. "I only found out

about Aidan a couple of years ago." He was too calm as he inched backward, which made me wonder what he was up to. "You couldn't have killed all those women in Boise."

Judd looked pleased with himself. "I didn't. I killed his wife though. Hell, she fought like a wildcat." He aimed a smug smile toward Aidan. "Wasn't hard to resurrect the Hangman after he vanished."

"Why'd you do it?" McFayden asked.

"You weren't there for me, but you jumped to protect them." Judd blinked, and moisture trickled down his cheeks. "Pretty fucked up that I had to commit murder to get your attention."

"I *tried* to protect you. Your mother left with you—I didn't know where you were. I never stopped looking, but I couldn't find you."

"You're lying! She told me you didn't care. *He* told me." His voice had changed, reminding me of the way he'd sounded as a child in my vision. He pulled up his shirt to reveal an ugly pattern of scars—the kind that made me think someone had burned him.

"Look at them, Dad. You weren't around to stop this. He did worse. So much worse. You don't know how many times he held me down and—"

"Please, Judd." McFayden interrupted, blinking rapidly as his mouth trembled. He shook his head. "This isn't the way to deal with it. Let me get you the help you need." He paused for a moment. "Let them go."

"It's always about them!" Judd waved the gun around and advanced on his father, who pushed Lila behind him. Aidan tensed, and I was terrified he was about to do something that would get him killed.

"Nobody's leaving here," Judd said. He sneered as his dad and Lila slowly backed toward Aidan. "That's right—go protect your *perfect* son."

Lila dropped next to Aidan and held onto him. I heard her soft cries from where I was restrained to the bed, and I accepted that we were all going to die. You couldn't reason with someone so far gone. I closed my eyes, not wanting to watch when it happened, and listened as the sheriff continued to stall Judd.

"I won't hurt you, son. Despite what you've done, I love you. But I won't let you hurt them either. You'll have to kill me first."

The blast shocked us all. My eyes popped open, and Judd was crying, looking on the verge of being sick as he stared in horror at his father. McFayden gazed at the blood oozing from his arm, mouth agape as Judd staggered back. Lila cried harder.

Where the hell were the police? As if in answer to my silent question, sirens sounded outside. Judd froze, listening as they drew closer. The echo of slammed doors penetrated the walls, and almost instantly, a cell phone rang.

"Fuck!" He paced a circle in front of the bedroom door.

"Come on, son. Put the gun down before you get yourself killed."

He stomped to his father and stuck the barrel in his face. McFayden closed his eyes.

"Jeff!" Lila shrieked. She jumped to her feet, trying to launch herself at the sheriff, but Aidan trapped her between his thighs.

"No, Mom!"

"Kill me," McFayden said, still grasping his injured arm.

"If killing me will dull the pain inside you, do it." A tear slipped down his cheek. "I should've been there."

Judd stumbled back again, and time stalled as he turned the gun on himself.

Everyone seemed to hold their breath, frozen in a sequence of events that only seemed possible in the movies. McFayden fell to his knees, pleading with him to drop the gun, and someone's cell went off again but was ignored. "Please, I'm begging you. Don't do it."

"I won't let them take me," Judd said, chest heaving, his hand shaking as he held the weapon to his temple.

"I love you," the sheriff choked. He hurtled himself at him, knocking him to the floor with a loud grunt, and they struggled amongst a tangle of limbs. Aidan jumped to his feet, his body ready to leap into action, despite not having the use of his arms.

Lila was screaming at them to stop. The bedroom door flung open, and several deputies swarmed inside. She rushed across the room and fell next to McFayden. He gathered her into his arms as the deputies detained Judd, who was openly bawling. They hauled him to his feet and dragged him from the room.

Someone unlocked the cuffs around Aidan's wrists, and he wasted no time in untying me, his fingers working fast to free my hands and feet. He pulled me into the safety of his embrace.

"If I never let you go, it'll be too soon."

# CHAPTER FIFTY-THREE

"Do you want me to go in with you?" Aidan asked, gesturing toward the precinct's entrance.

"No, I'll be okay. Doing this alone...I think it's something I need to do."

Aidan slid his palms along my cheeks. His lips met mine, and for a few moments our surroundings faded. We broke apart just as an officer moved past, decked out in a uniform that was such a dark shade of blue, one might think it was black.

"I'll be right here when you're done." He let go, and I could tell by the strain on his face that he wanted to go with me.

"I won't be long."

A detective escorted me into the back of the station. She opened a door to an office that was small and cluttered in a disorganized way that probably made sense to her.

"Have a seat," she said, gesturing toward the only chair facing her desk. She sat across from me and brushed the blond curls from her forehead. She seemed too young to be a cop, and I wasn't even sure why.

Judd hadn't been much older. I swallowed hard and silently recited the mantra that had gotten me through the past ten days: *He's in jail. Don't waste a thought on him.*

Too bad some part of my stubborn mind refused to listen.

"I know this isn't easy for you," she said, and I blinked, reminding myself how I was in the here and now. I had something important to do—something that wasn't easy, as she'd said, but it needed to be done.

"Take your time," she said. "I'm here as long as you need."

The next forty-five minutes picked at the scab covering my emotional wound. In light of what Judd had put us through, talking about my rape didn't inflict as much pain as it once had, but it still cut deep.

Difficult or not, I couldn't remain silent any longer. Professor Keely's other victim was locked in a her-word-against-his battle, and from what Joe had told me, his father was likely going to beat the charges.

I couldn't let that happen.

"You were very brave for coming forward, Ms. Hill."

We stood, and I quietly thanked her as she opened the door for me. She led me back to the lobby, and almost immediately I found myself in Aidan's arms.

"How did it go?"

"Good."

"How do you feel?"

"Better. I never realized how much I needed closure." I hesitated. "Maybe you're right. I think counseling might be a good idea."

He inched away to look at me. "I am so proud of you."

Catching sight of my mom standing nearby, I gave Aidan a funny look.

"The sooner you clear the air with her, the better. Trust me."

I scowled at him. "A little hypocritical, don't you think?"

He grinned. "I just got off the phone with my mother. Things are far from resolved, but we're working on it."

"This is so not fair," I grumbled.

He kissed my cheek. "You still love me." He gestured toward the exit. "I'll wait for you in the car."

"Okay." I watched him go before closing the distance between my mom and me. "Hey."

"Hi, Kenz." She pulled me into her arms and held on tight. "I've missed you."

"Me too."

She let go a few seconds later, and we watched as two officers hauled in a scruffy blond guy who twitched every few seconds. "With everything that happened over Thanksgiving and afterward, I never got a chance to tell you something," she said.

"What's that?"

"That you can tell me anything. No matter what."

I rubbed the toe of my sneaker over warn linoleum. "Part of me was ashamed."

"You have no reason to be ashamed. If I ever get my hands on him..." I peeked up and caught her wiping beneath her eyes. "I wish you would've told me. Over the summer, I sensed something was wrong, but I would've never imagined this, and then when you dropped out of school and moved —" she broke off, shaking her head. "I couldn't make sense of it."

I wandered a few steps, too uncomfortable with our conversation to stay in one spot for long. "I knew how much you liked and respected his dad." I lowered myself onto a bench and peered up at her. "Joe knew me better than anyone, and even he didn't believe me."

"I would have believed you. You're my baby—I'm always going to be on your side."

"Even though I'm with Aidan now?"

She sat beside me. "I don't have anything against him. It's true, I always thought you and Joe would get married someday and make me grandbabies." She smiled. "But I can see how much Aidan loves you. Now that we know you're not related..." She turned pink at the reminder.

"Yeah, can we not talk about that?" Bringing up that particular memory would only make reconciling things more difficult.

"Deal." She glanced at my stomach, and I thought about the months ahead—soon my belly wouldn't be so flat. "Looks like you're going to give me grandbabies after all."

"Grand*baby*," I said, laughing. "Don't hex me—Marcus already gave you twins." Joe walked through the entrance, and I abruptly stopped laughing. "You didn't." My head swerved back to her, and I shot her an accusing glare.

"Hey." She held up her hands. "I can honestly say I had nothing to do with this." She stood, adjusting her purse strap. "I'll let you two catch up. I told Marcus I'd babysit for him and Alicia. They're down from Salem for the weekend."

"Tell them I said hi." I was much too distracted by Joe's presence as he waited across the room, his eyes straying to me every so often.

"See you soon," Mom said. She gave me another hug

before taking off toward the exit where she stopped to greet Joe on her way out. He didn't waste time in ambling to my side.

"Hi, Mac."

"Hi."

He gave me a quick hug, and I was certain we both sensed the awkwardness between us. "How've you been?" he asked once he'd stepped away.

"Coping, but things are getting easier."

He stuffed his hands into the pockets of his coat. "Your mom told me the news about you and Aidan. Must be nice to know you're not being scandalous."

I clenched my teeth. "Why are you here, Joe?"

He pointed a thumb toward the front desk. "They called me. Guess they have more questions for me or something." His gaze swept my body from head to toe. "You seem... content."

I managed a smile. "I'm getting there." Probably the most at peace I'd been in months, despite things still being up in the air with Aidan and me. Despite the nightmares. Ten days since Judd had been arrested, yet we hadn't talked about our future. We'd talked about the baby some, but everything else was off-limits, lest we disrupt the tenuous balance we'd created since everything had gone down.

"Promise me something," Joe said, his voice dropping in that familiar way that told me whatever he had to say was important.

"What is it?"

"Come to me if you're ever in trouble, no matter what. I'll always be here for you, Mac."

"I will."

He shook his head. "No, I mean it. You're always gonna be apart of my life, and yeah, I hate that I lost you, but I don't want what happened to come between us. Promise me you won't close the door on us."

"I'm not the one who shut it in the first place." I paused, biting my lip. "We can't go back. You know that, right?"

"You say that, but I can't throw thirteen years down the drain. I hope you can't either." He frowned. "If he wasn't in the picture, would you give me another chance?"

"I've gotta go." I moved around him, incapable of uttering the word "goodbye" because it just seemed wrong.

"Hey, Mac?"

I turned, and he met me with a sad smile. "Congratulations on the baby. You're gonna be an amazing mom."

"Thanks." My mouth turned up the slightest bit, and the balance of my world evened out a little more in that moment. Everything was going to be okay; for once I believed it.

Aidan was waiting for me in the car. I settled into the passenger seat, and every tear I hadn't cried in the past few days seemed to gush from my eyes.

"What's wrong?" he asked. He placed his hand on the nape of my neck, his fingers tracing circles, and my body flushed and chilled at the same time.

I held my breath, but uncontrollable laughter bubbled up and spilled over anyway. I glanced at him through my tears. "Nothing. Everything. Probably just hormones." I wiped my face. "I'm glad we came here today."

"I figured you needed this." His fingers lingered on my skin for a few seconds longer before he started the ignition. After several stoplights and a few turns, we were speeding down the highway toward Watcher's Point. My throat ached with a new fear—one I knew we needed to talk about. The words wouldn't come though, and the questions I needed answers to remained unasked.

What was going to happen to us now?

Was he staying in Watcher's Point or did he want to go back to Boise? Would he ask me to go with him?

I'd follow him anywhere.

"The last time you were this quiet and distant, you broke up with me," he said. "Your mother didn't have any more confessions, did she?"

My mouth lifted at the corners. If he was worried, then maybe that was a good sign. "No. I think all her skeletons are out now." God, I hoped so. "And I definitely don't have any plans to break up with you." I sent him a sidelong glance. "You're too good in bed." Even with a gunshot wound slowing him down.

He laughed. "At least I've got that going for me, seeing as how you're insatiable."

"Like you aren't?"

"Guilty as charged." He laughed again. "But I can't help myself. The view is especially good when you're on top."

"You better eat it up now because I hear sex goes downhill after the baby is born."

He shook his head. "No way. I can't imagine that—not possible with you."

"Speaking of the *after*...what's going to happen with us?"

"What do you mean?"

"I guess I'm wanting to know...if you're planning to go back to Boise? You left your life there, Aidan."

He grabbed my hand. "I realize we have things to talk about, but I thought I was clear on my intentions."

"I need to hear you say it."

"I put the house in Boise up for sale. I'm not going anywhere, unless you do, and in that case I'll follow you." He glanced at me. "Though the Watcher's Point Herald did offer me a job, if you want to stick around."

"If you weren't driving, I'd jump your bones right now."

"Don't make me pull the car over."

I smiled, nibbling on my lip to keep from telling him to do just that. The remainder of the ride home passed in companionable silence. It was weird, how the word "home" seemed synonymous with Watcher's Point. With Aidan. He was my home.

We pulled onto his street, and the sight of the beach house made me shudder. We hadn't been back since Judd had snapped his last frail thread of sanity. Yellow tape hung from the staircase, flapping in the breeze and calling attention to the fact that something horrible had almost happened there.

"You sure you're ready to come back?"

"No," I said as he came to a stop in the driveway, "but we'll have to face this place sooner or later."

"True, but it can be later. We don't have to go inside yet." He let the engine idle. Normally, he would have opened the garage by now.

Half of me was tempted to return to the hotel where we'd hidden for the past ten days, taking the time to recover, the time to adjust. His wound would heal, but the ones left on our souls would hurt for a long time. We'd chased the pain away by wrapping ourselves in each other. The outside world hadn't existed within that room.

I took a deep breath. "Okay, let's go in."

He reached for the garage opener but halted as a gray pickup pulled in behind us. A door squeaked open, and I turned in my seat and saw the sheriff get out.

Aidan and I exchanged a look, and I could tell he was just as surprised by McFayden's arrival. He killed the engine, and we got out of the car.

McFayden greeted us with a tentative smile. "Your mother mentioned you might be here."

"How's your arm?" Aidan asked.

"It was just a flesh wound." McFayden jammed his hands into his pockets. "I'm a coward. I've thought about contacting you every day since that night."

"Why didn't you?"

"Wasn't sure what to say. What I should tell you."

"How about the truth?"

McFayden gestured toward the house. "Mind if we go inside and talk?"

"Sure." Aidan led the way up the stairs. He flipped on the light in the foyer and chased away the evening shadows. The sun had begun its languid dip below the horizon, and the sky was already darkening through the skylight.

I willed my heartbeat to slow as memories rushed me. I held onto the good ones, and the warmth of Aidan's hand at my back calmed me.

"Would you like something to drink, Sheriff?"

"Call me Jeff. You got coffee?"

Aidan nodded as he ushered us into the kitchen. He prepared the coffee pot, and the sheriff and I took seats at the center island. Aidan leaned against the counter on the other side and studied the granite for a few moments, seemingly lost in thought.

"Why didn't you tell me? I can understand why my mother wouldn't after all these years but to find out you have a kid and not say anything?"

"I wanted to. You don't know how hard it was—" McFayden drew in a breath as he brushed his hair back, and the bags underneath his eyes gave away his sleepless nights. "We knew we needed to tell you eventually."

His answer seemed to irritate Aidan. "Eventually as in another thirty years?"

"No, Aidan"—the sheriff quickly shook his head—"your mother didn't want to involve you, but considering everything that's happened, I think keeping you in the dark is a bad idea. Promise me you won't repeat what I'm about to tell you."

Aidan stood straighter. Something about the sheriff's tone put us both on alert.

"I guess that depends on what it is."

McFayden nodded. "I suppose that's fair. Your mother came to me a couple years ago. She was here in town for old man Davis' funeral."

"Yeah, I remember. Dad didn't show. He couldn't stand my grandfather."

"Well, she came to see me afterward. She was terrified, said she found something on Hamilton and that he threatened her."

Aidan narrowed his eyes. "Threatened her how?"

The sheriff clenched his hands. "He threatened to have her killed."

"My father is a lot of things," Aidan said, pushing away from the counter, "but he's not a killer."

"There's a lot you don't know about him. I've been investigating him since."

"Why?"

"That day when she told me about you, she swore me to secrecy and begged for my help. She didn't have to beg hard. I've always loved her, Aidan."

"Why come to you?" Aidan folded his arms. "She could've gone to the police in Seattle or the FBI. She could've told *me*."

"She wanted to protect you. Hamilton Payne is a powerful man. I'm sure you're aware of just how powerful. He's got his fingers in every corner of law enforcement, even the FBI. She didn't know who to trust."

"So what does she have on him?"

"I can't say."

"This is bullshit! You expect me to trust you, but you won't tell me what's going on?"

McFayden's gaze darted to me. "I can't blame you for being hesitant to trust me, but I came here to warn you. Be careful. Keep Mackenzie and your child away from him."

His words froze my heart. Aidan and I exchanged a worried glance.

"I don't understand," Aidan said as he pulled three mugs down from a cupboard. "I've never gotten along with him, but I can't imagine him hurting any of us, not in the way you're suggesting."

McFayden seemed to chew over his words as Aidan poured coffee into two of the mugs and hot water into the third for me. He added a tea bag to mine before setting the mugs on the counter.

"Let me put it this way," McFayden began. "At first, your mother suspected he was behind your wife's murder." He lowered his head, taking a moment to sip from his cup. "I sensed something was off about the whole thing, was sure it was a copycat even though law enforcement in Boise ruled it out. I never would have suspected Judd." He paused, and a flash of pain entered his eyes—eyes that looked so much like Aidan's now that I thought about it. "Just like you can't see that Hamilton is capable of such things."

"How can I help if you won't tell me what's going on?"

"I don't want your help on this. I want you to steer clear of him—keep your family away from him." His gaze landed on me. "Protect that baby of yours."

"Well that's a given," Aidan said. "He won't get near either one of them."

McFayden took another sip and then glanced at his watch. "I need to get going." He rose, and Aidan appeared uncertain. I understood what he was going through. I'd experienced the same uneasy feeling upon meeting Hamilton Payne for the first time after I'd learned the truth.

Except, according to McFayden, my father was evil incarnate. I should have listened to my mom—should have kept going, blissfully unaware.

The sheriff rounded the center island and pulled Aidan in for a hug. "I'm glad you know."

Aidan's eyes went wide, and slowly he lifted his arms and returned the gesture.

"There are no words...I can't tell you how sorry I am for what Judd did to you. Both of you." McFayden stepped away, never quite meeting Aidan's eyes, and I glimpsed the broken man I'd seen in the hospital. Judd's actions had affected us all.

The sheriff left, promising to keep in touch, and the

silence in the house unnerved me. Though he was there with me physically, Aidan's mind was elsewhere.

"Hungry?" he asked.

I finished my tea before standing, and our eyes met and held as I neared him. I entwined our fingers before leading him downstairs. The hall was dark, and the shadows threatened to close around me. I squeezed his hand and told myself there was no reason to be scared. Judd was in jail, and whatever threat Hamilton posed, we'd deal with it later. Right now, in this moment, I wanted to chase away the bad with the good.

Neither of us spoke as I pulled him into the bedroom. We stopped in the middle of the room, and I undid the buttons on his shirt. The material slid over his shoulders before whispering to the floor. His wound was healing. I gently brushed my fingertips across the skin below it.

"Does it still hurt?"

"Not really," Aidan said, his voice thick as he curled his fingers around the hem of my sweater. His knuckles grazed my sides as he lifted it up my body, and he tossed it somewhere in the vicinity of his discarded shirt before unbuttoning my jeans.

"You might have seen me coming," he began, dropping to his knees and slowly dragging my zipper down, "but I can't say the same. You knocked me on my ass." His eyes were bright as he gazed up at me. "We haven't known each other very long, but I have every intention of marrying you."

A smile played on my lips as I weaved my fingers through his hair, and I thought about how wrong he was. I'd known him for years—he just hadn't realized it.

# About the Author

Gemma James is a *USA Today* bestselling author of sexy contemporary and dark romance. She loves to explore the darker side of human nature in her fiction, and she's morbidly curious about anything dark and edgy, from deviant seduction to fascinating villains. Readers have described her stories as being "not for the faint of heart."

She warns you to heed their words! Her playground isn't full of rainbows and kittens, though she loves both. She lives in Florida with her husband, children, and a gaggle of animals.

Visit Gemma's website for more info on her books:
**www.authorgemmajames.com**

Made in the USA
Columbia, SC
28 May 2025